THE ILLUSION OF POWER

PASSION AND POLITICS
BOOK 1

J.L. SEEGARS

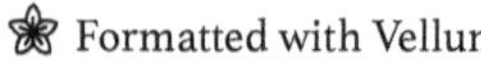 Formatted with Vellum

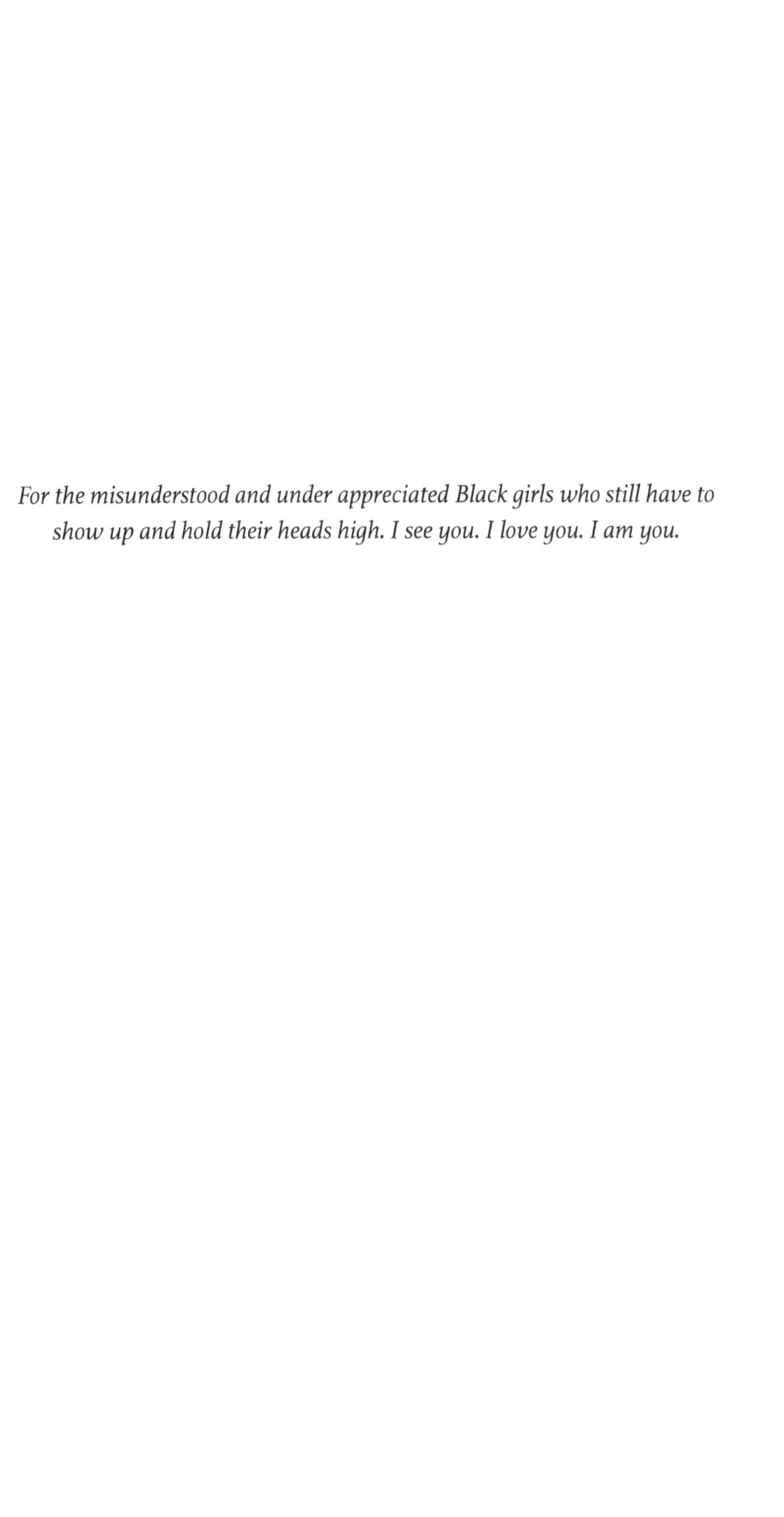

For the misunderstood and under appreciated Black girls who still have to show up and hold their heads high. I see you. I love you. I am you.

"I'm no longer accepting the things I cannot change...I'm changing the things I cannot accept.

— ANGELA DAVIS

AUTHOR NOTE

Honestly, I didn't know if I could write this book. We're all so tired of the world of politics right now, worn out from living in a world where the breaking news is also breaking us.

Despite being steeped in the world of American politics and centered on a Presidential election, I hope Selene's story will still be a place you can find solace. I hope the love, devotion and safety she finds in her men's arms will envelop you as well.

<u>Content and Trigger Warning:</u>

Please be aware this story involves sensitive topics such as **gun violence, racism, misogynoir, loss of a child, school shootings, online harassment, infidelity, stalking and kidnapping.**

While I always endeavor to be thorough when compiling this list, I'm aware that there are things I might have missed. Please charge it to my head, and not my heart.

I strongly advise you to consider your own health and well-being before diving into this story.

THE PLAYLIST

Find it on: Apple Music | Spotify

1

SELENE

I cringe when he reaches for me.

The reaction to my husband's attempt at affection is involuntary. A quick tensing and releasing of muscles I have no control over, but will be blamed for anyway, because everything is my fault. The strands of my hair yielding to the humidity in the late August air and reverting back to their natural curly state?

My fault.

My husband's wandering eye?

My fault.

My body recoiling when he reaches for me with his adulterous hands?

**My. Fault.**

The injustice of it all flares in my gut. A hot and insistent sensation that makes me want to be anywhere but here. Here, being the freshly erected stage on the front lawn of the home Aubrey and I have shared for the duration of our eighteen-year marriage with a bloodthirsty press corps at our feet, waiting for Aubrey Taylor—Democratic nominee and Presidential hopeful—to admit to something they already know he's done. I mean, weren't the photos of him spreading his former speech writer out on the conference room table in his campaign headquarters admission enough?

I swallow the question down, making sure not to let it show on my face because I don't want to give Jordan St. James—Aubrey's campaign manager—yet another thing to critique me on when this press conference is over. She'll already be on me about moving away from him, and it won't matter that it was just an inch, barely noticeable to the naked human eye, because Jordan St. James is far from human and she notices everything.

Which is how I know she knew this day would come.

Her knowledge might have felt like a betrayal if I hadn't accepted a long time ago that she isn't here for me. Aubrey is her primary concern. His political career and the viability of his Presidential bid are all she cares about. It's all *anyone* cares about. The Oval Office is the frame through which everything is viewed, and there's no room in the frame for my humanity. For my pain, humiliation, or anger.

There's only room for stoicism that comes too naturally. For relaxed features that give nothing away to the cameras that have come to capture everything. To broadcast yet another moment in my life where I have to stand tall when all I want to do is give in to the urge to crumble. I gaze into the crowd of reporters, as familiar with them as they are with me, and my mind conjures the memory of the first time I stood in front of this many cameras. Outside of my son's school, with droves of sobbing and worried parents at my back and police and paramedics at my front.

Aubrey was at my side then too, but I'd leaned into his touch instead of away, using the strong lines of his frame to hold me upright when the senior officer on the scene let us know that AJ, our only son and Aubrey's name sake, was one of the twenty-eight students who died in the bullet ridden hallways of the public high school we enrolled him in because his father didn't want being a Senator's son to stop him from having experiences in the real world.

AJ's death had thrust me into spotlight I never wanted to stand in.

Photos of me and Aubrey graced the covers of magazines and newspapers for days on end, and in every one of them, I was weeping.

Open mouth, body wracking, sobs frozen in time. My grief a commodity, available for public consumption. I refuse to feed them today, to let them see the insecurities Aubrey's affair with Sutton Ellsworth—the young, bubbly, blonde speechwriter—have awakened in me. Because I know this time around, there will be no national outpouring of sympathy, no empathetic messages from mothers who also go to bed with images of blood-soaked textbooks clutched by lifeless hands they grew inside of their bodies, filling their heads.

No, this time there will be think-pieces, blog posts, podcast episodes, and social media threads that will turn a conversation about Aubrey's infidelity into a discussion about my perceived shortcomings.

Aubrey reaches out again, and this time, I let him catch me. His hand cups me just above my hip—a practiced gesture of decency everyone now knows is a lie—and I turn my head to give him a thin smile. One that spells solidarity but not happiness, just like Jordan asked me to. And for just a second, as he stares down at me, his blue eyes soft and creased at the corners, his mouth a tender line of contrition, he looks a little like the man I married.

Serious but sincere.

Young but experienced.

Fierce but fair.

My heart squeezes, plagued by nostalgia and past potential, and I force myself to look away from him, back into the crowd of vultures hungry for my heartbreak. Aubrey follows my cue, and, thankfully, releases me from his hold as he turns back to the podium to shuffle through the papers of the speech he's already memorized.

I thread my fingers together and let them come to rest in front of me. As I scan the crowd, photographers snap pictures of my face, and I have to fight the urge to smile. I don't feel happy right now, but smiling when a camera is pointed at me is a reflex at this point. A result of a four years of press training that began the day after Aubrey was re-elected for a third time as a U.S. Senator for the state of Virginia, and not even a full year after we buried our son. Everything changed after that. He fired his previous campaign manager and hired Jordan, who brought on a team of women tasked with turning me into a Stepford wife with just a bit more personality, and I went from being a Senator's wife to a future First Lady.

Aubrey clears his throat softly, but the microphone in front of him picks up the sound and carries it across the stage and into the crowd gathered on the sprawling lawn of our five-acre estate in McLean, Virginia. The idea of building a stage and holding a press conference at your own home might sound ludicrous to some people—okay, *most*, people—but when Jordan pitched it, no one batted an eye. Aubrey's mother had raved about how incredibly smart it was to do it here, where we could drive home the idea that we have the same values as every other American family.

"Thank you all for being with us today," Aubrey says.

He's a skilled orator, and everyone hangs on his every word as he drones on about honor, temptation, and overcoming challenges meant to keep you from your destiny. I bite the inside of my cheek when he says that part. It's the only way to hold in the bitter laughter threatening to break free from my chest. How he can stand here with a straight face, painting his choice to break his wedding vows as a personal challenge that required Herculean effort he wasn't in possession of is beyond me. Staying faithful has never been particularly challenging for me, but perhaps I'm made of stronger stuff.

"I'd like to thank my family and friends for standing beside me during these trying times, and last, but certainly not least—" he pauses, and I turn to look at him because I've listened to him rehearse this speech a million times. Jordan made him practice until *I* knew every word, every inflection, every pause by heart, and this pause does not belong here.

Dread coils deep in my belly as I watch him fold the paper in half, making the words I was most looking forward to hearing disappear. To my left, I see Jordan shaking her head, her green eyes narrowed underneath fire engine red brows that are curved with disapproval. She looks as if she's trying to will Aubrey to go back to the carefully constructed script, to read the paragraph where he states how deeply he regrets breaking his wedding vows and betraying me, where he finally says he's sorry.

Aubrey presses his lips together, fighting against the words he should be saying and replacing them with ones that will do nothing to mend what's broken between us.

"Last but not least," he repeats, flicking guiltless blue eyes over to me before turning them back on the crowd. "I'd like to thank *you*, the American people, for your constant support and understanding. I am, admittedly, an imperfect man, but I'm also a man who loves this country. A man who cares about the person behind every vote. A man who, if given the chance to serve as President of the United States, will never stop working to make this country a place we can all be proud of."

2

SELENE

"The motherfucker didn't even apologize to you," Monique Walker exclaims for what feels like the hundredth time since Aubrey's speech two weeks ago.

"I know, Mo. I was there." There's a marked lack of patience in my response that causes my best friend of over twenty years to pause. Even though we're on the phone and not face to face, I know her full lips are pursed in a regretful frown.

"I'm sorry, Sel." She sighs, relenting for just a second. "I just get so pissed off every time I think about it. He had you move an entire product launch for that press conference, and he couldn't even be bothered to acknowledge you?"

Monique's anger tries to seep its way into my bones, but I don't let it. I simply can't hold another ounce of negative emotion. There's no room for it in my body. I tilt my head back and close my eyes, allowing the buttery leather of my headrest to cradle my skull while my best friend and business partner continues her diatribe. Nothing she's saying is wrong. Every point she makes about Aubrey's remarks during the press conference is an echo of truths I am resigned to hold deep inside of myself because if I let them out, I will explode and destroy everything in my path, including America's next President.

Aubrey wasn't even supposed to run this year. The plan was always for 2028. That's what we'd settled on when AJ was born the same year Monique and I started Culture Code—a digital firm operating at the intersection of technology and social justice. At that point, Aubrey was a low-level state senator with a dream, but I always knew where he wanted to end up. We made a plan. A timeline we dedicated our lives to and never deviated from, but then AJ died, and everything changed.

The loss of our son became cannon fodder for Aubrey's political career. Suddenly, everyone, including Scott Warner, the President at the time, knew who he was and what we'd lost. Out of the haze of our grief, Aubrey emerged. A bright and shiny star with enough political capital to launch a Presidential campaign a whole election cycle early.

"You can't stay with him," Monique is saying now, her voice cutting through my thoughts. "Please tell me you're not going to stay with him."

"Mo, I don't know what I'm going to do, okay? I'll think about it after we get this facial recognition software on the market."

"This is the part where I remind you that software would already *be* on the market if it weren't for your cheating husband."

"I don't need a reminder, Monique. I'm well aware."

Canceling the launch had hurt me and frustrated the hell out of my team. We've been working on this software for nearly six years. Writing and rewriting lines of code, building an extensive and diverse database of photos for the software to compare faces to, sacrificing sleep and sanity, all to get to a day Aubrey and Jordan stole from us without a second thought.

"You only call me Monique when you're mad at me."

"I'm not mad at *you*." I sigh, opening my eyes and looking at the house that no longer feels like home to me. "I'm just mad in general."

"Good. Anger is good. You can use it to pack up all your shit and leave that cheating asshole in the dust."

Sometimes I love how Monique can make everything that feels complicated seem simple. When I tend to overthink things, a rare but not unheard of occurrence, she comes swooping in with an outstretched hand, ready to lead me down a path she cleared for us. This is not one of those times, though. Because we're not conducting a cost-benefit analysis for a new community outreach program or determining how many new employees we can take on, we're talking about me leaving my husband of eighteen years.

Yes, I'm angry at Aubrey for cheating. Furious at him for denying me the public apology I have more than earned, but leaving him just doesn't feel like something I can do when I don't understand why any of this happened in the first place. I need answers, and Aubrey is the only one who can give them to me. Not that he's been particularly forthcoming these days. Every time I try to ask him about the photos, about the affair, about what drew him to Sutton in the first place, he shuts down, denying me access to the information I need to solve the problem in our marriage, I wasn't even aware existed.

Monique won't understand any of this. She's a heart-first person. Driven by emotion, especially in relationships. As soon as she starts dating someone, logic is a foreign concept. Reason a distant memory. Everything is angst, high stakes, and a burning passion that fizzles out fast. Monique has always enjoyed the thrill of those kinds of bonds, but they've never been for me. I've always appreciated the calm, steadiness of my marriage. Aubrey and I are both solution-oriented people. We have never faced a problem we couldn't sit down and parse out a solution to.

Until now.

"Goodbye, Monique." I lean forward, allowing my finger to hover over the red button on the display screen in my dashboard that will end the call.

"Thought you weren't mad at me?" She tosses back, not bothering to say goodbye before ending the call herself.

It takes me ten minutes to work up the energy to go inside. Every day, I come home from work and walk into something new and unexpected. Campaign staffers using my dining room to make calls to unregistered voters. Jordan, Aubrey, and Torrance Belford—Aubrey's running mate—having a working dinner in my kitchen. A news crew on my front lawn, getting shots of the house and property for a profile piece they're doing on Aubrey.

It's always something, and today it's a strategy meeting in my living room that includes Aubrey, Torrance, Jordan, and a large group of serious-looking men in black suits that I've never seen before. I take one look at the scene and turn the other way, opting to go work in my home office instead of subjecting myself to another long, drawn-out meeting where no one wants or needs my opinion on anything.

When I sit down at my desk, I release a deep breath to ground myself, so I can actually get some work done. Pushing back the software launch has created an intricately tangled web of complications I've been trying to unwind on my own for the past two weeks. The process would move a lot quicker if I allowed my assistant, Nichelle, and the launch team to help me, but I need the small sense of fulfillment that comes with resolving at least one issue in my life, and they need to be moving on to other projects. Once I start working, finding the stride of productivity I was unable to access at the office, time moves quickly.

Two hours pass with my eyes fixed on the screen of my computer and my fingers flying over my keyboard. I pay invoices for the new venue space and a steep cancellation fee for the old one, approve a marketing campaign and the associated print materials that had to be updated to reflect the new date and location, and reply to email after email from investors and stakeholders who don't think adultery is a sufficient reason for a delay. By the time I'm done wading through my to-do list, my head is hurting, and my eyes are begging for a break from blue lights and screens.

I begin to shut down my computer, intending to grab a quick snack from the kitchen and go up to bed, only to be interrupted by the chime of an incoming video call from my mother. An involuntary groan slips through my clenched teeth as I glance heavenward, praying today's call will be shorter than yesterday's and less invasive than the call we had on the day before that.

"Hey, Mama."

I force the words to come out even and free of the annoyance I feel building inside of my chest. Daily communication with my mother isn't something I'm used to. Our relationship is nothing like the one she has with my younger sisters, Robin and Jessica, who live all of five minutes away from the house we grew up in and visit or call our parents every day. Mama says the difference between her relationship with my sisters and her relationship with me is need.

My sisters need her, they've always needed her, and I don't.

Apparently, I've always been that way—strong, independent, *apart*. The child she never had to worry about. She's worried now, though, and it shows in every line of her round face and mahogany skin. It hangs on the corners of her downturned lips and lingers in the creases of her almond-shaped eyes, winking at me from the depths of brown irises with toffee colored puddles sprinkled throughout. They're my eyes. One of the only things my mother gave me while everything else came from my father.

"The baby girls are all you, Justine," the ladies who frequented my mother's hair salon used to say, *"but that oldest girl? She's all Albert."*

While I'm sure they meant well, the sentiment created something of a division between me and the rest of the women in my family. My mom and my sisters were always a unit. Their similarities made it easier for her to see them, to identify their needs and meet them, while my differences made me a puzzle no one tried to solve except my father. And even he gave up sometimes, opting to stash me in front of the old desktop in the back of his auto shop to play Solitaire when I refused to spend another day sweeping up hair and organizing perm rods by size and color in Mama's salon.

The corner of my lips quirk as the image of me at the makeshift desk floats through my mind. I wrote my first program on that computer. It was a crude but efficient piece of software meant to help Dad keep track of his inventory. Pride I'd never seen before had shone in my father's eyes when I showed him how it worked.

"You're smiling," my mother says, her head tilting to the side as she assesses me. "Are things getting better with Aubrey?"

"Things with Aubrey are exactly as they were when you called yesterday." Maybe worse. Every day that passes without us having an actual conversation lodges the knife in my back a little deeper.

Her frown deepens. "Well, what are you going to do about it?"

"The only thing I can do: wait."

"Wait?" The word is more of a shriek than a question, coated in disapproval and the type of confusion I've come to accept my mother will always have when it comes to me.

"Yes, Mama. Wait." I rub at my forehead, trying to dispel the ache growing behind my brows. I am so tired of talking about Aubrey, of being subjected to inquisition after inquisition, while he gets to keep living as if nothing happened. Besides being officially kicked out of our bedroom and having to hire a new speechwriter, Aubrey's day-to-day life is unchanged. He gets to work without interruption, to wear his wedding band without questioning eyes staring at it and making snap judgments about his state of mind and sense of self-worth. "Things have been hectic around here, what with the campaign and—"

"The news of the affair," she adds, cutting my sentence short. I watch her move through the hall that leads from her bedroom to the kitchen. Her pursed lips an indication of her waning patience. "Waiting don't make a lick of sense to me, Selene, but if that's how you want to live your life, then I guess there's nothing I can say to change your mind."

"*I* don't make a lick of sense to you."

Tears gather in the corner of my eyes, and I push them back. My mother stops walking, coming to rest in front of the wall of family photos she made us take every year on Easter Sunday, with the heat of the Georgia sun bearing down on us. In every one, my sisters and I are wearing matching outfits, and in every one, they're smiling big and bright while I grimace because the stockings are itchy and the tag in the dress my mother refused to cut out is rubbing against my skin.

Each image is a confirmation of the validity of my statement. It's not my marriage or the way I'm choosing to deal—or not deal—with this affair that doesn't make sense to my mother. It's me. It's always been me. My career. My husband. My sensory issues. My autism diagnosis. All my life, I've been one big question mark to her.

"*Baby.*" Her voice is a quiet, regretful whisper that does nothing to soothe the pain of spending my entire life being loved but not understood.

"I have to go, Mama. Please don't continue to call me every day. I will let you know when there's a change in my marriage you'll find satisfactory."

Before she can respond, I disconnect the call. As soon as her face disappears from the screen, a wave of shame washes over me because I know I hurt her feelings. Whatever else she might be, Justine Grant is a sensitive woman who loves her children with all of her heart, and she doesn't deserve my frustration or anger. I grab my phone from the wireless charging stand on my desk and send her a quick text, apologizing for my behavior. Afterwards, I send an apology to Monique as well.

When that's done, I set my phone down and place my head in my hands, pressing my palms into my eyes to try to curb the sudden urge to cry. I have people in my life who love me, who are worried about me, and for the past two weeks, all I've done is get mad at them for caring, for wanting to know my next move, so they can see me through it. All of the anger and frustration I've aimed their way has been misplaced. There's only one person it belongs to, and I'm going to give it to him whether he wants it or not.

"Are you planning on joining us in the living room anytime soon?"

My head snaps up, and I'm greeted by the familiar blend of classic European features and the manufactured ruggedness of a red-blooded American I've been looking at for years. Aubrey Taylor is a beautiful man, but he's nothing like the husband I pictured for myself when I was growing up.

I thought I would have what my mother and father have.

A beautiful, Black family with varying shades of melanin and textured hair. Babies with brown eyes instead of the cerulean blue Aubrey passed down to AJ. The color had been a shocking contrast against his brown skin, but at that point, I was used to being surprised by my life with Aubrey. He's been surprising me since the first time we met in the library during my first year of undergrad at Stanford.

At first, it was all positives like his patience and understanding, or the way he never treated my quirks like things to be tolerated instead of outright accepted, but now they feel overwhelmingly negative. This campaign has changed him, altered the way he treats me. He's critical, impatient, and... unfaithful.

The last word pulls all the air from my lungs. It leaves me in a weary sigh that Aubrey ignores. His brows lift, and his eyes stretch, a silent reminder of the question I've left unanswered. "I'm working," I lie, gesturing at my computer. "Trying to get the launch rescheduled."

"Can it wait? I need you out here."

His question hits me like a blow to the chest, exploding in a cloud of searing pain and annoyance. How can he ask me that? *Me.* The woman who just rescheduled one of the biggest days of her career to stand beside him while he admitted to betraying me.

"Can it wait?" I repeat the question, testing the words out, weighing them to see if they hold the same level of audacity when they come off my tongue. They don't. "No, Aubrey, it can't wait. *I* can't wait. I can't keep pushing my career to the wayside in service of your political aspirations."

"Political aspirations?" He huffs, stepping deeper into the office. "Is that really how you want to refer to the campaign I've given the last four years of my life to?"

Something inside me is breaking. Maybe it's been broken for a while. Maybe *I've* been broken for a while, and I'm just feeling it now. Right now, as I listen to my husband speak of his Presidential campaign as his own personal sacrifice, dismissing everything I've given.

My time.

My energy.

My dignity.

All of my work is done, but I turn back towards my computer, wiggling the mouse to awaken the screen. "We've both given a lot to this campaign, Aubrey. I've already rescheduled the launch date once. I won't do it again."

He rolls his eyes. "No one is asking you to move your precious launch again, Selene."

"But you are asking me to stop working on it to sit in a meeting no one needs me for."

"I just said you were needed."

I lift a brow, sparing him a glance out of the corner of my eye. "Who decided that?"

"What?"

"It's a simple question, Aubrey. Who determined I was needed? You? Jordan? Torrance? Which one of you do I have to thank for wasting more of my time?"

Because when I leave my office to go into the living room and sit in on the rest of this meeting, it *will* be a waste of my time. There might be one question meant specifically for me, something small that could be answered in an email to my assistant, but the rest of it will have nothing to do with me.

"The Secret Service agents who were just assigned to us."

My attention is divided between the email that just landed in my inbox and this pointless conversation with Aubrey, so it takes me a moment to process what he's just said. When I do, I give him all of it. Every ounce of my scrunched brow, open-mouthed attention.

"The who?"

Aubrey's lips twitch like he wants to smile but doesn't want to waste the action on me. He's happy my interest has been piqued because it means he's won tonight's battle of wills and importance. It seems to be a regular occurrence these days.

"The agents from our Secret Service detail."

"We don't have a Secret Service detail."

And with less than ten weeks left until Election Day, I don't understand why we would get one now. Once Aubrey got the Democratic Party's nomination, we were offered a detail, and he'd refused it because Jordan said it didn't align with the image they were trying to cultivate of him as a man of the people. They wanted to show voters that Aubrey wanted the Oval to make a change, not to take advantage of the perks that came along with it.

"We do now," Aubrey says, splitting his gaze between my face and the watch on his wrist. Clearly, he has somewhere else to be. "Come meet them, so we can all move on with our evening."

Reluctantly, I rise from my desk and make my way to the doorway Aubrey is crowding. He steps back, making room for me to pass through so we don't have to touch. The subtle rejection stings even as it satisfies the part of me that doesn't want Aubrey's hands anywhere near me. I step into the hallway with Aubrey at my back. He's several steps behind me, and every inch between our bodies is a reckoning. A private appraisal of the physical and emotional distance between us, I can't ignore anymore.

I round the corner that leads to the living room and notice two of the broad-shouldered, black suited men I spotted earlier moving towards me on long legs that seem to be locked in step. My own stride falters, and I stop short, pausing to appreciate the synchronicity of their movements, the symmetry of their existence.

They don't look alike—although they both are well over six feet tall and have deep, umber complexions. One stands an inch or so above his counterpart and probably outweighs him by a good twenty pounds of muscle. There are specks of gray peppered throughout the temples of his low fade, which suggests that he's older than his partner with the freshly shaved head, but not by much.

The differences are obvious, making it easy for anyone to view them as two distinct individuals, but still, something about their features insists they were meant to be viewed together.

One's firm jaw designed to enhance the sharpness of the other's.

One's full, sensual mouth created to highlight the lushness of the other's lips.

One's pair of onyx eyes crafted to make you contemplate whether the man at his side has ever been told his irises are a unique mixture of copper and brass.

Aubrey cuts the corner mere seconds after I do and runs into me, hitting me with a force that sends me flying. Even as I lose my balance, my body pitching forward while my brain calculates how hard I'll hit the floor, I find that I wouldn't be surprised to learn he didn't slow down at all because it's just not his way. When something is in his path, it doesn't occur to him that the decent and polite thing would be to go around.

He always chooses to go through.

I'm thinking about how absolutely messed up it is that I'm not even an exception to that rule when his hands go to my waist, steadying me with a loose hold that smacks of our estrangement.

There's no tenderness or familiarity, no lingering touch or question about if I'm okay. There's not even an apology. Just a frustrated curse and a roll of his eyes. I brush him off, looking up to find two sets of eyes on me. The moment I'm settled in the weight of their gazes, I want nothing more than to go back into my office and hide because those eyes see more in one second than I've ever willingly revealed to anyone in an entire lifetime.

3

CAL

The Taylors *look all wrong together.*

That's the first thought that runs through my head when my eyes land on them in the hallway. The second is that the wrongness my brain is registering has nothing to do with the way they actually look, because they're both attractive people.

Aubrey is an All-American, blonde-haired, blue-eyed man in good shape for his age and still managing to hold on to all of his hair, and Selene is, well, gorgeous. She's all sable skin and soft, round features, deep-set eyes shaped like almonds and the color of browned butter. Midnight strands that hang down her back when they're straight, and—based on the pictures I've seen of her before her husband's campaign manager or some press training expert demanded she change it—caress the back of her neck when it's curly.

By all counts, looking at the two of them together should be a visually pleasing experience, but all I feel right now is uneasy because there's an awkwardness in the air between them that makes being in their shared presence painful. After the press conference and the lack of apology, I expected their energy to be a little off. Aubrey's affair is national news, and his failure to give his wife a public apology has been a topic of discussion for two weeks. It's even bleeding into the polls, with the Black, female demographic Selene has helped him secure throughout the campaign expressing doubts about giving him their votes. Apparently, when Aubrey lost Selene's trust, he'd forfeited his right to theirs as well.

So, yeah, weird makes sense, and awkward is to be expected. But what's really catching me off guard is the hostility swirling around them because it doesn't feel new. It's too *settled*, completely at home in the space Aubrey puts between him and his wife when she pushes his hands away. Loud in the absence of yet another apology, he's denied her. An overbearing tree with thick branches, deep roots, and a fully formed trunk that speaks of consistent sustenance, showcasing the fact that someone has been feeding it for years, keeping it alive with a silent disdain that turned into public infidelity.

My training requires me to walk the fine line of trusting my instincts and keeping an open mind in every situation. It requires me to treat people as both predictable and unexpected at the same time, because it's the only way to get the full picture of what we're dealing with. I remind myself of these facts as I set aside all my assumptions about the Taylors and their marriage. The only thing I allow myself to hold on to is the knowledge that this couple is unlike any of the other pairs Beck—my best friend and the only man I trust to have my six—and I have guarded in the years since we left the FBI's Counter Terrorism unit and joined the Secret Service.

Our past assignments have had us dealing with couples who were deeply in love and weren't afraid to show it. Hell, even the buttoned-up, frowns-at-public-displays-of-affection types had a certain air of devotion around them. They might have hid it in simple gestures like a hand on the small of the woman's back or a loving glance from across a crowded room, but it was there.

It's not here, though.

I try to convince myself that it doesn't matter, even though I know it does. We can't protect people if we don't know the truth, and the truth of Aubrey and Selene is nothing like the picture his team painted in the security briefing we had in the living room. His campaign manager had assured us there were no domestic concerns to contend with while Aubrey tapped away at his phone like his primary goal for the meeting was to convey how bored he was with the topic of his marriage and infidelity.

The only time he seemed particularly invested in what we were saying was when our team lead mentioned the role Beck and I played in foiling the attempted assassination of President Scott Warner. The case, much like Aubrey's affair, was national news, and Aubrey seemed to recall every detail of it, except, apparently, our names. His face had turned red when he admitted to forgetting, but we'd taken no offense, introducing ourselves and shaking his hand.

Now his face is red again, and I bite back a laugh as I watch him stumble over his words, trying to introduce Beck to Selene even though it's clear to all of us he doesn't remember his name. We all watch him snap his fingers and frown as he tries to recall it, and in the silence we leave him lingering in, I feel something like camaraderie among the three of us. It snaps into place, holding firm even when Beck finally decides to put the man out of his misery.

"Agent Beckham, ma'am," he says, holding his hand out to Selene. He focuses all of his attention on her, hiding his annoyance with her husband in a friendly smile.

Her pupils dilate slightly as his raspy baritone washes over her, and I clench my jaw to hide my smile. Beck is quite the charmer when he's not being a cynical asshole.

"And this," he's saying now, slipping his hand out of hers and turning toward me, "is my partner, Agent Drake."

"Nice to meet you, Mrs. Taylor."

Her skin is still warm from Beck's palm when her hand slips into mine. I'm impressed by how firm her shake is. Most women in this world like to go with a delicate, bent wrist with fingertips that barely graze your palm because someone, somewhere, told them power and femininity don't go hand in hand. Selene clearly isn't a proponent of that mindset. There's strength in her grip and intensity in the eye contact she forces herself to give me, and I have to admit, if only to myself, that all the conservative old white men who spend their days online comparing her to Aubrey's mistress are right.

Selene Taylor is nothing like Sutton Ellsworth.

The speechwriter is youthful, naive exuberance while Selene is regal, exquisite wisdom. She's the beauty of aging, a walking testament to the glorious embrace of passing time and lessons learned. She's calm and quiet power that isn't afraid to get loud. Over the course of our threat assessment, which included an in-depth look at Selene's online presence, I came across posts that talked about Sutton's soft, feminine energy and described Selene as hard, and she is hard. The set of her jaw. The sharp line of her brows. The harsh slope of her shoulders. She is hard, but only in a way that tells me she knows all too well that this world isn't a safe place for a Black woman's vulnerabilities, that softness and warmth are not luxuries she can afford.

"Selene." She pulls her hand out of mine, splitting a commanding look between Beck and me. "Please call me Selene. Mrs. Taylor is my mother-in-law, and I've always hated being referred to as ma'am."

Beck nods, but his jaw has gone rigid. I can practically feel his prim and proper upbringing and the training protocols that warn against getting too close to the people you're guarding rebelling against the request.

"Of course, Selene," I answer with an obedient smile. "It's nice to finally meet you. Thank you for welcoming us into your home."

"I didn't have much of a choice in the matter." She cuts an accusatory eye at Aubrey, who keeps his features set in a mask of indifference. "But I'm glad to have you all the same."

The awkwardness is back, and this time it reaches out, pulling Beck and me into the bubble of discomfort. Beck shuffles his feet, and I know he's anxious to get on with it. He doesn't like small talk.

"Well, we should keep moving." Beck aims his words at me, but they're meant for everyone. "We're supposed to be ensuring the floor plans we received from Mr. Taylor's assistant last week match the actual layout of the house."

Selene's brows fall in on themselves as she turns to her husband. "You sent them plans for the house last week? I thought this was a recent development."

"I never said that." Aubrey flashes an annoyed glare at us, like it's somehow our fault that he didn't tell his wife they were getting a security detail even though he's known for weeks. After the press conference, there was an uptick in threatening language aimed at Selene from the same people celebrating her husband cheating on her, which made our presence less of a suggestion and more of a requirement for Aubrey to continue campaigning safely.

His team had been reluctant to accept a detail, something about it not fitting with his established image, but the powers that be insisted, telling him it wouldn't be good for his image if his wife was harmed and it came out he was aware of the threat and did nothing to prevent it. Judging by the perplexed look on Selene's face, it seems none of this information was passed along to her.

"I could fill an entire book with the things you never said, Aubrey."

He lets out a long, exasperated sigh, and I get the sense this isn't the first time they've had this conversation.

"I'm not doing this with you, Selene." He glances at his watch, impatience gathering in the corners of his eyes. "Now, you can either stand in this hallway and embarrass yourself in front of two perfect strangers, or you can come and meet the rest of the team, so you can get back to your work. The choice is yours."

I knew the moment Beck and I were assigned to this detail that I wasn't going to like Aubrey Taylor, but I never expected to want to punch him in the face on day one. Actually, I never thought *I'd* want to hit him at all. Out of the two of us, Beck's the one that's usually curbing the urge to commit an act of violence, but in this moment when Selene's skin has taken on a red undertone indicative of embarrassment and hurt is causing her lips to tremble the way my mother's used to when she'd talk about how my dad left her? I want to lay him out. I want to grab him by his throat and squeeze until he gives her the apology she deserves, not just for his current transgressions, but for past ones as well. For everything he's ever said or done to make her feel the way she feels right now.

The desire builds inside of me even as I watch Selene quell the emotions that inspired it. She pulls in a deep breath and crosses her arms, squeezing herself tightly. Then she turns to Beck and me, hitting us with a smile that's polite and distant, but somehow still dazzling.

"Agent Beckham. Agent Drake. It was so nice to meet you."

And without another word, she steps around us, continuing her journey to the living room where the rest of the team will be waiting. Aubrey stalks off behind her, leaving us standing in the pungent cloud of loathing and misery wafting off of him and directed at his lovely wife.

Beck looks at me and raises a brow. "*This* should be fun."

4

SELENE

I prefer my hair curly.

Decades of begging my mama for relaxers or the burn of a hot comb and being denied every time had left me with no choice but to appreciate the volume and fluff of my natural hair, to learn how to wash, deep condition, detangle and style it without getting overwhelmed by the feel of products on my hands and wet hair clinging to my neck and shoulders. By the time Aubrey established his campaign fund, I'd mastered the art of the wash and go, using only two products to give myself perfectly defined curls that lasted all week long.

I was loathe to give those curls up, to subject myself to the hell of finding a stylist who could keep my hair straight while maintaining the health and integrity of the curls underneath, to set aside a day out of every week all so I could fit the mold Jordan St. James told me I needed to exist inside if I wanted to be accepted as America's next First Lady.

Can you imagine?

A red-headed white woman without of hint of a wave or whisper of a kink in her hair sitting in my face touting the *power of the silk press* and sliding me a list of salons she thought would be able to meet my needs.

As if she had a clue in the world what my needs were.

As if she cared.

Like most conversations between me and Jordan, the one about my hair turned into an unnecessary argument. The two of us locking horns, both of us relentless and unyielding, reminding me that if any other circumstance had brought her into my life, Jordan would have been a friend of mine. I admired her confidence, how she pushed and pushed until she got what she wanted. I just hated when I was the one she was pushing, especially when it was on behalf of Aubrey.

In the end, I didn't consider any of the salons Jordan suggested. Instead, I asked Monique to make me an appointment with the stylist she's been going to for years: Diane Hastings, an old-school hairdresser with a shop on 7th street that's just a short walk from the Shaw-Howard metro stop. I was skeptical at first—about the other clients I'd have to encounter or the small talk I'd have to endure while Diane coaxed my hair into submission—but after years of being a regular, and receiving the gift of an after hours appointment with minimal chatting from Diane, I've come to appreciate the routine of it all, to value the sacredness of this space.

Which is why it feels like such a violation for Jordan St. James to waltz in here and take a seat in the chair across from me like she's waiting for someone to press her hair.

Diane goes still, her hand hovering over the handle of the marcel irons warming in their holders. "I don't know if you missed the sign out there, little girl, but we're closed," she says, her tone all sass and censure.

Jordan's eyes narrow with humor as she flips straight, red tresses over her shoulder. "I'm here for Selene, not your services."

Diane huffs, and out of the corner of my eye, I see her hands move to her hips. "Doesn't change the fact that the sign on the door says closed. And how'd you get past those big, burly men in black outside? I thought they were supposed to stop randoms from getting too close to *Mrs. Taylor.*"

I knew I liked Diane as soon as I met her. She's a straight shooter who has never flirted with the idea of holding her tongue. But when Jordan's emerald eyes start to glitter with discomfort, I decide I might love her. I've only ever seen Jordan completely at ease, confident in her ability to own the attention and command the actions of every person around her. Seeing her like this, questioning the validity of her presence in this space, is refreshing, and I don't mind if that makes me petty.

"It's okay, Diane. Jordan is my husband's campaign manager."

"Which is why the men in black had no problem letting me through," she says, flashing a condescending smile at the older woman fuming behind me, already fully recovered from the rare bout of feeling like she doesn't belong. "Feel free to continue your work, Mrs. Hastings. I don't want to interrupt."

I arch a brow. "Too late for that, don't you think?"

Diane huffs her agreement, but she resumes her work. Jordan watches with a distant kind of interest as Diane parts out another section of hair and picks up the marcels. The first bit of residual heat tickles my scalp before the iron glides down my blown-out strands, turning them into silken midnight. Most of the time, there's a kind of peace to be found in the monotony of the process. The parting, combing, and pressing.

But with Jordan here, that peace is eluding me.

I feel exposed. Like I'm standing in the street with only half of my clothes on and someone I don't know or trust is watching me struggle to make myself presentable, taking pleasure in seeing me out of sorts.

A pang of annoyance runs through me as I realize that's probably why Jordan chose to corner me here. She could have done it anywhere. At my home. In the offices of Culture Code. Hell, in my inbox. But she came here to send me a message: *I'm in control, and you're not.*

"What do you want, Jordan?"

She tilts her head to the side, taking her time bringing her eyes back to my face. "Oh, I think you already know the answer to that, Selene."

"Aubrey Taylor in the Oval Office," I repeat the mantra I've been reciting and had recited to me for years now, my intonation flat and emotionless. "That still doesn't explain why you're here."

"Do you still want it?" Jordan asks. "Do you still want your husband in the Oval, Selene?"

My nostrils flare. I hate being interrogated, especially when the questions are as pointless as this one. Every day of my life for the past four years has been this campaign. I've lived it, breathed it, *bled for it.* Sacrificed my dignity and pride all because I believe in the man I married and the good we can do for this country.

"Of course, I want Aubrey in the Oval."

Jordan brings her hands to the lapels of her blazer, adjusting it slightly even though there's not a button or single thread out of place. "Prove it."

If Diane wasn't currently holding hot metal to my head, I would have given in to the urge to let my head fly back in offense. Because I can't do that without getting burned, I allow the outrage to show on my face.

"Do you know who you're talking to?" Her lips part, but I wave my hand to stop her. "No, don't answer that. In fact, don't say anything else right now. I'll let you know when you can speak again. Are we clear?"

There's a grimace riding high on the lines of Jordan's brows, and she nods like I need her permission to continue.

"From the moment Aubrey hired you, all I've done is prove that our goal is the same. I have ceded control of my life, my image—" I lift a hand, waving my fingers to indicate my rapidly transforming strands "—my hair. I've smiled when you told me to smile, dressed how you told me to dress, kissed babies I didn't even want to hold, hosted a fundraiser on my son's birthday instead of visiting his grave, rearranged my schedule and my life for appearances and meetings and every other event you have deemed it necessary for me to attend. Most recently, that had me canceling a launch for a product I've been working on since before anyone in the world knew who Aubrey

Taylor was and standing beside my husband while he admitted to the world he cheated on me."

Diane scoffs, disgust riddled through the sound. It's her preferred way to communicate her disdain for Aubrey. A scoff, a deep sigh, a roll of her eyes. Other than that, she stays quiet about it, letting me use her shop as the one place where I can hide from the world that's still talking about my husband's infidelity.

"Everyone likes to imagine that the man in the chair is the one who makes all the sacrifices, but we both know better, Jordan. We know it's the people behind him who give up everything, and I *have* given up everything. There is nothing left for me to prove." I take a beat, pausing to make sure she has fully absorbed my point before saying, "*Now*, you may speak."

Jordan doesn't respond immediately. I don't expect her to because that would be too much like obeying a person she views as her subordinate. I wait her out, refusing to repeat myself, hoping maybe she'll get up and leave, that she'll go home and think of another, more appropriate time and place to broach this subject with me.

Of course, I don't have that kind of luck.

"I appreciate your candor, Selene. Really, I do, but you're wrong."

"About?"

"Having nothing left to prove."

Diane is working on the front, left side of my head now, so I reach up and grab my ear, folding the top of it down onto itself to ensure it doesn't get burned.

"What is it you think I still have to prove?"

"Your love," she says, crossing her legs.

"I'm not sure I understand," I confess, threads of irritation burning through me as I search for the nuance I'm certain has evaded me. It's not uncommon for me to struggle to wade through subterfuge and get to the true meaning of what's being said. Jordan knows I prefer clear and concise communication, so I'm not sure why she's being vague about her point. "Aubrey cheated on me," I continue. "How does that equate to my emotional commitment being called into question?"

Some people would think I'm being deliberately obtuse, but it's a genuine question. Everything I've done since the news of the affair broke has been in service to a love I've carried with me for over half my life. I stayed in the house. I'm still wearing my ring. I've refused to disparage his character in conversations with my family, friends, and the press. Every night since I kicked him out of our bed, I've lain in it alone and recited the list of all the good things Aubrey has ever done for me.

I haven't just proven my love for Aubrey, I've fought to hold on to it. I've held vigil for it, waiting for answers and healing that might never come.

Jordan sighs, and her lips twitch. Impatience, my brain screams, supplying me with the name of the emotion I've come to associate with the micro expression.

"Aubrey is the first Democrat in years to run a campaign that focuses so heavily on family values. I tried to talk him out of it. You see, it's a hard sell when there are no little Aubreys or Selenes running around to really drive home the whole family part. But he insisted on it because—"

"Because not running on family values would have precluded him from talking about our son's death every chance he got," I finish for her, not bothering to address the subtle dig about Aubrey and me not having more children. It's been a point of contention between my husband and me for as long as I can remember, and now it's a regular topic in campaign strategy meetings, the nightly news, and trashy tabloid articles that speculate about whether we'll have a 'save the marriage baby' soon.

Jordan doesn't so much as bristle at the suggestion. One of the things that makes her the best at what she does is that she doesn't balk at indelicacy. Part of me thinks she thrives on it, that she loves the way it gives her permission to be indelicate as well.

"Exactly." She nods, and the smile she flashes at me is broad, reaching her eyes. I don't know Jordan's expressions as well as I know Aubrey's or Monique's, but I recognize this smile, and it's as close to pride or admiration as Jordan gets. It tells me she appreciates my continued understanding of the way politics work. "Speaking on AJ's death has helped Aubrey maintain his family man image."

"Aubrey," I correct, my voice hard. "Don't call him AJ. You didn't know him. You never met him. You don't get to call him AJ."

My son hated being called AJ.

He always introduced himself to strangers as Aubrey, and if he had been around to meet Jordan, he wouldn't have allowed her to call him by anything other than that. Only a select few people were permitted to use the nickname, and some days, I think it still bothered him when we did. Aubrey thinks it's stupid that I've grown so protective of the moniker, that I would fume and rage when he used it in a speech, when I saw it written in the papers, or heard it passing through the lips of complete strangers, but I didn't care then and I don't care now. That name, those letters, the boy they represent, it's all a sacred covenant I won't tolerate the desecration of.

"Aubrey," Jordan repeats, dipping her head in acknowledgment even as her lips tighten with the need to tell me that not using the nickname makes it harder to differentiate between my husband and son in conversation. I lift my brows, inviting her to say the words so we can reenact the last time she said that to me, and I told her the solution to that problem was for her to never speak about my son again.

She pushes the words back down and clears her throat before continuing. "My point is, the family unit we're selling the world is only comprised of two people: you and Aubrey, and if things with you two continue the way they have, then we're going to keep losing customers."

I don't like metaphors, especially when they make me sound like a thing to be consumed and frame people who should be focused on making the right choice for their futures as grubby-handed vultures vying for the most popular thing, but I think I understand what Jordan is saying. Aubrey has taken a hit in the polls recently, and I'm guessing the independent data she has compiled has identified the specific demographic he's lost the most of.

Silently, I run through and eliminate the possibilities. If he'd been losing ground with white men, she'd be overseeing a photo shoot on a golf course with Aubrey, his brothers—Timothy and Simon—and their father, Arthur. If older white women were turning their backs on him, Jordan would be coordinating a string of appearances for him to attend with his mother, Hillary, as his date.

But she's not doing any of that.

She's here with me, which can only mean one thing.

"Aubrey's losing the Black vote."

Diane covers her laugh with a cough, but she doesn't say a word. If I didn't know she'd signed an ironclad NDA, I'd suspect that she was saving all of her commentary for someone else.

Jordan nods. "Black women, specifically. They're having a hard time forgiving him for the infidelity, for hurting you."

I would ask why they care, but we've gone over parasocial relationships a million times already. Despite working in tech, I'll never quite understand the Internet's ability to make complete strangers feel like they know you just because they've absorbed every moment of your life that's been posted across various platforms. Some of them so heavily edited, so perfectly curated, they don't even resemble what you lived through.

It's not all bad.

I know some people have been able to build beautiful communities and friendships through social media, but that has not, and will never, be me. My personality would make it difficult, but my life now —with Secret Service agents trailing me everywhere I go and standing in between me and the world—makes it so I'll only ever have this insulation, this pressure from an outside world I'll never get to live in that will dictate how I operate in my day to day life. They'll tell Jordan they want me to jump, and she'll use her data and statistics to tell me exactly how high to go.

Of course, I'm not mad at the Black women who are angry for me. I'm grateful that there are at least some people in this world who aren't blaming me for the mess Aubrey made. I am, however, mad that their collective anger will take precedence over mine. That it will become Aubrey and Jordan's focus and my responsibility to fix.

Maybe I should threaten to take away my vote, too.

"And you think I can change their minds?" I ask.

"I know you can."

Her confidence isn't in me, per se. It's in the data. In the numbers that tell her Aubrey only had Black, female voters to lose because of me. Their affinity for Aubrey is based on the strength of their connection to me. They trusted him because I trusted him, and now, their faith in him is shaken because mine has shattered irreparably.

I pull in a breath, trying to expel the hurt that's rolling through me. "The first rule of sales is belief, Jordan. You have to believe in the product you're selling. You have to have an unshakable confidence in its worth before you can convince someone else of its value. I don't have that in me and Aubrey right now, so, no, I don't think I can. Whatever ground Aubrey's lost with Black women will have to be recovered without me. I can't sell a lie."

"So you're saying that our goals are not the same."

"Not at all. I still want Aubrey in the Oval. I just think you two are going to have to figure out a way to get him there without me."

As I say the words, I feel relief wash over me. For weeks, everyone has been asking me what I'm going to do about all of this, and I've told them I was going to wait. I thought I meant for Aubrey to give me the answers I needed or the apology I've been craving, but now I know I was just waiting for the right moment to say what I've been thinking since I realized I had to postpone my launch.

"I'm taking a step back from the campaign," I announce. "I'm going to focus on myself and my business, and I can't do that if I'm being trotted out like a prized horse for every Black voter-related emergency. Aubrey and I will address our issues privately. We'll heal on our own terms and at our own pace, and you will do what you can to help him recover in the polls."

Jordan leans forward in her seat and squares her shoulders, her eyes taking on a hard glint. "That's not an option, Selene."

My spine stiffens at the harshness of her tone. "Of course it is."

"No. Your options are as follows." She holds up her right hand, extending one long index finger to indicate my first option. "One.

Remember that a life in the public eye is what you signed on for, and commit yourself to doing whatever I tell you is necessary to make the American people believe in the solidity of their future, First couple." Slowly, she brings up her middle finger to represent my second option.

"Two. You file for divorce. Move out of the house. Sever all ties with Aubrey and allow him and his campaign to move on from all of this nonsense. This is my least favorite option," she says, her nose scrunched. "It's messy and leaves room for too many variables, but I could make it work. I'll have Aubrey and Sutton married with a baby on the way faster than you can change your last name back to Grant. She'll make a beautiful First Lady, don't you think? Young and blonde, with just the right amount of naivety to make her easy to handle. Trust me, no one will remember the affair or the scorned ex-wife when the pictures of the First Couple taking little AJ to visit his big brother's grave come out in the Times."

Horror and shock roll through me, combining with pain and anger to render me speechless. I know this was Jordan's goal: to paint a picture so ugly, so vivid, it would paralyze me before catapulting me into action, but it still hurts.

It hurts so fucking bad.

"That's enough!" Diane shouts, slamming the marcels back into their holder. They clang loudly, making me jump, but I still can't move, so I watch helplessly as she rounds the chair and grabs Jordan by her arm, forcing her out of the shop. With her point made, she goes without a fight, shrugging out of Diane's hold at the door and tossing a smile at me over her shoulder.

It's the same one she gave me the first time she saw me with my hair straight, and I don't have to sort through my knowledge of her expressions and the emotions they're meant to convey to know that smile can only mean one thing.

Triumph.

5

SELENE

Even on the worst days of my marriage, of which there have been a lot of late, I have never been able to picture myself outside of Aubrey's orbit. Our lives are too intertwined, our vision for this country too similar, and our grief far too familiar. So when Jordan pushed me to leave him, I knew, just like she did, that I wouldn't.

That I can't.

And it doesn't have anything to do with love or jealousy, although something ugly and bitter had unfurled inside of me at the mention of Sutton taking my place as Aubrey's First Lady. No, my reason for staying, like everything else in my life, is about my son.

There are memories I have of AJ that I only share with Aubrey.

Like watching the lines on every test turn pink, still not believing it was real, and going to the doctor to do blood work and confirm. Aubrey had paced endlessly, his fingers raking through his hair, leaving tunnels of angst I smoothed over again and again.

I can't even put a number on the amount of times I performed that same soothing motion over the short years AJ was alive. Aubrey was always the emotion-driven worrier, while I was the solid, steady one who leaned on statistics and logic. We made a great team, balancing the demands of raising our son together, and now, carrying the sweet, suffering burden of remembering.

It's too much for one person to hold on their own, and I need Aubrey's hands. I need his strength, his pain, and his understanding.

I need *him*.

Because at his side, and before things went bad, in his arms, are the only places I feel safe enough to wade into the murky waters of grief, the only places I know I can let myself sink into the memories of AJ's smile, the sound of his laughter, the weight of his little body wriggling on my chest the day he was born, and trust that I'll be pulled out before I drown.

And if I walk away from Aubrey, if I lose him, then I'll lose AJ all over again because I'll never be strong enough to visit those places on my own.

I try to explain this to Monique when our weekly one-on-one turned, as it always does, into a conversation about our personal lives, but she doesn't get it. Her eyes should be focused on the reports spread out in front of her that say the delayed launch of the facial recognition software has tanked our fourth quarter projections and probably will prevent us from hiring the one hundred and fifty Black women who just graduated from our in-house coding academy but instead they're squeezed tight as she lets out an exasperated sigh.

"So let me get this straight, you're staying with Aubrey so you can suffer together?"

"That seems like an oversimplification."

With her eyes open and on my face, she rubs at the wrinkle forming between her brows. "Is it, though? You've basically just told me you don't want to leave Aubrey because he's the only one you can grieve AJ with, which is a lie, by the way. I miss him too. I will grieve with you. I *have* grieved with you."

Her lips tremble a bit, the way they always do when she speaks about her godson, and I feel bad for striking a nerve even if I don't fully understand which one I've hit.

"I know that." I reach out for her, offering my hand because years of friendship have taught me physical contact helps soothe her in more emotional moments, especially when I'm out of my depth. "I didn't mean to suggest that Aubrey is the *only* person. I know he's not. I just—" I sigh, hoping the words will find me. "He's his father, Mo. I look at Aubrey and I see him. The man he would have grown into if his life hadn't been cut short. It's like glimpsing into a future I'll never get to see."

"Or shackling yourself to a past that might destroy you," she returns, squeezing my fingers to soften the blow of her reproach. "You don't need Aubrey to remember AJ. You're his mother, Sel. Everything he is, everything he could have been, started with you, and it still lives in you. *He* still lives in you."

I blink away tears as her words wash over me, but refuse to soak into the battered flesh of my heart. They can't because they feel all wrong on my skin.

"Thank you for saying that."

"You're welcome."

Monique pulls away, reluctantly accepting that I'm past the point of absorbing her kindness because she knows me as well as I know her. Maybe even a little better.

"Don't you need to be leaving?" she asks, gathering up the reports scattered across the table and placing them in a folder.

Frowning, I glance at my watch and, seeing that it's nearly eleven, push to my feet. Monique rises too. She has a full day of meetings ahead of her, and I have to leave the office to attend an appearance with Aubrey at Children's National Hospital in the district. I push down the annoyance bubbling in my chest at having my day cut short in service of Aubrey's campaign. I've repeatedly asked his team not to schedule things during my work day, but they have yet to comply. They don't seem to know or care about my endeavor to create space between my life as Selene Taylor, CEO, and Selene Taylor, future First Lady.

"Will you let me know how the shareholder meeting goes?" I ask Monique as she makes her way to the door.

"You got it, boss," she says jokingly, breezing out the door as my assistant, Nichelle comes through it.

"I already know I need to be leaving," I say, hurrying over to my desk to grab my purse and phone. "Can you have them bring my car around front?"

"Umm." Nichelle bites her lip, glancing over her shoulder at something or someone I can't see. "About that—" she starts before taking several more steps into the office, making room for the imposing presence of Agent Beckham in my doorway. He doesn't linger there, though. He keeps moving, making an anxious-looking Nichelle step further into the room with nothing but the force of his will.

At the sight of him, I immediately straighten. Suddenly, I understand why Nichelle looks out of sorts. Why she's stumbling through an explanation about not knowing if she should call down for my car because Agent Beckham said he's here to take me to the event.

I hold up a hand, silencing her unnecessary explanation. "Please call for my car, Nichelle."

For the first time in all of her years in my employ, Nichelle hesitates to honor my request. Wide brown eyes shift between me and the agent, and she actually looks more stressed about disappointing him than me. I can't say that I blame her. Agent Beckham is formidable. He stands a few away from Nichelle, his long legs shoulder-width apart. His arms folded in front of him, onyx eyes sweeping over the room before landing on my face.

"That won't be necessary, Ms. Durant," Agent Beckham says, addressing her without looking away from me. "You'll be riding with me, Mrs. Taylor."

"No, I won't. I drove here, and I don't have any intentions of leaving my car."

Of being left with no choice but to ride back home with Aubrey.

"I have orders to bring you to the hospital, ma'am. If you'd like, I can have another agent pick up your vehicle and bring it back to the residence."

"I would *like* to be on my way to this speaking engagement instead of standing here arguing with you about something as trivial as me driving myself. I drove into work just a few hours ago. What's changed between now and then?"

Surely, it's not an active threat or anything of that nature. If that were the case, someone would have told me. Jordan's assistant would have reached out to Nichelle, or Aubrey would have broken the silence in our text message thread to let me know something was up.

At least, I hope he would.

Agent Beckham blinks, his expression still. "I'm just following orders, ma'am."

"And I appreciate that, but this—" I gesture around the room, indicating the building at large before continuing, "—is my domain, and that means I'm the one giving the orders, not blindly following them." I narrow my eyes at Nichelle, trying to quell the anger burning its way up my throat because she doesn't deserve to have it aimed in her direction. "*Please* place the call for my car. Tell them I'll be down in five minutes."

To my surprise and annoyance, Nichelle looks to Agent Beckham, waiting for the slight incline of his head before she scurries out of the room. I roll my eyes, gripping the edge of the desk while he stares at me.

"Why are you here?"

His jaw clenches, and I know he has to be tired of repeating himself. "To escort you to your scheduled appearance, ma'am."

"Selene," I insist, even though at this particular moment I don't really care what he calls me because I don't want him here. I told Aubrey, Jordan and Agent Daniel Hicks, the man in charge of our Secret Service detail, that I didn't want agents in the building. Up until today, they've respected that wish, but now that respect seems to have flown out the window, and it dawns on me that it's happening now, just a day after my conversation with Jordan.

She probably orchestrated this, sending Agent Beckham here as a proxy—a tall, frustratingly handsome pawn in her power play. Just the thought of it has me digging my nails into the bottom side of my desk, threatening to ruin my manicure, which would only give Jordan another thing to harp on when she starts breathing down my neck about showing up late.

He shakes his head, a silent refusal to grant my request to use my first name, and I huff out a sharp laugh before grabbing my things and rounding the desk.

"You can storm into my building and order around my employees, but you draw the line at calling me by my name. That's great." I stride past him, my steps short, my spine straight, and he follows me out of the office, pausing right behind me when I stop at Nichelle's desk. "Did you call for the car?"

"Yes, ma'am."

I don't thank her. I'm far too annoyed with this entire situation to be polite, too aware of the weight of Agent Beckham's sharp gaze on the back of my neck to do anything but give her a curt nod and move to the elevator bank where another man in a black suit with a gun on his hip is waiting. When he sees us approaching, he lifts his wrist, speaking into the microphone attached to his cuff before pressing the button to call up the elevator.

It's not Agent Drake, which surprises me because I've never seen the two men apart. The thought distracts me from my anger at having my building invaded, but only for a moment.

"You should consider a private elevator," Agent Beckham says, standing with his back to me and his eyes scanning the floor. "It'd be more efficient from a security standpoint."

My foot taps impatiently, and I track the progress of the car via the numbers on the screen above us. "It'd also limit my interactions with the people who pass through this building on a daily basis for work, use of our co-working space, or to attend our coding academy."

Interacting with most people is a painful experience for me, but that's not true here. The people who come into Culture Code are like me. They value the work as much as I do, and they don't take it personally when I'm too engrossed in a task to even utter a word or stop to eat. I get them, and they get me. I've spent a long time searching for that kind of understanding, and I won't give it up just because some gun in a suit says I should.

The elevator arrives with a ding that prompts him to spin around and step in front of me, blocking my view of the people pouring out of the parted doors. When they're all out, the other agent leans inside and does a cursory sweep of the space before nodding to Agent Beckham that it's safe. Once we're inside, with him in front of me and the other agent at my back, he replies.

"The whole point of security is to minimize risk, which, yes, means limiting your interaction with the public. That's not a bad thing. You're too exposed here. It's not safe."

"We've never had so much as a misplaced package here, Agent Beckham. My building is perfectly safe."

And the fact that he'd suggest it's not makes me even more annoyed with him and this entire situation.

"You've never been the First Lady before, Mrs. Taylor; that comes with different risks."

I cross my arms, giving myself a subtle squeeze to try and push down the sudden and persistent feeling that the walls are closing in on me.

"I'm not the First Lady right now."

And if things keep going the way they're going for Aubrey in the polls, I probably never will be. He's not recovering as quickly as Jordan would like, so the stress is on. At this point, it never seems to turn off. Everything, including this appearance I don't want an escort to, is important. A situation that could either make or break the campaign.

The pressure of it all is intense, but having a place to hide from it, a place where I can just be myself, has helped a lot. It scares me to think I could lose it, that my safe place might be pried from my hands by someone who doesn't understand what it will do to me to see it change in even the smallest way.

"But one day you might be," he says, his tone flat. "It's illogical to hide from the possibility and leave yourself at risk."

My jaw drops. I don't think I've ever been called illogical, and the word lands like a blow in the center of my chest, splitting my sternum and leaving the anger I've been holding in no choice but to come spilling out.

"Illogical is assuming that you or anyone else can predict the outcome of an election that's still weeks away," I grind out. "*Illogical* is coming into a building where you weren't invited and have no authority and assuming your suggestions would be honored or appreciated."

The man behind me, who I now remember is Agent Harris, coughs and shifts on his feet like he can't wait to be out of this small space and away from the hostility rolling between his partner and I. The elevator finally arrives at the lobby floor, and when the doors pop open, I rush around Agent Beckham, intending to beat him to the exit and spare myself whatever response he's cooking up.

Of course, my version of rushing is no match for his quick reflexes, and he catches me.

"*Mrs. Taylor*," he barks, wrapping his hand around my wrist and pulling me back to keep me from passing through the doors. Agent Harris moves past us, probably stepping outside to secure the perimeter or something, while Agent Beckham and I glare at each other.

I pull my arm away, and his eyes flare with indignation. I'm not sure if it's because I've left him with no choice but to release me or if it's because he had to grab me in the first place.

"My apologies, ma'am." He resumes the rigid stance he held in my office, which I'm realizing is as close to relaxed as he gets, and swallows. "You should always remain between agents whenever possible. I can't keep you safe if you insist on breaking formation."

"That's just the thing, Agent Beckham. I don't need you to keep me safe. I don't need you here at all." I turn on my heel and shove my way through the doors, heedless of the eyes on me or the glowering man at my back. All I want to do is get to my car and away from him.

Agent Harris's cheeks are red, and his eyes are shifty when I come to a stop in front of him. He's standing at my driver's side door, blocking my entrance even though the engine is running and time is of the essence.

"Please move out of my way, Agent Harris."

I try for calm, but I fail. My voice shakes with frustration and the need to be alone, to have a moment to decompress before my senses are overloaded with the snapping of cameras and the constant buzz of chatter that surrounds events like these.

"Mrs. Taylor—" Harris starts.

"Let her go, Wyatt," Agent Beckham says from behind me, and it's only then that he moves, clearing my path and closing the door once I'm safely inside. Unlike everyone else today, I don't wait for Agent Beckham's approval before I pull away from the curb, easing my way into traffic without looking back to see if they're following because I know they are.

THERE ARE MORE agents waiting for me at the hospital.

They greet me at the entrance, forming a tight circle around my body while reporters and photographers clamor for candid shots and sound bites they'll spin and manipulate to fuel whatever narrative they're peddling about me today. I allow the men in black to lead me to a small conference room, where Jordan and Aubrey are waiting, along with Alexis Ritter, the head of the hospital, and a group of other people I don't bother to identify. They all look up when I enter the room, but only Aubrey stands. I'm shocked by the small gesture of civility, and even more stunned when he crosses the room and holds his arms open, allowing me to decide if I want to step into them or not.

Today has been a lot, and it's not even noon yet, so I stand there for a moment, staring at the arms I've needed and been deprived of for far too long, and then sinking into his embrace. He squeezes me hard, applying a perfect pressure that instantly regulates my nervous system. A memory hits me, taking me back to the first time I asked him to hug me like this. It was my senior year at Stanford, and finals had me spiraling in the worst way. All I wanted was one of my daddy's bear hugs, and all I had was Aubrey and his willingness to try to replicate it.

Over the years, he perfected it, learning how tight to hold me and for how long. Eventually, he got to the point where he could take one look at me and know that I needed one. Before this very moment, I assumed that knowledge, or at least the desire to act on it, had been lost somewhere in the sordidness of the affair. But now Aubrey is silently communicating to me that it hasn't, and that brings tears to my eyes. My arms circle his waist, and I nuzzle into his neck, melting at the physical contact.

I can't remember the last time he hugged me like this, and I can't bring myself to care that it might only be happening because we're in a room full of potential voters who are eager to buy into the image Jordan wants us to sell.

"Are you okay?" he whispers into my ear, his voice tender.

"I am now."

Aubrey pulls back, and my heart sinks at the loss of proximity, thinking the moment is over. But he surprises me again, keeping his arms around me as he makes eye contact with someone, probably Jordan, over my head.

"Give us the room, please."

All at once, everyone is on their feet and moving out the door, leaving us alone.

"Thank you for being here," he murmurs, sending another wave of shock rolling through me as he urges my head back to his chest.

"Jordan didn't exactly give me a choice."

"She didn't give me one either. I told her I hate hospitals, and she told me to suck it up."

"She's been spending too much time around your dad. I'm pretty sure that's what he told AJ when he said he was scared to get his tonsils removed."

Aubrey snorts, and I bury my smile in the crisp lines of his white button-up, relishing in the sound of his heartbeat, strong and sure, in my ear. The levity of the moment, the lightness of a fond memory of

AJ, won't last long. I know that. There's just too much left unsaid between us.

"This is nice," he says, rocking me back and forth a little. "It's been too long since you let me hold you."

Sensing the moment slipping away from us, I untangle myself from his hold. "It's been too long since you've *wanted* to hold me."

He runs his fingers through his hair, exasperation written into the lines of his face. "I always want to hold you, Sel. You asked me to leave our bed."

Every negative emotion he soothed with his touch comes rushing back to the surface. I don't know why he's choosing today of all days to broach this topic when he's spent weeks avoiding it, but I'm not going to shy away from it. I want to talk about it. I need to. It's the only way I'll be able to heal.

"Don't do that, Aubrey. Don't make it seem like I just woke up one day and kicked you out of our room. I asked you to leave because you—"

His hands fly up, palms facing outward in a show of surrender. "I know. I know." He closes the space between us, taking my face in his hands and staring into my soul with blue eyes that were designed to turn me into a puddle. "I know what I did, and I'm sorry, Sel."

The pads of his thumbs run gentle lines over my cheeks. "And you deserve so much better than this rushed moment, this short apology. I know that. You deserve a real conversation, and I want to give that to you. I *will* give that to you. I promise."

I'm stunned into silence.

This is the first time he's apologized since the news of him and Sutton broke. And as much as I appreciate it, as much as I want to soak it all in, I can't stop my brain from screaming: *why now?*

Before the thought can find life on my lips, my heart whispers: *Does it matter?*

And I decide in an instant that no, it doesn't matter at all.

6

BECK

"**S**he's impossible."

I toss the words over my shoulder, and even though I can't see his face because I'm digging through the refrigerator to find the steaks that have been marinating all day in preparation for our first night off in weeks, I know Cal is smiling.

He's amused by my agitation with Selene Taylor and has taken every opportunity to let me know it. I've been ranting about my run-in with the future First Lady for hours, starting the moment I passed through the door of his home after stopping by my place for a quick shower and a change of clothes. It's not rare for us to spend our nights off together, even though we spend all day by each other's side, but it is rare for me to still be talking shop when I'm on the cusp of consuming one of his culinary creations.

The bowl I've been hunting is sitting on a shelf below the one Cal said it would be on, and I pull it out, setting it on the counter so the steaks inside can come down to room temperature.

"You don't agree?" I ask, arching a brow as I scoop up my glass of wine. It's the only one I'll have tonight. Usually, I would save the small indulgence for the food it's meant to be enjoyed with, but I couldn't bring myself to wait.

Nothing goes with venting like wine.

"I didn't say that."

"You didn't *say* anything." My eyes are on his hands, watching the fluid motion of the knife rocking against the wooden cutting board as he minces garlic and slices shallots.

When he's done, he slides everything into the stainless steel pan on the stove. They hit the olive oil with a quiet sizzle that makes him smile.

He loves to cook.

That's the first thing I learned about him, and I gained that knowledge at a time in my life when I didn't want to know anything about anyone new because I'd just had my entire world ripped from me in the most brutal way. I was trying to rebuild, and despite transferring to a new unit within the Bureau and integrating myself into a team I didn't know or trust, I was hellbent on doing it alone.

Cal wouldn't let me.

We were partnered up on my first day in the Counter Terrorism Unit. I knew it was because he was the only other Black man, but I didn't mind. I was glad to be paired with someone who'd spent more of his life than I had carrying the badge. I relished his wisdom even as I resented him for forcing his way into my life, infiltrating my bubble of grief with his quiet strength, constant support, and meals, even a recently widowed man out of his mind with anger and self-loathing couldn't refuse.

Now he cooks for me all the time, and I have no qualms about letting him.

We share meals and vent our frustrations about being Black men in America who have spent our lives in service to a country that was never meant to serve us back. Most of the time, our frustrations are shared. The two of us volleying complaints back and forth until we both feel light enough to wake up the next morning and do the job all over again.

I don't need the camaraderie, but I do wonder why it feels like I'm alone in my frustration with Selene Taylor, especially when I gave Cal the complete play-by-play, including the acrid smell of burnt rubber that stuck to me long after she peeled out of the driveway in front of her building.

"Why aren't you saying anything, Cal?"

"Because you need me to listen more than you need me to talk, Beck," he says, copper eyes flicking to my face with humor shimmering in the brass puddles of his irises.

"That's never stopped you from adding in your two cents before." Curious, I study his face, watching for something. I'm not sure what, though. He rolls his eyes, turning his back to me. I slap my hand on the counter, taking the break in eye contact for the tell that it is. "You think I'm in the wrong, don't you?"

When he spins back around with the bowl of spinach I washed earlier in his hand, I see the truth written all over the perfectly symmetrical lines of his face. "I was following orders," I explain through clenched teeth. "It came directly from Hicks. What was I supposed to do? Say no?"

"Of course not. You're already on thin ice with him as it is."

I grimace, hating that he's right. Daniel Hicks and I have butted heads since Cal and I made the move from the FBI to the Secret Service together. Years later, not much has changed except for the fact that he's my boss, which means I can't over rule him when he's wrong, which is far too often, or punch him in his shit when his mouth gets a little too reckless.

"Well then? What was I supposed to do?"

Cal sighs, stirring slowly to fully incorporate the heavy cream he's just added to the pan of spinach. "You were supposed to remember that everyone reacts to having their lives invaded by strangers differently. Selene has made it clear from the beginning that she didn't want us in her building. Did you honestly think she was going to respond well to you showing up and strong-arming her?"

"I wasn't strong-arming her," I grumble as the frustration that had my chest all puffed up and my shoulders high around my ears dissipates. Cal watches me deflate, a knowing smile curving his full lips as he adds a mixture of freshly grated Provolone and Parmesan into the pan.

"You were, and you probably got all stern and formal when you realized she was intent on standing her ground."

Damn, the man knows me too well.

"How many times did you call her ma'am?"

"Shut up, Drake."

Cutting the heat to the eye, he huffs out a laugh that only grows louder when I flip him off, and I busy myself with taking another sip of my wine. Cal's smile fades, his expression growing a bit more serious. Over the rim of my near-empty glass, I watch him cover the pan of creamed spinach and move it off the stove. Then he's crossing the room to me, wiping his hands on the kitchen towel he keeps slung across his shoulder when he's cooking.

"All I'm saying is you could have adjusted your approach when you realized she wasn't receptive."

"Is this the moment where you give me the speech about getting more flies with honey?" I ask, setting my empty glass down.

As the more cynical and outspoken half of our duo, I've heard the speech from Cal a thousand times before. They weren't as frequent when we were in the Bureau as they are now, but I wasn't as unsatisfied there as I am here.

He sets the towel down on the counter. His hand still resting on the blue cotton with white lines threaded through it, the tips of his outstretched fingers stopping mere inches from mine. I obsess over that distance while he considers my question.

"No," he says finally. "I don't think you need to hear it today. I do think you need to come to terms with the reality of this detail, though. You've already made it clear you think this assignment is below you. You don't have to let that belief spill out into every interaction with the Taylors or the rest of our team."

Cal has always been the more diplomatic of the two of us. I'm not sure if it's wisdom from the few years he has on me or just ill-placed humility, but he's always so cool about everything, including not getting what he deserves. I, unfortunately, have never had a diplomatic bone in my body. I push and push and push for what I deserve. When it's not easily given, I take it. And I'm a million times worse when it comes to what I believe the people I love deserve.

"I don't think the assignment is below me. I think it's below *us*."

"Beck, we've been through this."

He's right. We've been through this a million times, and the conversation is always just me trying to figure out how we went from decorated FBI agents preventing a domestic terrorism group run by a gun-loving white supremacist named Leland Marsh from murdering a sitting President to doing whatever it is we're doing now.

Our unit, but more specifically Cal and I, had been building a case against Marsh and the Brothers of Confederate Pride for years. Leland was methodical and surprisingly intelligent for a man so ignorant, so it had been a slow process. Every time we thought we were about to catch a break, the witness we flipped would turn up dead, or the agent we put undercover would double-cross us.

The assassination attempt was a lucky break. It had come out of nowhere, though. A result of President Warner's outcry for gun control laws in the wake of the Taylors' son's death. Like most things involving politicians, I'd taken the President's speech about our government needing to do more than send thoughts and prayers with a grain of salt. However, Marsh and his cronies took it as a sign that the government was finally banding together with minority groups to prevent white Americans from protecting themselves.

When I put the cuffs on him, Marsh admitted he considered gunning for the Taylors instead of Warner, but ultimately decided a dead President would make a bigger splash. It was a dumb risk, but I'm glad he took it because it allowed us to put him and the majority of his organization behind bars for a long time.

Cal clears his throat, pulling me out of my head and prompting me to reply. "I know we have, but that doesn't make me any less angry about it. Five years ago, you and I were the only thing standing between a sitting President and imminent danger. They came to us, do you remember? They fed us all of this shit about valor and patriotism and asked us to leave the Bureau, promising renowned details and distinguished assignments worthy of our sacrifices. We should be guarding Presidents, Cal, not babysitting future First Ladies who don't even want our protection."

"Of course I remember, Beck," Cal says, his voice too soft in the wake of my harsh rambling. "I was the one laid up in the hospital bed."

My eyes fall shut as the image hits me. Not of him in the hospital bed, but of his face the moment the bullet that put him there went through his vest, entering just below the front plate. His expression had been so calm, even as he hit the ground hard, bleeding from his abdomen. The moment he realized Cal was hit, President Warner scrambled to him, applying pressure to the wound while I shielded them both with my body and returned fire, striking the gunman—a young, inexperienced shooter who had just joined Marsh's militia a few weeks prior—right between the eyes.

"Hey," he murmurs, his fingers wrapping around my wrist and tugging until my eyes pop open and my feet begin to move. "I didn't mean to take you back there," he says when I stop in front of him, our mouths inches apart, our bodies close.

I know he's referring to that day specifically, but the truth is, that's not the real problem. The problem is the way any mention of it acts as a key, unlocking the part of my brain where the long list of losses I've endured lives. They're written in chronological order.

At the top are my birth parents, who didn't want me.

The middle is littered with the names of foster siblings and friends I gained and lost as a result of being constantly bounced around the system.

Near the end are the names of my adoptive parents, Edgar and Delores Beckham. The wealthy, elderly white couple who found me when I was eight years old and, despite not knowing a thing about raising a Black boy in the upper echelon of society, gave me the best of everything.

The last names are the freshest wounds, my wife and the little boy in her belly who died when she did. It had nearly killed me to add them in, to live every day in the bleak reality of losing them. And when Cal went down, when his blood ran red and thick under the soles of my shoes, I felt that darkness descending on me again. I felt the loss of him and wondered why I thought I'd be able to keep him when life had taught me that goodness doesn't stick around for long.

It's that thought, that memory, that sends my hands to his waist, my fingers searching for the hem of his shirt and tugging up to expose the smooth burnt umber of his skin and the cut lines of his stomach. As delicious as they are, I'm not here for his abs. No, I'm here for the jagged flesh that marks the bullet's entry and the line of scar tissue that tells the story of the doctors cutting him open to remove it. Cal sucks in a sharp breath through his teeth when my fingertips trace over them, and I tear my gaze away from his stomach to look at his face, needing to know if he wants me to stop. If tonight is one of the nights that the lie we tell in public will permeate the private truth of us.

It happens sometimes.

When the lie is too loud and the truth is too quiet. When we've risked being found out for the reassurance of a brush of our pinkies or a lingering look and reality sets in, reminding us that being lovers puts our partnership and careers at risk.

One second of eye contact tells me there's no reluctance to indulge on Cal's part. The hiss was more surprise than anything else, probably because I'm not usually the initiator. I let my worry, my frustration, and the constant fear of losing him bleed out of my eyes along with a silent plea for the physical expression of his affection, for a tangible reminder that he's still here with me and not another name on my list.

"I'm right here," he assures me, reading the look with ease. One of his rough, warm palms comes up to cup the back of my neck, urging me forward until my lips are on his. We both sigh into the connection, and Cal holds me firm, refusing to let even a millimeter of space between our mouths. The kiss is bruising, and his tongue is demanding as it pushes past my lips, conquering my mouth with rough sweeps that soothe every word of worry I've spoken or let die on my tongue.

My hands begin to move again, fingers greedy as they traverse the familiar terrain of his torso and chest, freeing them from the clinging fabric of the black workout shirts he wears even when he's not in the gym. I break the kiss for a split second to pull the shirt over his head, and he growls his disapproval, smashing his lips back to mine as I toss the offending fabric over my shoulder.

We stumble over it on our way out of the kitchen. Me, walking backwards while Cal haunts my steps, tugging on the tied strings securing my sweats to my waist. By the time we make it upstairs to his bedroom, there's a line of clothing in our wake and two raging erections pressed between our naked forms.

Cal releases me with a wet smack and smiles wickedly. "On your knees, Beckham."

My dick pulses at the dark promise laced in the order, and I lower myself to the ground immediately, eager to please, desperate to taste. I reach for his dick with eager hands, and he steps back, a tsk of disapproval hitting the air. Confused, I look up and find him staring down at me with hard eyes and his hands behind his back.

"Just your mouth. Do you understand?" he tells me, lifting one leg and placing his foot on the edge of the bed.

Fuck is he sexy like this. All the diplomacy and carefully constructed control he exhibits in his day-to-day life morphing into something new, rising to meet the unspoken demands of my desire.

"Do you understand?" he repeats, reaching down to stroke his dick with the same hand that was just cupping my neck. Entranced and irrationally jealous of his palm, I nod, which makes Cal smile. "Good. Now, put your hands behind your back and come here."

I do exactly as he asks and shuffle forward, moving slowly so I don't lose my balance. When I'm close enough to see the bead of precum creeping out of his tip, I rise on my knees and flick out my tongue, catching the evidence of his arousal just as it emerges. The creamy, salty flavor of him explodes on my tongue, and I moan, setting the sound free to meet Cal's grunt of approval in the air around us.

A glance up at him reveals his eyes squeezed shut and his chest heaving with anticipation. I keep my gaze on his face, wanting to see his reaction when I take his length into my mouth, grazing his shaft with my teeth. His shifting expression is everything I hoped it would be, and I close my eyes, pride swelling in my chest when he starts to rock his hips, fucking into my mouth with soft, helpless groans that make me want to touch him. I know better than to disobey him, though, so I keep my hands behind my back, digging my nails into my flesh as a constant reminder to leave them there.

"Fuck. That's it," Cal pants, breaking his stance to cup the back of my head and pull me down further, effectively choking me on his dick. "That's right. Get me ready for you."

My mouth waters at the thought of him inside me, so my next pull on his length is a wet slurp that makes him grip both sides of my face. Reverent fingers stroke the lines of my jaw before applying an almost painful pressure that forces my mouth to stay open at that exact angle. Cal is a perfect picture of rapture when I look up at him again, marveling at the juxtaposition between his tender expression and his savage movements. He's looking at me now, fucking my mouth like an animal while he holds me hostage with those eyes.

"I'm right here, Beck," he says, pulling back until only the flared tip of his dick rests on my lips. "Do you feel me?" he asks, pushing back in forcefully, hitting the back of my throat and still going further until his balls slap my chin and I gag around him, moaning my understanding because it's not possible to verbalize it.

I do feel him.

I feel him everywhere.

In the burn of my jaw and the ache in my knees.

In the sting of my fingernails digging into my wrist because I still can't touch him, and the heavy pulsing of my dick against my thigh.

But most of all, I feel him in my chest. In every skipped beat of my heart and swell of affection. In every I love you, explicitly spoken or discreetly expressed.

Satisfied with my understanding, Cal draws back once again, but this time he doesn't return. Instead, he pulls me up to my feet and kisses me gently, massaging my aching jaws.

"You're never going to lose me."

He whispers the promise into my lips and leaves me at the foot of the bed, going to his nightstand to retrieve a bottle of lube from the drawer and returning just as I'm climbing onto the bed. The sensitive tip of my erection grazes the sheets, leaving a trail of unspent desire for Cal to follow. He's at my back in seconds, pushing me down and nudging my knees apart. My elbows sink into the plush mattress, and I sigh as the familiar sounds of him lubricating his fingers echo around me.

In moments, he's parting my cheeks, rubbing impatient but careful fingers over and into the ring of puckered flesh we're both desperate to have wrapped around his length. His index finger is first, sliding in and out of me slowly, a gentle intrusion that acts as the prelude of what's to come. Every time we're together like this, the process is the same. The slow build up, moving from one finger to the subtle burn of two, and then the aching stretch of three. Cal's fingers are long and thick, so the combination of his index, middle, and ring fingers is a near-perfect replica of his girth.

"Breathe," he reminds me, running a soothing hand down my spine as he squeezes more lube between my cheeks. I push out a breath, and the exhalation relaxes me enough to ease his next advance.

Cal presses a prideful smile into my shoulder blade, rotating his wrist slowly even as he continues to work his fingers in and out of me. "That's it. You're doing such a good job, love. Fuck my hand so that I can fuck you."

My head lolls forward, eyes rolling back as I rock back on his fingers, helping him reach the bundle of nerves inside of me that's already swollen with arousal. Cal curls his fingers inward, massaging the spot repeatedly until I'm lost, disappearing into the familiar haze of pleasure that has every muscle in my body floating on the edge of tension and relaxation. It's a familiar balance, one I know is necessary to achieve the goal Cal and I are working towards: our shared release.

"I'm ready, Cal. Please. *Please*," I plead, as another trickle of precum leaks out of me, adding to the rapidly growing puddle underneath me. To my shock, and utter joy, he relents, kissing my shoulder as he removes his fingers and replaces them with the tip of his dick, giving me no warning before he pushes inside, seating himself in one stroke.

"FUCK!" I shout, rising up on my knees until my back is plastered to his chest. "The fuck do you have against issuing a word of warning?"

The bastard huffs out a laugh. "You said you were ready," he breathes into my ear, ghosting his fingers over my hips and sides, kneading my flesh to encourage my muscles to relax while kissing up my shoulder and neck. He's not moving yet because he's waiting for me to adjust to the feel of him inside of me. Even with all the prep work, it still takes a second.

A result of infrequent indulgence, I guess.

Cal shifts, shoring up his stance, and when I tense again, dreading the bite of the next stroke as much as I'm looking forward to it, he pauses. "Do you want me to stop?"

Every cell in my body revolts at the thought of him leaving me like this. My dick hard, the head swollen, precum trailing down my shaft and balls onto the comforter under us, my mind fuzzy with lust.

"*Fuck no*," I moan, forcing myself to relax into his hold. I don't just want this. I *need* it, and I show Cal that by dropping back down onto my elbows, burying my face in pillows that smell like him and surrendering to the weight of his dick in my ass.

Cal grips my hips with sure hands and rears back, swinging forward in the very next second with enough force to knock me off balance. Even though that wasn't his intention, he takes full advantage of my prone position, using the new angle to hit the spot he was massaging with his fingers just minutes ago. My lips part on a guttural moan that fills my mouth with Egyptian cotton and the smoked spice scent of my partner and best friend.

"Do you feel me, Beck?" he asks again, treating me to another jarring stroke. "I'm right here."

Turning my head so my words aren't muffled by the pillow, I nod. "I hear you"

I push back, meeting his next thrust with a smirk. "But if you want me to feel you, fuck me harder, Drake."

My challenge is met exactly how I expect it to be. With a feral growl and wicked words that accompany life-altering strokes that threaten to destroy me. Cal chuckles darkly as I fight to return everything he's giving me. The force. The momentum. The sheer power of hips that won't stop driving into me, even as my hands find purchase on the mattress, and I rise up on my knees, toes digging into the bedding as my feet come to rest on either side of Cal's legs.

He bites down into the muscle between my shoulder and neck, reaching around to grab hold of my dick. His thumb circles around my tip, gathering precum and spreading it around the flared head before dragging his fist down to my base and bringing it back up over and over again, somehow managing to match every roll of his hips with the stroke of his hand.

It's a maddening layering of sensation. The constant press and glide of his dick. The slip and slide of his hand. And the moans. *Our* moans. Cal's moans in my ear, his teeth nipping at my lobe. My moans deep and desperate as he whispers, "I wish you could experience this. I wish you knew how fucking good you feel around me, how perfect it is when you let go and trust me to take care of you, to get you there. Keep trusting me, love," he purrs, reminding me to relax as the promise of my release climbs up my spine and the twitching of Cal's dick tells me his isn't far behind.

I melt into his rhythm, letting every advance of his dick push mine into the tight grip of his fist, creating a circuit of pleasure that chews us up and spits us out in minutes.

I break first, painting the dark, luxurious fabric covering the pillows with long ropes of cum that start strong and then taper off, the last of it coating Cal's fingers in messy streams that eventually end up on my hip. The result of him forcing me back down and holding me still so he can pound out his release. He comes inside me, the heat and force of his pleasure emphasized by a string of filthy curses that continue to spill past his lips even as he collapses on my back, panting.

I support his weight until he comes back to his senses and pulls out of me. We both groan at the slow drag of his spent dick over sensitive nerves. It feels good. Good enough to make me want to go again, but I know we won't.

We never do.

That's not how this thing between us works.

There are no second rounds, no cuddles, no aftercare.

There's just this.

The heat of the moment and the cool vulnerability we're left to sit in once it subsides.

The silence of cleaning off with warm, soapy wash cloths we only use on ourselves and the stripping of bedding soiled by desire.

The quiet slide of the nightstand drawer and the dull thud of the bottle of lube as it returns to its rightful place, waiting for the next time we break.

The imperceptible creak of the floorboards as we follow the trail of our clothes back through the house, returning to the kitchen as friends instead of lovers.

7

———

SELENE

My mama always used to say that love makes a house a home.

I never appreciated the adage until we had AJ, until his tiny little wails echoed in the foyer and the first steps of his fat feet slapped against the tile in the hall, until I'd come home and trip over book bags and sneakers at the door or find several lanky, endlessly hungry teenage boys raiding my fridge with AJ leaning on the counter, his floppy, black curls in his eyes as he scrolled through delivery apps to figure out what they were going to scarf down next.

I can be rigid about a lot of things, but raising AJ taught me how to be soft. I'd never yell or get annoyed with the mess, the missing groceries, or the dent their food orders put in my bank account. I'd just toss my bags down, kick off my shoes and join in on the fun for however long they'd let me.

My heart was happy.

My house was a home, full of people and love.

These days, the love is absent—although, since the appearance at the children's hospital a few days ago, I've glimpsed it a few times—but the people are still here. The house is always full of people I'd happily sacrifice if it meant having another movie night with AJ and his friends. They're all so noisy, but it's not the fun kind of noise that's created by uninhibited teenagers whispering about crushes and playing video games. It's the serious kind of noise that makes my house feel more like an office building than a home. Constant typing, the incessant ringing of phones, orders being barked over comms, and the quiet murmur of my movements being verbally cataloged.

It happens as soon as I emerge from my bedroom just after eight o'clock on Saturday morning. The low rumble of Agent Drake's voice from his post at the end of the hall.

"Hummingbird is leaving the primary suite."

We were assigned code names during our first meeting with our detail, and for the most part, I don't pay attention to when or how it's said, but when Agent Drake says it, it sends an idiotic rush of warmth through me that the severity of his gaze does nothing to dispel. Copper eyes sweep over me, making me acutely aware of the fact that Aubrey's text, stating his immediate need of my presence, left me with no time to get dressed, so I'm moving towards him with a freshly washed face and a careless low ponytail that's one swift movement away from coming undone. Worst of all, I'm wearing nothing but a black satin nightgown that stops well above my knee and the matching robe, which isn't much longer.

I didn't even bother to tie it. That's how much of a rush I was in. How determined I was to meet Aubrey's request and keep feeding the positive energy that's been swirling between us since that hug at the hospital. I don't regret my commitment to keeping things with my husband trending towards the positive, but I do regret not taking a second to put on some real clothes or at least a bra.

"She's heading for the kitchen," Agent Drake is saying now, his prediction based on his knowledge of my Saturday morning routine.

"Aubrey's office, actually," I correct him, lips quirking as he scrambles to relay the information. Even though it only lasts for a moment, seeing him out of sorts helps me feel less self-conscious, and my steps slow a little. The urgency that catapulted me out of the room leaving me in a quiet sigh that begs for just another second in the agent's presence.

If he thinks it's odd that I've come to a complete stop in front of him, Agent Drake doesn't let on. "You should still stop by the kitchen," he tells me. "Won't get much done on an empty stomach."

"I'll be sure to stop by the bird feeder before I get too distracted," I quip, watching as my poor excuse for a joke washes over him. It takes him a full second to give in to the smile, but when it happens, when his serious facade is cracked by radiant light that rains down on me, I'm left with the distinct feeling of standing in a puddle of sunshine.

I'm thinking about how I could stay in that warmth forever when it fades away suddenly, pushed out by the intrusive cold front that is Agent Beckham appearing out of thin air. He pauses outside the bubble surrounding his partner and I, looking between us with an unreadable expression before deciding to address me first.

"Ma'am." He dips his chin, and I wonder if it's his way of trying to make his demeanor seem less hostile. It doesn't. If anything, it makes his lingering annoyance with me even more evident. "Drake, I need you up front," he says, turning to head back down the hall and leaving Agent Drake with no choice but to follow. I watch them go, waiting for the broad span of their shoulders to disappear around the corner before finally resuming my journey to Aubrey's office on the main floor.

Outside the door, I hear shouts of excitement layered over the sounds of a newscast in the background and feel the soft trickle of disappointment roll down my spine. Part of me had stupidly believed Aubrey's desire to see me had to do with...well, with me, but I should have known better. Our entire life is about this campaign. I don't know why I thought this morning would be any different.

I step inside and find Aubrey in the middle of the floor, his hands linked together and resting on top of his head while he bounces on his toes with excitement. Jordan is perched on the edge of his desk, flipping through the channels on the television at a rapid rate. Every channel that comes up is a news station—FOX, ABC, CNN, etc.,—and they all have a different version of the same story running right now. Jordan is changing the channels too fast, so I can't hear what any of the broadcasters are saying, but I can read the words scrolling on the breaking news banner at the bottom of the screen.

Breaking: President Lucas Sanders rushed to the hospital after a sudden collapse.

"It's fucking everywhere," Aubrey remarks, his voice full of wonder as he pumps his fist in the air. He turns, probably intending to address Jordan, but his gaze snags on me. "Selene, baby! Finally. Have you seen this?" His right hand swings back, gesturing at the TV.

Jordan is no longer flipping through the channels, so the screen is still, an image of the President taking up all seventy inches. He looks healthy there, or at least as healthy as a white man pushing eighty can look. His pale blonde hair is thinning, the skin on his face sagging under the weight of age and the stress of spending decades of your life in politics. His eyes are bright, though. A luminous gray that reads as silver and speaks of wisdom.

I've never met the man before, and I don't agree with a single one of his political views, but in this moment, I feel for him. For his wife and their three children. For his grandchildren, who probably heard about their grandfather's collapse from the media instead of their parents or another loved one.

That's how I found out about the active shooter at AJ's school, on the news. A breaking story just like the one playing out on the television in front of me now, except there are several degrees of separation between me and this story, and that day, there were none. Since then, I haven't been able to watch a breaking news story without thinking about the horror the subject's family might be feeling at that exact moment.

Apparently, Aubrey doesn't have the same issue.

He scoops me up in his arms and spins me around, kissing my neck and cheeks and face while Jordan slips out of the room with her phone to her ear.

"Is she calling to check on President Sanders?" I ask, wincing as my back hits the door.

Aubrey is caught up. He's touching me everywhere, his hands greedy and rough as he grabs my thighs, forcing me to open for him, to make room for the span of his hips and the erection that makes me gasp in surprise.

Is he getting off on this?

"Aubrey." I push on his shoulders, forcing him to look at me. There's a raw, chilling quality to his gaze, the possibility of power spilling out of his eyes. His expression lingering somewhere between rabid desire and the presence of mind necessary to answer my question.

He shakes his head, attempting to clear the fog of lust I'm not sure is even really for me. "What?"

"Is Jordan calling to check on President Sanders?" I repeat, although I already know the answer. It's there in the lack of empathy in Aubrey's eyes, in the heaving of his chest, and the subtle rock of his hips between my thighs.

His brows fold in on themselves. "Of course not, she's talking to her team, having them update the campaign messaging and run the ad we shot that focuses on Sanders' failing health and...*highlights... my....virility.*" The delivery of the last three words is staggered, each one punctuated by a pump of his hips that nudges his tip into my center.

It's meant to be enticing, to stir up feelings of desire and excitement, but instead, it just makes me sick to my stomach. It feels wrong to be on the brink of a celebratory fuck when there's a life hanging in the balance. I open my mouth to say as much to Aubrey, but the words get lost between his lips and mine, and the opportunity to speak up, to ask for clarity, gets further and further away from me the longer the kiss goes on.

I try to want it, to relax into his hold, to appreciate the feel of his skin on mine, but it's hard. He's moving too fast. His hands are too rough, and my mind is everywhere but in this moment with him. My thoughts bounce from the President, to the new ad I'm sure will be playing on every major news outlet by the end of the night, and then —when Aubrey undoes his pants and his dick is a breath away from being inside of me—to Sutton fucking Ellsworth on her knees with her lips wrapped around the dick in question.

That snaps me out of it.

"Stop," I say firmly, pushing at him again. He pulls back and then advances again, so I shove him hard. "Aubrey, I said stop. Let me down."

He releases me, stepping back to allow me room to put my feet on the ground. "What's wrong?" he asks, tucking himself back into his pants and then running frustrated fingers through his hair.

I stare at him, wondering how many times Sutton saw him in this particular state of dishevelment. If she'd giggled and swooned at getting to witness a man like Aubrey in such a vulnerable position. *Of course, she did,* I think bitterly. *She probably relished every moment of seeing the raw, unfiltered version of him.*

For some reason, the word raw bounces around my skull, calling my attention to yet another question I need to ask my husband about his affair.

"Did you use condoms with her?" I blurt out.

Aubrey throws his hands up. "Jesus fucking Christ, Sel. You want to talk about this *now*?"

My jaw clenches, old resentments and new pain rising up inside of me. "Well, yes, Aubrey. I thought it might be nice to know if you're putting me at risk *before* I let you fuck me."

"I would *never* put you at risk."

"That's not an answer, Aubrey."

Another hand rushes through his hair, spawning more tunnels of agitation in the golden strands, and he sighs heavily. It's that sigh that tells me I won't get the answer I'm looking for today, if I get one at all.

"Selene, we're standing on the precipice of our dreams, of a future we've been working toward for years. In just a few weeks, we'll be poised to keep our promise to make sure no other parent loses their kid the way we lost AJ."

At the mention of our shared vow born of grief and the sensation of helplessness so strong we have gone to great lengths to never feel it again, I soften immediately. Aubrey steps forward, wrapping his hands around my wrist and pulling me into him. I tip my head back, looking up into his face, trying to decipher if this is manipulation or actual care. His eyes are gentle, wide with something I can only call sincerity.

"We've been different since the hospital," he whispers. "Better than we've been since the news of the affair broke. I don't want to go backwards, Selene, only forward. Only with you."

"I want that too, Aubrey, but there is no forward for me without answers about how we ended up here in the first place."

"Aubrey, we have a call in five minutes," Jordan says, her voice and sudden appearance in the doorway behind me interrupting whatever he was about to say. She marches into the room, accompanied by several other staff members. They don't spare us a second glance as they make a beeline for the conference table in the far corner.

With the moment broken, I start to pull away, but Aubrey stops me.

"Have dinner with me on Monday. We'll go to our favorite spot and talk about everything. I'll answer all of your questions, tell you whatever you need to know, so we can leave all of this ugliness behind and focus on our future."

I bite my lip. "I don't know if a public setting is the best place for us to…"

"I need you, Aubrey," Jordan calls from across the room, pulling his attention from me.

"Just give me one damn second to speak with my wife," he barks over his shoulders before looking back at me. "Then we won't have the conversation at dinner. That will just be the start. You'll get all dolled up. I'll wear the same shit I always wear." His lips curve in a self-deprecating smile. "We'll have good food and even better wine, and then, once I've proven that I love you and remind you why you put up with me, we'll come home and have the hard conversation in private."

Jordan clears her throat loudly as the tell-tale chime of a person entering a video call sounds out around us. Aubrey doesn't move. He just stands there, silently pleading for me to accept his offer with wide, imploring eyes.

"Aubrey!" Jordan shouts, her tone incredulous. She's never seen him put me before his work, before her.

He arches a brow. "Selene."

Behind him, Jordan apologizes to the person waiting for Aubrey, assuring them that the call will start soon. She doesn't know that, though, and the uncertainty written into her features when she glances over her shoulder at me says as much. Just like at the hair salon, I feel a rush of pleasure roll through me at the sight of her discomfort. It hits me like a shot of tequila, burning its way down my throat and into my chest before leaving me with the heady sensation of freedom.

This freedom is laced with power, and I get drunk on it, holding on to it for long seconds before I set Aubrey free and put Jordan and the rest of her anxious colleagues out of their misery.

"Fine, I'll have dinner with you."

Aubrey's smile is straight rows of brilliantly white teeth that fill my line of sight for a second when he comes down to kiss me.

"I love you," he murmurs the words into my lips before pulling away, leaving me to wonder if maybe, just maybe, we can make our marriage work.

8

CAL

Part of me wants to force Beck's raised hand back down under the table where it will be free from the scrutinizing gaze of our boss, Daniel Hicks, who has just asked if anyone has anything to add before our Monday meeting concludes.

Everyone, but especially Beck, knows the question about having more to add is rhetorical. Any items Hicks wanted to hear or needed to address have already been discussed at length, and the point Beck is about to raise was not one of those things. It doesn't help that he has already mentioned it to Hicks and been told his assessment of the situation was incorrect. I don't agree with that take, but I also know calling our boss out on his bullshit in front of the rest of the team won't help Beck no matter how right he is.

Hicks scoffs, sitting back in his seat with his fingers laced in front of his stomach. "What is it, Beckham?"

Beck stands with a stack of papers in his hand. They're memos containing all of the pertinent information for the threat he discovered at the Taylors' residence. I know this without having looked at the paper he dropped in front of me because I was there with him when he put it all together. My chest bare, my tone cajoling, my hands busy with the need to soothe. Still, I pick up the paper, acting just as surprised by the information it relays as everyone else.

"On Saturday morning at approximately 0800 hours, I performed a perimeter check at the Taylor residence and spotted this vehicle—" he slams the memo down in front of Hicks, lingering for a second longer than he did with the rest of us to jab at the paper with his index finger, indicating the printed photo of a red Honda civic with South Carolina plates on the road right outside the Taylors' gate. Hicks snatches his paper out from under Beck's fingertip, nearly ripping the memo in half.

"We've already discussed this," Hicks gripes, balling the paper up and tossing it onto the table. "I reviewed the footage myself and concluded that there was no viable threat."

Beck is back at my side now, sinking into his seat with a grimace while the rest of our team looks on with thinly veiled excitement. They love to see Beck and Hicks go at each other. They love it even more when Beck is inevitably punished for insubordination.

"With all due respect, sir, your conclusion was wrong," he says, clenching his fist together to maintain some semblance of calm. I'm proud of him for trying, but I can't let it show on my face. "The vehicle was parked on the street for hours. I spotted it on my first perimeter check at 0700, and it was still there an hour later on my next sweep."

"The windows are tinted, though, how do you know anyone was in there?" Jim Ortega, Hicks' right hand, asks, leaning around his best friend to lay skeptical eyes on mine. I glare at him, warning him to tread carefully.

"The photo is a still taken from video footage, so it's a bit darker in the picture than it was in person," I say, addressing the other man directly. "There was enough visibility for him to see the silhouette of the driver. I believe that's stated in the brief, Ortega, along with a first-hand account from Agent Beckham and me about how the driver took off when we tried to approach."

Anderson, who's sitting closest to me and therefore the last person who should be lending his voice to a contrary opinion, scoffs.

"If I'd seen two big motherfuckers that look like you coming my way, I would have peeled off too."

My head whips around so fast, the asshole doesn't have time to hide his flinch. "The fuck did you just say, Anderson?"

His face turns red, but I know it's not remorse he's displaying, or even embarrassment, it's just plain ole fear that I might actually introduce his face to the clenched fist my hand has turned into. He slides away from me, holding his hands up with his palms facing outward.

"Chill, Drake, I was just joking."

"Which part of that was funny, Anderson?" I tilt my head to the side as he flounders for a response, looking to his friends for help. I grab hold of his chair, spinning it around so Beck and I are the only things in his line of sight. Glancing back at Beck, I ask, "Did you get the joke?"

He grips his chin lightly, pursing his lips. "I didn't. Why don't you explain it to us, Anderson? Break down all the nuances that people who look like us might have missed."

"Oh, well, I just meant...you know—"

Hicks slams his hand on the table. "Enough!"

I can tell by the reckless thread of energy running between Beck and I that neither of us thinks its enough. It won't ever be enough, not until fuckers who try to pass off racism and microaggressions as humor start losing their jobs for it.

"Drake, let go of his chair," Hicks orders, his voice cracking like a whip. I do as he asks, releasing Anderson and then shoving hard to get him the fuck away from me. Once Anderson is settled in his spot around the table, Hicks looks between Beck and I. At first, I think he's going to ream us out, but he surprises me by sighing and rubbing a hand at the back of his neck.

"I wasn't aware that the two of you tried to approach the vehicle," he admits.

Beck places his elbows on the edge of the table, steepling his fingers together. "I thought you reviewed the video footage?"

"I did!" Hicks insists. "I guess I must have missed the part where you two made your approach." He won't meet either of our eyes, focusing instead on unfurling the piece of paper he scrapped just moments ago. "Says here you went into the residence to retrieve Agent Drake instead of radioing for backup."

Beck nods. "I did."

He'd found me in the hallway having a rare moment alone with Selene. She was fresh-faced and relaxed, her feet bare and her smile wide as I laughed at her bad joke. There was a moment, after the joke and the crack in my professional persona, when I wanted to move past the formalities and tell her I wanted more of this side of her. The silly, corny woman with eyes that sparkle with delight at someone else's amusement. I wanted to tell her that the remote, withdrawn woman who wears a suit of strength every time she leaves the house is lovely, but I know she's not real because I watched my mother don the same armor when my dad left. She never got to take it off because she never found anyone she trusted enough to be vulnerable with. I want Selene to know she can trust that part of herself with me, to believe that if she wanted to shed it, I'd be there to shield her.

All of those desires evaporated into thin air when Beck appeared, which was just as well because I had no business wanting any of those things. My job is her physical safety, not her emotional well-being. It's a fact I have to remind myself of constantly these days. A mantra I repeat every time I scroll through her mentions on social media to log threats and run background checks on potential perpetrators and find myself wondering how she feels when she sees the things I see. How it feels when the hate shows up in places I can't be, like her personal inbox or the mail she gets at Culture Code, when the whole world feels like a cavern with sharp teeth, mouth open and waiting, ready to eat her alive.

When Beck and I first met, I found myself wondering about him in the same way. I would go to sleep and dream of him, wake up and worry about him, about the grief he wore like a second skin and the wardrobe of pain and loneliness he layered over it. I felt for him then what I feel for Selene now: a pressing need to be there for him, to hold some of his pain, so I insinuated my way into his world until he accepted I wasn't going anywhere.

Doing that with Selene isn't an option, though, because she's married to the next President of the United States, and the oath I'm bound by only permits me to kill for her. To die for her. It doesn't allow me to know her.

And even knowing that, I still indulged in that short, stolen moment and hated having to walk away from it. If it had been anyone else asking, I would have found a reason to say no, but it wasn't anyone else. It was Beck, and I took one look at his face and knew denial wasn't an option.

It never is with him.

He gave me the rundown on the situation on our way out of the house, and I followed his lead, covering him while he approached the driver's side window, pulling him back when they sped away suddenly.

We called it in to Hicks immediately, not because we wanted his opinion—we knew something was off—but because we needed his permission to abandon our posts to give chase. Of course, he declined almost instantly, never letting Beck give him the complete picture.

This time when Beck tries to explain the interaction, Hicks lets him, nodding when he ends his recount by saying, "I think we should have the local PD put out a BOLO and bring the driver in for questioning. At the very least, we need the incident documented."

"I'll make note of it," he says, rising from his seat, which puts an end to the meeting. The rest of the team stands too, and Beck and I follow suit. I'm about to congratulate him on making it through the meeting without ending up in Hicks' dog house when he squares his shoulders and lets out a dark chuckle.

"Hey, Hicks," he calls out, stopping him in his tracks. Hicks turns, and his cronies turn too. All of them are wearing similar looks, anticipatory smirks pressed down into feigned serious expressions. They know the train we've just managed to get back on track is about to go flying off the rails. "You didn't write it down."

Hicks' brows furrow. "I'm sorry?"

Beck leans over, plucking a pen from the cup in the middle of the table and grabbing a fresh notepad. He strides over to Hicks, his expression calm, nothing like you would expect from a man who's toeing the line of losing his job. He shoves the pad and pen into Hicks' chest, holding it there until the other man places his hands around the materials.

"You didn't write it down," Beck repeats. "You can't make note of something you didn't fucking bother to write down."

Hicks looks past Beck, making eye contact with me. His gaze is hard with the silent order for me to get Beck out of his face, but I don't move a muscle. Beck's approach might differ from mine, but it's still better than doing nothing when there's a potential threat on the horizon. Plus, me intervening now would only feel like a betrayal of my knowledge of Beck's history with nonchalant supervisors and the lives they leave hanging in the balance. I would never do that to him.

Sensing that I will be of no assistance, Hick returns his attention to Beck. The large vein in the center of his forehead that indicates his emotional state pulses angrily as he takes the pen and paper and tosses them back onto the table.

"I'll tell you what, Beckham," he sneers, getting into his face. "I'll do a full report on this little incident, and it'll go into the Taylors' file, but it'll also go in yours as an attachment to yet another write-up due to insubordination. And when I'm done writing that, I'm going to grab my pen, go to the bulletin, and put you down as the cover agent for the next month." Hicks glances back at his snickering flunkies and grins. "Who needs a shift covered?"

Anderson's hand flies up. "I need my shift for tonight covered, Beck. The Taylors are going on a date, and I'm still recovering from the second-hand embarrassment from the last time I had to watch them share a meal."

My brows lift at the mention of a date. I guess it makes sense that I wouldn't know anything about it since I'm off tonight, but it still strikes me as odd to think about Aubrey and Selene doing anything together that wasn't mandated by Jordan St. James. I guess things with them are better than I thought.

"Provide him with the details. He'll take care of it." Hicks swings his gaze back to Beck. "Won't you, Beckham?"

Beck shrugs. "As long as you make note of the incident and put in the BOLO request with the locals, I'm happy to fill in where I'm needed."

There's a serenity to his response that fills me with pride I can't let show. Every time Beck pushes, Hicks pushes back, trying to hit him where it hurts. It's funny to me that he never learns, that in all these years, he's yet to realize that for Beck, a win is a win. It doesn't matter if he gets punished or written up or never has another day off in his life because he got Hicks to fold.

The would-be standoff ends unceremoniously. Hicks backs away from Beck, turning on his heel and storming out with his shoulders high around his ears. Every member of our team follows behind him, leaving Beck and me alone. When the door closes, I move to stand in front of him, reaching up to cup a hand at the back of his neck and pull him in close. He's stiff at first, railing against my touch because of where we are, but I need to touch him, to reassure him that even in the moments when he was standing against Hicks alone, I was in his corner. It takes a minute, but eventually he gives, resting his head on my shoulder.

"You did good," I tell him, eyes on the door in case someone doubles back.

"I fucking hate this. We shouldn't have to fight tooth and nail to have our concerns acted on. It shouldn't be this fucking hard, Cal."

"You're right. But we can't focus on that now. You need to go home and get some rest, and I need to convince Ortega to let me work his shift tonight."

Beck's head snaps up, his eyes wide. "No, you don't—"

I silence him with a short, chaste kiss. "It's already done, love."

ORTEGA DIDN'T NEED CONVINCING.

As soon as I approached him, he agreed and went to call his wife to tell her he'd be available to take her out to dinner for their anniversary after all. And now, hours later, Beck and I are standing side by side in the Taylors' circular driveway waiting for them to emerge so we can get this date night started.

Beside me, Beck is more relaxed than he's been all day. He leans against the car, long legs stretched out in front of him, arms crossed over his chest, and I smile to myself, knowing that relaxation is a direct result of the work I put in this afternoon after we left headquarters. At first, he protested the idea of me coming to his place after I finished talking with Ortega, but then I promised to feed him and walk him through a recollection protocol to help him get back any details of the incident that might have been lost over the last few days. That had resulted in him telling me the driver had his window down when he did his first perimeter check. Only slightly, but enough for him to know something about the person felt familiar to him, like he'd seen him before, which pointed us to our old case files to figure out where their paths might have crossed.

After an hour of looking, we decided to call it quits for the day and try to get some sleep. That was a fruitless endeavor, but I don't think either of us regrets it.

"Stop thinking about it," Beck orders through clenched teeth just as the front door of the residence opens, and Selene steps out, wiping my brain clean for a moment.

She's absolutely stunning, and I'm aware that I'm staring, conscious of the fact that I shouldn't be. Still, I'm afraid that if I look away, then no one will appreciate the amalgamation of small details that come together to create one exquisite picture.

The form fitting black dress with a slit up her thigh.

The gold stilettos with straps that wrap up her calves and match the thin, diamond-encrusted gold chain at her throat.

The artfully messy bun at the top of her head with a few curled strands left out in several places. My favorites are the ones that frame her face, highlighting her cheekbones and the sharpness of her eyes.

Every piece is more captivating than the next, holding me in the painful space between reality and a possibility I can never entertain.

It takes me too long to realize that Beck is there too. He's gone still beside me, and I pull my gaze away from Selene just long enough to watch him watch her. To see his eyes trail up her leg, swallowing hard as if every inch of smooth, sable skin exposed by the slit measures the difference between the buttoned up, reserved woman he claims he can't stand to the distinctly sexual being standing in front of us.

I've never dated women, although I've been attracted to them, but Beck has. Beck *does,* but I've never seen him with any of them before, so I've only ever theorized what attraction for the opposite sex might look like on his face. I didn't think I'd like to see it, fearing that it would only make me realize how fragile the thing between us is. But when the subject of his focus is Selene, it only seems to amplify what I feel for him. In this moment, with the thread of focus extending between Beck and me reaching out to envelop Selene, our bond feels stronger than ever.

Just as I'm growing used to the connection, it fractures under the weight of Aubrey's sudden appearance at her side. Selene smiles, a genuine smile that's meant for him and no one else, but he doesn't see it because he's too preoccupied with his phone. He breezes past her, heading to the car we're standing in front of. Beck jumps into action, opening the door for Aubrey while I move over to Selene. She's still standing in the same place, her expression a broken mix of hurt and annoyance because of her husband's lack of attention.

"Mrs. Taylor, you look lovely tonight." Aubrey's last name tastes like ash on my tongue, but I fight the sensation to gag, choosing instead to extend my hand to Selene. She stares at it for a long moment before taking it, allowing me to help her down the steps and to the car.

The physical contact only lasts for a few seconds, but I relish every one, wondering if she feels it too—the electricity buzzing between the lines of our palms.

The regret that courses through my veins and causes my hands to shake when I have to let her go.

9

BECK

From my post in the far right corner of the dining area, I catch Cal's eye and discreetly hold two fingers to my chest, prompting him to move to a closed channel so we can have a conversation without any of the other agents working tonight overhearing. He dips his chin in acknowledgment, and in seconds, his gravelly timbre is filling my ears.

"What's up?"

"You're distracted," I say by way of greeting, opting out of a gentle approach because a situation as serious as this just doesn't allow for it. Cal's brows shoot up, but I know it's not my delivery that's caught him off guard. It's my message.

"I'm sorry?"

He's right to be confused, and maybe even a little offended, because tonight he's as focused as he's ever been. The problem is, he's too focused on her. Even now, as he's waiting for my response, his gaze lingers on the table towards the back of the room where Aubrey and Selene are being served their entrees and getting their glasses of wine refilled. Of course, it's our job to check in on them from time to time, but Cal isn't checking in.

He's staring.

Spending long seconds studying Selene's profile, his jaw clenched with annoyance every time his gaze lands on Aubrey, who seems to be making up for his lack of attention at the beginning of the night by turning on the charm. He's been making Selene laugh, and while I can't deny that it's nice to see genuine joy written across her face, I can't help but worry about Cal being so affected by it.

"You're distracted. Every time I look at you, you're looking at her."

A ghost of a smirk plays on his lips. "Jealous, love?"

Heat creeps up my neck, and I barely resist the urge to flip him off for intentionally trying to fluster me. "No. I'm not jealous, I'm concerned. All of your focus is on how their date is going when you should be paying attention to what's happening in the rest of the room, where threats are more likely to come from."

My words have a harsh bite to them, anger and maybe a little bit of jealousy, coating each one. I knew Cal liked Selene. It was clear to me in the way he toed the line of indifference on the day of the children's hospital event. But I didn't know exactly what that meant until tonight. When I saw him staring at her, his eyes shimmering with things he shouldn't feel, his throat tight with things he could never say, I realized there was more than the friendly but distant interest you can't help but garner when you spend your days around a person.

There was forbidden affection.

There was career-ruining attraction.

There was the soft pull of distraction, and in our line of work, distraction gets you killed.

"You don't need to be concerned because I'm not distracted, Beck. I'm aware of everything happening in this room and your head," he says, emphasizing the last part with a wiggle of his brows that tells me he doesn't believe for a second I'm not jealous.

"What color dress is the woman in the booth to your left wearing?" I ask, glaring at him. I don't need to tell him not to look because he already knows better than to cheat in a game meant to test his recall and focus.

"Green. She's paired it with red heels." His nose scrunches with disapproval. "A bit too Christmas-y for my taste, but to each their own. The man she's with is a banker, and he doesn't seem to share her passion for art."

"How many people have come through the door since we moved to this channel?"

"Six. A group of four being seated in the booth closest to the door, and two women who opted for seats at the bar. One of them is approaching you now, probably on her way to the bathroom."

As if on cue, a woman in a cream wrap dress walks up. Her eyes lock on mine, a flare of panic in them when she realizes I'm blocking the hall leading to the restrooms. I step aside, giving her a tight smile and a wide berth to move past me. Once she's out of earshot, I resume my stance and reluctantly give Cal his props as I do a cursory scan of the room.

"Fine, maybe you're not distracted, but it doesn't change the fact that you're too focused on Hummingbird. You need to reel it in before someone who's not me notices."

I expect his response to be immediate, but it's not. The line is quiet, and when I look at Cal, his face is warped with tension, all traces of humor gone. At first, I think it's in response to what I've just said, but I eliminate that possibility quickly. Cal and I both value the pure honesty that years of friendship and love have afforded us. We don't get upset when we're called out by the other, and even if we do, the reaction is never as visceral as the one Cal is having right now.

Certain the source of his agitation isn't me, I turn my attention outward, scanning the room for any signs of a threat. That's when I see him. The man in the opposite corner of the room. He's short, probably no taller than five feet, seven inches. White, with black hair and brown eyes. He's wearing a brown tweed jacket with patches on the elbows and a white button-up underneath. The jeans he's wearing are a bit casual for the setting, but I don't really care about his fashion faux pas. I'm more concerned about the phone in his hand pointed at Selene and Aubrey. From that angle, he has a perfect, unobstructed shot of them, so I'm certain he has his camera on, taking photos, or maybe even worse, videos of what's supposed to be a private moment. Thankfully, he's being discreet, so no one, least of all the people currently having their privacy invaded, has noticed.

Unfortunately for the voyeur, Cal has noticed, though, and he's already moving toward him. It's a slow approach, and it would look casual if it weren't for the tense set of his shoulders and the unwavering death glare he's sending the man. I match the pace of my approach to Cal's to avoid drawing the attention of the rest of the diners, and the poor fuck is so focused on what he's doing, he doesn't realize we've closed in on him until Cal is casting a shadow over his uneaten meal and I have my hand on his shoulder, forcing him to stay seated.

"Hey!" he whisper-shouts, his head snapping up, wide brown eyes looking between us. I study his face, trying to see if he could possibly be the man who was in the car. I can't say for certain whether he is or isn't, and that bothers me. I thought I'd gotten a good look at the guy, but apparently it wasn't that good. It doesn't matter, though, because this man is here, and he's guilty of something.

Whether it's the small crime of bringing his phone into a space where it's strictly prohibited or a larger offense like stalking has yet to be determined. Normally, I wouldn't be so quick to conflate separate events, but two incidents happening just days apart hardly seems like a coincidence, and I refuse to treat it as such. Especially when I know what I know about the online vitriol that only seems to be aimed in Selene's direction. Things calmed down for a bit after the children's hospital appearance led to an increase in Aubrey's poll numbers, but for every positive comment about the couple, there were five more negative ones, all focused on her.

They came for everything—her clothes, her hair, her business, her smile—nothing was off limits, not even her son. Posts about him are the worst, followed closely by those hoping Selene will die so Aubrey and the speechwriter can finally be together. Those posts are usually accompanied by disgustingly detailed and badly written torture porn that makes my stomach turn and dredges up memories of a time I'd rather not revisit.

It was those memories that had made me push Hicks this morning. Those posts, and that old fear of an innocent woman being caught in the cross hairs of some maniac, that sent anger rolling through my gut and landed me here, which is exactly where I need to be in order to keep Selene safe from those who would do her harm.

Without proof, I've decided the man squirming under my hand fits the bill, and everything about Cal—from his demeanor to the snarl curling his lips—says he agrees.

"Put the phone down," I issue the order in a low growl the man has no choice but to obey. He drops the device, and I see his screen is open, the camera still rolling even though it's no longer focused in Selene and Aubrey's direction. It's all the confirmation I need. *"Get up."*

He's not moving quickly enough, so I decide to help him out, gripping him under the arm and lifting him from his seat. Cal grabs his phone and begins swiping almost instantly, which makes the man protest loudly.

"That's private property!" he shouts, drawing the attention of everyone in the room. Most of them look concerned at first, but when they see the official-looking suits and the American flag pins on our lapels, they look away. "You can't just go through my phone without my permission!" The man is screaming now, all his venom for Cal, even though I'm the one dragging him out of the dining area toward the kitchen. "I know my rights," he insists. "I'm a member of the press!"

On any other day, his announcement would have meant something to me. Not much, but something. It might have been enough to get me to loosen my grip on him or allow him the dignity of standing on his own two feet to leave the room, but unfortunately for him, today is not one of those days.

Today, I'm impatient and running on little sleep. Today, I'm fed up with assholes who think they can do whatever they want and get away with it. Today, I'm coming to grips with the fact that my partner is emotionally invested in the woman whose well-being we've been entrusted with, which means I don't just have to protect Selene, I have to protect Cal, too.

"Did you hear what I said?" The man asks as I release him, pushing him through the kitchen door. For a second, everything in the busy kitchen stops, and everyone looks at us, watching our impromptu processional to the administrative office with vivid interest.

"Your press pass won't save you," I mutter, herding the man into the office with Cal hot on my heels, still swiping through the man's phone. I know he's made it through the photos and videos by now, moving on to the man's messages and call logs, gathering any pertinent information for the report we'll have to file and submit to Hicks.

I roll my eyes just thinking about the flak we'll get for bringing yet another incident to his attention. I'm sure he'll treat this one with even less urgency than the first.

"What's your name?"

The man opens his mouth, probably preparing to spout off some line about not having to tell me anything, but Cal beats him to the punch. "His name's Franklin Landry. He's a reporter for The Daily, and according to this text from his ex-wife, he's supposed to have his son tonight, but he flaked at the last minute to grace us with his presence."

Franklin pulls at the lapels of his ugly ass blazer and frowns. "I had to work. My son understands."

"I don't know, Frank. He looks pretty upset to me," Cal says, turning the phone towards us. On the screen is a photo of a little boy who has the misfortune of looking like his father. There are tears streaming down his face and bubbles of snot coming out of his nose.

Franklin lunges for Cal, and I stop him with a hand on his chest. "Don't."

"Those messages are private!"

"So is the dinner the Taylors are having," I tell him, forcing him down into the rolling chair behind the desk. "How did you know they were going to be here?"

"And how did you get a reservation?" Cal adds, setting Franklin's phone on the desk and planting his palms on either side of it.

Franklin runs a hand through his hair. "I got a tip, and the reservation wasn't hard to come by. The owner owes me a favor."

"A tip from who?" I cross my arms, not liking the sound of someone giving up Selene and Aubrey's location. Information like that is a precious commodity, which means someone is always looking to buy and sell it. Obviously, Franklin is the buyer in this scenario, and I want to put hands on the seller.

"I can't reveal my sources."

I look at Cal, silently asking how he wants to play this. He shakes his head, and despite my frustration, I agree with his choice. We both know we can't legally compel him to give us answers, and we don't have the time or privacy necessary to do it any other way.

"Fine, then you've left us with no choice but to arrest you for harassment."

Franklin's jaw drops. "What?! You can't do that. Harassment is a misdemeanor at best, and you're only authorized to make felony arrests."

"You're right, but we have you scheming your way into this restaurant and violating the phone-free clause in the reservation contract for the sole purpose of recording the Taylors without their permission," Cal tells him. "Add in the disparaging comments you've made about Mrs. Taylor in your paper—"

"I've only ever written the truth," Franklin cuts in, crossing his arms. "I can't help it if it's not always flattering."

I wave a hand, dismissing his bullshit excuses. "It doesn't help that Mrs. Taylor is the primary focus of most of your shots. Remind me, Agent Drake, does the targeted victim being a Black woman help or hurt Franklin's case?"

Cal smiles, the lines of his face turning into harsh angles that are sharp enough to cut through bone. "Oh, it definitely hurts his case, Agent Beckham. See, Mrs. Taylor being Black and a woman means she falls into two of the seven groups of protected characteristics. That intersectionality is really fucking you up, Frank, because it's what takes your harassment charge from a misdemeanor to a felony."

Franklin turns pale, and I know we've got him. He pushes out a harsh breath through his nose, and I wait for an answer that gets delayed when the door swings open behind us and Agent Harris steps inside. Harris is a tall, balding white man in his mid-thirties who tries to stay neutral when it comes to our fucked up team dynamics. I don't like or dislike him, and I get the sense he feels the same way about Cal and me.

That indifference is in his eyes when they pass over the scene in front of him. "Mr. Taylor would like a word," he says eventually, stepping back to make room for Aubrey crossing the threshold.

Harris leaves the office, and the door snaps closed behind him while Aubrey moves around Cal and me to stand next to Franklin. His hands are tucked into his pockets, and his lips are pressed into a flat line.

"What's going on?" he asks, looking between the three of us.

Cal straightens. "We caught this man taking photos and videos of you and Mrs. Taylor. Apparently, he's a member of the press."

"We're trying to figure out how he knew you would be here," I add, turning back to Franklin. "Who's your source?"

Every ounce of cooperative energy the reporter previously possessed has left him. He's not even looking at us anymore. All of his attention is on Aubrey, and I can see the desire to seize the opportunity in front of him brimming in his eyes.

I snap my fingers in front of his face. "Don't even think about it. Mr. Taylor is not here to answer your questions. You're here to answer mine."

Aubrey frowns. "Is that tone really necessary, agent?"

Cal balks, and I step in front of him, placing myself between him and Aubrey despite being annoyed myself. The last thing I need right now is someone else telling me how to do my job.

"We're trying to determine if there's a leak in your camp, Mr. Taylor."

"And I appreciate that, but there's no need to mistreat a revered member of the press." He edges around me to lean on the desk in front of Franklin, clapping him on the shoulder. "I'm sorry about all of this, Mr…"

"Landry," Franklin provides, flicking a smug gaze to Cal and me.

"Mr. Landry." Aubrey smiles, clapping his shoulder again. "Please accept my sincerest apologies for these overzealous agents."

"*Overzealous*?" My voice is rough with disbelief. "We were doing our jobs, Mr. Taylor."

Aubrey spares me a single glance over his shoulder. "With unnecessary force," he says. "I'll be sure to report this to your supervisor."

The statement is directed at me, but I know it's for Franklin's benefit. Aubrey is hoping to buy some goodwill with the reporter by making a common enemy out of us.

"Make sure you let him know that they also took my phone and went through my personal messages and photos," Franklin adds, practically preening under Aubrey's attention.

"That's completely unacceptable." Aubrey reaches back, holding his hand out. "Give me his phone."

Cal is vibrating with anger, so instead of handing the phone to Aubrey, he shoves it across the desk. It hits Aubrey in the hip, but Franklin is the one who scoops it up. His eyes are alight with opportunity as he opens a recording app.

It's almost laughable how quickly it happens. Aubrey's shock and Franklin's intense focus as he peppers him with question after question. Some of them come out so fast, I can't even catch them. Aubrey stands, shaking his head and laughing in a way that suggests he doesn't think any of this is funny at all. Franklin follows suit, and Cal and I both take a step back, satisfied to let this nightmare play out for just a bit, even though we both know we won't let him lay a finger on Aubrey.

"Mr. Taylor, what does your wife think of Sutton Ellsworth still being on your campaign's payroll?" Shock colors Aubrey's features, but Franklin is relentless, saving the best question for last. "Does Selene know Sutton wrote the moving speech she delivered at Children's National Hospital?"

A heavy silence falls over the room, and it's not Aubrey who breaks it. No, the voice that fills the space, breaking our bubble of perceived privacy, is softer. We all turn to find Selene standing in the doorway in the gorgeous fucking dress that will now always be associated with this night, with this embarrassment, with this pain, her mouth agape as she sputters,

"I'm sorry, *what*?"

10

SELENE

It's evident none of the men in the office were expecting to see me.

Aubrey looks angry that I'm not at the table where he told me to wait.

The man behind him, who I assume is a reporter because of the recording app open on the screen of the phone he's pointing at Aubrey's face, looks so pleased with himself. His eyes are wide, bright with glee and opportunity when they land on my stunned expression.

Agents Drake and Beckham look horrified to be standing at the site of yet another mortifying moment in my life. Underneath those twin expressions of horror is some other thing I don't quite understand. I don't get the chance to process it either because as soon as everyone, including me, accepts that I am here, and I did hear the last question, the reporter starts to move towards me.

The agents move in perfect synchrony, with fluid, unhurried movements that bring the span of their broad shoulders together to form a wall between me and the vulture squawking questions in my direction.

I don't even look at him because this hurt, this pain, this rage, is all for Aubrey. His eyes are liquid, rippling pools of cerulean that are meant to soften me, but I don't have an ounce of give left. I can't bend any more truths or talk myself into being satisfied with the drops of hope for my marriage that have been sustaining me since our conversation the morning President Sanders collapsed. For days, I've been looking forward to this night, knowing a single dinner wouldn't fix everything but hoping it would be the start to mending a festering wound.

But now I feel more wounded than ever, and God, I hate that it's happening here in front of these men, but I'm bleeding out.

My eyes narrow into slits, and Aubrey swallows, holding his hands up, ready to plead for mercy I don't have to give. "Is it true?"

"Sel." He glances around, shaking his head. "Let's not have this conversation here."

"Is. It. True?!" I stomp my foot, knowing it might look childish, but loving the way the force of my stiletto colliding with the floor sends vibrations reverberating through me. Aubrey hangs his head, but it's not shame that weighs it down. It's frustration. It's the burning need to raise his voice and shout back at me. It's the war waged by the desire to reel me back in and the need not to cause a scene.

"Yes, but—"

I want to scream. I want to hit him. I want to let the dam holding back the rage that's been building and building inside of me finally break.

"Why the fuck would you do that?" I grit out, pushing the broken syllables past clenched teeth. "Why would you do something so stupid as to continue to work with that woman?"

Aubrey flounders for an answer. His thin lips parting and then coming back together before anything of substance can pass through them. I know there's nothing he can say to make this right. Nothing he can do to justify an ongoing professional, and probably personal, relationship with Sutton.

And the worst part about it is, he doesn't have to. He doesn't have to explain his choices or justify his actions because there has never been a consequence if he didn't. I've never given him a consequence.

He cheated, and I stayed by his side, turning myself into the kind of woman I swore I'd never be: jaded, disconnected, placated by small promises, soothing wounds with tattered scraps gathered from the feet of men who were supposed to love and care for them. Men who spend all their time congratulating themselves for conquering the world and don't bother to mention the women who carried burdens that left their greedy hands free to hold the riches they have no right to.

Wave after wave of resentment surges through my veins, bolstered by the realization, fed by the stupid fucking look on Aubrey's face when he says, "No one was supposed to find out."

A bitter laugh breaks free from my chest, and one of my hands flies up, gesturing at the reporter who is still recording. "Well, obviously, that didn't go to plan."

Something about the wild wave of my hand prompts Agent Drake to take action. He pulls the phone from the reporter's hand, swiping long fingers over the screen, probably to delete the recording. The reporter protests loudly, screeching about his civil rights and privacy. Aubrey turns to him, issuing an unnecessary apology that prompts both agents to respond loudly.

Suddenly, the small room is filled with bickering over the agent's duties and the public's right to know what's happening with elected officials. At my back, there's the clinking of dishes, the chopping of knives, the whining of metal heating up over open flames, the hum of constant communication between a team that works with the efficiency of a machine.

It's too much.

The voices saying everything and nothing at all.

The sounds pressing in on me from all sides.

The harsh swelling of emotions in my chest.

The echo of my heartbeat in the base of my skull.

The heat of shame rising high on my cheeks.

Overwhelmed, I turn away from the men and the mess of my life and march out of the restaurant. I know Aubrey won't chase me. He doesn't do that. Even when he's wrong, he remains firmly planted in his position, literally and figuratively. I highly doubt he's even noticed I'm on the move, but the agents on our detail have.

More specifically, Agent Drake has.

Everyone and everything I pass on my way through the dining area and lobby of the restaurant is a blur, barely registering through the haze of overstimulation, but his steady presence at my back makes it impossible for me to ignore him. Surprisingly, his proximity doesn't grate on my already frayed nerves. Instead, it feels more soothing to know he's here with me, keeping me physically safe while I'm emotionally destroyed.

We reach the black SUV, and I'm moving too fast, leaving no time for the agents inside the vehicle to step out and open the door for me. I reach for the handle, but once again, Agent Drake is there. The heat of him at my back. His long fingers brushing against mine, gently moving my hand out of the way so he can open the door.

"Let me," he murmurs, his voice a low rumble against my ear.

It's not intentional.

I know he's far too professional for that, but it still feels like he's offering me something more than this small but expected gesture. I swallow the thought and slip past him and into the backseat. He closes the door and rounds the car, ordering the two members of his team who are sitting in the front to get out, and then sliding behind the wheel. When he's settled in his seat, the door clicks closed behind him, shutting out the rest of the world, making the soft sound of my thumb flicking against my index finger repeatedly all the more obvious.

The action isn't new. It's been one of my stims for a long time, but I don't usually give in to the urge to perform it, especially not in public. I've always been adept at masking. That's part of the reason why I got my diagnosis so late in life, but I got even better at it when AJ died and the eyes of the world were on me, eager to witness the spectacle of my grief. Stimming on top of the constant public breakdowns would have only made things worse, inspiring questions to which no one had the right to want answers. It occurs to me that I'm opening myself up to those same questions now, just from a smaller audience.

Agent Drake is quiet in the front seat, but I know he's watching me. I can feel the weight of his gaze on my overheated skin, which forces me to make the concerted effort to calm myself by squeezing my eyes shut, pulling in jagged huffs of air, and pushing out smooth bubbles of breath that carry some of the anxiety out of my body. Then, and only then, am I brave enough to open my eyes, to raise my head and meet those dark, inquisitive eyes that don't shift away from mine in the rear view mirror.

It feels like the moment on the porch earlier tonight. When he wouldn't look away from me, and I didn't want him to. I thought that desire was just because of Aubrey's lack of attentiveness in the moment, but now I know it wasn't. My response had nothing to do with Aubrey at all. He could have been staring right at me, and I think I would still prefer the intensity of the elusive agent's gaze. I would still want to unearth the thoughts hidden behind his unreadable expression.

Maybe that's why I give in to the urge to goad him, to force him to divulge some part of himself, because every bit of me feels like it's on display.

"I know what you must think of me," I whisper quietly, afraid of the question hidden in the words even as I crave his answer.

"It's not my job to think anything of you, ma'am."

Through the mirror, he searches my face, and I wonder if he's ever looked at me for this long before, if we've ever been alone for this long before. Everything about this moment feels like it exists outside the bounds of our professional context, and I'm reluctant to be dragged back into them by his half-answer.

"Well, you'd be the only person in the world who doesn't have an opinion of me." A humorless laugh slips through my lips as the nasty beliefs that exist somewhere between my thoughts and the words I've read online rush through my mind. "There's a wide range of them," I continue. "Opinions, that is. A lot of people think I'm stupid for staying with Aubrey. Others think I should be thankful that this is his first time stepping out on me. Within that group, there's a sector that likes to theorize about my bedroom performance because, of course, me being bad at sex gives my husband license to cheat." Agent Drake swallows and shifts in his seat. I know I'm making him uncomfortable, but I can't stop. "I saw a post on Reddit once. There were photos and videos, none of me smiling, though. An entire album full of frowns and rigid posture with a caption that read 'No wonder AT had to find some new ass. It's no fun fucking a cold fish.'"

He grimaces. "That kind of language has no—"

"I don't care about that," I say, cutting him off even though there's a part of me that craves the visceral nature of his reaction. There's protection in it, censure and outrage that doesn't blame me for reading the post the way Aubrey had. It lets me believe that he's on my side. It makes me desperate to hear him say it. "Tell me the truth, Agent Drake, what do you really think of me?"

There's no dancing around a question phrased so plainly, and I see the resignation to give me my answer throbbing in the muscle of his jaw, feel it in the seconds that pass slowly, marked by nothing but the sound of my finger flicking.

"Cal," he says finally, rolling his head from one side of his neck to the other.

"What?"

"You're asking me to breach a professional boundary. Agent Drake won't do that." He shakes his head regretfully. "Agent Drake *can't* do that, so please, Selene, call me Cal."

Something sharp and demanding jabs me in the heart at the sound of my name on his lips. A blade of intimacy that cuts through my sternum and makes me gasp audibly at the first taste of this new familiarity on my tongue.

"*Cal.*"

"Yes." He nods, copper eyes shimmering with approval. "It's short for Callan."

"Callan." My brows dip inward as I sort through the information in my mind to place the word. "It's a Gaelic name that means 'powerful in battle.'"

He isn't the least bit put off by the random fact that's just popped out of my mouth. "If you say so."

Humor that has no place in the cloud of devastation looming over me causes my lips to quirk. "I say so."

Silence pools between us, and it takes a second for me to realize that he's waiting for me to ask again, this time using the shortened version of his given name. The question swirls in my mind but stalls on my lips for a moment.

"What do you really think of me, Cal?"

He sighs, and there's relief in the sound that suggests he was afraid I had lost my nerve. His eyes burn into me through the glass of the rear-view mirror. "I think the only flaw you possess is your love for him."

Just as quickly as the moment began, it ends with the sudden appearance of Agent Beckham. He pulls open the passenger side door and climbs inside, slamming the door behind him. His brows are furrowed into the same hard line of agitation they were in inside the restaurant when Aubrey kept apologizing on his and Cal's behalf.

I know that agitation all too well. I get how it sits with you, a heavy weight in your gut pressing down on you, making you doubt your own convictions and actions, leaving you with the distinct feeling of being wrong when you know that you're right.

"We've been given orders to take Hummingbird home," he grumbles, securing his seat belt with a sharp click before his eyes find mine in the rear-view mirror. It's a different feeling than being stared down by Cal. There's no softness to be found in the onyx pools, just the harsh, sterile sting of metallic indifference. "Mr. Taylor is staying behind to handle the situation. He'll be along shortly."

I nod and sit back, hooking my seat belt as Cal pulls away from the curb. There's no point in questioning the decision to leave Aubrey behind, especially when I know Agent Beckham isn't the one who made the call. Aubrey isn't either. He wouldn't dare handle a situation like this without Jordan. He probably called her as soon as I was out of the way. I can see it now. Him, on the phone panicked and agitated at my outburst. Her, dropping whatever it is she does when she's not up his ass to talk him through containing the reporter until she arrives on the scene to do damage control.

As Cal drives me back home, I think about what level of problem-solving a situation of this magnitude will warrant. Since it's a member of the press and a damning recording of my unfiltered reaction to a new piece in the sordid puzzle of Aubrey's affair, I assume Jordan will come out of the gate swinging. She'll coddle him with the promise of some exclusive or another, making promise after promise until he agrees to forget this all happened.

And even though there isn't a promise she can make that won't involve me in some way, shape, or form, I know there won't be a single moment in those negotiations where I'll truly be considered. Not by the reporter. Not by Jordan. Not by my husband. Because the truth is, they don't care if I'm embarrassed about my husband's continued betrayal or hurt by being blindsided once again.

They only care if I'm compliant, perfect, and quiet, and by the time I'm alone again— standing inside a bedroom that still holds all the remnants of the hope and wistfulness that colored the time I spent getting ready for dinner—I've decided I'm just about done being all of those things.

While I undress, I consider what this new resolution actually means. Several answers come to mind while I'm scrubbing off my makeup and pulling bobby pins out of my hair, but I'm too exhausted to truly consider any of them. As I run a bubble bath to soothe my nerves, I decide that just the knowing is enough. I smile as the words filter through my mind, reminding me of my mama and the way she used to always fuss at me for wanting to have a solution to a problem as soon as I became aware of it. The fond memory sparks the desire to reach out, and I grab my phone from the dual vanity and dial her number before I can curb it.

Despite the late hour, she answers on the first ring, worry curling like vines of creeping ivy around her greeting. "Selene, baby, are you okay?"

I take a seat on the edge of the tub and push out a calming breath that's a partial wince because of the cold bite of the marble surround colliding with my bare skin. "I'm fine, Mama," I assure her, even as my chest burns at the tenderness in her tone.

She's quiet for a moment, no doubt battling with the desire to know what my husband has done this time and the need not to have another phone call end in an argument. "Oh," she says, finally. "What are you doing up? Working?"

"No, ma'am. I just got back from dinner, and I'm running a bath. I was just thinking of you."

There's no mistaking the smile in her voice. "Well, isn't that nice. You've been on my mind today, too. Your sisters and I were talking about coming up to visit when you have some time in your schedule."

Twisting around, I run my fingers through the bubbly water to test the temperature. "That would be nice."

"No, it wouldn't. You hate hosting us."

"No, I don't," I insist, then pause and laugh when Mama snorts. "Okay, fine. I do hate hosting, but that's not specific to y'all."

She hums her approval at my confession, and I feel the tension in my muscles ease. I missed that sound. I missed this, these rare moments of easy connection. I miss her.

"I can come down instead," I offer. "It's been too long since I've seen everyone, and I know Daddy hates to travel now with his hip."

"Yeah, he's been a whiny little brat ever since the surgery."

"Mama!"

"What?"

"Don't talk about my daddy like that."

"I'm the one who has to hear his mouth, Selene. I'll talk about him however I please. Besides, he's right here listening."

I smile, picturing the two of them in the living room. Daddy, in his big, leather recliner, while Mama and her crossword puzzles, knitting needles, and other random assorted items take up the couch.

"Hey, Daddy," I call out just as the door to my bedroom opens and closes hard. I push to my feet, standing just as Aubrey barges into the bathroom. "Mama, I've gotta go."

My rushed goodbye layers itself over whatever she's saying now. I end the call abruptly and set the phone down on the edge of the tub, fighting the urge to cover my naked form.

Aubrey is quiet, and his eyes rush over my bare skin, greedy and unapologetic as he watches me step into the steaming water. The tub is too full, so water sloshes over the edges as I sink down, using the bubbles to hide myself from the signs of desire I've learned to recognize on my husband's face. They haven't changed at all since we met at Stanford, but now, instead of being excited, I'm disgusted and thoroughly confused by his audacity to display them.

Dragging my foot from one side of the tub to the other to create some waves, I let out a long sigh that conveys just how annoyed I am at having to be the one to start this conversation.

"Are you going to stand there all night staring at me, or are you going to grow some balls and explain yourself?"

Aubrey presses his lips together, trying his best to look contrite. "Selene, you have to understand. Sutton...she," he pauses and lifts a hand to rub at the back of his neck. "She grew up with nothing, and she has no one to fall back on. She moved here for this job, and I couldn't just cut her off completely. You know how it is when you're young and fighting to survive. All it takes is one thing—" He holds up a finger, and his features collapse onto each other in the way they do when he's trying to appear sincere and spark an emotional response in his audience. "—one small thing like an unexpected bill or something huge like losing your job and then suddenly your whole life falls apart. I couldn't have that on my heart. I couldn't just send her away knowing that the whole scandal is making it impossible for her to find another job."

He shakes his head like the thought of his mistress suffering in any way would absolutely gut him, and for the first time in a while, I'm buying what he's selling. He looks genuinely distressed, which only adds to the rage simmering inside of me at the moment.

I tilt my head back, allowing it to rest on the cool tile behind me, and look at him through low eyes. "That's very thoughtful of you, Aubrey."

Relief spreads across his features like wildfire, and I douse every ember with my next words. "It's nice to know you're capable of that kind of care and consideration. What I would like to know, however, is where the fuck that concern was for me? Did you even think about what it would do to me to find out you're still working with her? Did you stop and ask yourself how I would feel to stand in front of the world and speak words written by your mistress? Did you even think about me at all?"

"Sel, you have to understand…"

"No, I don't!" I scream. "I don't have to understand anything. I don't have to filter my pain and embarrassment through the lens of your flawed logic. Everything you've said is based on emotion, Aubrey, it's rooted in care and concern, you've gone to great lengths to extend to a woman you haven't been with in months, but haven't tried to give to your wife, who's been by your side for years!"

Something about the way his eyes refuse to meet mine sets off my internal alarm bells. I turn my words over in my head, searching for the thing I said that would have made him go from open and pleading to avoidant. The only thing that stands out is the comment about how long it's been since he last slept with Sutton. When the news of the affair broke, he assured me it had been over for months. He swore on our son's grave. That was how he'd gotten me to agree to the press conference.

I sit up, heart pounding with fresh betrayal. "You're still sleeping with her."

The answer is in his eyes and on his face before it ever leaves his mouth. In fact, it never actually leaves his mouth. He's too much of a coward to say it, and I'm too fucking weak to hear it. I draw my knees up and wrap my arms around them, planting my chin on my forearm as the pain washes over me in cold waves that set my teeth on edge.

"When did it start back up?" I ask, wincing as Jordan's comment about how easily she could slide Sutton into the First Lady role takes on new meaning. "Did it ever stop?"

"Of course, it stopped." Aubrey scoffs, and the sound burns through me. Suddenly, there's rage on top of the pain.

"Don't do that, Aubrey. Don't act like me asking if you ever stopped fucking the woman you're still cheating on me with is some affront to your character. You don't get the benefit of the doubt from me. You haven't earned it."

His entire demeanor shifts at that phrase, and I shouldn't be surprised. Aubrey is as entitled as they come. The concept of earning anything is foreign to him. He thinks everything, even the highest office in the land, is his birthright. His shoulders drop, and the golden lines of his brows pull together into a harsh line of resentment.

"Is that what I have to do, Selene?" he sneers. "I have to earn it? I have to get down on my fucking knees and beg you for your forgiveness? Do I have to lie and tell you I'm never going to fuck her again? Is that what it's going to take for us to get past this?" My lips part, my tongue heavy with responses to his rhetorical questions, but he continues, stealing my chance for rebuttal. "You've made this entire thing impossible, you know that, right? Even Jordan, who gets paid a handsome fee to manipulate facts and craft narratives that lead to the forgiveness of the most egregious crimes, couldn't come up with a sentence perfect enough to make you *get the fuck over it*!"

The sharpness of his tone as he speaks, no, *shouts,* those last words, makes me jolt, but it doesn't stop me from holding his gaze. This is the most candid he's been in weeks, and even though I hate him in this moment, I appreciate the view of his true face.

"Is that what you want, Aubrey? For me to get the fuck over it?"

"What I want is to be President, and nothing, not even your feelings, begins to outweigh that desire because I was born to lead this country, Selene." He runs his fingers through his hair, shaking his head as he looks down at me. "I thought you understood. I thought you, of all people, would know sacrifices would be made along this path."

"Time. Money. Energy. Those are the sacrifices I signed on for, Aubrey. Not my dignity, not my pride."

"Don't you get that your pride is the problem? Your pride is the reason we can't move past a minor indiscretion."

"It wasn't minor or singular."

Aubrey frowns. "What?"

"You had an affair on the world's stage, Aubrey. That's major." Deciding the time for cowering in my pain is over, I stretch my legs back out in front of me and lie back again before continuing with my point. "And you slept with Sutton multiple times, so there wasn't *an indiscretion,* there was a series of indiscretions. Every time you fucked her, every time you sexted her, every time you thought of her while you jerked off in the shower was an indiscretion, a betrayal you have yet to explain or truly apologize for."

He stares at me for a moment, astounded and annoyed by my explanation. Then he throws his hands up in the air. "Jesus fucking Christ, Selene! You really want to know why I won't talk to you about the affair?" Another rhetorical question, but this time I don't even try to answer because he's practically salivating with the need to express the hateful things running through his head. "Because every conversation based on emotion goes like this. You treat our marriage, and my infidelity, like a bug in your software you have to run a diagnostic to find and fix. And you did the same thing when AJ died, studying the crime scene photos like some sort of sociopath."

When this conversation started, I didn't think there was anything else Aubrey could say to hurt me, but clearly, I was wrong. The comment about how I handled AJ's death strums across the strings of my grief, creating discordant chords I refuse to let him hear. I steel my spine and school my features into a mask of neutrality as he rants about how disgusted he was when I asked for the photos I only wanted to see so my brain would stop filling in the blanks of an already horrific day with images worse than the reality of what happened in those halls.

At the time, Aubrey had said he understood, but I knew he didn't. I knew he couldn't. Still, I never imagined he was disgusted by it, by me.

He goes on and on, his cruel honesty bolstered by the high of that first confession until his complaints come full circle, looping back around to the affair, linking my apparent character flaws to his infidelity.

"You always have to be in control. Even in the bedroom. You know sex is supposed to be fun, right? You're not supposed to be counting strokes or reaching down to adjust your partner's head when he's eating you out."

The need to defend myself rises in my throat, but I bite it back down. I don't need to tell Aubrey I've never in my life counted strokes or justify the time I got so fed up with him mistaking my labia for my clit that I physically moved his mouth where I needed it.

"So that's why you cheated? Because we weren't having fun in the bedroom?"

Aubrey is intent on selling the lie, on laying the blame at my feet, so he nods. "Yes. And I don't understand why you're so determined to punish me for something that was bound to happen anyway."

Despite the burning sensation in my chest and the desperate desire to pick up something heavy and chuck it at his head, I smile. The inappropriate act is accompanied by a snorting giggle that makes Aubrey's eyes go wide with confusion.

"What's funny?" he asks.

"I'm sorry." I cover my mouth, pressing the manic chuckle back between my lips. "I don't mean to laugh because you're right." His eyes get even wider now, and I take several calming breaths before I go on. "About the affair," I clarify, nodding my head solemnly. "It was always going to happen. Not because I'm woman enough to ask for what I want in the bedroom, but because small men like you always cheat with little girls who make them feel big."

Aubrey balks, and I lick my lips, tasting retribution made sweeter by the patience I exhibited during his tirade. "Question. How do you think you'll fare as the leader of the free world when you haven't come up with a single original idea since you started working with Jordan?" I tilt my head to the side, arching a brow. "It makes you wonder, doesn't it? Like was it even your idea to fuck Sutton or was it just a seed your campaign manager planted?"

I snap my fingers as another thought lands in my mind. "Or maybe it was a direct order!" I nod, liking that line of reasoning better. "That sounds like something she would do. She'd have to be desperate to risk the scandal, which means you must have been in dire need of a confidence boost, someone to make you feel manly because your wife was too busy working for her success to stroke your tiny little ego."

I lift my hand, holding my thumb and index finger together to indicate the size of the ego in question, while a faux pout tugs at my lips. Aubrey glowers at me, and for a second, he looks like he wants to strangle me. Instead of being afraid, I find myself wondering.

If he'd actually take the risk with a house full of staffers and Secret Service agents.

If I'd even have it in me to fight back.

If Jordan would swoop in and help him make my murder look like an accident.

If anyone would bat an eye when Sutton fucking Ellsworth went from being an adulterous, former speechwriter to the First Lady of the United States of America.

11

SELENE

None of the scenarios I pondered in the bathtub on the night my marriage fell apart for good came to pass. Aubrey left the bathroom in a dramatic huff, deciding to spare my life, no doubt for the sake of his political campaign, and I finished my bath, grateful to know there is a limit to my husband's depravity after all.

Something about knowing that left me feeling brave and destructive, and in the days since, I've dedicated my time to getting on his nerves.

I started out small: skipping events and appearances, liking and sharing get-well-soon posts for President Sanders, and, when he failed to give me the desired reaction, creating one of my own and sharing it across all my platforms. Needling him in such small ways has been fun, but after days of minor nuisances, I'm ready to become a big fucking problem for him.

That desire is what leads me to his headquarters on the Friday after our doomed dinner date. I stride in on sure feet with my shoulders square, my head held high, and my favorite white pantsuit hugging my frame. Jordan forbade me from wearing it years ago, telling me that I should never wear the same thing twice after a fashionista dedicated an entire series of posts to the outfit, documenting every time I'd worn it. Being the dutiful wife, I pushed the suit to the back of my closet and haven't touched it again.

Until today.

I knew it would be the first non-verbal communication to Jordan that I was done taking her and Aubrey's shit. And when I walk into the conference room in the center of the headquarters, interrupting what I'm sure is a strategy meeting dedicated to the continued exploitation of President Sanders' prolonged hospital stay, I can tell she's gotten the message. Her green eyes narrow, and those perfectly arched brows curve with interest and annoyance as she watches me move to the end of the table closest to the door, directly across from Aubrey.

"Give us the room," I say. My voice is laced with authority that leaves no room for question. Everyone but the two people I need to speak to rises to their feet and scrambles out the door behind me. When we're alone, I drop into a chair and place the manila folder I've been holding in my hand on the table. Jordan and Aubrey both eye it suspiciously. I pat it and smile. "Don't worry. We'll get to that eventually."

"What the fuck are you doing here?" Aubrey asks, rolling up the sleeves of the crisp white button-up he's wearing today. The navy blue tie he paired it with is already loose, a sign that his day has been filled with agitation. For years, I've let that sign and so many others be the difference between me walking on eggshells or moving and speaking freely around him. I won't be extending him any such graces today.

I lean forward, placing my elbows on the table and steepling my fingers together. "I'm not happy."

"So make an appointment with your therapist," Aubrey retorts.

I bare my teeth in a sharp smile. "This *is* therapy, Aubrey. Coming in here, interrupting your day. Forcing your world to bend to my will for once. It's quite intoxicating, I can see why you two like disrupting my life so much."

Aubrey glances at Jordan, but her eyes are on me. Her expression unreadable as she studies my face. I want to know what she's thinking, but I don't ask because I know she'll lend her voice to whatever is on her mind soon enough. She won't do that until she knows exactly why I'm here and what I want, though, so I fight past the rush of agitation that runs through me at the thought of my delayed launch and all the other ways they've interrupted my life over the past few months. I'm not here to rehash the past. I'm here to talk about the future.

About *my* future.

Turning my head, I hold Jordan's gaze. "You told me I should file for divorce if I wasn't happy."

She nods, eyes lighting up as the wheels in her mind start to spin. "I did. Is that what you—"

"No." Jordan visibly deflates. She tilts her head to the side, trying to understand my angle. I laugh. God, I enjoy her when she's confused. "I'm not filing for divorce." I swing my gaze back in Aubrey's direction. "I thought about it. I thought about it for a long time, but then I decided that that would be too easy for you."

"A divorce in the middle of a presidential campaign on the heels of a cheating scandal?" Aubrey huffs incredulously. "There wouldn't be anything easy about that. It would likely cost me the election."

"We both know she wouldn't let that happen," I toss back, nodding in Jordan's direction. "She's already got it all planned out, Aubrey. They'd paint you as a victim in all of this. The poor, misunderstood patriot who made one small mistake that his frigid wife would never forgive. They'd practically hand you the Oval and then you'd hand your mistress the role *I* bled for."

Just the thought of it has me hiding my hands in my lap so no one can see them turning into clenched fists. It's not about Sutton. Not really. It's about the causes she would choose to champion. They'd be all lighthearted and easy to stomach, just like her. She wouldn't push for any real change. The platform, the influence, the proximity to power would all be wasted on her.

I swallow, feeling the burn of the edges of my nails cutting into my palm. "You would move on, Aubrey. You'd have everything you wanted, including your mistress. I'd be crucified in the media even more than I already have been, and everything I've done to further your career, to get you here, will have been for nothing. There will be no payoff, no reward, just more suffering." I shake my head, a rueful smile on my lips. "I can't abide that. *I won't.*"

"So what is it that you're proposing?" Aubrey asks as red rises from the collar of his shirt up his neck. He's been growing more agitated the longer I've been in the room, commandeering his time and attention.

"A political marriage," I pause, letting the offer sink in. "We stay married in name only. There will be no physical intimacy. No attempts at reconciliation or emotional connection. You don't love me anymore. I don't know when it happened or how, and truly, I don't care because I'm not in this marriage for you anymore. I'm here for our goals, for our vision, for the promise we made to each other when we lost our son. Do you remember that promise, Aubrey?"

"Of course, I remember that promise, Selene."

I nod, never having doubted his answer to that question. "Then you won't have any problem backing my First Lady initiative to place mental health professionals trained to create emotionally safe environments in schools to help prevent school shootings. You will be vocal about your support and use all your presidential influence to persuade AJ's school to be the first to implement it. You'll also guarantee the $ 1.2 billion in funding that my team estimates we'll need to implement it nationwide and promise continued funding for this program through the presidential foundation you'll establish after your term, or terms, are over. Lastly—" I look between him and Jordan, hardening my stare, "—all messaging around the start of a First Family is to be discontinued immediately. I will not bring any more children into this world with Aubrey as their father."

My last declaration is followed by several seconds of silence that are pierced suddenly by the sound of Aubrey's bark of laughter. "What the fuck makes you think we'd ever agree to something like—"

Jordan places a hand on his arm, and I read the silent order for him to shut up in the subtle shake of her head. He ignores her, though, pushing his chair back from the table and rising to his feet. He plants both palms on the table and leans forward like he wants to climb across it and rip my throat out.

"Extortion? This is low even for you, Sel," he growls. "I should have known it would always end up this way with us. My father warned me—the day he wrote the check that helped you start Culture Code—*he told me* that you were only in it for the money. That all you wanted was the power and prestige that came along with my name. I didn't speak to him for weeks afterwards, do *you* remember that? I told him you loved me, that you'd never use me like that. I loved you. *I made you.* The business you keep crying about my campaign interrupting wouldn't exist if it weren't for me." He lifts his left hand and slams it into the table. "My money." Another hard slap. "My name." One more collision between his open palm and the glass. "My connections and power. You don't get to sit here and make demands of me, Selene. You don't get to tell me how this is going to go. That's not how this works."

Every word, every sentence comes with a rise in his volume. Jordan places a hand on his forearm, attempting to calm him. "Aubrey. You need to lower your voice and sit down."

He shakes her off, but he does sink into his seat. "I'm not agreeing to it. I'm not agreeing to any of it, do you hear me?"

"You will."

His chest is heaving, and the redness that was creeping up his neck has now overtaken his face. "What makes you so sure?"

"Because you need me, Aubrey. You've always needed me. My face. My name. My melanin. I've lent credibility to your stances on racially charged issues like police reform. Without me, you would be nothing more than another white man throwing buzzwords like 'equality' around. I made your messaging more poignant. I'm the reason it hit home and brought in the voters who carried you in the polls, who qualified you for debates, and got you the Democratic nomination. You wouldn't be here without me, and if you want to make it to the Oval, you'll do the smart thing and keep me around."

"She's not wrong," Jordan says. "After the children's hospital appearance, you regained some of the ground you lost in the polls. Voters respond to the two of you together. They like it when you appear to be on solid ground."

"And if we keep the act up, we can both get what we want. We couldn't keep our vows. We don't have AJ, but we can have the Oval, Aubrey."

Aubrey shakes his head, and I'm not sure if he's objecting to the entire proposal or my most recent statement. He scrubs his hand down his face. "*No.*"

There's no reasoning with him, so I turn my attention to Jordan as I grab the manila envelope I sat down with before. I don't even open it before I slide it down the table to her. It stops just short of her fingertips, and she pulls it the rest of the way, unwinding the piece of twine wrapped around the button to keep it closed. Nothing ever spooks Jordan, so there's no gasp of shock or horror when she pulls the pictures out, even though only the first one is familiar to her.

It's the one that hit the press and blogs first. The one that made Aubrey come forward and admit to the affair with Sutton. Up until this very moment, no one knew the ones underneath it existed except for me and the person who sent them to me. There are fifteen in total, and Jordan flicks through the rest of them quickly, taking in each frame that displays all the ways Aubrey fucked Sutton throughout this very office and a wide array of discreet hotel rooms throughout the city.

"How do you even have these?" she asks, setting the photos down and sliding them over to Aubrey, who is now the color of a ripe tomato.

"Someone sent them to my office."

What I don't say is that the photos arrived over a week before the first one hit the press. When the news broke, I acted just as shocked as everyone else was. In a way, I was. I was shocked that the person who sent me the photos hadn't chosen to share a more graphic image or publish all of the pictures at once. Now, I'm grateful that they didn't because it's given me the leverage I need to navigate this moment.

Aubrey shoves the folder and the photos away, causing the images to scatter across the table. "You think this means anything? The world already knows I'm fucking her. I can't admit to an affair twice."

"No, but if you refuse to give me what I'm asking for, I'll make sure you're destroyed by it this time. I'll send those photos to your most critical political pundits and give a comment to every reporter who asks for one. I'll write a tell-all book and have it out before the election. You know how I am, Aubrey, when I'm hyper-focused on something, I can have it done like that." I snap my fingers. "Jordan can tell you how many publishers are chomping at the bit to tell my story. I'll sign the first deal that comes with an expedited release date and puts the book on the shelves before Halloween. And do you know what happens when you put a book out, Aubrey? Press tours. Normally, I hate the press, but I'll make an exception for the chance to ruin you. I'll do interview after interview until the only thing anyone sees when they turn on the news is my tear-stained face and your poor execution of every pose in the Kama Sutra."

Aubrey and I stare at each other, locked in a silent battle of wills. He's used to me losing, but today I'm not walking away with anything less than a win. I let that determination show on my face, let it bleed out of my pupils and drip off of my lashes. With nothing but my eyes, I remind him that the only reason the affair didn't end him before is because *I* chose not to let it. I wanted to see him succeed, but if he refuses to give me what I want, thereby ensuring that I'll fail to keep the promise I made in my son's name, then I'll make sure he fails too.

And no one, not even Jordan St. James, will be able to stop me.

Aubrey is still in denial about that fact, but Jordan? She knows. For the first time since the day we've met, she's looking at me with a flicker of admiration in her gaze. She gathers the photos up and puts them back into the envelope.

"Thank you for this proposal, Selene. Aubrey and I will discuss it and get back to you."

After I leave Aubrey and Jordan, I return to work and have the most productive day I've had in months, feeling lighter than I've in years. That feeling is aided by the update Monique gave me during our one-on-one about how getting the product launch back on track has impacted our plan to hire the coding academy graduates. Our initial hope was to hire them all, but the delay and the associated setbacks meant that wouldn't be possible. Now that we're back on solid footing with our stakeholders, our quarter four projections indicate that we'll be able to bring on at least 90% of them, which is a significant increase from last year, when we were only able to take on half of the cohort.

It's not quite the full sweep I was hoping for, but it's close enough, and today I'm allowing myself to take the small win because I know there's a bigger one on the horizon for me.

When I arrive home that night, the win comes to me in the form of Aubrey and Jordan waiting for me inside my office. They're gathered at the small conference table to the right of the door, so I spot them immediately and clock the stack of papers with signature tabs on the side shortly after.

Contracts.

The sight of them makes me smile, and the sight of my smile sets Aubrey's teeth on edge. He hides the grimace curling his lips behind the rim of the tumbler of whiskey in his hand, taking a long, deep gulp as I sit down across from him.

"Didn't take you long to convince him this is the best option," I say to Jordan, dipping my chin in acknowledgment of the feat she accomplished in such a short time. I'd expected it to take at least a day for her to get Aubrey back to the table.

Her smile is thin and tight as she cuts straight to the chase. "We've reviewed your offer, and Aubrey accepts your terms." She picks the first set of pages up off the stack in front of her and slides it over to me. "But we have some stipulations."

I flip through the pages, scanning the lines and absorbing their meaning. "Stipulations?"

"Just caveats that will help protect the truth of your new dynamic," Jordan assures me. "You're required to attend all campaign-related events, including photo shoots, interviews, trips, etc.; you have to continue living in the residence and wearing your wedding ring. You're also required to continue the utilization of the Secret Service detail to maintain appearances, and you must not..."

Jordan continues reciting the clauses, but I tune her out so I can fully absorb the words in front of me. For the most part, the demands are reasonable, and they will go a long way towards protecting the image I want to help Aubrey sell. I'm not even mad at the clause forbidding me from speaking publicly about any political beliefs that contradict Aubrey's because we're in alignment on everything that matters.

What does give me pause, though, is the last bullet point. My eyes move over the words just as my brain begins to acknowledge the sound of Jordan's voice again.

"Lastly, you are prohibited from engaging in any physical or emotional relationships outside of your marriage."

My jaw drops, and my eyes leave the contract to find a smug grin on Aubrey's face as he tosses back the last of the whiskey in his glass. Starting a relationship with anyone is the furthest thing from my mind right now, but I still feel a fresh wave of annoyance roll down my spine at the inclusion.

"Are you serious right now?" I hiss at him, rolling my eyes when he chuckles and nods.

"As a heart attack," he tosses back nastily, making me wish, for just a second, that a cardiac event would strike him down, so I don't have to.

"You cheated, Aubrey. You're *still* cheating, and you have the nerve to add this in like I'm the one who got caught with my pants down."

"Selene," Jordan calls in a calm but demanding tone. "Everything that applies to you applies to Aubrey."

This subtle appeal to my strong sense of justice works just as she intended. My shoulders relax, and I study Aubrey, realizing that his shitty mood has less to do with me and more to do with having to break up with his mistress for real this time.

"So you're done with Sutton?"

Jordan doesn't even give him time to answer. "For good. She is no longer affiliated with the campaign in any fashion and is currently aboard a flight to Kentucky, where she plans to quietly rebuild her life."

"I'm sure the large check you gave her will make that a lot easier."

Aubrey doesn't appreciate my musing or the irony behind it. Just this morning, he was accusing me of wanting his money, but in the end, it was his little girlfriend who made off with it.

"Just sign the damn contract," Aubrey growls, rising from his seat to pour himself another drink.

"There's also an NDA," Jordan adds, sliding the last stack of papers in front of me. "It just ensures that you won't disclose the true nature of your relationship to anyone, including, but not limited to, the media, your family, friends, or colleagues."

I gather both sets of documents and place them side by side. "And how do you plan to enforce these contracts? There are no penalty clauses here."

Aubrey snorts as he returns to the table. "Because no one is stupid enough to write down threats."

My brows rise in surprise as I look between the two of them. "Threats? What exactly do you think you know about me that you could use to threaten me?"

"We don't have to know anything," Jordan says, leaning back in her chair. "That's the amazing thing about power and influence, Selene. You can say anything, and all of a sudden—" she holds up her hands, using her fingers to mimic an explosion "—it just is. I can make anything, even the most outlandish lie, seem like a fact, and when you're talking about things people don't understand, like the inner workings of a tech firm, it's easy to create panic and distrust. I have an entire folder of stories ready to run about Culture Code, complete with media placements and witnesses who'll corroborate any story I want them to tell."

Aubrey grins, clearly enjoying this little shake down. "My favorite is the one about your company mining and selling American user data to China."

"China, seriously?"

"Or Russia." Jordan shrugs. "Whatever country Americans are most afraid of that week is who you'll be in bed with. We'll plant the seed, and misinformation and fear will do the rest."

Sadly, I know that she's telling the truth. The years I spent at the side of a political animal like Aubrey have shown me just how easily politicians can use the media to manipulate the public. They could destroy my business whenever and however they want, and there wouldn't be much I could do about it.

That thought should scare me.

And the fact that the two contracts in front of me all but guarantee the loss of the leverage that got us to the negotiating table should make me want to back down, but as I pull a pen from my purse, there's no fear or desire to retreat. There's only the exultant rush of achievement stemming from securing the necessary support to honor my son's memory and the heady knowledge that I won't ever be in danger of breaking this contract.

I have no reason to.

Aubrey's campaign is already dictating my schedule.

I never had any intention of leaving the house I made a home.

And most importantly, there isn't a single man in this world with whom I want an emotional or physical connection.

12

———

SELENE

A week after signing the contracts that gave me my new lease on life, I'm at the office working late, preparing for the biggest day of my career. The launch of Smart Sight—the facial recognition software we've been developing since the inception of Culture Code—is just three days away, and I couldn't be more excited about bringing this software into the world even though I'll have to schlep around the country with Aubrey immediately after. He's already on the road, beginning the first leg of a series of rallies, town halls, and interviews that Jordan has put together with the hope of drumming up voter interest and early ballots being cast in his favor.

We'll be together for weeks, making stops in Georgia, Wisconsin, Nevada, and Michigan before returning to Virginia for a fundraising gala for the campaign. It's not exactly how I want to spend my time after the launch, but I'll make the best of it because of my contractual obligations.

Sighing at the thought, I push back from my desk and roll my head from one side of my neck to the other in an attempt to relieve the tension building in my muscles from another long day. Between preparing for the launch and my extended absence, I've been burning the candle at both ends to make sure everything and everyone has gotten their fair share of my attention. Unfortunately, that's left me and my needs neglected.

My muscles are aching and begging for a massage.

My eyes are dry and strained from squinting at the screen.

And my attention is constantly split between a million different tasks, leaving me in a persistent state of overstimulation, something that's not at all helped by the sound of the news broadcast blaring through the speakers of the television mounted across from my desk. I meant to turn it off hours ago, but I'd gotten caught up with troubleshooting a server issue for Smart Sight, unable to break free from tunnel vision long enough to turn the volume down or shut the TV off altogether. Now that the task is complete, my brain allows me to reach for the remote that's been on the edge of my desk the entire time, mere inches away from my hands but miles outside of the realm of possibility as far as my executive dysfunction is concerned.

Just as my fingers wrap around the sleek controller, the screen shifts to accommodate an update on a story that apparently ran earlier. I don't know how I missed it. I must have been too distracted with my work to pay attention, but now my eyes are on the screen, and my heart is in the pit of my stomach. The camera pans across a crowd of adults standing just outside the police tape holding a flimsy perimeter outside of a school where a group of sobbing children— some of them covered in blood that probably belongs to their classmates or teachers—are being escorted to their anxious parents by police officers in tactical gear.

On the screen, below the images of tearful reunions coupled with the crestfallen expressions on the faces of all the people realizing they won't have one, is a line of scrolling text summarizing what we're seeing:

Hours-long standoff with active shooter at Bright Hall Middle comes to a tragic end.

A dull, but incessant, ringing starts in my ears as I will myself to look away from the familiar pain on strangers' faces, even though I know I won't. I won't turn the channel yet, and even when I do, I won't put the parents, children, or teachers out of my mind. I'll obsess over their grief, let it transport me back to the harsh, bitter waters of my own. I'll be destroyed by it, and somehow, some way, find it in me to remake myself again.

"The shooter killed himself." A deep voice laced with somberness says from somewhere to my right. I turn to find the agent I can now identify by the notes of his gravel and velvet tone, and jump when I realize he's closer than I expected him to be.

Cal.

I haven't had the nerve to call him by his name since the night he gave me permission to, but I still think it in my head every time I see him. I like the familiarity of it. The way it makes me feel like we're friends, or, at the very least, not just strangers bound by proximity and duty.

His features, which were just hard and serious, shift into something softer as his eyes rove over my face. I hold my breath as he appraises me, unsure if I want the vulnerability of being witnessed or the dissatisfaction that comes with not being seen. In those same silent seconds, I search his face, trying to get a sense of what's happening in his head, but he gives nothing away.

"I'm sorry for startling you," he says, finally meeting my eyes. "I knocked several times, but you didn't answer."

I click the power button on the remote, and the television screen goes black, dropping us into a silence I have to fill with words that I hope will smooth out the disapproving notch sitting between his brows.

"I didn't hear you. When I'm working, I tend to tune everything else out."

He could easily point out that I was knee deep in the trenches of emotion and not working when I ignored his knocks, but he doesn't. I appreciate him for that, especially since I'm one hundred percent certain Agent Beckham wouldn't have hesitated to call me on it.

"Everything, including your stomach?"

"My stomach?"

"Yes, your stomach. You haven't eaten since I came on shift hours ago, and there are no notes in the log indicating that you received food deliveries. As far as I can tell, the only thing you've consumed today is the cup of coffee sitting on your desk."

It shouldn't mean anything to me that my eating habits, or lack thereof, have garnered his attention, but for some stupid reason, it does. For some stupid reason, his words and the frown pulling at the corners of his mouth as he delivers them send a warmth reminiscent of what I felt that night when we were alone in the car spreading through my chest. My hand rises on its own volition, landing with an open palm over my heart, and I rub at the spot until the heat and emotion are dispelled.

"I didn't even finish the coffee," I tell him, forcing levity into my tone to make light of what's rapidly becoming another one of those weird moments I keep ending up in with him. "Pretty sure they burned the milk, so the latte tasted off."

Cal tilts his head, concern etched into the lines of his forehead as he reaches for the cup, testing its weight and the validity of my state-ment. When he finds it full, his frown turns into something close to a scowl. It doesn't fully erase the concern, so the two expressions sit together on his handsome face, a perfect marriage of wrath and care that makes me wonder, for the briefest of seconds, what it would look like if it were real and not just a byproduct of the correlation between my well being and his job.

"You need to eat."

"I will when I get home."

He glances at my desk, eyes lingering on the stack of abandoned papers I set aside to deal with the server issue. "That won't be for another few hours," he says matter-of-factly. "You need to eat some-thing. I won't have you passing out on my watch."

I pull the stack in front of me and begin sorting out what's urgent and what can wait until tomorrow. "You won't be responsible. I will, and I'll be happy to sign a waiver or anything else you need to assure the higher-ups that you warned me against continuing my day without proper sustenance."

My voice is hard with a touch of finality to it that should send him retreating back to his post, but it doesn't. He stays exactly where he is and blows out a breath of frustration. Out of the corner of my eye, I watch him reach into the pocket of his perfectly tailored pants and pull out a cell phone. Within seconds, he's got Agent Beckham on the phone, their voices a brilliant blend of dark velvet and sumptuous smoke that makes me wonder if everything about these two men is better when experienced together.

"I need you to make another stop. I'll get Ortega to stay on until you're back." A brief pause where I can hear the other agent complaining about owing his teammate a favor. "It won't be your favor to owe. It'll be mine," Cal assures him while I pretend to be too busy working on the edits to my speech for the launch to care about what either of them is saying. I do care though, so despite my best efforts, I'm tuned in to their frequency, and I hear everything from the coaxing lilt in Cal's voice as he convinces his friend that coming back from his break a few minutes late won't be an issue to the husky notes of authority in his tone when Agent Beckham finally agrees to make the stop and he tells him where to go.

My pen, which had been crossing out a statement I felt was repetitive pauses when Cal says the name of a Jamaican restaurant I've been frequenting a lot lately and recites my current hyper fixation meal perfectly, right down to the bottled ginger beer I always pair with my curry shrimp, rice and peas, and coco bread. When I look up from my work, I find that his eyes are already on me. He lifts a brow, mouthing, "Anything else?"

I shake my head because I don't trust myself to speak, don't trust my voice not to shake or tremble or do some other thing that would convey how deeply his knowledge of my likes and needs has affected me. Since signing the papers that effectively ended my marriage, I've been plagued with this sense of loneliness, an intrinsic sadness stemming from the teenage girl inside of me who met and fell in love with Aubrey, who wanted things with him she'll never get to have, who worries what the world will look and feel like now that she doesn't belong to anyone. Now that there's not a single person in this world who loves her, who cares if she eats or sleeps or hurts.

I thought I had put that girl away, stuffed her and all of her feelings down into a box where her worries and wants could no longer bother me, but here she is, right on the surface, ready to shed tears and spill truths to a man who only cares because he has to.

Cal ends the call, pocketing his phone. "Beck should be here soon. Would you like me to get you something to hold you over while we wait?"

I drop his gaze, wanting nothing more than to be alone with my wayward emotions. "No, thank you."

This time, he takes my dismissal for what it is, rapping his knuckles on the desk before turning on his heel. "I'll leave you to it."

When he's gone, it takes me a while to get back into the groove, but I manage to eventually. By the time Cal comes back—with Agent Beckham and bags of food in tow—I'm done with my speech and my stomach is wrapping itself around my spine. All of which means I'm feeling incredibly grateful when Cal hands me my food. That feeling, coupled with the warmth and weight of the plate in my hand, plus the subtle savory and spicy scent wafting into my nostrils, has me moaning with delight.

"Mmmm. This smells amazing." I hit a little shoulder shimmy that would be embarrassing if I weren't too starved to care about such things. "Thank you," I say to Cal as he hands me my ginger beer.

"Beck's the one who made the stop," he reminds me, tipping his chin in the direction of the other man who's been standing near the door, quietly watching our exchange. I catch his eye, holding his steely gaze for as long as I can bear to.

"Thank you, Agent Beckham."

"You're welcome, ma'am."

A tense silence follows our exchange, and I can see both men preparing to retreat. For some reason, the idea of them leaving me here to eat alone when they're probably going to sit down and consume the food they ordered together doesn't sit right with me, so I find myself issuing an invitation I probably shouldn't.

"You could eat in here if you'd like," I start, holding out a hand to gesture at the conference table where Monique and I usually share lunches.

Agent Beckham looks to Cal, giving him a subtle shake of his head. "I don't think that's appropriate."

Heat creeps into my cheeks with every second that passes with my hand still hanging in the air, so I bring it down and pray the embarrassment isn't showing on my face. Confirmation that it is comes in the form of Cal's tight smile.

"That's a generous offer, Selene. We'd be happy to take you up on it, but only if you join us." He crosses the room to the table, looking at Agent Beckham, who grimaces but moves over as well. While I gather my things to move over to our makeshift dining area, I hear the low murmur of Cal's voice along with the soft rustle of plastic bags from a different restaurant. I can't make out everything, but I can tell he's trying to inspire a change in his partner's attitude.

Whatever he says works because Agent Beckham's demeanor is noticeably more relaxed when I sit down in the seat they left for me at the head of the table. It's odd being between them. Hell, it's odd seeing them seated, but the feeling doesn't last for long as we tuck into our respective meals. Cal forces us into a conversation that's stilted at first but grows more comfortable when both Agent Beckham and I accept that he won't allow us to exist in silence.

Because I'm starved and ravenous, I finish my meal before both of them, which gives me the chance to sit back and observe the two of them together. I find myself equally captivated by the men, desperate to know more than what's right on the surface of their bond. It's harder than it should be for someone like me who's been perfecting the skill of decoding people for decades. I started doing it as a kid, memorizing the hallmarks of normalcy in order to fit in better with the kids around me, using that information to paint different faces on the masks I used to hide my own quirks because people were more comfortable around me when I was nothing more than a reflection of them. Miming the way they spoke, repeating their jokes, telegraphing their mannerisms.

It became a vital skill, one I could use to blend in or ease my transitions into new spaces, to ensure that people felt comfortable around me, even if I never truly felt comfortable around them. This isn't that, though. I'm not using the skill because I feel like I need it to survive this interaction; I'm using it because I want to understand why, in my mind, they are two pieces of the same whole.

I search for an answer to that question in the inside jokes that reveal the depth of their history, in the smile lines that crinkle the corners of Cal's eyes and the spark of rare openness that flashes across Agent Beckham's face when they tell me about the first case they closed together in their days at the Bureau. But even with all that, I feel dissatisfied, unable to point to any quantifiable reason that explains it.

Monique would roll her eyes if she heard me say that. Then she'd launch into a whole speech about how you can't break people and their bonds down into neat little science terms like negative and positive charges or chemical bonds. She'd tell me that some people just work.

And there's no denying that these two men work. They belong together in a way that makes me ache with envy, that makes me want to insert myself between the two of them, not to disrupt their bond, but to be a part of it.

13

———

CAL

Beck and I work best as a unit.

There's a rhythm to us, a synchronicity that can't be taught or replicated with anyone else. It's why we always work the same shifts and take assignments together, completing tasks as a team. It's why we're alone doing a sweep of the green room located in the back of the Ronald Reagan Building and International Trade Center's amphitheater—Selene's chosen venue for the launch of her facial recognition software—why I'm aware of the sudden shift in Beck's energy when I mention her name.

It's not exactly hard to miss when it's accompanied by a roll of his eyes and a heavy sigh that comes from deep in his chest as he slams the door to the green room's en-suite bathroom.

"You've got to stop, Cal."

"Stop what?"

"You know what." Onyx eyes flick to the doorway, making sure it's empty before Beck continues, his voice pitched low. "This thing with Selene. It's reckless, unprofessional, not to mention dangerous."

"There is no thing with Selene," I insist, pulling open the drawers on the vanity situated on the wall across from the bathroom.

"Really?" he asks, crouching to check underneath the couch for any items that shouldn't be there. "Then why can't you stop talking about her?"

I push the last drawer on the vanity closed and straighten to my full height, considering his question. The answer is simple, and it sits on my tongue, ready to emerge and turn my previous statement into a lie. It wasn't my intention to be dishonest, especially with Beck. I never lie to him about anything, but it's hard to tell him the truth when it's something I don't even want to acknowledge myself.

Beck stands, dusting off his pants and suit jacket as best as he can. I move over to him, getting the spots he missed. "Answer the question, Drake," he says, turning to face me when we've successfully rid him of the small specks of dust and dirt. Everything about his expression suggests that he already knows the answer, and I'm not the least bit surprised that he does. He's good at reading people. Years spent in the foster care system taught him to read a person's intentions in a split second. His graduate degree in behavioral psychology and years spent in the Behavioral Analysis Unit in the Bureau did the rest.

Which means there's no real point in deflecting or holding back.

"I can't stop talking about her because I can't stop thinking about her," I admit, shaking my head as one belated confession rolls into another. "Sometimes she's a complete mystery to me, and other times I can see her as clear as day. Her loneliness and her strength. Her beauty and the sadness that lingers in her eyes even now, when it seems like things with her and Aubrey have evened out."

When I would interrogate suspects, I'd always tell them they'd feel lighter once they told me the truth. I'd stolen the tactic from my mom who always used it to get me to confess to doing dumb shit like punching a hole in a wall when my dad broke yet another promise to come and pick me up for the weekend. Back then, small admissions did lead to relief, but today the unburdening makes me feel ten times heavier because with it comes the acceptance that Beck is right about me being reckless and unprofessional.

He stares at me, waiting for me to continue. I lift a hand, rubbing at the back of my neck, self-conscious under the weight of his gaze. "I know you don't like her," I say finally.

"This isn't about how I feel."

But it is.

There's no way it couldn't be when we are what we are to each other. Not just partners and friends, but that third, secret thing that usually has no place in our work dynamic but is present here, in this conversation. Beck doesn't want to acknowledge it yet, though, so I push on, moving around the emotional grenade to get back on track, reaching for words that might lead to a shared understanding.

"She's like us. Alone. Apart. Other. Surrounded by people who are committed to misunderstanding her, who don't want to take the time to know her."

"She has a best friend whom she's known for decades and an entire building full of people who are just like her that she sees on a daily basis."

I dip my chin, acknowledging his point. "You're right. She does. But that's when she's in her world. When she's in his world, she has no one."

Beck strokes his chin as a rare flare of possession laces itself around his reply. "She can't have you."

The moment Selene and I shared in the car after the failed dinner flashes through my mind. Her soft voice lined with steel as she asked what I thought of her. The curve of her lips when she said my name. Those gorgeous brown eyes going wide when I said loving her husband was her only flaw, and the way she lingered outside of her bedroom door when I escorted her to her room later that night, like she was as reluctant to leave my presence as I was to let her go.

All those tiny little things come together to prove one thing: Selene already has me.

She has my attention.

She has my interest, my care, and concern. She has infiltrated the same part of my brain that Beck did when he first came into my life, and now she's on the path he carved out that leads to my heart. I don't know how to stop it. I'm not sure that I would, if I did. All I know is I'm here, once again wanting something with someone I can never really have.

There's pity in Beck's eyes as he studies my face, reading my thoughts so easily. "You're going to get hurt," he warns me, using the same words he spoke after we shared our first kiss. He wanted me to know then, just like he wants me to know now, that what I want will never truly be mine. I don't need the warning. I know the bleak reality I've resigned myself to existing inside of. I live it every day with him.

Sometimes it's easy. It's just the two of us operating inside the messy parameters of our undefined relationship. And other times, like when I have to watch him get dressed for a date, it's harder.

It's not even the dating that's the problem, because I date too, mostly to distract myself from images of him being out with someone else. The problem is that the someone else is always a woman. I know it sounds ridiculous, especially since an intoxicating amount of pride swirls through me every time I think about being the first and only man he's been with, but his exclusive interest in women hurts me in a way that my exclusive interest in men has never wounded him.

It forces me to face the shame that lives at the core of our connection, to remember Beck questioning if being with me meant he never truly loved his wife or wanted his son.

Reaching up, I dust a speck of dust off his shoulder and smile. "I'll be fine. I won't ever cross the line with Selene, and I'm well-versed in the art of hiding my feelings. After all, no one we know is aware that I'm in love with you."

Our conversation in the green room casts a somber cloud around Beck and me that hangs over us for the rest of the day, refusing to be dispelled by our attempts to pull each other into conversation and exacerbated by Selene's request to have us drive her to the venue that comes in just an hour before she's due on stage.

It's clear to me Beck is agitated by the request, that he's added it to the list of reasons he has to be worried about me and Selene, and even still, I can't bring myself to be anything but glad that out of all the men on our team, she feels most comfortable with us. The thought has the corners of my mouth lifting into a small smile that I hide from Beck by turning my head toward the window while he navigates through evening traffic.

"What's funny?" he asks, cutting his eye at me as he slows to a stop at a yellow light.

His voice is low, barely loud enough to be made out over the sound of Selene rehearsing her speech in the backseat, but I hear him because even when we're out of sorts, I'm always tuned in to his personal frequency. The same is true for him, which is how he caught the stupid smile in the first place.

"Just thinking about a joke Riley told me when I talked to her this morning," I return quietly. I regret the lie, but I don't regret the effect it has on Beck. As soon as my niece's name leaves my mouth, his eyes light up, and his shoulders relax. All of the confusing, off-putting energy between us dissipates, making me wish I had thought to invoke her name sooner.

Beck is as obsessed with the headstrong ten-year-old as I am. When we went to New Haven this summer to visit my younger brother, Hunter, and meet the daughter he'd only found out about a few months prior, we both dove headfirst into an adoration that's only rivaled by the love her parents have for her.

"How's my girl?"

"She's great, already asking when we're coming to visit her again. Hunter says she's started going to the gym with him for classes."

Beck snorts, letting his foot off the brake when the light turns green. "Is she going as an instructor or a student?"

"Probably a little of both."

We share a laugh that melts away all the tension in my chest, only for it to come back in full force when Selene speaks. "How old is your niece?"

I meet her eyes through the rear view mirror, seeing that she's put her note cards down and is rubbing her thumb against the side of her index finger. It's the same thing I watched her do after her last date with Aubrey, and I now know, from research I did that night, that the small action is one of her stims.

"She's ten," Beck says when I'm quiet for too long, and Selene's eyes shift away from mine, presumably to hold his gaze. She smiles, and it's a small, genuine thing that adds a dreamy quality to her already ethereal features.

"Ten is a good age. They still have a lot to learn about the world, but they're also capable of teaching you so much. It's a beautiful exchange, if you know how to appreciate it."

Her wistful tone leaves no doubt in my mind that she's speaking from experience. That she's thinking of every bit of knowledge she gleaned from the son she lost when he was only a few years older than Riley is now. Neither Beck nor I responds. I don't know what to say, and the pulsing of his jaw tells me he's mind is on the fact that he never got to know or appreciate the gift or challenges that come along with any age.

I'm not sure which is worse. Being robbed of the possibility of a life before you could ever hold it, or spending fourteen years nurturing a spirit, only to have it ripped away. As I look between the two grieving parents, I decide that there is no better or worse. There's only the bitter fruit of their misfortune, and my burning desire to stand between them and more pain.

"Yeah, Riley is a great kid," I offer, my voice rough with emotion. "She's smart and headstrong."

"The girl has an opinion on everything," Beck adds. I'm shocked that he's still participating in the conversation, but I don't let it show.

"AJ was the same way. He came out of the womb judging every-thing and everybody." Her eyes are back on me now. "My mama always says whatever personality they're born with is the one they keep. Was Riley the same way?"

My mind tries to conjure thoughts of a baby Riley, but I come up empty because the sad truth is I never got to see it.

"I'm not sure. I only just met her a few months ago."

Selene's face falls. "Oh. *Why?*"

There's genuine confusion wrinkling the usually smooth skin

between her brows as if she really can't think of a single explanation for my absence from Riley's life.

"Because my brother, Hunter, didn't know that she existed until recently. We didn't grow up together and haven't always been close, so I was one of the last people he shared the news with."

It's a short statement to summarize a long, sordid story about Hunter's struggle with addiction that led to his girlfriend leaving him when she found out she was pregnant and coming back into his life years later to reveal that they had a daughter. I don't feel the need to elaborate on it because it's not really my story to tell.

"I'm sorry," she says, wincing slightly. "I probably shouldn't have asked you that."

"It's okay," I assure her.

And it is because I know Riley now, and our mutual love for her has become a bridge that Hunter and I have used to find our way to each other. For years, we've been the only real family the other has had, and still, we walked through the world alone, holding each other responsible for our father's sins.

Before I left New Haven this summer, we sat down and had a long talk about Nicholas Drake and all the ways he contributed to the rift between us. I admitted to resenting Hunter for getting all the time and attention I stopped receiving when he abandoned me and my mom. Hunter confessed to hating me for always being the perfect, older son he was constantly compared to.

We both realized that we had never had a chance to truly know or love each other, and we promised to do better. And we are doing better, not just for Riley, but for the two little boys inside us who still need each other.

"Sibling relationships can be hard," Selene offers, twisting her lips to the side thoughtfully. "My sisters and I aren't all that close, and we did grow up together."

No part of me is willing to leave her admission hanging in the air, so I meet it with a question I've been wanting to know the answer to for some time.

"Has it always been that way, or has life gotten in the way?"

By life, I mean Aubrey. Selene isn't a weak-willed woman, so I know one man couldn't keep her away from her family, but Aubrey isn't just a man. He's a political animal with a single-minded machine behind him. It would be easy for anyone's needs and desires to be overlooked and disregarded by it.

"It's always been that way," she says, shrugging. "They exist inside this bubble with my mom that I constantly find myself outside of."

Beck shifts in his seat, his eyes flitting to the rear view mirror to catch a glimpse of Selene's face as she unknowingly speaks directly to the child inside of him who spent the formative years of his life feeling the exact same way. Before he was adopted, several of his placements had him living with families that had biological children who never let him forget he was the outsider. For him, that hell ended when he found two people who took him in and made him their entire world, but Selene is still there.

Alone. Apart. Other.

He turns his head, his gaze snagging on mine, and I see the words I used to describe Selene earlier dancing behind his eyes as reluctant understanding etches itself into his features. It's not approval, not by any stretch of the imagination, but it's something.

The car slows as we approach the blockade around the venue. Beck rolls down his window, and we both present our credentials. We're waved through quickly, driving the short distance between the gate and the back door Selene will enter through in silent observation of the vulnerabilities divulged over the course of the ride.

When Beck parks, I exit the vehicle first, moving to Selene's door to let her out. I offer her my hand, and she takes it even though she doesn't really need it, allowing me to pull her out. I take a step back to give her space to gather herself, watching with vivid interest as she smooths the hand that's not in mine over the jacket of her pale, yellow pantsuit and squares her shoulders like she's preparing to take on the world all on her own.

It takes me a single second to realize that, in a way, she's about to do exactly that. Her husband isn't here. Her parents and siblings are hours away. I can't help but wonder if any of them have called to offer their congratulations or sent a text with words of encouragement to soothe any last-minute nerves. I'm not sure, and since I can't be certain, I'm unable to fight back the urge to offer some up myself.

Selene begins to pull away, and I hold her tighter when I absolutely should be letting go. Out of the corner of my eye, I see Beck rounding the car, and his questioning gaze is heavy and heated as it burns into the side of my face. Selene's is equally hot and just as confused, but she doesn't try to break free. She just stands there, waiting patiently for me to do or say something to justify the delay.

Suddenly, I'm nervous, and my voice tries to shake as I lend it to the only words that feel appropriate to say to her right now.

"You should be so proud of yourself."

14

SELENE

There's an uncomfortable warmth in my chest, and it has nothing to do with the lights flooding the stage, illuminating my entire body and highlighting the expensive fabric of my pantsuit, and everything to do with Cal's words ringing in my head.

As I deliver my speech, they play in the back of my mind, sparking questions about how he knew I needed to be reminded to think of myself in this moment. All day I've been preoccupied with thoughts of who wouldn't be here and why—my sisters had to work, my daddy doesn't like to fly, my mama hates to travel without him, and Aubrey...well, Aubrey's not here because he's an asshole who decided the clause about attending events and showing up for each other only applies to me. I wasn't exactly chomping at the bit to share space or spotlight with him, but I'm annoyed by his absence and the double standard it represents.

Of course, I didn't bother to communicate any of that to him and Jordan before their flight to Atlanta to meet with Cordelia Barnes, a Georgia Senator who's best known for losing the Republican nomination to President Lucas Sanders in the last election. I also didn't bother to ask what business Aubrey could possibly have with the woman whose every belief flies in the face of his because I knew he wouldn't bother to explain. Instead, I channeled all of my energy into last-minute preparation for the launch, and now I'm here, in this glorious moment, and it's everything I hoped it would be.

There are hundreds of people in this room—my employees, peers, members of the press, and of course some naysayers—and they're all hanging on my every word, listening as I take six years of hard work and condense it into small, manageable selling points that will hopefully result in the purchase and implementation of Safe-Sight everywhere.

Clicking a button on the small remote in my hand to change the slide, I pause at the podium I've barely used and take a sip of water. It's a strategic move. One that allows me to get my bearings as I prepare to wrap things up and leaves the audience with no choice but to look at the array of Black and brown faces frozen in time for mugshots by police departments all over the world. The room is so quiet that the sound of me setting my glass down sends an echo through it. I back away from the podium, splitting a severe, challenging gaze over the faces in the crowd. Some of them shift uncomfortably under the weight of it, relieved when I turn my attention back to the screen.

"This is the data set our competitors use to train their facial recognition software." I sweep my arm through the air, gesturing grandly at the visual representation of the infuriating fact before continuing. "Mugshots. Photos taken at the lowest point of a person's life and then fed, without their permission, into an algorithm that will spit them back out as a viable match, whether they meet all the criteria or not. Think about the implications of that for a second. A biased dataset where Black and brown faces are overrepresented, an algorithm that refuses to acknowledge error and provides a match that is then used to generate warrants and lead to arrests that sometimes turn fatal."

I purse my lips, shaking my head as I think about a case where that exact thing happened almost a decade ago. The tragedy prompted me to write the source code for this software.

"As our global dependency on technology grows, we must remain cognizant of its limitations and imperfections. We must acknowledge the human element of its creation that leaves it open to fallacy and do everything we can to decrease the possibility of lethal mistakes." Another press of the button shifts to the next slide, this one displaying hundreds of tiny squares filled with the smiling faces of people of all shades, shapes, and walks of life.

"This is just a small sampling of the ethically obtained photos Smart Sight was trained on. As you can see, we prioritized equal representation across the board to create the largest and most diverse dataset in the world, and the only one composed entirely of photos and videos taken with the subject's express consent. This is the future of facial recognition software." I click the button one last time, and the photos move away, shifting to make room for the logo the marketing team spent months conceptualizing. I hold my arms out wide, my heart beating wildly in my chest as I say, "*This* is Smart Sight."

The room erupts into thunderous applause, and I expel a harsh breath, turning my head to share a triumphant smile with Monique. She beams at me from her spot in the wings, and behind her, there's Cal. His expression is severe, features trained into a hard mask of indifference, but his eyes? They shine with approval and a secret pride that sets off sparks of pleasure inside of me. They explode quietly, melting into a pool of liquid warmth that trickles down my spine and makes me forget myself for just a moment.

Monique's brows furrow with confusion when the applause dies down, and I'm still looking in her direction.

"Q&A," she mouths at me, waving a hand to urge me to get back to the crowd. With a small laugh and heat creeping into my cheeks, I do as I'm told, stepping up to the podium to address my audience.

"I'd like to open the floor up for questions."

As expected, several dozen hands fly into the air. I wade through them slowly, choosing people from the front rows first and working my way to the back where the members of the press are, because I know their questions will have nothing to do with Smart Sight. For the most part, the reporters play nice, congratulating me on the launch and questioning which state I'm most excited to visit in the upcoming weeks, but I know better than to think that will last.

I point at an older white man with thinning silver hair and thick glasses, who is standing near the center aisle. He's been patiently waiting for me to get to him with a hungry glint in his eye.

"What's your question, Mr…" I trail off, leaving space for him to identify himself.

"Hughes," he provides. "Jason Hughes from The Daily. I believe you're familiar with us," he chuckles, and everyone else in the room laughs too. I don't so much as smile, a wariness settling over me at the name of the paper that works overtime to belittle me and resorts to nasty tactics like infiltrating private dinners to get a story.

My fingers grip the edge of the podium. "Your question, Mr. Hughes?"

He digs a small notebook out of his back pocket, flipping the cover open and tucking it behind the worn pages. "Are you familiar with the recent bill introduced in Congress this week to fund the purchase of AI-enhanced security cameras for schools that would use facial recognition software and other physical and behavioral markers to identify school shooters before they get the chance to kill?"

"Of course. A reactionary piece of legislation written by Republicans after the shooting at Bright Hall Middle to pacify their constituents who are tired of their grief and pain being met with thoughts and prayers."

Hughes' brows shoot up, reaching for his hairline as he lets out a whistle. "That's some harsh criticism. I take it this bill doesn't have your support."

I've already given him his sound bite, but he's still fishing for more, trying to herd me into a corner with a soap box in it that I'm all too happy to stand on. I'll give him what he wants, but only because doing so will allow me to reiterate the points I just made about responsible use of technology.

"We've just established that technology is fallible and subject to producing unanticipated outcomes. I think using it in that way would only result in the inequitable disruption of the lives and learning of Black and brown students who'll be flagged by those cameras for 'suspicious activity' more often than their white counterparts even though we know white males make up 81 percent of shooters in the K-12 setting."

I begin to back away from the podium, intent on ending the conversation there, but Hughes steps forward, his voice a touch louder than before.

"Would you feel that way if Smart Sight were the software used to make the identifications?"

A deep sigh leaves me as I level him with a flat stare. "Technology could not have prevented the school shooting that took my son's life. It could not have prevented what happened at Bright Hall Middle. Technology is not the solution to a problem that is largely human. We don't need AI-enhanced security cameras in our schools; we need mental health professionals and a comprehensive network of support for those at risk of committing these horrific acts."

It's as close as I've ever come to publicly discussing my First Lady initiative, and I have to force myself to stop there because it's not supposed to be widely known until after the election. Hughes, along with every other reporter in the room, is writing down what little I have said, and I know they'll hold on to it for later, using it to speculate about what I'll use my title for.

"If your husband wins the election, is that where you'd tell him to start?" he asks.

All of the reporters perk up, and just about every phone in the room is pulled out and pointed in my direction, the cameras set to record. In the back of my mind, I hear Jordan's voice reciting the clause that prohibits me from voicing political views that might oppose Aubrey's. It echoes like a warning that I ignore because I know we are united on this front.

"No. If my husband wins the election, I would advise him to start with a nationwide ban on assault weapons and high-capacity magazines. Then, I would suggest he lend his support to those lobbying for gun control laws that will require background checks for all weapons sales, keep them out of the hands of domestic abusers, and remove them from the possession of people who are proven to be a danger to themselves and others."

Murmurs ripple throughout the crowd, making the fire in Hughes' eyes burn brighter. He's finally gotten whatever it is he was looking for. Suddenly, Monique appears at my side, inching herself between me and the podium.

"That concludes the Q&A portion of the evening. Thank you all for being here tonight. Refreshments are available in the lobby."

The prompt but polite dismissal gets people moving, but Hughes stays glued to his spot, watching as Monique grabs my elbow and tries to maneuver me off stage.

"Mrs. Taylor," he calls, smirking when I turn to the microphone. "Do you think he'll do any of those things?"

Lately, all Jordan does is preach to me about the importance of solidarity in front of the press, and I've upheld my end of the bargain without much of a struggle. Still, I'm relieved to be faced with an opportunity to expound on my belief in Aubrey without a single ounce of doubt threaded in my answer.

I hold my head up high, painting on a small smile for the photographer to Hughes' right, and nod. "We lost our son in an act of senseless and preventable violence. I can't think of a single reason why my husband would shy away from the chance to spare another parent from that same fate."

"Is that a yes?"

"Yes. I am confident my views are in alignment with his plans."

"*WHAT THE FUCK WERE YOU THINKING?*"

The harsh words brush against the shell of my ear as Aubrey rocks me back and forth in his arms. The embrace and the smile plastered on his face are all for the sake of the cameras lining the tarmac to document my arrival in Georgia mere hours after I left the stage.

I'm still wearing my suit from the launch, and the bun at the nape of my neck is too tight, but I still smile when he spins me around to face the photographers. Light from the flashes on their cameras creates spots that blot out my vision, and Aubrey's nasty tone rings in my head, but still, I smile.

I smile, and I wave, and I allow him to kiss me on the cheek and place his hand on the small of my back, leading me to the black SUV he arrived in. The agent I recognize as the team lead, Hicks, is behind the wheel, so another agent, whose name I don't recall, is at the door, holding it open for us. Aubrey gestures for me to slide inside first, and he follows closely behind, his face red. Before he can speak, I turn to get a look out of the rear window, curious about the fact that we're alone.

"Is Jordan not riding with us?"

She was standing beside Aubrey on the tarmac when the plane door opened, but I haven't seen her since.

Aubrey scrubs a hand down his face as Hicks places the car in drive and hits the gas. "No, I asked her to take the other car."

"That's odd. Usually, you two like to extract your pounds of flesh at the same time," I muse.

"So you know what you've done?"

"When I landed, I got a text from Monique telling me to stay offline. I assume a statement I made at the launch has been misconstrued in some way or another, and now you're concerned about how that will affect you in the polls."

"Misconstrued?" Aubrey sneers, pulling his phone out of the interior pocket of his suit jacket and tapping the screen. "Presidential hopeful Aubrey Taylor will ban assault weapons once in office, per his wife. Selene Taylor disparages the proposed solution to mass shootings in schools, promising a Taylor administration will bring real change in the form of strict gun control."

My brows collapse into each other as Aubrey continues reading headline after headline, his voice shaking with fury. There's hostility rolling off of him in waves that make no sense to me.

"I'm not sure I understand what the problem is," I admit, casting a sidelong glance in his direction. "Those headlines sound accurate to me."

Aubrey scoffs and tosses his phone down on the seat between us. "The accuracy is the problem, Selene. You taking it upon yourself to shit all over a bill with bipartisan support and give your opinion on one of the biggest issues in this country is the problem. *Who the __fuck__ do you think you are?!*"

I flinch at his raised voice, and when the agents in the front seat stiffen but don't say a word, I find myself wishing for the two men who are never far from my mind, knowing at least one, but probably both, of them would have had something to say about the way my husband is speaking to me right now.

"It's not about who I think I am, Aubrey. It's about who I know you are, what I know you believe. You are a proponent of gun control. It's one of the smaller tenets of your campaign promise and, in case you've forgotten, one of the larger tenets of our life. And we both know that bill and every other one like it won't do a damn thing to change things."

The more words I say, the harder his leg bounces. I don't understand it. This reaction or his growing agitation, and I don't have the patience to sort through it when the facts are what they are.

He pinches the bridge of his nose, shaking his head. "You have no idea how any of this shit works, Selene. You're supposed to stand there and look pretty. You're not supposed to rip apart bills or make promises about what I'm going to do."

"I would never make a promise on your behalf, Aubrey," I retort, crossing my arms over my chest and leaning my head against the window. "I don't have enough faith in you for that."

Any chance for him to respond is lost in the vibrating of his phone against the seat, indicating an incoming phone call. Whispering a prayer of thanks that the discussion is over, I close my eyes and try to tune Aubrey's conversation out.

I'm unsuccessful.

Mostly because I'm put off by the sudden shift in his tone when he picks up.

"Cordelia, to what do I owe this pleasure?" he coos, his voice oozing with friendliness and familiarity.

I can't hear her response, but I do pay close attention to Aubrey's end of the call. My ears perk up when they begin to discuss the bill, and my eavesdropping affords me the knowledge that Senator Barnes was the one who brought it to Congress. Clearly, that's part of the reason why Aubrey is so upset with me. If Senator Barnes is his friend, or at the very least a political ally, my public disparagement of legislation she is trying to get passed would create complications between them.

The added context is nice to have, easing some parts of my confusion while simultaneously creating more questions. Aubrey ends the call, promising to speak with the Senator again soon. I sit up and open my eyes, settling an inquisitive gaze on his face. He's still angry, that much is clear by the tension in his jaw, but his mood is a little better.

That'll change.

"Since when are you in bed with the Republicans?" I ask.

He glares at me, offended that I'd dare question him, but he answers anyway. "Since I've come to understand that bipartisanship is integral to the success of this country. Sanders has had almost four years to bring both sides of the aisle together, and he's only managed to divide the country further. I won't make the same mistake. I plan to take over the Oval with people on both sides in my corner, and accomplishing that goal means keeping people in my camp from shitting all over initiatives backed by my would be allies."

When his little speech is over, he shifts his focus to his phone, leaving me to wonder if his definition of bipartisanship is compromising his beliefs, bending his morals until they're small and insignificant enough to fit neatly in the palms of those allies' hands.

15

BECK

I wake with sweat dripping down my back, and the late dinner Cal and I shared when we arrived in Atlanta last night making its way up my throat.

It's been months since I've dreamed of Diana and Cameron, our unborn son, longer still since their deaths were the topic of my unconscious musings. Normally, I'm able to keep all thoughts of them locked away and my focus on my work, but exhaustion and the mental imprint of the beginning of recurring grief has rendered me weak. Susceptible to subconscious torture that's left me sick to my stomach.

Turning over onto my back, I squeeze my eyes shut and fight against the heavy weight pressing down on my chest, against the hot, sticky swell of nausea in my gut. I inhale slowly, taking four counts to fill my lungs and then holding for another four before taking the same amount of time to exhale.

It doesn't help.

Nothing ever really does. Nothing except for Cal's calming presence and the heat of his skin. The soft press of his lips against my sweaty forehead and the reassurance that I'm not alone anymore.

Except I am alone right now because I wouldn't let him stay with me last night.

He'd offered. He even promised to sleep on the couch to minimize the chances of us being tempted to do anything that might be overheard by the people sleeping on either side of the thin walls. I knew he meant it, that he'd be here with me, but I still denied him because I thought I would be okay, because I hoped that even if I wasn't, I'd be able to deal with it on my own.

I'm swimming in the regret of that decision when a short, quiet knock sounds out against my door. I lay still, straining my ears to be sure that it wasn't just my imagination, and the knock sounds again, followed by the long, dull beep of the lock disengaging. The door opens and closes with a soft thud, and I listen to his near-silent footsteps as he crosses the room, pausing to shed his clothes and hang them in the closet next to the ones I'll put on when I'm ready to face the day.

The mattress sags under the weight of his knee as he hovers above me, silently commanding me to move over to make room for his slightly larger form. I shift until he has enough space to settle comfortably, and he slips underneath the covers, pulling me into him. I rest my head over his heart and sigh my relief into his bare chest.

"You're only supposed to use the key for emergencies."

Cal presses a kiss to the top of my head. "This is an emergency."

I want to argue with him, but I can't because he isn't wrong. While there might not be any looming threat of physical harm, the scent of my emotional crisis is permeating the room, and Cal has sniffed me out, marking me as the emergent situation in need of his immediate attention.

"I'm sorry I didn't let you stay," I mutter, regret twisting itself into the words.

"Hush, love," Cal whispers, running a soothing hand over my side. "Try to rest."

But I can't rest because I'm guilty and sad and sick about losing my wife and son, about what my grief for them has brought me and what it might cost me if I can't find a way to let it go. It feels wrong to think those words today of all days, but today isn't just the anniversary of Diana and Cameron's death, it also marks Cal and I's beginning.

Six years ago to the day, I visited my wife and son's graves. I laid down flowers for Diana and secured five white balloons to Cameron's headstone, and later on that same day, I made love to my best friend for the first time, creating a convergence of life-altering grief and the most affirming love that I sometimes struggle to believe I deserve.

Tears crowd my eyes but refuse to fall, so I choke on the lump they create in my throat instead. "I still miss them so much," I croak. "I still love them so much, but I love you too, Drake. *I love you too.*"

"I know, Beckham," Cal murmurs, his assurance providing a peace that rushes over me in a sudden wave. "I've always known."

We lay in silence until the sun comes up and it's time for our morning run. Cal eases out of the bed first, making his way over to the closet to dress again while I head to the bathroom to complete my morning hygiene routine. When I emerge, he's sitting on the edge of the freshly made bed with his phone to his ear. Judging by his clipped tone and the responses that consist of 'yes, sir' or 'no sir', I'm assuming he's speaking to Hicks.

As I get dressed, I keep an ear out for any indicators that our morning plans will be disrupted and let out a sigh of relief when Cal hangs up and there's no look of resignation on his face.

"All good?" I ask, strapping my phone into the band on my arm.

Cal pushes to his feet and nods. "Yep. Hicks was letting me know Selene requested us to drive her to the rally this afternoon. Apparently, Aubrey is going ahead of her."

A quiet hum of acknowledgment is all I have to offer in response until we're outside, fully stretched and away from anyone who might care to listen to our conversation. Cal's pace is even, his features tight with concentration that doesn't break when I speak.

"You do a shit job of hiding how happy the thought of being around her makes you."

Just a day ago, I was struggling with the idea of Cal's feelings for Selene. In some ways, I still am, but I've also resigned myself to the fact that nothing I say or do will change his mind about her. I'd be lying if I said I didn't completely understand the appeal. Selene is a beautiful, broken thing, and Cal is a fixer. A nurturer by nature. He wants to help, to heal, and to pour his love into someone, watching it transform them. I just hate that he keeps choosing to direct that love in the direction of people who aren't truly available to receive it.

Selene.

Me.

It's a cruel fate, and he deserves so much more.

A full minute goes by without a response from Cal. Nothing but the pounding of our shoes on the pavement, our synchronized breathing, and the soft sounds of a rapidly awakening city greet my observation.

"It's not a good look for us to be taking requests from her," I huff, grimacing when we round a corner and Cal hits a sprint. He's smirking when I'm finally able to match his stride, and I bump him with my shoulder.

"Asshole."

"Not my fault you can't keep up," he quips.

"Yeah, whatever, old man."

We pause at a crosswalk, jogging in place while we wait for the signal to cross safely. Cal squints against the sunlight bouncing off the tall glass buildings around us, shielding his eyes with one hand.

"Hicks gave the order. I accepted it. It's as simple as that."

"But it isn't simple. Nothing about this is simple." At the first flash of the 'walk' signal, we take off, crossing the street and turning left towards a stretch of office buildings, coffee shops, and cafes.

"He's our supervisor, Beck. What was I supposed to do? Tell him no?"

We both know insubordination is more my thing, so I'd never expect it from Cal. What I do expect is for him to have a little fucking perspective on this situation. "No, but you could have asked if someone else could do it. You could have told him we were hoping for a chance to build a rapport with Aubrey."

"*You* want to spend time with Aubrey Taylor?"

I frown, knowing that being around the man is the last thing I actually want to do. "I want to guard a President, Cal. Aubrey is the candidate; getting on his detail should be our primary focus."

He cuts an eye at me, trying to decipher my mood. "Is this about the trajectory of our careers or about putting some distance between Selene and me because I already told you, you don't have to worry. I can keep my feelings in check."

"The two things aren't mutually exclusive. Your feelings for Selene could be the end of both of our careers."

"Beck, you know I would never—"

Normally, I'd be soothed by a Callan Drake promise because I've only ever known him to be a man of his word, but today, I can't even let him finish the thought.

"You can't control everything, Cal. You can't even keep the hearts out of your eyes when you look at her, and don't even get me started on how you look when you have occasion to touch her."

My agitation is apparent, evident in the rising volume of my voice, and Cal slows down, wrapping his fingers around my bicep to force me to do the same. We come to a reluctant stop in the middle of the busiest stretch of sidewalk, and people move around us, tossing questioning glances in our direction as they do.

Cal pulls me to the side, his chest heaving as he studies me with concerned eyes. "What's this really about, love?"

I squeeze my eyes shut at the term of endearment, pinning him with a hard stare when I open them again. "Don't. Not now."

He recoils at the rejection, and a wave of shame washes over me. I hate hurting him. Hate putting that dejected look on his face. Hate the way he steals his features and crosses his arms, closing himself off to me, even though it's what I deserve.

"Sorry," he says, his eyes on any and everything but my face.

"No, I'm sorry."

We both take a beat to compose ourselves.

"It doesn't change anything with us," Cal murmurs quietly. "I still..."

He trails off, bringing a searching gaze to my face, and I nod. "I know. This isn't jealousy, Cal. This is a concern for my partner, for my best friend."

"Concern, you seem more adamant about expressing today than yesterday." He tilts his head to the side. "Why?"

It was never my intention to bring this conversation to him in this way. I wanted our morning to be calm and quiet, free from my anxieties about all the shit in this world I can't do a thing to change. That ship has sailed, though, so I have no choice but to tell Cal what I heard.

"Last night on the plane. You were sleeping, and I guess they thought I was asleep too, otherwise they wouldn't have said a word, but I overheard Ortega and Anderson talking shit."

"About?"

"You. And Selene. Specifically, about the moment before she walked into the venue when you were holding her hand. Apparently, there are pictures, and they were wondering what you said to her. From there, it devolved into speculations about her using you to get back at Aubrey for cheating."

"What did you say?"

"Nothing. I would have wanted to defend you, which would have only made it look like you're doing something you need to be defended from."

The muscle in his jaw pulses. "I hear you."

For the first time in a while, I believe he's listening, that he's taking my concerns seriously. "I know you care about her, Drake, but a little distance might be good. We should talk to Hicks about it."

"He won't put us on Aubrey because he wants the Presidential detail for himself." He scrubs at his jaw roughly. "I'll just have to do a better job of keeping my shit together around her."

"Cal."

"I can do it, Beck. I promise."

There's no point in arguing with him, especially when he's right about Hicks trying to parlay leading this detail into the most coveted one in the Service, so I concede with a resigned sigh that puts an end to the entire discussion. We resume our run in silence and the tension that hung between us yesterday joins as an unwelcome third, sticking around through two miles, joining us at the table when we stop at a cafe for water and a light breakfast.

Unlike last time, there's no talk of adorable nieces to dispel the negative energy, so we have to sit in it, eating our food without exchanging a word until Cal curses and throws his phone onto the table, sliding it towards me.

"Look at this shit."

Picking up the phone, I study the screen, arching a brow when I realize that he's on Selene's Instagram page. "This is your version of doing better? Stalking her online?"

He glares at me. "I check her socials every day to keep an eye out for any potential threats. You know this."

I do know. Usually, we go through them together, splitting up the platforms and comparing notes, making sure the tech guys, whose job it actually is to sort through it all, didn't miss anything important in their daily reports. From the looks of the comments underneath the post Cal has pulled up on his phone, today's report is going to be a fucking mess.

"Holy shit," I whisper as my thumb moves over the screen, revealing one hateful comment after the other. "How have none of these been flagged or reported yet?"

"I don't know."

Cal's leg is shaking so hard it's making the table vibrate, and I would try to calm him down, but I don't have a shred of calm inside of me. All of it disappeared when I saw the first response to Selene's post celebrating the successful launch of her facial recognition software. In the photo, she's on stage with her best friend Monique and the rest of their team. Everyone is smiling and happy, proud that years of work have come together in this moment.

The positivity and light radiating from the digital still stand out in stark contrast against the darkness of the death threats below it.

Death threats.

Hundreds of them. Hundreds of people wishing for the end of a person's life because she dared to speak out about the need for gun control in a country where someone murdering children with assault rifles is a common occurrence. Some of them are simple and lacking in creativity, but others are more graphic, racially charged torture porn that's ripe with depravity.

As I scroll, a red, hot anger flares in my gut. Building and burning its way through me until all I can see, all I can taste, all I can feel is a primal surge of protectiveness that makes no sense to me because, as far as I know, Selene isn't in any real danger at the moment. When it threatens to overtake me, to send me sprinting back to the hotel to put eyes on her, I toss the phone back on the table and rub at my temples.

"Hicks needs to see those," I growl.

"He probably already has. He gets the same reports we do. The question is, is he going to do anything about it?"

We share a look, both of us knowing that the answer is no.

Hicks actively ignores those reports and refuses to account for them when he's allocating security resources. Everything he does relays his belief that Selene's safety is not a priority. It's not uncommon for spouses or family members to be designated as secondary in details like this, but the threats posed to Selene online are the whole reason why we were assigned to the Taylors in the first place. That her safety is now treated as an afterthought by everyone but me and Cal pisses me off.

For what seems like the millionth time since he spoke them, Cal's words from the green room ring in my head. *Alone. Apart. Other.* He'd been trying to tell me then that Selene was like us, and I see his point now. But I also see something else.

The similarities between the brilliant, beautiful Black woman we've been tasked to protect and the brilliant, beautiful Black woman I grieve every day.

The one who would still be here if it weren't for the same kind of inaction and nonchalance that poses a threat to Selene's life today.

Part of the reason why I don't get along with Hicks is because he reminds me of my old supervisor, Robert Spring. We started off on the wrong foot on my first day as a behavioral analyst, and we never found the right one. That mutual hostility was at an all-time high when we started to investigate a string of murders happening right in our backyard. All of the victims were white, female sex workers with a history of drug addiction. The killer raped and strangled them before displaying their bodies in parks around the city. It was a high-profile case, but it took us forever to catch a break. Finally, a witness, a girl who'd survived an interaction with the killer before he'd gotten his MO down, came forward, leading us to a man named Alan Valinsky.

I knew Valinsky was guilty from the moment we met, but we could never pin anything on him. The guy got a kick out of coming in after every new kill, volunteering airtight alibis and playing the good, helpful citizen, always refusing to talk to anyone but me. After months of coming up empty, Spring ordered me to leave Valinsky alone, but I didn't listen. I kept digging into him, finding and interviewing everyone who ever knew him, including his first wife, who left him after the birth of their son.

The next time we saw each other, I brought up her name, and his cool, calm demeanor broke, exposing a nasty temper. I told him that was why his wife had left, and then asked him what it was like knowing he'd never see her or his son again. He'd only grinned and walked away, leaving me with a warning about how quickly others' misfortunes could become our own.

That's when I knew Diana was in his crosshairs.

I begged Spring for a protective detail, only to be reprimanded for harassing an innocent civilian, and two months later, my wife was dead. I still remember the smile on Valinsky's face when I walked into our bedroom and found him standing over her. The way he laughed when I cuffed him and broke crime scene protocol just so I could hold her one last time.

Spring came to the funeral to pay his respects and pulled me aside, telling me there was no way we could have known this would happen. I punched him in the face and proceeded to try and tear him apart with my bare hands.

My transfer paperwork was filed the next day.

That transfer led me to Cal. It put me on a path to Selene, made it so I have no choice but to stand between her and the world in a way I never got to do for Diana.

16

SELENE

"And you're staying offline?" Monique asks, her brows furrowed with concern as she searches my face through the screen of my phone.

"Yes. I've deleted everything but my email."

"Don't check that either! Nichelle is screening everything and forwarding the important stuff to me."

I grimace. "Monique, I can't just fall off the face of the Earth days after our biggest launch. I can stay off of social media, but I need to be present at Culture Code. I need my work. I mean it's not like people are sending death threats to my e—"

My voice trails off when Mo presses her lips together, and I run frustrated fingers through the freshly curled strands of my hair and sigh. There seems to be no end to the fallout from my gun control comment. Since arriving in Atlanta, I've had to contend with Aubrey's anger, Jordan's disapproval, death threats online, and now, apparently, in my inbox, and I'm just tired. Of course, I'm not a stranger to online vitriol, but this feels different. More hostile. More vicious. More like millions of strangers are actively thinking of ways to kill me as opposed to hoping I'll just drop dead so they can have their blond hair, blue-eyed First couple.

As strange as it sounds, I was fine with the passive act of wishing me dead, but the intentionality behind these threats has me more scared than I care to admit. I feel like there's a target on my back and a shooter around every corner. Fear coils around my ribs, causing my stomach to churn anxiously.

"You'll have to make sure to tell Nichelle to send the threats to Jordan, so she can forward them to the Secret Service," I say, running my fingers through my hair again and then wincing because I won't have time to fix it before I need to leave for the rally.

"She's already on it, Sel."

I nod, rising from my spot at the foot of the bed to cross over to the vanity and assess the damage I've done to my hair. Thankfully, it's not too bad. If anything, my fretting has added some volume, making the style look lived-in instead of stuffy and too perfect. Propping my phone up against the mirror, I rake my nails through the curls on the other side to achieve the same effect. Monique nods her approval.

"You look beautiful."

"Thank you."

She stares at me, and I see my own fear reflected in her gaze. It lingers for a second before she pushes it away, projecting confidence. "You're going to be okay."

"I'm going to be okay," I repeat, coaxing a thin smile to the surface to put Monique and me at ease. "I'll text you later. Love you."

"Love you too, bye."

The screen goes dark, and I allow my features to crumple into a mask of distress for just a second before tucking it away and grabbing everything I need to head out the door. The suite Aubrey and I are sharing is empty and still as I move from my bedroom to the living area. Everyone of importance has accompanied him to a meeting with Senator Barnes that I didn't know about until they were all marching out the door. A flurry of voices and magnified importance that left me to dwell in my anxiety and prepare for the rally all alone.

I didn't expect anyone in Aubrey's camp—especially not him or Jordan—to be of much use to me on either front, but I still found myself annoyed as I watched them leave, ignoring my comments about us arriving at the first major event of this travel season together. Apparently, our contractual obligations shrink to become mere suggestions where Aubrey is concerned. The unfairness of it burns in my chest, threatening to singe the soft, sheer fabric of my cream blouse and the lapels of the lavender blazer of my pantsuit.

Pushing out a slow, even breath, I wrap my fingers around the handle of the door and pull it open, bringing myself face to face with Agent Harris. His hand is raised, prepared to knock, and even though I've surprised him, he doesn't let it show on his face as he lowers his hand to his side.

"It's time to go, ma'am."

He steps back, leaving me space to move into the hallway. There's no one else on this floor, so Agent Harris gives me a wide berth as we make our way to the elevator, and he doesn't say a word for the duration of the ride down. The chill of his reserved presence is immediately dispersed by the warmth of the two gazes that land on me when we step out under the awning where three large, black SUVs are waiting in front of the hotel.

There are other people looking at me besides them.

The local cops standing on either side of their slanted black and whites to prevent cars from the adjacent street from turning into the hotel's circular drive glance over their shoulders to catch a glimpse of me.

Drivers from the halted vehicles on the road toss exasperated glares in my general direction.

One of the valets leans against the wall, trying to appear casual even though he's got his phone in his hand and is clearly recording me.

All those eyes. All that attention, and yet, the only thing I feel is the shock of onyx and the familiar, smoldering heat of copper and brass.

Since the first day I met them, I've been obsessed with decoding the pair in front of me, determined to understand the symmetry of their existence. In all that time, I never thought I'd get to experience what it would be like to stand in the middle of it. I've craved it, of course, hypothesized that existing between two people, so sure of who they are together, would make me feel like I belonged.

I never thought I'd have it, though, but for one small, blissful moment, I do.

I have the perfectly balanced weight of their shared attention pressing in on me from all sides, heavy and tight like a twenty-five-pound blanket with compression capabilities.

I have Agent Beckham's soft, but curt, greeting and a cursory sweep of his dark eyes over my face as I pass between him and the door to climb into the backseat of the car.

I have the rough caress of Cal's voice as he explains how long it will take for us to get to the venue and the low rumble of his quiet exchange with Agent Beckham once he's settled in the passenger seat.

And when we pull out of the hotel driveway, following closely behind the lead vehicle, I have the first taste of calm I've experienced since I arrived in Atlanta last night.

We don't talk enough about how exhausting anxiety is. How it steals your ability to reason, leaving your brain free to run a mental marathon your body didn't agree to or train for. How, once that marathon is over, fatigue sets in, sending you plummeting into paralysis, a numb kind of relaxation that costs too much to bring so little relief.

That's the state I'm in for the duration of the ride. My body is fused to the backseat. My bones are liquid underneath my skin. My eyelids are heavy. I'm in the middle of trying to coax them back open when the long and loud blare of a horn pierces the air. The sudden, jarring sound is more than enough to put my body right back on high alert all on its own, but when it's accompanied by the sound of screeching tires and the acrid smell of burning rubber, my heart lodges itself into my throat, thrumming wildly against my esophagus as the disembodied voices of the agents in the cars behind us shout through the comms that our formation has been broken.

Agent Beckham, who's spent the whole ride monitoring our surroundings, spins in his seat at the same time I do. Both of us were stunned and quiet as we observed the beat-up blue sedan with windows dark enough to rival the tint on ours accelerate, drawing close enough to make my muscles seize from the threat of impact.

"The fuck is this guy doing?" Cal growls as the engine revs and the SUV lurches forward, creating space between us and the unknown car that's quickly deleted when he slams on the brakes. Confused, Agent Beckham and I both turn our attention back to the front of the car just in time to witness the second break in our procession. The tail lights of the compact, red car flash rapidly, indicating that the driver is pressing and releasing the brake in quick pulses meant to keep them from colliding with us and the lead SUV.

"Get over, Drake," Agent Beckham issues the order between calm breaths, even as his head swings wildly from the front to the back.

The other agents on the comms are telling Cal to do the same thing, and when I am no longer frozen in fear, I'm able to turn my head and see that the other SUVs are now in the far left lane with a large gap between them where we're supposed to be. Cal doesn't bother with his signal. He just checks his blind spot and begins to shift the wheel to take us to safety, only to be cut off by the roar of several motorcycles who choose that exact moment to take up residence at our left side. The riders are decked out in traditional biker garb. Bulky helmets that hide their faces, leather pants and jackets free of emblems, which strikes me as odd because they move like a group, and that usually means distinct markings or signage, right?

"Only if they want to be easily identified."

The answer to what I thought was a silent question comes from Agent Beckham, who now has all of his attention on me. Onyx eyes rove over my features, taking in what I'm sure are obvious signs of helplessness and fear. His jaw tenses and his nostrils flare, signs of annoyance I've grown used to seeing on his face. I can't tell if they're for me or just a byproduct of this unusual situation, and I guess it doesn't really matter because focusing on him gives me the ability to turn my silent anxiety spiral into voiced concerns.

"Why wouldn't they want to be identified?" A small, horrified gasp passes through my lips when silence greets my question, and I balk, pressing my body into the door on my right as images of gun-wielding assassins on bikes flash in my mind. "You think they're trying to…"

I can't say the words, and I don't need to because they know. They've seen the death threats and prepared for the possibility of someone trying to turn words into lethal action. I thought I'd prepared for it too, but as I peer out the window, searching for any sign of a gun or a bomb on the bikers who haven't even looked in our direction, I realize how foolish it was to think that. Agent Beckham follows the unspoken thread of my thoughts, and his face softens marginally.

"We don't have any reason to believe anyone on this road is trying to hurt you," he says. His voice is low, his gaze severe, demanding me to believe him. And despite the tight grip Cal has on the wheel and the constant barrage of commentary spilling from the comms that tell me this is all a show of bravado to keep me calm, I want to take this gift he's offering me. I take too long to accept it, though, so he reaches for more words. "For all we know, these are just impatient Atlanta drivers in a rush to go nowhere fast. Isn't that right, Cal?"

Cal gives an enthusiastic nod of his head. "Yeah, that's right."

As if to prove their point, the red sedan in front turns on its signal light and moves over to the right, crossing two lanes of traffic to take an exit at the last second. Moments later, the lead SUV with Agent Harris at the helm picks up speed, passing the bikers and crossing lanes to take up residence in front of us, which earns him a bevy of leather-clad middle fingers as the motorcycles peel off. Over the comms, I hear Agent Anderson confirming that he was able to reclaim his position behind us. He doesn't mention where the blue sedan went or when it left, and I find that I don't really care to know.

"See? We're all good," Agent Beckham says, forcing the tension out of the muscles in his shoulders as he turns back around in his seat, putting an end to our tenuous connection.

"Yeah, all good," I agree, sinking back into my seat with a sick feeling in my gut that remains firmly in place for the rest of the ride. When we arrive at the venue, I push it down and away, tacking on my future First Lady smile that only falters when I come face to face with Senator Cordelia Barnes.

She's holding court in the middle of the small space behind the stage, where Aubrey and I will be in just a matter of minutes. Everyone who should have been at the door to greet me is standing around her, hanging on every syllable of her exaggerated southern drawl. To my surprise, Aubrey notes my approach before anyone else does, and he parts the crowd surrounding the Senator to meet me with open arms. I have no choice but to step into it.

He squeezes me tightly and places his lips to my ear. "*Behave.*"

I swallow my snarky response as he lets go, spinning me around to face the group of awaiting onlookers. Senator Barnes has stepped forward, placing herself ahead of everyone else. Aubrey urges me toward her with a firm hand on my back, and I fight the desire to swat him away.

"Well, if it isn't our aspiring politician," she remarks, extending her hand.

I glance at Aubrey, a silent inquiry about why he didn't issue the same warning about behaving to his cohort. He stretches his eyes wide and laughs at the Senator's bad joke along with everyone else. Her blue eyes glow with the pleasure of shared humor at my expense, and her blonde bob swishes with condescension as she tilts her head to the side to await my response. I square my shoulders and take her hand, squeezing harder than I need to just to get her attention.

"You must have me confused with someone else, Senator. I'd never waste my time, talents, or intellect on a career as frivolous as politics."

There are fine lines in the pale, thin skin around the corners of her eyes that grow deeper when they narrow into slits. All the laughter dies down, leaving nothing but a heavy silence as everyone but me holds their breath waiting for the Senator's response. I watch her weigh her options, deciding whether she wants to continue this catty exchange or retreat to safer ground.

She drops my hand unceremoniously and frowns as she wipes her palm on her pants. "My apologies. I assumed someone with so much to say about legislation and policy would have a desire to do the work, not just publicly dissect the approach of those of us who are actually trying to make change."

"That was your second mistake."

"*Excuse me?*"

"I said—"

"Oh, no, I heard you just fine, Mrs. Taylor," she says, forcing the words out between the narrow spaces of her clenched teeth as her left eye twitches. "I don't make mistakes."

Last night, when I was in desperate need of a distraction from the hate being thrown my way, I kept myself busy by doing a deep dive into all things Cordelia Barnes, so I know that's not true. I know every mistake she's made publicly, from her fumbles in the stock market to the inaccurate Gloria Steinem quotes in her speeches. I even know the exact series of missteps she made that cost her the Republican nomination in the last election. I don't have time to run through all of those things with her now, though, so I focus on what's relevant to this conversation.

"You're human, Senator, of course, you make mistakes. In this instance, you've made two." I hold up my right hand, lifting my index and middle finger with a smile. "Your first mistake was writing a bill that was more about performance than real progress, and your second was assuming that I, or any American, has to be an elected official in order to voice valid concerns in a public setting."

"Selene," Aubrey hisses, censure laced in every syllable of my name.

Cordelia holds up a hand to stop him from saying more, but her eyes never leave mine. "It's fine, Aubrey," she says, a sinister smile curving her thin lips. "I like this one. She's feisty."

Her unnecessary stamp of approval seems to soothe Aubrey, but it unsettles me, adding to the sick feeling I've been carrying with me all day and leaving me certain of one thing: nothing good will come from Cordelia Barnes being in our lives.

17

CAL

Rustling papers followed by Beck's sighs woke me from the short nap I allowed myself to have on the private plane taking us from Atlanta to Madison, Wisconsin. I check my watch and find that we're forty-five minutes into the two hour flight, and then glance at Beck who has used every second of that time to continue sorting through our old case files to see if anyone we came across at the Bureau looks even remotely similar to the man he caught a glimpse of outside of Selene's house weeks ago.

Since the night of the rally, he's been on what I can only call a rampage. Going toe to toe with Harris and Anderson for letting the formation get broken right after we dropped Selene off that night, getting in Hicks face again about the lack of urgency where Selene's concerned, spending every moment of his spare time trying to find a connection between the first incident and the last.

I've been behind him every step of the way—voicing my support of his theory, urging him to rest, quietly admiring the rage driving him because I know the place it's coming from. That place exists inside of me, too, and only a handful of people get to live there. Beck is one of them, and Selene...well, for better or worse, Selene is another.

"You're up," Beck rasps, leaning his head against the seat and fixing low eyes on me. "How was your nap?"

I lift my hands above my head and groan through a stretch. "Short. Find anything?"

"No. If I had, I would have woken you up."

I watch him dig his fingertips into his temples, a surefire sign that he's fighting off a headache, and wish that I could do something to soothe him. Normally, I'd take his head into my lap and force him to close his eyes while I take over the temple massage and pepper kisses over his furrowed brows. For now, all I can do is give him a sympathetic look.

"You should get some rest."

"Cal, I—"

"I know, Beck, but you still need to rest. Tired eyes miss important details."

Something about my insistence only makes him more determined to ignore me. He sits up, long fingers stretching towards the papers he's probably read a hundred times at this point.

"There's something here," he insists, casting a sidelong glance in my direction. "I haven't found it yet, but I can feel it in my gut. The red car that was in front of the house is the same make and model as the one that cut us off on the highway."

We've gone over this line of thought a million times. If the cars are the same, then it stands to reason that the driver is the same. If the driver is the same, then we can confidently link one incident to the other and connect the danger looming around Selene to one of our past cases, putting this whole thing to rest. There's only one problem.

"The plates didn't match."

Beck scoffs. "People change plates all the time. You know that as well as I do."

My fingers brush his as I reach over and close the file he's reading. It's not intentional, but it does get his attention. Wide eyes try to leave my face to see if anyone is watching us, but I shake my head, ordering him to keep his gaze fixed on me.

"You're right. I do know that. I also know that you haven't had a solid hour of uninterrupted sleep in days." I trail my hand up his arm and place it on his chest, pushing him back into his seat. "Rest, Beckham. That's an order."

"You're not my superior, Drake," he grumbles, eyes already falling shut.

I wait until his breathing has evened out to move my hand, and then I spend a minute just staring at him, hoping an hour of rest is enough to make up for the ones he's missed.

He never sleeps well in the days leading up to the anniversary of Diana and Cameron's deaths. The nightmares and the guilt eat away at him, making it impossible for him to find solace in his subconscious. Normally, it subsides within one to two days. If we're on a job, it takes even less time, but this year it's different. The lines between the personal and professional are blurring for him.

This isn't something I need to bring to his attention because he's already aware of it, already found a suitable explanation for the visceral reaction he's having to the thought of Selene being harmed. When we talked about it last night, he made it sound like some sort of quest for redemption, as if keeping Selene safe would somehow soothe the part of him that torments him for not being able to do the same for Diana.

While I know there's some truth to that line of thought, I know it's not the whole truth because when Selene was afraid, when she was in fear for her life, Beck lied to her.

He lied because he knew that the truth wouldn't give her any comfort, and he's never done that with anyone under our protection before. I'm usually the one with the gentle touch, the one who'll mince words to make the facts seem less scary and offer assurances I can't guarantee. Beck is the realist. The cynic. The truth speaker at all costs.

But he lied to Selene, and that lie made my heart sing. It catapulted me back to the night of Selene and Aubrey's date night when the three of us were suspended in a moment only I gave its proper appreciation. Beck would never admit it, but he was just as enamored by Selene as I was, just as affected by the nameless, impossible thing we've fallen into against our will.

Every second we spend together, where it's just the three of us, feels like a prelude to what can never be. A cruel teasing of forbidden perfection where Beck and I get to cherish and care for Selene, to engage with her in a way no one else in this part of her life—but especially her husband—seems to want to. Even now, at the front of the plane where Aubrey Jordan St. James, Torrance Belford— Aubrey's running mate—and his wife, Anne, are huddled around a table trading jokes and sipping champagne, she is alone. On the outside of their bubble, while her partner makes no attempts to pull her in, letting her linger on the margins like she's less than an afterthought.

To her credit, Selene doesn't seem to care that much. She has noise-canceling headphones in and is focused on the book in her hand. She's about halfway through what looks to be a romance novel. My brows lift in surprise, and I bite back a smile. I wouldn't have taken her for a romance reader. The small, stolen detail makes me greedy for more, and soon I'm staring and unable to stop myself from conducting a distant but appreciative perusal of her.

My eyes touch every inch of her face, lingering too long on her pouty lips that are free of lipstick or gloss but still look perfectly kiss-able before moving up to study the slight flare of her nostrils as she turns the page in her book. I'm in the middle of admiring the fullness of her eyelashes when her eyes suddenly latch onto mine.

The instant our gazes meet, I feel it.

That life-threatening, career-ending current that passes between us, threatening to unearth every root I've ever lain. To steal my integrity. To swallow my ambition. To obliterate my oaths and promises and reveal my secrets and regrets. To expose me for every- thing I am and all the things I never will be.

I should be afraid. I should be anything but excited at the prospect of standing in the path of a live wire, but that's all I ever am when she looks at me.

Excited.

Heart racing, pulse pounding, all of my senses tuned in to her and only her.

Which is why I don't notice Harris looking at me from across the aisle until he clears his throat. I jolt, breaking Selene and my mutual trance as I turn in his direction.

"You good, Drake?" he asks, adjusting the hood on his head.

"Yeah."

"You sure? Looked like you were kind of zoned out there for a moment."

Harris has always been a neutral party on the team. He's not really a member of the good ole boys club Hicks runs, but he'll never a part of the impenetrable unit that is me and Beck. He seems fine with that, with being able to flow effortlessly between the two groups inside our team. I don't begrudge him his chameleon abilities, but they make it hard for me to read him, which means I have no idea if he's genuinely checking in on me or if he caught me staring at Selene with—as Beck would say—hearts in my eyes and is trying to be fucking funny.

"Positive," I grunt, pushing to my feet. "I'm grabbing a cup of coffee, do you want one?"

"No, I'm good." He waves me off, leaning his head against the seat and pulling his hood down further before closing his eyes. Pretty much everyone at the back of the plane is sleeping or trying to sleep, so there's not a soul paying attention to my agitated expression on my trek to the kitchenette.

The flight attendants take one look at my face and make themselves scarce, leaving me alone with my bad mood. As I grab a paper cup, I find myself laughing at how quickly they got the hell out of dodge, and the small bit of private humor grounds me, allowing me to forgive myself for potentially letting Harris see the crack in my mask.

"I'm sorry for staring."

Her voice is a familiar rush of warmth trickling down my spine, and I have to push down every errant thought and inappropriate emotion it inspires in me away before I turn to face her. She's standing just inside the doorway, her expression still and her eyes fixed on a point above my head as she speaks.

"I can never really tell how much eye contact is too much. I apologize if I made you uncomfortable."

"No apology necessary. Technically, I was looking at you first."

"Why?" Her brows sink together, and it occurs to me then that she is genuinely confused, like she can't think of a single reason why anyone would want to spend time studying the masterpiece that is her face. "Was there something in my teeth? I hope you would tell me if there was something in my teeth."

"Of course, I would." Since she's so serious, I can't give in to the humor bubbling in my chest as I watch her step into the narrow space to look at her reflection in the stainless steel refrigerator. "There's nothing in your teeth, Selene."

She straightens and crosses her arms. "Then why were you looking at me, Cal?"

I gave her permission to call me by the shortened version of my given name weeks ago, but she hasn't used it since. Hearing it pass through her lips now, when we're alone and she's close enough to touch, adds a weight to this moment, turning it into something that should be commemorated by truth.

They're there on my tongue. The words I can't give her. And I swallow them whole, banishing the speech that would tell her I was staring because I couldn't bring myself to look away, because I was trying to decipher how many shades of brown there are in her irises and if there's some joy beneath the sadness that washes out everything else most of the time.

Selene watches me do it. Her expression calm and patient, her eyes unblinking even as I taint this precious moment with a lie.

"Because I was trying to make sure you weren't still shaken up by what happened yesterday on the way to the rally."

I take a sip of my coffee to wash away the bitterness of dishonesty, and she smiles.

"Oh. I'm fine." She reaches up and tucks a strand of hair behind her ear. It's got a slight wave and puffiness to it, like her natural curl pattern is starting to stage a rebellion. "I meant to thank you and Agent Beckham for keeping me calm and safe."

Another sip of coffee, this time to quell the urge to dedicate my life, and Beck's too, to doing exactly that until she takes her final breath. The liquid burns its way down my throat, searing the vow to my flesh.

"You don't need to thank us," I tell her. "We were only doing what we're supposed to do."

"Right," she says, her head bobbing up and down. "Well, you're both exceptional at your jobs."

I don't know how to accept a compliment based on the execution of duty when I'm talking about obligations of the heart, so I don't. The silence that follows only lasts for half a second before Selene speaks again.

"I was surprised by how...kind Agent Beckham was in that moment. He's typically very impatient when it comes to me."

"Beck's impatient when it comes to most people, but he knows how to dial it back sometimes."

"I don't think he likes me very much."

"I'm sure that's not true."

"You're just being diplomatic."

I chuckle. "No, I just know Beck well, which means I know he can be standoffish and little bit of an asshole sometimes, but I also know that he has a good heart. He's just lost a lot in his life, so he's hesitant to put it on display."

She twists her lips to the side, considering my words. "I suppose that makes sense. This isn't really a heart-first job, is it?"

"No, Selene, it isn't."

At least, it's not supposed to be.

18

SELENE

Cal has me draped across his lap.

My back is arched, the curve of my ribcage kissing the hard muscles of his thighs as he runs a callused palm over my ass. The first slap makes me gasp, and he chuckles darkly at the sound. I wish I could see his face, but the room is pitch black. All I have is the incendiary sensation of his touch, the intoxicating smoke and spice scent of him, and the desperate whimpers leaving my lips that are soon drowned out by the sound of his fingers dipping into my drenched sex.

He groans and leans down to plant a kiss on my back as I rock against his hand. My pussy is already spasming, the hot pressure of an impending release rolling down my spine.

"I'm going to come, Cal."

"Let go, sweetheart," another voice purrs into my ear as a new set of hands urges me up off of Cal's lap so they can palm my breasts, tweaking my nipples with a roughness that's in sync with the gentle push and pull of Cal's fingers moving in and out of me. "Let him know how good he's making you feel."

I reach for him blindly, fingers cupping the back of his skull, caressing the smooth skin that would have told me who he was if I hadn't already identified him by his voice. He allows me to pull him closer, drawing his lush lips into the crook of my neck where he bites down on gently.

"*Beck.*"

Cal's nickname for his partner is a broken moan that's part confusion and part delight. It leaves my throat in a low, shocked whisper and hits the air, greeting me as I move from the carnality of my dream to the cold loneliness of my empty bedroom.

"Seriously?" I throw an arm over my eyes as the flame of embarrassment heats my cheeks. It grows hotter when I squeeze my thighs together and feel the slickness gathered between them. The moment I acknowledge the moisture, my pulse starts to throb. A soft, incessant beating that's concentrated in the bundle of nerves begging for attention, for friction, for the version of my two sentries that only exists in my head.

With one arm still shielding me from the shame of my dream, I slip the other underneath the covers and spread my thighs. I gasp softly when my fingers glide through the evidence of my arousal and drag it up to my clit, circling it several times before allowing myself the pleasure of direct touch. The first swipe across the sensitive nub is like a bolt of lightning, striking hard and fast, forcing my back to bow and my legs to jerk. The second isn't as jarring, but it's just as delicious, and I know it won't take me long to finish what dream Cal and Beck started.

Seconds later, I'm digging my teeth into my arm to stifle the cries of satisfaction that are the last thing I hear before I fall into a deep, dreamless slumber.

THE NEXT MORNING, I wake feeling refreshed and in as good a mood as I've been since the launch of SafeSight. To my surprise, that good mood extends beyond the confines of my bedroom, persisting even as I enter the living area of our suite and find Aubrey at the dining table reading a newspaper. There's a spread set up behind him that's enough to feed a small army, which means the suite will be brimming with people shortly.

He doesn't look up as I move to the breakfast bar and begin fixing my plate, which is fine because he doesn't deserve to bask in a bit of my post-orgasm glow. Heat creeps up my neck as images from my dream rush through my mind in rapid flashes, and I bite down hard on the inside of my cheeks to dispel them.

"How did you sleep?" Aubrey asks, the sudden sound of his voice making me jump hard enough to send several of the grapes I'd just placed on my plate flying off. I spin around, a grimace on my lips, when I find him staring at me. His head tilted to the side like he's trying to figure something out. The question and the intensity of his gaze make something ugly and bitter bloom in my chest. It rattles against my ribs, making me squint as I try to determine what it is.

Discomfort.

Guilt.

Shame.

I square my shoulders, silently resolving to sort through those feelings once I'm alone again, as I raise my chin. "I slept great," I return, and then, since we're playing at cordiality, I add, "How about you?"

Aubrey rests his back against his seat and crosses his legs, stroking his chin. "Are you sure? No complaints about your mattress or the air conditioning? I know how restless you get when you're hot at night."

"Yes, I'm sure, Aubrey." I set my plate on the table and crouched down to pick up the runaway fruit. "I think I'm capable of accurately reporting the quality of my sleep."

He raises his hands in mock surrender. "Don't get all snappy with me. I was only asking because I thought I heard some noises coming from your room."

All of my muscles tense, rendering me motionless with a handful of grapes hovering over the empty trash can next to the breakfast bar. One endless second ticks by before I'm able to force myself back into action. I drop the grapes, and they land with dull thuds at the bottom of the trash.

"I don't know what you heard, but it wasn't me," I say evenly, turning back around to grab my plate. "I got a full night's rest, which means I'll be more than prepared to participate in whatever events you and Jordan have committed me to for the day."

Since I don't have access to my email, I've had to rely on direct or written communication from either Jordan or Aubrey to inform me about my day. I've insisted on weekly schedules, so I could have more time to prepare, but they've pushed back, stating that things are changing from minute to minute, so there's no point in making one. The lack of organization and consideration for my time is a constant source of agitation for me, which is probably why they continue to leave me in the dark.

Aubrey picks up his glass of water and takes a long sip, still eyeing me like I'm a puzzle piece he's trying to determine how and where to place. He takes a few sips and then sets it back down, making a show of keeping me waiting.

"We'll be in strategy meetings for the day, so you won't be needed."

A rush of relief washes over me, so sudden and intense that I almost smile at him. It fades quickly, though, once I realize that no campaign commitments plus no work for Culture Code means a day of boredom for me. Without another word to Aubrey, I return to my room and eat my breakfast at the small table in the corner that gives me a view of the park outside the hotel.

My phone buzzes with a text from Monique.

> Monique: Get off your phone, hoe!

> Selene: I wasn't on my phone until you texted me.

> Monique: But you had it near you, which means you were about to be on it, scrolling through those social media apps I told your ass to delete.

> Selene: I did delete them! Which is probably
> why I'm sitting here bored out of my mind.

Monique: Bored? I thought there was a tightly
packed itinerary that demanded your
attention and presence.

Taking a bite out of my chocolate croissant, I snort out a derivative laugh and type out my reply.

> Selene: Apparently not today. Aubrey said
> they're having strategy meetings, and I'm not
> needed.

Monique: No Aubrey. No campaign events.
No work responsibilities. I'm not seeing the
problem here.

> Selene: The problem is, I have nothing to do.

Monique: Selene, you're a grown woman with
free will. Go out and enjoy your day. Get a
massage, go shopping, rent out a theater,
and go see a movie.

Only one of those options sounds truly appealing to me, so I thank Monique for her suggestions and set a plan for an outing into motion.

An hour later, Aubrey's strategy meeting is well underway, and I'm walking out of the suite to meet Cal and Bec—Agent Beckham, in the hallway. My heart does this weird half-beat when I see that they're both dressed down, wearing dark jeans and well-fitting t-shirts that match the casual look of my white button-up, light-washed denim, and sneakers.

Almost like we're going on a date, my brain supplies giddily. I cringe at the thought, reminding myself that the two men in front of me have never given me any indication that they are interested in me romantically or otherwise. They have only ever been the picture of professionalism, and any lapse in their professional personas—such as the meal we shared in my office or the moment when Cal told me my only flaw was my love for Aubrey—was orchestrated and prompted by me. Frankly, it's concerning that I even need to be reminded of those facts, that I'm so lonely I'm having inappropriate dreams and projecting romantic feelings onto people who are paid to be around me.

The line of thought dampens my mood slightly, leaving me sullen and withdrawn as we navigate the streets of Madison, heading towards downtown, where my research has told me all the best shops are. When we arrive at the boutique I requested to visit first, I see that Agents Harris and Anderson are already there. They salute us from the inside of their car parked right in front of the store, watching as we head inside the store, which is empty save for the overzealous owner who begins to fawn all over us as soon as we enter.

"Please let me know if you need *anything*, Mrs. Taylor," she says, trailing my steps as I peruse the rack closest to the door. "If there's something you like that's not in your size, don't worry. I can have it altered and delivered to your hotel in twenty-four hours."

"That's very sweet, Dana. I will be sure to let you know."

She clasps her hands together, and the bangles on her arm jiggle as she bounces on her toes. "Oh, I'd just love it if you found something today that you'll want to wear while you're here in Madison. My customers would go crazy if they saw me tagged in one of your posts." She pauses and turns to Cal, who's standing closest to us. "She can tag me, right? I mean, I know I can't post anything saying she's here, but if she wears something from my store, I'll get some kind of credit online, right?"

Amusement swims in the pools of copper and brass that search my face for a clue as to what he's supposed to say, and I take pity on him by supplying my own answer.

"Of course, you'll be tagged. Would you mind grabbing your business card for me, so I can make sure I get your information exactly right if I need to post?"

Dana squeals. "Yes! I can absolutely do that. I just need to make a business card first."

We watch her disappear into the back of the store, and the room instantly feels calmer once she's gone. Cal even steps back, leaving me to browse the racks while he and Agent Beckham watch from their respective posts in the small space. By the time Dana is back—with a makeshift business card printed on regular paper, I have several pieces in my hand that I want to try on.

She takes them from me and nods approvingly. "You've picked some great pieces. Would you like to try them on?"

Since my sensory issues don't allow me to buy a piece of clothing without knowing exactly how the fabric lies and feels against my skin, I nod. "Yes, please."

"The fitting room is just through there." She tips her chin in the direction of a gauzy, lavender curtain to the right of the checkout area, which is where Agent Beckham is standing. "Come with me. I'll get you set up."

I follow her determined steps, but we both stop short when Agent Beckham steps into our path. His expression is severe but not unkind as he says, "I need to clear the area first."

Dana glances at me and then back at him, her brows folded in confusion. "But the other agents already cleared the store. There's no one back there. I would never put Mrs. Taylor in any danger, I swear."

"It's protocol, Dana," I explain, sparing her the speech I'm sure she was about to get because the last thing I need is Aubrey and Jordan on my ass because some young, white girl is crying on the internet about getting yelled at by a Black Secret Service agent on behalf of the most hated Black woman in America.

Dana nods as if she actually had a say in the matter. "Okay, that's fine. I guess."

I swear I catch Agent Beckham rolling his eyes at her as he turns to go through the curtain, but I can't be sure. It takes him all of five seconds to give the all clear, and less than that for Dana to hang all the pieces I chose in the dressing room and shut the door, giving me the illusion of being alone even though I can still hear her trying to pull Agent Beckham into conversation he clearly doesn't want to have. Dana's endless chatter and his reluctant hums of acknowledgment become the soundtrack to my outfit changes, making the process feel less harrowing.

Somewhere between the third and fourth piece, the energy in the boutique changes. I don't notice it at first, the stillness and the quiet that seems to take over, but then, as I'm standing in the dressing room in nothing but my bra and panties, I hear Cal's voice, loud and urgent.

"BECKHAM! GET EYES ON HER NOW!"

At first, I think the her in question is Dana, and I immediately begin questioning where she's gone and what she's doing, but then the door to my dressing room bursts open, and I'm not alone anymore. Agent Beckham slams the door closed behind him, and there's a moment where we just stare at each other. Onyx eyes slide down my frame, taking in the sheer lace of my bra and the thin lines of my thong that rest high on my hipbones. It's not a creepy, leering kind of study, but I wouldn't call it indifferent either.

I'm searching for a word to accurately describe it when Cal comes back on the comms, asking for confirmation that I'm safe. That seems to snap Agent Beckham out of his trance, and he turns towards the door to give me some belated semblance of privacy while he assures his partner that I'm fine.

"What's going on?" I ask, voice shaking as thoughts of the erratic cars and faceless bikers in Atlanta take over my mind. Fear rolls through my body, gripping me with long skeletal fingers that tighten when he glances at me, his face grim.

"Anderson and Harris heard gunshots. Get dressed, so we can move when it's time."

There's a command to his voice that all but forbids me from disobeying him, but I still can't bring myself to move. "Who's shooting? *Why* are they shooting?"

Are those bullets for me?

The silent inquiry steals all the breath from my lungs, meaning I'm not even able to gasp when the gunshots go from a distant concept to a reality that's far too close for comfort. Three loud pops pierce the air, and my body quakes with each one. I back myself into a corner, while my brain uses my terrified state to conjure more questions like: Is this how AJ felt when he heard those first shots echoing in the halls of the school we told him he'd be safe at? Did his heart stop beating altogether for just an instant and then kick into overdrive, sending adrenaline and cortisol through his system and forcing him into action? Or was he like me? Paralyzed, wishing like hell he could be anywhere else?

"He must have been so afraid," I murmur, covering my ears with my hands when the sound of gunfire and the constant stream of voices over the comms gets to be too much. My mind is racing, flitting between the present and the final moments of my son's life, and I'm mumbling incoherently, unable to understand or process anything that's not horror and pain.

"Mrs. Taylor," Agent Beckham calls, rounding on me with wild eyes. "You have to get dressed."

"I've never heard gunshots before, Beck."

Tears blur my vision, hiding his reaction to my use of his nickname, and I'm too afraid to care if it's inappropriate to call him that. "I don't think AJ had ever even seen a real gun before the day he died," I continue, my voice muffled in my ears. "*He must have been so scared.*" My heart squeezes, and my throat constricts. I'm crumbling under the weight of it, the thought of how wrong gunshots must have sounded in a space meant to hold laughter and the unique brand of hope associated with youth and forming friendships, of how wrong it sounds here, and Beck's voice is growing more urgent. His 'Mrs. Taylors' getting louder and louder until finally he shouts, "*SELENE!*"

The use of my first name jars me, pulling me out of my head just long enough to bring his face into focus. He's mere inches away from me, patience and calm radiating off of him in soft waves, even as evidence of the escalating situation outside fills the air. I hear one of the agents say that police are still eight minutes out as glass shatters somewhere in the store, and the small bit of solace I'd found in the sharp bite of Beck's tone when he said my name dissolves because now all I can see is my son laying face down in a pool of blood littered with the shattered glass of his classroom window.

A lot of the images and sounds I associate with AJ's death originate in my mind, but this one is real. I saw it with my own eyes when Aubrey secured me access to the crime scene photos. And my perfect recollection of every detail in the picture sends me to my knees with my lost child's name on my lips.

Beck sinks with me.

His hands are on my elbows so I don't go down too fast.

His long legs bracketing my body, offering support to my trembling form when it hits the floor.

His arms wrap around me, tentatively at first, and then more firmly when I don't pull away.

"Tighter," I beg, and I don't have the presence of mind to be embarrassed or ashamed at the need evident in my voice. "Squeeze me tighter, please."

He obliges without hesitation, using all of his strength to reset my overactive nervous system while he instructs me to breathe and tells me we'll be fine in the same deep, rough timbre he used in my dream. When I'm no longer struggling to breathe, he loosens his grip, but doesn't let me go.

"I had a son too," he says, the confession a delicate whisper against my temple that makes me afraid to breathe for fear that he won't say more. "I *lost* a son, too, in the most horrific way. I never got to know him, not like you got to know Aubrey, but I loved him. I still love him so much, it makes it hard to breathe. You know?"

"Yeah," I gasp, fresh tears falling from my eyes as I remember Cal's words on the plane about all the loss Beck has endured. "What was his name?"

"Cameron." His lips curve slightly, a result of a small, involuntary smile. "Diana." He swallows hard. "My wife. She, uh, she liked the name, pulled it out of some baby book, and never even considered another. She said it felt like him, so that's the name I put on his gravestone."

It doesn't escape my notice that he's using the past tense when talking about his wife, which suggests that she's also gone. And because he said he never got to know his son, I'm left with no choice but to believe he lost them at the same time.

"I'm so sorry, Beck. I wouldn't wish this pain on anyone."

He sighs and begins to pull away, signaling the end of this moment. I want to thank him for talking, for bearing a piece of his tattered soul in an attempt to soothe mine, but there's no space for gratitude in the quiet I hadn't even noticed settling around us.

"Is it over?" I ask, watching him push to his feet, taking his hands when he reaches for me. He pulls me up with little to no effort and nods.

"The cops just arrived on the scene. Cal, Anderson, and Harris apprehended the suspects. They're giving their statements now. Get dressed, so we can get you back home."

I'm so out of sorts, so shocked by what we've just shared and impressed by his ability to be present with me while actively collecting the pertinent details of what was happening with his teammates that I don't even think to argue with him. I just slip back into my clothes and follow him out of the dressing room, allowing him to guide me through the empty store with his fingers linked in mine.

19

***

BECK

Selene's palm is soft, and her fingers are long and elegant, gripping me like I'm a lifeline she doesn't want to let go of. I'm considering what it might be like to continue to hold on to her when Cal meets us at the front door of the boutique. I do a quick sweep of his body, making sure he's unharmed, while he stares questioningly at the link between me and the woman that's going to ruin us both.

"Ready?" he asks with raised brows and humor-filled eyes.

"Yep."

I should let Selene go. I whisper the words to myself a million times on the short trek from the door of the boutique to the door of the car, which I open with one hand to prolong the contact between us, but I don't let go until I have to. She slips into the backseat and *smiles at me.* It's not a full-blown, mega-watt grin; she doesn't really do those, but it is a gentle curving of her lips that's filled with gratitude.

"Thank you, Beck."

Unable to speak, I dip my chin and close the door, allowing the dizzying wave of relief that comes with putting a barrier between her and the dangers of the world to wash over me while Cal stands a few feet away with a slack jaw.

"Beck? Since when does she call you Beck?"

"Shut up, Drake," I grumble, pulling open the passenger door and climbing inside. His eyes are still laughing at me when he gets behind the wheel, and I make a show of ignoring him, focusing instead on trying to gauge Selene's mood through the rear-view mirror. I see her and Cal share glances in it sometimes, and I spend the duration of the ride back to the hotel hoping for the same thing.

It never happens.

She stays quiet and keeps her eyes focused on her hands, never once looking up, not even when Cal explains that the gunshots were a result of a bank robbery gone wrong and had nothing to do with her. I thought that information would give her some comfort, especially since she's been so anxious about the increase in online threats, but she barely reacts to it.

I try not to take the withdrawal personally, especially because I know how unnerving the trauma we just experienced can be, but it does feel personal. Everything with her feels personal, and I'm kicking myself for only just now realizing it. For spending weeks trying to reel Cal in without acknowledging that I fell into the water right along with him. Once again, we're side by side, swimming in a sea of trouble, wading into forbidden waters with linked hands and interwoven hearts. It feels just like it did when we first started, when Cal kissed me and my whole life changed.

The thought of my world changing again, especially in a way that can never happen and would upend everything we've worked so hard for if it did, scares the shit out of me.

Hours later, when we've fully debriefed Hicks on the incident, filled out all of the requisite paperwork and handed the responsibility of Selene's safety off to someone else, I'm in my room alone. Cal wanted to hang out, but I put him off, knowing he'd convince me to divulge every detail of my time with Selene before I even had a chance to process it for myself.

I planned to process it, to dig into what it meant for me to be so affected by Selene's pain, for me to talk about Cameron and Diana to her when I haven't spoken about them to anyone but Cal and

Erin, Diana's mom, in years. Still, I got afraid of acknowledging the obvious truth and decided to hide at work instead. I hoped that working would stop me from thinking about Selene, but my work is all centered around her, so it just places her at the front of my mind.

Sighing, I close my computer and throw myself back on the pillows of my bed. I'm seconds away from breaking down and calling Cal to see if he wants to go out for a late dinner when my phone rings. I smile as I pick it up off the nightstand, thinking it's him reading my mind in that odd way he does, and then groan out loud when I see my mother-in-law's name displayed on the screen instead.

Guilt, inspired by my unfair reaction, blooms in the pit of my stomach. Erin doesn't deserve my apathy, especially when I'm the asshole who forgot to call her on the anniversary of her only child's death. Now that Diana is gone, I'm the only family she has, and I do a shit job of taking care of her, of being there for her, of reaching out and holding space for her feelings about the most significant loss of her life.

And despite all of that, she still loves me.

I can hear it in her voice when I answer the phone.

"Lance! How are you doing, sweetheart?"

My eyes fell shut at the deep, rasping lilt she passed down to her daughter. The first time I heard Diana speak, I was captivated by it, certain I didn't want to go another day without her throaty laugh or the breathless huskiness that made it sound like she smoked a pack a day even though she hated the smell of cigarette smoke.

Some days I wish I'd never heard it. That the correspondence surrounding the foundation she was tasked with running after my parents' death had happened over email instead of over the phone, and then—because I had to put a face to the stunning voice that rivaled the depth and timbre of my own—in person. If we'd never met, if we'd never fallen in love, if I'd never asked her to marry me, she'd still be here and Erin wouldn't be stuck with me.

"Hello? Lance? Did I lose you, baby?"

There's shuffling on her end that suggests she's pulled the phone away from her face to make sure the call is still connected, which makes me smile. "No, ma'am, I'm here."

"Thank goodness. I thought I had put it on mute again. You know us old ladies don't know how to work technology."

"Now, Erin, you know you're still getting carded at the bars. Ain't nothing old about you."

She sucks her teeth. "Lance, please. I can't tell you the last time I set foot in a bar, let alone had to show my ID for a drink. I'm old, and I know it, so don't go trying to convince me I'm a spring chicken."

This is as close as she ever gets to scolding me. In all the years that I've known her, I've never heard her raise her voice, never seen her speak a hateful word to anyone. Not even to me when I called and told her Diana was gone and it was all my fault. She dropped everything she was doing and got on a flight, stayed with me for weeks, held me when I cried, forced me to pour the bottle of liquor I was drowning my sorrows in down the sink. She even came back for Valinsky's trial, held my hand through every testimony, and acted as my visual touchstone when I had to take the stand.

She is every good thing her daughter was and my son would have been, and I don't deserve her. That knowledge threatens to cave my throat in, to stop the apology I owe her from being heard.

"I'm sorry I didn't call."

I don't try to offer an excuse because there are none. I can't bring Diana back, can't take away the years that grief has swallowed up, can't fill in the hole her loss has left in both of our lives, but I can call. I *should* call.

"Oh, honey, please." I can practically see her pursing her lips and swiping a dismissive hand through the air. "I don't need a phone call to prove to me that you carry her with you every single day." My eyes burn with tears I don't allow to fall. "Besides," she continues, "I know you're busy guarding the President."

The confidence with which she delivers that misinformed statement pulls a reluctant laugh out of me. "I'm not guarding the President."

"Might as well be. Everybody knows the Taylor boy is going to win the election. President Sanders is too damn old to be trying to go for another term. He don't look like he got four more years left to live, let alone to work. Watch and see, Lance, that man is going to the White House, and he's taking you with him."

A day ago, a proclamation like that would have spoken to every hope and dream I've had for myself and Cal over the last four years, but today it gives me pause. It makes me think about Selene, the complexities of our rapidly developing situation, and the likelihood of Aubrey keeping either of us around if he finds out how we feel about his wife.

How __we__ feel.

The words ring in my head, and I have no choice but to sit with them. To acknowledge their presence and the truth they tell. To wonder when I went from warning Cal to guard his heart against Selene to opening up mine.

I rub at the notch forming between my brows and sigh. "If you say so."

"I do," she pauses, and I know we're about to transition into the part of the conversation that feels more like an interrogation. "You sound tired. Are you getting enough sleep?"

"Yes, ma'am," I lie.

"Eating well?"

"Of course."

"Drinking your water?"

An exasperated chuckle passes my lips as my heart swells with love for her. "Yes, I'm drinking my water, brushing my teeth after every meal, stretching every night, and taking all my vitamins. I'm taking care of myself. I promise."

"Mhm hmmm," she hums skeptically. "You know I'll be able to tell if you're lying when you come home for Christmas, right?"

We never formally agreed to spend the holidays together. It's just something that happened. A tradition forged in mutual despair and need. It was easier to get the holidays off when I was still at the Bureau, but it's more challenging now. She knows this, but she still acts like my presence is a sure thing. I guess it's her way of staving off the threat of loneliness until she has to accept it. And because I owe her hope, I always play into her innocent delusion.

"I know you will, which is why it's a good thing I'm telling the truth."

"Are you coming alone this year?"

"Who else would I come with?" I ask, wondering if this is the start of what is sure to be an uncomfortable conversation about my love life. I've never mentioned any of the women I've dated to her, mainly because it's never been anything serious, and she's never asked. I've always just assumed she didn't want to know, didn't want to think about someone taking Diana's place in my bed and in my heart.

"I don't know," she hedges. "Maybe your special someone."

"My special someone? What makes you think I have a special someone?"

It's as close as I can get to a denial. Saying I don't have someone special in my life would fly in the face of everything Cal is to me, but confirming her suspicion would open up the door to questions I don't know how to answer. Not because I'm not sure how I feel about Cal, but because I'm not sure how Erin will feel about me confessing to being in love with a man she's only known as my best friend and partner.

I don't think she'd bat an eye at me being with a man—she's surprisingly open-minded for an older, Southern woman who was raised in the church—but the thought of her knowing about Cal still gives me pause. Still scares me. Still makes me wonder if she'll look at me the same if I say I loved Diana with everything in me, but I know my soul was forged at the same time as Callan Drake's.

If I have to explain that, I'm currently trying to figure out where the future First Lady of the United States of America fits into that equation.

"Mothers have their ways, Lance," she tells me, pulling me out of my spiraling thoughts. "I knew about you before Diana even told me your name. Don't think you're exempt from that just because we only see each other a few times a year."

"Oh, I wouldn't dare doubt your abilities."

She tsks her disapproval at my obvious sarcasm. "Don't patronize me, boy. Am I preparing my house for you and a guest or not?"

I try to picture it, bringing Cal to Diana's childhood home with me. His hand in mine, the truth of what we feel for each other in our eyes. I want that. I want it more than anything, but I'm just not sure I'll ever be able to have it.

"No," I say finally, letting the image fade away. "It'll just be you and me."

20

SELENE

Monique and Nichelle's squeals of delight threaten to burst my eardrums. They're so shrill and go on for so long that I have to mute the sound on my computer and massage my temples to stave off the headache I'm sure they've just activated.

When I'm certain my head won't explode, I turn the volume back up so I can hear what Monique is saying, which has Nichelle nodding so enthusiastically.

"I had to mute you, so I missed part of that," I cut in. "Can you please start over? And at a normal volume this time."

"Silencing a Black woman is crazy," Monique complains.

"I'm not trying to silence you, heffa. I'm just trying to walk away from this call with my hearing intact."

"Anywaysssss," she drawls, rolling her neck for dramatic emphasis. "I was saying that you've had a crazy week. First, you survive a shoot-out, and now you're about to be giving a TED talk!!!"

News of the bank robbery broke a few days ago, turning Aubrey's rally in Madison into a public spectacle that brought out the entire city and seemingly every news crew in the state. Everyone was desperate for a glimpse of me, conducting visual inspections of my body for any proof of the incident and coming up empty. Apparently, some folks, mostly Aubrey's new supporters who despise me for existing, were disappointed that I wasn't walking around with a gunshot wound. They turned to social media to express those feelings, even going as far as to speculate that my proximity to the robbery was a lie, some hoax to garner public sympathy and put a stop to the death threats.

As if I would ever expect a nation founded on racism and misogynoir to be moved by the thought of a Black woman being in imminent danger. They thirst for our tears, gorge themselves on our pain. They want nothing more than to see us humbled by violence, destroyed by hate, erased and abused. A society like this? People like that? They wouldn't even know how to begin to feel sympathy for me because that would mean seeing me as human, and all I have ever been to them is expendable.

"It wasn't a shoot-out, Mo."

"There were guns and bullets, Sel. It was a shoot-out."

"But enough about that!" Nichelle says, stopping us before we get caught up in a pointless back-and-forth. "Let's focus on more positive things, like this exciting email from the TEDWomen team!"

The email is the entire reason for this impromptu video call, and it feels like a beacon of light, breaking through the dark cloud that has been hanging over my head for days. At first, I thought I was fine. I even managed to smile and thank Beck for getting me through the whole ordeal, but once I got in the car, I felt myself shutting down. Retreating into the silo of my anxious mind, wondering if any of this —the campaign, the election, the White House, my First Lady initiative, Aubrey's campaign promises and this farce of a marriage—is worth what I might be giving up to have it.

I had a taste of it, all of the things I could be missing, when I was in Beck's arms on the floor of the dressing room. And although the presentation was new, the preparation different, the flavor of the dish was familiar on my tongue. I'd sampled it before in the quiet, rare moments I spent alone with Cal.

Care.

Compassion.

Empathy.

Basic ingredients of human interaction that I've been starved of for so long, that I've agreed to live without. And for what? To stay attached to Aubrey?

To honor AJ.

The voice in my head supplies, dousing every scrap of my doubt in gasoline and striking a match. The fire warms my skin, and I breathe in deeply, pulling in lungfuls of self-loathing and smoke as ash rains down on my head.

"Sel? You good?" Monique asks.

I split a forced smile between her and Nichelle. "Yes, let's focus on the email."

Nichelle shares her screen, displaying the email that was sent directly to my inbox, which I haven't been allowed to check in what feels like forever. "Alright, essentially, they're asking if you would be interested in giving a talk in Houston. As you know, the topic is up to your discretion, but they would love it if you could tie in some points about the coding academy. They'd want to see an outline of the talk beforehand, but it'll be up to you what makes the final cut."

"That all sounds good."

Giving a TED talk has been a dream of mine for as long as I can remember. The thought of being able to check this item off my professional bucket list has my leg shaking with anticipation. I'm already formulating my talking points when Monique chimes in with a question I didn't think to ask.

"When is the Houston event?"

Nichelle scrolls to the bottom of the email, using her mouse to highlight the date that is underlined and capitalized: JANUARY 27, 2025. My heart sinks, and Monique curses.

"Why the fuck would they ask you to speak at an event that's a week after Inauguration Day?"

"Maybe they think Aubrey won't—" Nichelle folds the rest of her sentence between her lips, and I don't know whether to laugh or cry at the thought of Aubrey losing the election. "Forget I said that," she murmurs. "I'm sure they're just as hopeful for a Taylor presidency as we all are."

Monique pulls a face but keeps whatever disparaging comments swirling around in her head about Aubrey to herself. "Email them back, Nichelle. Ask if they can move the date of the event."

"We can't ask them to do that."

"Why the hell not? They came to you, Selene, which means they should be willing to accommodate your needs. On January 27th, you'll either need to be settling into your role as the First Lady of the United States, or, God forbid, hiding from the world and tending to Aubrey's wounds while President Sanders starts his second term."

She shudders at the thought of me comforting Aubrey, which only serves to remind me that we're doing such a good job of selling the lie of reconciliation that even my best friend believes it. Everyone does. When my mama called to check on me after the boutique incident, she ended the call by saying she was glad to see that we found our way through such a trying time.

This lie is so isolating, and the act I volunteered to put on for the world has already cost me so much. I'm not the least bit surprised that it's going to cost me a TED talk.

"Tell them no, Nichelle."

"Selene, don't be stupid," Monique growls, leaning closer to the camera. "You've wanted this for so long. We're not going to let a damn scheduling conflict stop you from having it."

"I'm not being stupid, Mo. I'm being realistic. If the opportunity came around once, it will come around again." Pulling my gaze away from the square on the screen vibrating with my best friend's disappointment, I focus the last bit of energy I have for this call on Nichelle. "Keep the email brief. Decline the invitation and make sure you let them know how much I appreciate them thinking of me."

Monique's disappointment is palpable, and it clings to me when I end the call without waiting for Nichelle to acknowledge the directive. She's right to be disappointed in me. I'm disappointed in myself. I admit that to myself as I climb into bed and pull the covers back over my body. I've been hiding out in here for the last twenty-four hours, refusing to do anything besides play games on my phone I know I need to delete because I've resorted to spending actual money to purchase virtual coins that can be redeemed for extra lives and special tools that make it easier to beat more difficult levels.

My thumb is poised against the button on the side of my phone, ready to double click to make yet another ill-advised purchase when a text from Monique pops up at the top of my screen. Sighing, I open our message thread and prepare myself for another argument. Honestly, I'm surprised it's taken her so long to reach out. It's been hours since I abruptly ended our video chat with Nichelle, and she's usually so much quicker about letting me know how much of an asshole I am.

The text isn't long, just a few lines. The first of which includes the phrase 'stupid bitch' and makes me smile.

> Monique: If you think I'd let you give up on this dream, you're one stupid bitch. The TED team agreed to let you pre-record your speech. You'll do it at the event space in Houston for continuity's sake. They'll have it ready to go in 48 hours. Aubrey and Jordan have already been notified. You're welcome.

A mixture of emotions flows through me, and I take a slow, deep breath, then release it as I identify each one. There's excitement, of course, a little bit of shame at having given up so easily, and finally, an overwhelming kind of love for my best friend that my two-word response doesn't even begin to convey.

> Selene: Thank you.

LESS THAN TWENTY-FOUR HOURS LATER, I'm walking into a spacious, two-story farmhouse in the heart of Houston and listening to Cal and Beck grumble about me being the first person in the house as they bring our luggage in from the car.

"I promise I'll let you clear every room in the house before I go any further." I hold up my hand, trying to look repentant but failing miserably because I can't stop smiling. Being away from Aubrey and knowing that tomorrow I'll be fulfilling one of my lifelong dreams has done wonders for my mood. It also doesn't hurt that my travel companions are the only two people this campaign has brought into my life that I trust.

Usually, we'd have more members of the team with us, but before we left this morning, Aubrey informed me that Harris and Anderson would be staying with him to fill in for two of the men on his detail that came down with food poisoning. He was oddly giddy about delivering the news, probably hoping that having less security would deter me from going. Still, I just smiled and said okay, which only annoyed him more. He left the room after that, only emerging when Cal and Beck showed up to escort me to the car, sending us off with a comment about being sure they would take good care of me.

Neither man seemed to doubt the truth of that statement until we arrived in Houston, and I revealed that we wouldn't be staying at the hotel Jordan's assistant had booked for us. Now, they seem different, not less confident, per se, but on edge and maybe a little mad?

Cal places his bag by the door, and Beck drops his beside it. My suitcase and the matching duffel on top of it are lodged between their bodies. Both of them have a hand on the handle like they're ready to grab it, and me, and bail at any second.

"Remind me again why we're not staying at the hotel with a dedicated security team and a police station two streets over." This comes from Beck, who is doing his best to suppress the agitation weaving itself through each word.

There's still a tenuousness to our dynamic that makes me uncertain about how to interact with him. I know he takes his job very seriously, that he's a stickler for protocol and doing things by the book. I don't think there's anything I can say that will make him okay with this, so I don't bother with a lie.

"Because I'm tired of hotels," I say simply, which makes the corners of Cal's mouth quirk.

He attempts to hide his amusement with a swipe of his hand down his face. "I get that, Selene, but the hotel is exponentially safer than a home we haven't had a chance to secure that's owned by someone we haven't vetted."

Beck's head bobs up and down, the sunlight filtering through the window bouncing off the smooth skin of his scalp. "Exactly. There could be any number of cameras, listening devices, or—"

"There aren't."

His eyes narrow at my interruption. "You can't know that for sure."

"Yes, I can." I shrug off my backpack and set it in one of the chairs around the massive dining table that separates the living room from the kitchen. Both men watch me warily as I round the couch and plop down. As I make myself comfortable, I glance over at them, taking in their rigid forms. "Will you two please sit down? I promise no one is going to jump out and attack us, okay? This house belongs to one of my professors from Stanford. It's been in her family for years, and she keeps it up even though she hasn't been to Texas in years. I trust her implicitly."

A fact Monique is aware of, which is why she had Nichelle reach out to Dr. Tia Bloom the moment she decided I was going to do this talk, whether I wanted to or not.

"Honestly," I continue, "I should be offended that you two think I'd be careless with my own safety, but I'm too tired to care." My eyes fall shut on their own accord, but I can still feel their piercing gazes on my skin. I roll my neck in their direction, squinting at them through one eye. "Nothing you say is going to convince me to spend another night in a hotel before I absolutely have to, so you might as well do whatever it is you need to in order to feel comfortable sleeping here."

I don't know how long it takes them to secure the house, but I keep my promise and stay put until they're done. They return to the living room looking a little less stressed and, to my surprise and delight, sit down in the armchairs across from me.

"All clear?"

"All clear," they say in unison.

Once settled in his seat, Cal stretches his long legs out in front of him, linking his fingers together and resting them on his stomach. Beck remains upright, his arms crossed over his chest. Both of them are dressed down today, wearing nondescript athletic wear. Beck is wearing a black sweatsuit, and Cal is dressed in a pair of dark gray joggers with a matching moisture-wicking shirt that showcases his biceps. They both seem so human outside the armor of those black suits and the context of the world that brought us together, and I feel human too. And it's not just because I'm wearing yoga pants and the oversized Stanford hoodie I've owned for decades.

No, it's more than that.

It's my imperfect posture and my messy ponytail.

It's my bouncing knee and the absence of the desire to hide the stim.

It's my flat expression, and my quiet brain that, for once, isn't screaming at me to emote before the people I'm sharing space with start to think I'm a sociopath.

It's the comfort of silence I don't have to fill, and the intimacy of being allowed to simply exist, to just be a woman relaxing on a couch in a room with two incredibly handsome men who can't take their eyes off of her.

Suddenly, I'm incredibly aware of the fact that it's just us here.

Me and the only humans on Earth I've ever had a sex dream about.

21

CAL

Selene rises from her seat abruptly.

"I should get some work done," she announces, grabbing her bag from spot where she left it and heading towards the hallway to her right, which leads to a home office. Just before she cuts the corner, she stops. "Monique had groceries delivered. Please help yourself to whatever you like."

And then she's gone, rushing off with her shoulders raised and wracked with tension.

"Is she okay?" Beck asks, glancing at me like I have a fucking clue what just happened.

"I don't know."

"Should we go after her?"

That he even considers that an option makes me smile. I have to hide it, though, since he's still reluctant to talk to me about whatever it is that's developing between them. I know he'll bring me into the loop eventually, and I'm trying to be patient, but it's been hell waiting to find out where his head and his heart are at.

I push to my feet. "No. We should call Hicks and let him know the situation has changed and do another perimeter check."

Beck stands, too. "Divide and conquer?"

"Let me guess, you'll do the perimeter sweep while I call and update Hicks?"

"Precisely." He claps me on the shoulder twice before stepping around me and heading out the front door. I dig my phone out of my pocket and dial our supervisor, already knowing he won't be happy with this development. As much as I like the thought of time with Selene where outsiders are not constantly monitoring us, I'm not psyched at her choice of accommodations either. The house is lovely, don't get me wrong, but the property is far too big for Beck and I to effectively monitor on our own. We'll have to sleep in shifts and pray the lack of rest doesn't impede our ability to keep Selene safe.

"This is Hicks."

Ready to get the inevitable reaming over and one with, I explain what's going on in short, succinct sentences that leave no room for misinterpretation or confusion. When I'm done, he groans.

"Are you fucking kidding me?"

"I wish I were."

"So now I have to go and tell Mr. Taylor that his wife of twenty some odd years has run roughshod over not one, but two, Secret Service agents and convinced them to take her to an unsecured location despite their training, and common fucking sense, telling them that was a bad idea?"

"All due respect, sir, what you tell Mr. Taylor is none of my concern. Beck and I have been entrusted with Mrs. Taylor's safety, which means we go where she goes. She's here, so we're here. That's the situation."

"Well it's a shitty situation, Drake, and I can guarantee you there will be hell to pay if anything goes wrong."

"Less chance of that happening if you send us two more bodies. Travel protocol mandates at least four agents—"

"I know what the fucking protocol is, Cal," he barks, slicing my sentence in half. "Just like I know you heard me when I said Ortega and Bennett are down. Any good agent knows that when resources are spread thin, you prioritize the primary. Correct me if I'm wrong, but that would be the man currently running for the office of President of the United States, wouldn't it?"

There it is again. That insinuation that Selene's life is less important than Aubrey's, even though she's the one under constant threat. That's a casual justification for playing fast and loose with a Black woman's life. Beck probably thought I would do a better job of keeping my cool when faced with Hicks' bullshit, but my patience for this man and this conversation is a rapidly unraveling thread.

My nostrils flare as I push out a frustrated breath. "Correct me if I'm wrong, Dan, but if anything goes left while we're out here, that would not only reflect badly on Beck and me but you and the rest of the unit as well, wouldn't it? Tell me, how likely do you think Mr. Taylor is to select you to run his Presidential detail if his wife is injured or killed because you sat around playing with your dick instead of *getting me some fucking back up*?"

The last part of my sentence is a growl that I deliver through clenched teeth. Hicks' side of the line is silent for a second, and I'm certain if I could see him right now his face, neck and even the lobes of his ears would be red. That's how he always looks when Beck takes him to task, and I smile at the thought of getting the same reaction from him.

After a full minute, he sighs. "I'll put a call into the local PD and see if they can send some uniforms over to assist."

"Six for day shift, six for night shift."

"Four for day shift, two for night shift."

It's not enough, but it's better than nothing. At the very least, we'll be able to focus on the interior of the house while putting the officers in charge of exterior security. In the morning, we'll have one team from the day shift secure the venue where Selene is recording her speech, while the other team tails us when we leave.

"Fine. We need them here as soon as possible, Hicks."

He grumbles something about me thinking I'm his boss under his breath and then hangs up the phone, leaving me with no choice but to hope he'll keep his word.

Beck comes back into the house via the back door while I'm rummaging through the fridge to figure out something for dinner.

"All good?"

He crosses over to the sink and washes his hands. "Yep. All exterior doors are locked. The windows on the ground floor are closed and secure. The back gate is latched. I did see a snake near the back patio, though."

"A rattlesnake?" I ask, turning around with all the ingredients for a simple pasta dish clutched to my chest. Beck, who knows about my fear of snakes and, more specifically, rattlesnakes, nods and gives me an impish grin as I set them on the counter. My eyes narrow as I study his expression. "You're lying," I declare finally.

He throws the towel he was using to dry his hands down. "Damn! I hate how good you are at that."

"Maybe you should hate how bad you are at lying," I muse, crouching down to pull the cutting board I saw earlier out of one of the cabinets underneath the expansive marble countertop of the island. When I rise, I'm greeted by his middle finger.

"Fucker," he says.

I pull a knife from the block next to the gas range and slice open the package of crimini mushrooms, shrugging off his insult. He rests his elbows on the counter. "You're not even going to try to deny it?"

"What's the point? You know I'm a fucker. I know I'm a fucker." My eyes meet his, and my voice drops down low. "You like how I fuck you."

His lips part, and his brows shoot up in surprise. I chuckle, admiring the effect my words have on him and appreciating that he doesn't immediately tense up or turn around to check and see if anyone heard me, even though he knows Selene is in the house.

Almost like he doesn't care if she learns the truth about us.

Almost like he's accepted that our feelings for her and each other could very well make that a question of when and not if.

Beck clears his throat. "How did the call with Hicks go?"

For some reason, the change in subject doesn't bother me as much as it usually does. I recount the details of the call for him as I rinse the mushrooms, and he vents about Hicks while I pat them dry with a paper towel. Listening to Beck talk is probably one of my favorite things to do while I'm cooking. His passion and candor make the process feel like it's going faster, and when he jumps in and helps, it does.

"It's like they don't care if she lives or dies," he's saying now, watching the faucet tied into the tile above the stove gush water into the stainless steel pot on the back eye. "She deserves so much better."

The shift in his attitude regarding Selene since the last time we cooked a meal together is so drastic, so poignant, I can't stop myself from diving headlong into a topic we've been tiptoeing around for days.

"She has better. She has us."

He cuts the water off and turns the dial up to its highest setting. He's always so impatient when it comes to waiting for water to boil. I want to tease him about that, but now isn't the time. Aside from the soft sizzle of the mushrooms browning in the pan in front of me, there's not a single sound in the kitchen. Beck's avoidance is loud in the face of that silence, and so is his resigned sigh when he turns to face me head-on.

I study him more closely than I did earlier when he was lying about the snake. I can always read him easily, but he tries to block me, to erect walls in the onyx pools of his eyes. I reach for him, linking our fingers together.

"Can we please talk about it?"

"What's the point?"

The swell of love that blooms in my chest when he doesn't act like he has no idea what I'm talking about is the point. Confirmation that I'm not losing my mind is the point. Assurance that whether I act on them or not, my feelings for Selene won't cause a permanent rift between me and the man I love is the point.

I don't say any of that because it all feels too serious, and if things get any more serious, then Beck will get scared and shut down. Instead, I offer him a lifeline in the form of levity and a bad French accent.

"Folie à deux."

A shared delusion. A mutual agreement to indulge in the madness of possibility. An aching, forbidden echo whose weight is balanced between his hand and mine.

Beck snorts. "That's a great way to put it because we both have to be experiencing a break from reality if we think we have real feelings for her, if we think, for even a second, she would want one, let alone both of us."

The word both sparks a hunger inside of me that won't be touched by the food we're preparing. "You would want to share?"

His pupils dilate slightly, and he's nodding his head before he can stop himself. He drops my hand, taking a step back as if a few feet between us will make the desire swirling around us less potent.

Long fingers glide over his scalp and down his neck, gripping his nape tightly. "*What I want* is for you to stop acting like there is a single scenario where this thing between us and her happens."

"So, you *do* have feelings for her."

"Oh for fuck's sake, Cal," he hisses. "Do you need to hear me say it?"

My answer is immediate. "Yes."

Beck closes the distance between us with angry strides and places both of his hands on my shoulders. "You were right about her, okay? She's not at all what she seems. There's a softness and a strength to her that makes it impossible for you to want to experience anything that's not her. And she's so fucking smart," he pauses just to smile like he's disgusted with himself. "I could listen to her talk about coding and social justice and the implications of living in an increasingly technological world every day, all day, and never get bored."

"Me too," I admit, knowing that feeling all too well. I knew I was in love with him when I started reading the DSM-5, so that I could have a better understanding of the mental disorders he was always going on about. My first clue that I was fucked on the Selene front was the in depth research I did on autism, consuming everything I could about stimming, masking and low support needs versus high support needs in the span of a night.

"But that's not a good thing, Cal! Holding her hand in public is not a good thing. Cradling her half-naked form in your arms when your training tells you to always have one hand free and ready to access your weapon, and there's an active threat, isn't a good thing. Staying in a house alone with her isn't a good thing."

His logic is sound. I should be agreeing with him, or at the very least, telling him I appreciate the points he's just made, but I can't because my brain is stuck on something he's said.

"That's what happened in the dressing room? You held her?"

I wait for jealousy or bitterness to sweep in at the thought of the two of them wrapped in an embrace, but it doesn't come. All I feel is grateful that Beck was there for Selene in a moment when she was clearly in need.

"She was scared." He grimaces as the memory assails him. "She kept talking about how loud the gunshots were and calling her son's name, saying he must have been scared when he heard them the day he died. I couldn't bear to see her in that kind of pain." He searches my features for understanding. "I didn't have a choice."

"Of course, you didn't. She needed you. You set everything aside to be there for her."

"And I would do it again, without question."

"I know, so would I."

The snap of his fingers is loud, but the vast, accusatory stretch of his eyes is more audible. "That's the problem, Drake. Selene doesn't need us to set everything aside for her, to be everything to her. She needs us to do our jobs and do them well, and if we can't do that, then we both need to walk away."

My heart twists in on itself at the mere thought of moving in any direction that differs from the path she's traveling. "If we walk away, she'll have no one."

"If we continue to guard her with our hearts and not our heads, then she'll end up dead. Trust me when I say there's no amount of love, no depth of emotion that will make you okay with that kind of failure."

There's a grave certainty to his tone that brooks no argument, and

I know exactly where it comes from. That knowledge makes it so that the only thing I can do is nod solemnly.

"You're right."

A sad smile tugs at his lips. "I know."

And just like that, the promise is made, and everything we've ever felt for Selene shrinks in on itself, another torrid secret trapped between Beck's heart and mine.

A flower stomped out before it ever had the chance to bloom.

22

BECK

Growing up in the foster care system meant constant lies and broken promises. Promises to be a real family. Promises that the father with the harsh glint in his eyes and the beer in his hand won't get drunk and beat you within an inch of your life. Promises that the hand-me-downs and shared room and pallet of blankets on the floor that serve as your bed are just temporary.

Promises made.

Promises broken.

Promises, promises, promises.

I got to the point where I automatically became skeptical of anyone who uttered the word because I knew that, eventually, their actions would reveal their words as the falsities I already knew them to be. That only changed when Cal became a part of my life. I never knew anyone as steadfast and committed to doing what they said they would do when they said they would do it until him. It didn't take me long to realize that his dedication to making his word his bond stemmed from the stream of broken promises and half-truths his father fed him as a child.

Something about knowing the dark, broken place where this part of his personality was born made me inclined to take him at his word, and I haven't once regretted it because Callan Drake has never made me a promise he didn't intend to keep.

Until Selene Taylor.

Before I allowed myself to acknowledge the feelings I have for her, I was angry with him for not being able to keep his word regarding her. But now I'm intimately familiar with the magnetic pull of her, and I can't keep my word either. I promised myself that I wouldn't let us end up eating the dinner Cal made with her at the dining table because the low lighting, the simple yet decadent dish, and the quiet conversation would feel too much like the thing we both want but can't have.

But here I am, with Cal to my right and Selene across from me, watching her gather bucatini noodles covered in a creamy mushroom-based sauce on her fork with delicate twirls of her wrist. Cal and I are both staring, but she doesn't notice because her eyes are closed as she brings the first bite of food to her mouth. She hums softly when her lips close around the fork, and my muscles tense at the gluttonously carnal sound, remaining that way even after she's chewed and swallowed.

"Cal, this is delicious," she says, taking a sip of the glass of Chardonnay in front of her. I found the bottle in the wine fridge and opened it just for her to enjoy.

A gentle, proud smile curves his lips. "Thank you."

"You're welcome." She splits a gaze between the two of us, and it turns shy when her eyes land on me. There's a cautiousness between us that doesn't exist with her and Cal, and I know I shouldn't, but I want it gone. "You didn't have to go through all this trouble, though. Cooking for me is not a part of either of your job descriptions."

"It wasn't any trouble," Cal tells her.

"Our job is to safeguard your physical well-being. I think keeping you fed is a part of that," I add, making sure to soften my tone to make the words seem less impersonal.

Selene, who appreciates a logic-based argument more than

anyone else I know, chews slowly, considering my words. Eventually, she nods, accepting them.

"I guess you're right."

"I am," I assure her.

"Doesn't happen often," Cal jokes, and they both laugh when I flip him off.

I can't even bring myself to feel self-conscious about the show of unprofessionalism, because we're already so far out of bounds; it just feels right to let Selene step further behind the curtain. When the laughter dies down, we all tuck back into our food, falling into a comfortable silence that persists until all the plates are clean.

Selene sits back in her seat, her fork clanging softly against the edge of her plate as she sets it down. "That was one of the best meals I've had in a while. Where did you learn to cook like that, Cal?"

I already know the answer by heart because I asked the same question after the first time he cooked for me, but I still listen intently, watching the emotion behind Cal's eyes as he tells Selene the same story he told me.

"My dad left me and my mom when I was young. He was the love of her life, and losing him had broken something inside her. She tried to fix it, to hide it in random hobbies. I remember coming home from school one day and finding her in the living room with bundles of yarn and knitting needles, only to throw them in the corner with the materials from the rest of her abandoned interests."

Nostalgia shimmers in pools of copper and brass that stay focused on Selene's face. Her features are still, but the steady eye contact she's giving him makes it clear she's not just listening, but hearing him, catching the notes of vulnerability and years-old pain in every word.

"Cooking was the only thing that stuck," Cal says, continuing. "And I think that was just a matter of necessity. My dad used to do all the cooking, so when he left, we were getting by on frozen pizzas, sandwiches, and boxed meals. One day, she just woke up and decided she was done with it. She started buying cookbooks from second-hand bookstores and forced me into the kitchen to try out recipes with her. I hated it at first because neither one of us knew what we were doing, and most of the food was inedible, but eventually we got good at it. I started looking forward to our evenings together in the kitchen, and now every time I cook it feels like I'm back there with her."

A wave of sadness washes over his features, and I reach for him on instinct, placing my hand in his and squeezing gently. Cal's eyes are wide when they meet mine, surprise spilling out of his irises as we both realize what I've done and who I've done it in front of.

My heart thuds against my ribs as I look to Selene, who is, as usual, giving away very little. Her eyes trace the lines of our intertwined fingers, and it feels like Cal and I are both holding our breath as we wait for her reaction.

"When did she pass?" Selene asks softly, her voice free of disgust or judgment.

Cal's throat works as he tries to conjure the words, but they won't come. It's still hard for him to talk about losing his mom. She was all he had when his dad left, and he built his world around her. Her passing shattered him. I think that's how he recognized the fractures in me.

"It'll be sixteen years in January," I say, supplying the answer because he can't.

Selene's features soften ever so slightly, and shock rolls through me when she leans forward and her slender fingers find Cal's free hand. They're tentative at first, unsure if their elegance belongs against the roughness of his skin. It doesn't show on her face, though. The only thing I see there is an openness that's rarely present when other people are around and a spark of surprise when Cal's fingers close around hers, suspending us in a moment of connection that doesn't feel wrong, weird, inappropriate or any of the other words I'd convinced myself should be used to describe this thing between us.

All it feels is right.

Like the three of us were meant to share this moment, like Selene and I were supposed to comfort Cal, and Cal and I are supposed to protect her, and they are supposed to remind me what it feels like to have a family. What it's like to be vulnerable, to open up, to risk my heart because doing it once isn't courage, but doing it twice might be.

The moment ends a few seconds later, and to my surprise, it's Cal that severs it. He gives Selene and me gentle smiles before letting us go and pushing to his feet.

"Ready for dessert?" he asks, turning towards the kitchen before we even respond. Selene looks at me, a silent question passing between us about whether Cal is alright. I nod even though I'm not entirely sure and stand, quickly clearing our plates.

"I can—" she starts, her hand already reaching for a glass that I take from her because I don't want her lifting a finger. She huffs a breath of disbelief but remains seated, watching as I balance all three plates, glasses, and an array of silverware in one hand.

Cal turns when he hears me come into the kitchen. He's back at the refrigerator, but in the freezer this time, pulling out a pint of vanilla ice cream and putting it on the counter beside three bowls and the plate of freshly baked chocolate chip cookies waiting to be consumed. I place the dishes in the sink and leave them, knowing we'll come back to them later. And the entire time, we stare at each other, copper and brass meld into onyx as we engage in a silent conversation that we've gotten too good at having.

Without a word or a shift in his demeanor, he tells me that he's fine and asks if I am too. Knowing his inquiry is inspired by the promises I had just been contemplating as broken, I nod. And even though I'm unsettled by the moment we just shared and the vows lying in pieces at our feet, I know it's true. I'm fine because he's fine. After all, Selene is safe because we're here together.

Cal walks around the counter, handing me the plate of cookies while he carries everything else to the table, where Selene is still seated, waiting patiently for us with a carefully closed expression.

"I hope you like chocolate chip cookies," Cal says, lining the bowls up in front of him on the table.

Selene leans forward, examining the spread. "I love chocolate chip cookies, but I don't think I can eat another bite."

Cal pauses mid-scoop and lifts a brow at her, and I laugh. "Selene, you should know that Cal is very serious about dessert. He won't take no for an answer, and before you ask, yes, I am speaking from experience."

"Don't make me sound like a monster for wanting to share a sweet treat."

"You're not a monster. I'm just letting her know that saying no really isn't an option."

His jaw drops. "It's an option. Of course, it's an option!"

I shake my head subtly at Selene. Her lips part in a pretty, bewildered sort of pout as she looks between us, trying to process the sudden appearance of our less serious sides. She's never seen them before, just like we've never seen the side of her that concedes easily, gleefully.

"Can I have two cookies?" she asks between a laugh that sends warmth flooding my chest.

"Absolutely."

Cal's eyes are two pools of adoration as he adds a spoon to the only bowl with ice cream inside it and passes it to me. I place the still-warm cookies on top and extend it to Selene.

Her fingertips brush against my hand as she takes it from me, and a slow, liquid heat trails down my spine at the contact. "Thank you," she murmurs sweetly.

"You're welcome."

She waits until Cal and I have fixed our desserts and are seated again to take her first bite. Once again, the air around us is filled with the sounds of her enjoyment, sparking a desire in me to do nothing but feed her, not just food but more.

To fill her up with love.

To nourish her with the kindness and attention she's so clearly being starved of in her marriage. She's been playing the role of the happy wife well, but I know better, even if no one else does. I know what a woman who is having her heart, mind, and soul taken care of looks like, and that's not Selene. Not when she's around Aubrey.

Cal and I could get her there, I think to myself, not even bothering to fight off the ridiculous notion as I bite into a cookie and the nutty flavors of browned butter and semi-sweet chocolate explode on my tongue. My mind races with all the things we could do for Selene, what we could give her, what she could give us, while she and Cal talk. Their voices float around me, and I soak in the beauty of the blended melodies, appreciating his deep rasp and her soft lilt as they discuss the technique required to make a cookie with crisp edges and a gooey center.

For the most part, I stay quiet, just enjoying the easy flow of conversation, but when dessert is done and Selene insists on helping us clean up the kitchen, I find my voice again.

"You know there's a dishwasher, right?" I ask, eyeing her with thinly veiled wonder as she fills the freshly cleaned sink with hot, soapy water. Steam billows around her, obscuring her features a bit, but not enough for me to miss the scrunch of her nose.

"I know, but I grew up hand-washing dishes. Old habits die hard, I guess."

"So you never use the dishwasher?"

"Never," she says, scooping up all the utensils and placing them in the sink. The water has to be close to scalding, but she doesn't even flinch as she plunges her hands into it. "Even though I hate the feeling of food floating around in the water—" she shudders at the thought. "—and the dishwasher is quicker, and more efficient."

"It also uses less water."

"I know. I told my mama the same thing when cleaning the kitchen became my sole responsibility. She laughed in my face and told me to get to scrubbing. Didn't matter that we had a fully functional dishwasher."

"One of my foster moms told me I *was* the dishwasher. That's what her kids called me until I moved out a month later."

Cal is behind me, wiping down the counters and the stove, but I know he's tuned in to us, know that he's paying attention to the conversation. His surprise is palpable when those words leave my mouth.

"I didn't realize you grew up in foster care," Selene says.

"It's not something I talk about much."

Or at all, I add silently. The list of people who I freely discuss my upbringing with has only ever had two names on it: Cal and Diana. But now, I guess, there are three.

"That must have been difficult for you. The lack of stability. Being on the margins of existing family structures, trying to find your place in established dynamics when your world was always changing."

Her words are a perfect encapsulation of the struggles I faced during my formative years. For anyone else, they might have been too honest, too straightforward, but not for me and not from her. They hit me right in the center of my chest, all the more poignant because of how intently she's looking at me.

"I survived."

"Yes, you did," she agrees, a degree of pride woven through the words as she turns her attention back to the dishes.

Unable to pass up an opportunity to be close to her, I move over to the sink and start to rinse the items she's already washed.

"Thank you," she says, directing her gratitude at me for what feels like the millionth time today. No matter how frequently those two words come, I never get tired of hearing them from her.

"No problem."

We stand shoulder to shoulder, working through the dishes by category. Utensils first. Then her wine glass and our cups, followed by the bowls and plates. She resets the water before washing the cookware, and I dry it all, handing it off to Cal to put away once he's done sweeping the floor. When everything is clean, Selene washes out the sink again and dries down the counter around it, signaling the end of this shared moment of domesticity.

"I should get back to my speech."

My lips part on an attempt at protest, but Cal silences me with a hand on my shoulder.

His fingers dig into the muscle of my shoulder as he speaks. "And *we* should do one more perimeter sweep and check on the officers outside."

Selene's eyes move over the point of contact, but just like earlier when we were holding hands, her face gives nothing away. She steps back, preparing to turn on her heel to leave us.

"Goodnight, Cal. Goodnight, Beck."

I watch the sway of her hips as she goes, hating every step that takes her away from me. "Goodnight, Selene."

"Don't stay up too late," Cal adds, his soft command floating down the hall after her.

23

SELENE

Despite Cal's warning, I did in fact stay up too late putting finishing touches on my speech.

When my alarm for the day goes off, I wake up bleary-eyed and regretful, wishing for coffee and a few more minutes in bed. Knowing only one of those things is within the realm of possibility for me, I toss aside the bedding and stride over to the dresser on the other side of the room where my phone is still blaring. I shut off the alarm and then check my texts, smiling when I see a good luck message from Monique and a confirmation from Nichelle that my point of contact at TED x Women received the speech I sent over in the wee hours of the morning.

I respond to both of them before heading into the bathroom. After I'm showered and moisturized, I find myself taking longer than necessary to decide on an outfit. My teeth dig into my lower lip as I consider the three choices in front of me. The first two are not too different. Tailored pantsuits in colors and silhouettes I tend to favor that will pair well with a simple silk blouse.

The third is a bit different.

It's a soft cream with light brown pinstripes and a more relaxed fit. The blazer is longer than the ones I usually wear, with the hem hitting at my mid-thigh, flowing into the matching fabric of the wide-leg pants. What sets it apart, though, is the corset with the sweetheart neckline that cups and lifts my breasts, creating an amount of cleavage that the media will deem as obscene if I follow Monique's suggestion and leave the blazer open.

As I run the tips of my fingers over the lush fabric, I wonder why I bothered to include the option in the first place. Then I hear it, the answer to the question hidden in the deep rumblings of male voices just down the stairs, for them. I packed it for them, hoping it would grant me access to the soft, decadent place where the warmth of their attention washes over me, moves through me, makes me feel seen and understood.

Acknowledging that truth makes the time I spent considering the other two pantsuits feel like a waste of energy. I hang them back in the closet and make short work of unwrapping my hair and putting on some basic makeup before getting dressed. I allow myself a quick minute to take in the outfit in the full-length mirror in the corner of the bedroom and then rush out the door before I change my mind about leaving the blazer open.

The moment I'm outside of my room, my heart starts to thud against my ribcage, beating harder with every step I take down to the first floor, where Cal and Beck are waiting for me. I pause on the last step to catch my breath and end up losing it altogether at the sight of them at the counter, shoulder to shoulder. Neither of them are wearing the jackets to their standard black suits, so there is already an aching intimacy to this scene that melts into a forbidden sacredness when Beck passes the mug in his hands to Cal. He takes it, turning it until his mouth is aligned with the place where Beck's lips just were.

A tiny, shocked gasp tries to leave me, but I bite it back, not wanting to call attention to myself and lose a chance to observe the two men I can't help but wonder about. Last night, after the show of affection that had surprised me but seemed at home between the two of them, I found myself wondering if there was something more to Cal and Beck's relationship than the professional and platonic front they present to the world. I spent the few breaks I allowed myself from my speech questioning if they'd ever gone beyond a friendly touch, if they'd kissed, made love, if they'd shared a woman the way they had shared me in my dream....

"Selene?"

I jolt at the sound of Beck calling my name, and the gasp I had been holding back decides to leave me then, which earns me two tilted heads and four folded brows.

"Everything alright?" Cal asks, handing the mug back to Beck, who sets it on the counter. All thoughts of caffeine forgotten because I'm standing here acting weird. I force myself back into motion, striding across the room with a smile.

"Yeah, everything is fine. I was trying to remember if I'd sent my speech off."

The lie comes easily, and both men nod, allowing the tension to melt out of their frames. As I approach, they both step back, making space for me between them. Cal is on my left, and the heat and weight of his gaze is a familiar burn on my skin. Beck's is less familiar, but no less intense, searing my right cheek with calm focus.

"Did you?" he asks, sliding a mug I hadn't even noticed in my direction. The coffee inside is the perfect shade of brown, indicating the presence of the two small splashes of creamer I take mine with.

I wrap my hands around the body of the mug, enjoying the warmth against my palms as I bring it to my mouth. "Hmm?"

One corner of Beck's mouth tips up as he watches me drink, but it's Cal who speaks, posing the question as he produces a plate seemingly out of nowhere. There's an assortment of cut fruits in a small bowl to keep them from touching the toasted slice of sourdough bread, topped with mashed avocado, scrambled eggs, and sriracha.

"Did you send off the speech, Selene?"

I blink at the plate, stunned by its sudden appearance and the fact that everything on it is an exact replica of the breakfast I make when I have time to cook at home. Since we've been traveling, I haven't had a single rendition of it that's come close, but somehow I know that won't be the case with the meal in front of me.

"Yes, I sent off the speech," I say finally, closing out that point of discussion before moving on to a new topic. "You didn't have to cook again, Cal."

"I didn't. Beck did."

"Oh." My surprise is evident in my voice, and Beck seems to tense up when I set my gaze on him. We're growing more comfortable with each other every day—the evolution of our relationship helped along by the events of the dressing room and Cal's quiet influence—but we're both still being careful. Measuring every word, revealing the hearts underneath our hard exteriors with slow, deliberate movements, which is why I feel so bad when the following words out of my mouth are, "I didn't know you cooked," instead of 'thank you' or some other expression of gratitude.

Cal barks out a laugh, and Beck's brows lift high, reaching for his non-existent hairline. He shakes his head, but I've seen him upset enough times to know that he's not mad. Confirmation comes in the form of his low chuckle as he rubs his chin.

"I can do the basics. Toast bread, scramble an egg." He shrugs. "I hope it's to your liking."

"I'm sure it will be."

"You should sit down and eat before the bread gets soggy though," Cal tells me, picking up the plate and taking it over to the dining table. Beck grabs my coffee and puts one gentle hand on my hip to turn me away from the counter. I comply immediately, melting slightly at his touch and wanting to protest when he takes it away. They get me settled in with my breakfast—leaving me with strict instructions to finish the whole thing in preparation for the long day ahead—and set about securing the house for our departure.

By the time they're done with their duties, I've washed and dried my plate and both mugs. Beck comes to escort me out the door to the car, insisting on carrying my laptop bag and my purse. Cal is already waiting behind the wheel, and there are two uniformed officers in the squad car in front of him. They lead the way to the venue, and thankfully, the ride is uneventful.

When we arrive, I'm swept away by a team of people who move

far too quickly for Cal and Beck's liking. I can tell by the clipped cadence of their strides as they follow us to the green room, where a hairstylist and makeup artist are waiting.

"Mrs. Taylor, you're already perfect. I don't even know why they needed me here," she gushes by way of greeting as I sink into her chair. There's a twang to her words that makes it clear she's a born and bred Texas girl. "I'm Paris, by the way."

"Nice to meet you, Paris."

Usually, I'd opt to shake her hand, but she's already turned towards her work station, shuffling through brushes and makeup palettes we both know she won't need. She rounds the chair, obscuring my view of Cal and Beck, and places gentle fingers on my chin, tipping it upwards. I fight the urge to bristle at her touch, even though I hate having unfamiliar people touch me.

She turns my head to the left and the right, sparkling brown eyes assessing me. "I think we just need some gloss and a little highlight. You're so stunning in person. I mean that's not to say you're not that way in photos," Paris rambles, tapping a clear gloss onto a clean palette that's strapped to her wrist. "Just that you're—" she pauses, scanning my face again, this time to see if she's offended me.

"Prettier in person," I supply, hoping to put her at ease. "Thank you."

"I can't believe you came so prepared," she muses, swiping a fresh brush over my bottom lip. "I thought I was going to have a blank canvas to work with, had a whole look planned for you. Now, I'll have to tell my mama I only got to put some lip gloss on you."

"And highlighter," I add, rubbing my lips together at her silent instruction. "I'm sorry I didn't leave you any work to do. I wasn't sure if they'd have someone here capable of doing Black hair or accurately matching shades on melenated skin."

Paris' head bobs up and down as she swipes highlighter across my cheekbones and nose. "That's real. Some of these girls around here would have you going out there looking a hot mess, but not me. I would have got you right, Mrs. Taylor."

Judging by the expertly applied makeup on her face and the

smooth waves of combed-out curls in her layered hair, I know she's not lying. If I had known she was here waiting for me, I would have approached my morning differently.

"Is she ready?" A voice calls from behind Paris just as she steps back from me. Now that she's no longer in my line of sight, I see that the voice belongs to Stephanie Glass, the head of the TED x Women team. I'm surprised that she's taken the time out of her day to come and retrieve me from the green room.

"All done," Paris declares, stepping to the left so I can stand.

Stephanie's blue eyes roam over my features. "You're stunning, Mrs. Taylor. Beautiful job, Paris."

"Oh, I—" Paris starts, but I cut her off, leaning into the lie because I don't feel it's fair for her to potentially be reprimanded because I wasn't aware she was available. "Yes, she's amazing."

"You made it easy for me, Mrs. Taylor."

She comes in for a hug, and I tense at the promise of contact that never happens because Beck takes a step forward and clears his throat. Paris freezes, her pretty eyes growing wide at the non-verbal reprimand as she backs away.

"Let's get you to the stage," Stephanie says, breaking the awkward silence that's fallen over the room. She steps out into the hallway and begins walking, leaving us with no choice but to follow her clipped strides. The hallway that leads to the stage isn't all that long, but it seems to take us forever to traverse it because we keep getting stopped. By the time we reach the stage, I've met everyone on the film crew, all of Stephanie's team, and the head of the venue's janitorial staff.

They're all lovely and extremely accommodating, which is great because I spend the rest of the day surrounded by them, being told where to stand and encouraged to emote 'just a little more'. It's a harrowing and tedious process that makes me wish I could give the talk in person instead, because then my flat affect wouldn't really be up for discussion. We recorded my speech three different times, with Paris coming in to touch up my hair and makeup between the second and third take.

When it's all said and done, we have a product that I'm proud of, which is all that matters. Stephanie and her team seem satisfied as well, to the point that they insist on taking me out to dinner to celebrate. The part of me that's exhausted and ready to be done socializing wants to say no, but then Stephanie tells me it's a Black owned restaurant, and I feel compelled to say yes.

My agreement sets Cal and Beck into immediate motion. The tension in their shoulders as they escort me to the car makes me regret my decision.

"I'm sorry," I tell them when we're alone. "I wasn't thinking about the security aspect of it."

Beck is behind the wheel this time, and those onyx eyes burn into me through the rear-view mirror, reminding me of the last time we got into it about security formations and protection protocols. I half expect this to be the moment things go bad between us again, but instead, he shakes his head like it's normal for us to be heading into another public setting with only two uniformed officers to support them.

"That's not your job, Selene."

"My job is to make keeping me safe easier, not harder," I respond, aware of how wildly my attitude on this topic has changed. Weeks ago, I couldn't bear the thought of them in my home, at my work, in my life, and now I don't want to go anywhere without them.

"Well, you've never been any good at that, so we're used to pivoting for you."

Shock rolls through me as my jaw unhinges, trying to hit the floor. Beck doesn't even attempt to hide his humor at my reaction, and Cal, who is on the phone requesting more bodies with no success, barks out a laugh at my expense. The injection of levity makes me feel less guilty, and it also soothes my nerves when Cal and Beck explain that only one of them will be going into the restaurant with me.

"We'll have two officers on the exterior," Cal says, frowning as he eyes the industrial style brick building where Feast is located. "One on the front and the other on the back."

Beck runs a hand over his scalp and sighs. "I'll go in with you, and

Cal will stay with the car." He shifts in his seat, fixing an earnest gaze on my face. "Unless you want Cal to come—"

"No, I want you."

Truthfully, I want both of them, and I'm so focused on how those words would sound coming out of my mouth that I'm not paying attention to what does. Both men stare at me, and the hum of building intensity starts to resonate in my chest, causing my thighs to clench.

"I mean—" I swallow, desperate to clarify, fearful of making it worse. "You've already made a plan, and I don't see any reason to deviate from it."

They share a look I don't understand, and then Cal nods. "Okay, let's do this."

He hops out of the passenger seat and opens my door, offering his hand, which I take out of habit and the desire for physical touch that is usually a rarity for me, but seems to always exist when he and Beck are around. We round the car together, and as soon as I'm in arm's reach, Beck's hand is on the small of my back. He guides me away from Cal, who salutes us before climbing back into the driver's seat.

Stephanie meets Beck and me at the door of the restaurant, and he drops back, keeping a respectable distance as we make our way to the private dining area where the rest of Stephanie's team is. She runs through introductions again when I'm seated at the head of the table, and conversation starts to flow immediately.

I try to follow the topics, I do, but every word my companions say is pushed out by the thrum of impatience that rattles my bones and begs to be alone with my men again.

My men, when did I start to think of them that way? I muse silently, sipping my wine and allowing my gaze to wander to Beck. He's across the room near the doorway, eyes constantly shifting, moving over the faces and hands of the people at the table and the servers coming in and out of the room. It's too much for one person to keep track of, but he seems nonplussed. He's responding to Cal on the comms when he finally looks at me. I watch his lips form the word "Hummingbird," and my heart flutters at the thought of them discussing me even as my features remain still.

"He's pretty intense," Stephanie whispers, pulling my attention to her. She's too close to me, and her perfume, which smelled lovely earlier today, has started to sour a bit for me. The floral notes are too heavy, drowning out everything else. "I don't think I've seen him so much as sit down today. He doesn't even look tired. The man has *stamina.*"

I've heard Monique talk about enough men to recognize the lust infused into the last part of her comment. Objectively, I know that Beck is an attractive man. I know that many women speak about him this way, or even worse, but that doesn't stop my body from reacting negatively to Stephanie's words or feeling disgusted by her conspiratorial smile.

Sitting my wine glass on the table, I push to my feet. "Excuse me."

Stephanie's smile falters as I move away from the table, unsure of where I'm headed. Beck watches my approach with a slight dip in his brows, which spells curiosity. "You okay?"

Since I can't tell him I'm fighting the urge to strike a woman for even hinting at speaking about him in a suggestive manner, I nod and call up a reassuring smile. "I'm fine. Just going to the restroom."

He looks between the table and the hallway where the bathroom is, clearly weighing letting me out of his sight against leaving my food and drink unattended and vulnerable to tampering.

"I'll be okay," I tell him, taking advantage of his indecision and heading down the hall without him. The bathroom is empty when I enter it, and I take up residence at the sink furthest from the door, washing my hands with cold water and soap just so the trip doesn't feel useless.

As I'm drying my hands, the door swings open. I glance up and breathe a sigh of relief when I find that the woman I'm now sharing space with isn't Stephanie or another member of her team. The relief is short-lived, expiring quickly when the woman crosses her arms and scowls at me.

"I know you," she spits out. "You're the bitch that's trying to take away our guns."

My stomach turns at the pure malice she's managed to fit into the few words. In some distant part of my brain, I know I should be offended by her calling me a bitch, but I'm not. At this point, I've been called everything but a child of God by social media trolls and far-right media pundits.

The woman taps her foot. "What? You don't have nothing to say now?"

"No, I made my thoughts on gun control quite clear." I toss my paper towel in the trash can between us and start towards the door that she's deliberately blocking. "It's unfortunate that you don't agree with my stance, but I don't think either of our minds will be changed by a bathroom debate."

Her scowl deepens, lines appearing on the pale skin around her mouth as her cheeks flush with fury. She steps forward, cutting me off with a finger to my chest. I flinch, and she smiles maliciously.

"Unfortunate? You know what's unfortunate, Mrs. Taylor? That someone hasn't put a bullet between your eyes like they did your mixed-breed bastard of a son. Yeah, that's *real* unfortunate," she drawls, laughing when her mention of AJ pulls an involuntary whimper from me. "Don't worry, though," she coos, backing away. "There's still time for that."

It doesn't occur to me that she didn't even use the bathroom until the door swings shut, and I'm alone again, frozen in place, processing being terrorized in the place I came to seek reprieve.

I don't know how much time passes between the woman's departure and Beck's arrival, but knowing him, it couldn't have been long. He bursts into the bathroom without knocking and takes me in. I already know what he sees. Outside of my clenched fists there are no indicators of the emotions rioting inside me, and I wish that the pain would show on my face, that it would make itself plain, present itself "normally" so I didn't have to do the work of explaining how deeply I feel, how badly I hurt.

I wish that just this once, the evidence would be there, and I wouldn't have to do the impossible work of convincing people to believe in things they can't see. My entire life has been spent defending the apparent contradiction of my existence: saying I'm sad, yet being questioned about not crying, being happy, and yet being punished for not showing it with a smile.

I expect Beck to need that—the declaration of feelings to circumvent the abnormal presentation of them—but he never asks for it. He looks at me and knows that something is wrong.

"What happened?" He closes the space between us in two long strides, one hand on the holster on his hip and the other reaching for me. He draws me into him, squeezing me firmly against his body as he shifts us around, kicking the door of each stall open to make sure there are no lingering threats.

"She's already gone," I murmur against his chest. The words wheeze their way out of me, a result of the lovely vice grip he has on me. He's already raised Cal on the comms, and I hear him barking instructions for Beck to bring me out through the kitchen, but he's still listening to me.

"Who was she?" he asks, pulling the door open and popping his head out to make sure the hallway is clear. "What did she look like?"

"I've never seen her before." I close my eyes, conjuring her face. "She was white, shorter than me, but not by much. Dirty blonde hair and green eyes."

Beck repeats the description to Cal and rubs my arm. "That's good, Selene. That's good. Do you remember what she was wearing?"

"Black sweater, black pants, no jewelry." I squint against the light as I open my eyes to find Beck staring down at me. "That's not helpful, is it?"

"It's accurate, and that's all that matters." He gives Cal the last of the information and then tells him we'll be at the back entrance in five minutes.

"That should be enough time to say goodbye to Stephanie—"

"Fuck, Stephanie," Beck growls, the depth of his tone sending vibrations from his chest through mine. "What did this woman say to you?"

"It doesn't matter."

"Yes, it does, Selene." A muscle in his jaw jumps. "Did she threaten you? Did she touch you? Did she—" he flounders for another word, and I sigh, deciding to put an end to his search.

"She called me the bitch that was trying to take away her guns."

"Fucking Texans," he hisses. "What else?"

"She said she wished I were dead. Same old, same old. It's not America if someone isn't wishing for the death of a Black woman."

I'm paraphrasing, of course, but I'm honestly too tired to rehash it verbatim. Plus, no part of me wants to repeat those ugly words about my son to Beck of all people. I don't know how close his grief lingers to the surface, and I won't have some random woman's hateful comment triggering him.

"That's it?"

"Isn't that enough?"

He grimaces. "Yeah. That's more than enough."

"Do you think the officers will find her?"

"Probably not," he says, regret passing between us when he finally lets me go. "But Cal and I will."

24

CAL

There's a wariness to Selene's demeanor that weighs down her shoulders and makes her footsteps heavy as she climbs the stairs up to her bedroom. Beck and I watch her go, anger and concern dueling for precedence in my body while guilt flashes behind his eyes.

"Stop beating yourself up, Beckham." I place a hand on his shoulder to guide him to the office where Selene was working yesterday. He waits until the door is shut to respond, self-loathing wrapping itself around each word.

"Twice," he says, shrugging me off to pace the length of the floor. "Twice she's been in my care, and something has gone wrong."

I lean against the door with my arms crossed. Years of knowing and loving him have taught me how nasty and incessantly negative his thoughts can get. How necessary it is to combat that self-deprecation with facts. I never inflate them, never exaggerate his role in anything, just give him the cold, hard truth and let it work its magic.

"And both times you have gotten her out of harm's way without so much as a scratch."

"Don't do that, Drake," he scrubs a hand down his face. "Don't fucking patronize me. She shouldn't have been in harm's way to fucking begin with. That's the whole point of what we do."

"Beck, our job only exists because it is inevitable that people like Selene will find themselves in harm's way. We do what we can to prevent that, but sometimes prevention isn't possible, which is why we have protocols and procedures."

"Protocol dictates that you stay with your charge at all times."

"Yeah, well protocol also doesn't account for the bullshit situation Hicks has us in right now. You had to make a judgment call."

He lifts his hands, threading his fingers together and letting them come to rest at the nape of his neck. "Would you have made the same call?"

"Absolutely. Leaving her food unattended would have rendered it inedible and delayed the meal. The bathroom was in your line of sight. You stayed in the spot that made it possible for you to execute both of your responsibilities to the best of your abilities, and you were successful."

He blows a harsh breath through his nostrils. "I wasn't successful."

"Is she dead, Lance?"

My tone and the question make him flinch, but they also ground him in reality. He sighs and gives a resigned shake of his head, "No, but—"

"No buts. Just facts. She's alive. *Say it*."

His jaw clenches in a futile attempt to stop himself from obeying, and I march over to him, palming his defiance and squeezing gently. Desire and indignation flare in his eyes, and as much as I want to fan the flame of one, I'm more concerned about stomping out the other so we can get on to more important things.

"*Say it, Beckham.*"

I feel the flex and release of muscle, the hinging and unhinging of bone, and then finally, he gives me what I want.

"She's alive."

"That's right, and we're going to make sure it stays that way."

Now that his head is back on his shoulders, I have to tell him something that might send him spiraling again, but for different reasons. I remove my hand from his jaw, barely resisting the need to pull him in for a kiss, and take out my phone.

"Let's sit down, I need to show you something."

We settle into the armchairs in front of the desk, both of us perched on the edge of our seats so we can look at the photo displayed on my screen. It's a little dark and taken at a distance, but you can still make out the woman in all black climbing into an older model sedan with a man behind the wheel. Her hair is whipped around her face, hiding her features, but she matches the description Selene gave us.

Beck takes the phone from my hands, zooming in on the woman. "When was this taken?"

"Tonight. Around the time you found Selene in the bathroom. It's a still from some CCTV footage from a shop one street over from Feast."

"I don't remember seeing her. Are we sure this is the woman Selene described?"

"We can't be certain until we show the photo to her. Houston PD is working on getting an ID. That's not the important thing, though."

His brows wrinkle with confusion. "It's not?"

"No." I reach over and swipe to the left, bringing up another image. "This is from a red light camera on the same block."

Beck examines the photo closely, but his focus is only on the woman in the passenger seat. His tunnel vision makes sense to me. She's the one who slipped past him and got to Selene. She's the one who made him feel like a failure, but *she* isn't the problem.

"Look at the driver," I insist. "Does he look familiar at all?"

He's reluctant to pull his eyes from the woman, almost like he's scared she'll slip through his fingers again, but when he does, they grow wide with recognition.

"Holy shit. It's him!"

"Yeah, it's—"

"The driver of the red Honda," he says, completing my sentence with the wrong words.

"What? This is the guy you saw in front of the house that day?"

Beck's excitement wanes a little at my lack of understanding. "Yes, isn't that what you were going to tell me?"

"No." I run a hand over my head as agitation builds behind my ribs. This situation is growing more complicated by the minute. "I didn't get a look at the driver, remember?"

He frowns. "Right. Then how do you know him?"

"Because he's Leland Marsh's son."

The gravity of that statement makes the air in the room heavy with the kind of dread that can only be associated with the name of a man who plotted the public murder of a sitting President and almost killed me along the way. We arrested Leland Marsh years ago and left him to rot in a federal prison in Florence, Colorado, while the rest of his brothers in racist arms wound up facing charges for their role in the assassination attempt or died trying to avoid arrest.

Our years-long investigation into Marsh made it necessary for us to know everything and everyone in his life, but his son, Jacob, who was, by all accounts, estranged from his father, never garnered any true interest for us. We interviewed him once after the Warner incident, and he made it quite clear that he wasn't affiliated with Leland or his group. He was only twenty-five at the time, a quiet, but clearly angry kid with long, greasy hair that hung in his face and gave him a mean case of adult acne. In the photo taken today, he has a buzz cut, and, as far as I can tell, the acne has cleared up. With the close-cropped hair, he looks more like his father than he did before. I squint at the picture, wondering if maybe it's the hateful glint in his eye that's feeding the resemblance.

Beck rubs at his temple with one hand. "I don't understand. Why is Leland Marsh's kid stalking Selene? And who's the girl? How does she fit into all of this?"

His questions mirror the inquiries floating around in my mind, and I hate that I don't have answers. Hate that I don't have them for him, and I won't have them for Selene when we break this all down for her. Hate that I have to introduce another unsettling query into what's already a long list of unknowns.

"I don't know, but we're for damn sure going to find out. And we're also going to find out how the fuck they knew we were here."

Selene's trip wasn't advertised. As far as the world knows, she's still in her hotel room recovering from the stressful incident at the boutique. All of her socials are quiet, save for the constant influx of nastiness in her comment section, and the TED x Women team was forbidden from breathing a word to anyone about her being here. Of course, it's always possible that someone spotted her in the restaurant and posted about it...

"That wouldn't give Jacob enough time to get to Houston, though," Beck says, making me realize I was speaking out loud. "They were here waiting for a chance to take a shot at her. They were lying in wait at the restaurant."

"That doesn't make sense. That kind of preparation would mean access to proprietary and constantly changing information that is only available to our team."

"It makes perfect sense, Drake." Beck's eyes narrow, pools of onyx swirling with betrayal and murder. "Because we have a fucking leak."

It's not a question. It's an indictment, only we're not sure which member of our team is about to stand trial. My hands turn into fists, and I squeeze them tight, imagining the faces of every man we've worked alongside for the past four years. We're not a tight-knit group by a long shot, but I wouldn't have ever thought any of them capable of this, of putting the lives of their fellow agents and the person they've been charged with protecting in jeopardy.

There's no denying the evidence, though.

Only someone on our team could have obtained the information about the restaurant in time for Jacob and the mystery girl to arrive. Aubrey's camp hadn't received the report on the change of plans yet. Hell, knowing Hicks they might never get it because he didn't deem the communication necessary.

"Could it be Hicks?" I wonder out loud, my brain sorting through all the instances of nonchalance and weaponized incompetence.

"It could be any one of those fuckers," Beck hisses. "Or, worse, all of them."

"The whole team? Even Harris?"

"Maybe. It doesn't matter right now, though, because until we find out who it is, we can't trust any of them."

"Did you ever start?"

"Hell no."

Amusement feels out of place in this room, so I swallow the laugh his matter-of-fact response sparks in my chest and pluck my phone out of his hand. "How do you want to play this?"

He eyes me suspiciously, obviously wondering why I'm deferring to him when I'm usually the one who lays out a game plan. I don't feel like explaining that I don't like it when he doubts himself, when he acts like he's not one of the best agents and investigators I know, when he forgets that I trust him with my life and Selene does too.

"How do you want to play it, Beckham?" I ask again, demanding an answer with an arch of my brow.

"We start with Marsh. Looking into him will lead us to the leak in our boat. Keep everything off the books until we know who we can read in. Off the books means leg work we don't have time to do, though."

He's right. We'd be completely on our own and starting from scratch without the Service's resources. Tracking down Jacob's mom and friends and interviewing them in person, handwriting notes, and keeping hard copies of everything so none of it touches compromised servers. With Aubrey and Selene's travel schedule and public commitments keeping us busy, it'd be the slowest investigation in history.

"I could call Charlie," I offer, invoking the name of one of the few agents we keep in touch with from our old unit. Beck strokes his chin, nodding thoughtfully.

"She did always like you better."

"Yeah, cause you're an asshole."

"So is she."

Once again, he's right. Charlie Monroe is an asshole. It's what she had to become to survive as a twenty-something-year-old woman with her entire career ahead of her in an agency still dominated by old men who refuse to go out to pasture. Like Beck and me, she existed on the margins of the Bureau, passed over for promotions because of her age, denied coveted assignments because of her sex. I'd taken her under my wing, becoming something of a mentor to her, helping her find a path that fit her skills and career aspirations. It didn't take her long to figure out she liked undercover work, and she made her bones as a UC by infiltrating a sex trafficking ring operating in DC and bringing down everyone involved. After that bust, cases that required her to go under were her bread and butter.

When Beck and I left the unit, she was embedded in an arms dealer's entourage as the girlfriend of one of his lower-level runners. We didn't get to say goodbye, which is something she brings up every time we speak.

This time is no different.

"Well, well, well, if it isn't my so-called friend who abandoned me to go play with the big boys," she says by way of greeting, her voice deep and commanding. When we met, she talked like a cheerleader, all high-pitched and excited. She looked like one, too. Short, petite with brunette hair she always wore in a ponytail. Now, even when she's relaxed and playful, there are no soft lines or gentle notes, which speaks to the things she's seen and fits the severity of the short pixie cut she had the last time I saw her.

"It wasn't like that, Monroe," I recite my line in this worn-out script with ease.

"What was it like then, because—"

Beck groans, the little patience he had with Charlie and this conversation expiring. "A promotion," he growls. "It was like a promotion. Can we please get to the point?"

Charlie's tsk of disapproval rings through the speaker. "Glad to see nothing has changed with you, Lance. Still a total buzzkill."

He glares at me like I'm the one who just called him out, and I hold a hand up to stop him from digging into Charlie's ass over the phone. If he upsets her too badly, she won't help us, and we can't have that.

"Listen, Monroe. I need a favor."

The line goes quiet as she decides whether she wants to address me or further antagonize Beck. "I'm listening," she says eventually. I don't give her time to reconsider, rushing through the ask and all the pertinent details that led to us making it.

"What makes you think the Bureau has a file on Jacob Marsh?"

A derisive snort leaves Beck. "His father carried out an assassination attempt, Charlie. There's absolutely a file on him. Can you get it for us or not?"

"Let's say there is a file," she hedges, sounding like a true agent of bureaucracy. "Why can't you get the information inside of it another way? I'm sure the Service has access to the same databases we do."

I glance at Beck to see if he thinks we should read Charlie in. He shakes his head, so I pivot to the closest thing to the truth I can give her. "The usual channels aren't an option for us right now."

"You don't trust your team," she deadpans.

"We don't trust anyone but each other," Beck retorts.

"And you," I add, attempting to sweeten the pot. "We trust you, Charlie. Wouldn't have called if we didn't."

She heaves a long, deep sigh, and when she speaks again, I hear the reluctant resignation in her tone. "I'll see what I can find."

25

BECK

Hours after our call with Charlie, I'm a ball of anxious, unspent energy.

I take all of the perimeter sweeps just to have something to do, and clean the entire kitchen alone after we finish the dinner Cal cooked, and Selene refused to come down to eat. Most, okay, maybe, all, of the anxiety I feel has to do with her.

Her silence.

Her pain.

Her safety.

Cal tries to keep me grounded, but I can tell he's floating away on a cloud of worry, too. It's evident in the way he keeps staring at the book he took off the shelf in the office, never turning a single page.

We're on the couch with the TV on, but neither of us is watching the movie that's playing because our eyes are on the stairs, willing her to appear. And the volume is turned down low so we can listen to the shifting of the floorboards in her room as she paces back and forth. My entire body burns with the need to go to her, to see her, to hold her, and just when I'm about to reach my breaking point, the pacing stops, morphing into soft footfalls that, seconds later, hit the stairs.

We trace her descent with our eyes, a current of anticipation arching between us when she appears. She's changed her clothes, back in the soft Stanford hoodie she flew in, and a pair of shorts that leave everything below her mid-thigh bare. I hear Cal suck in a breath that matches the desperate gulp of air I'm holding in my lungs as we adjust to the feel of our bond stretching. Opening up just enough to envelop the delicate creature in front of us and then closing again.

I wonder if she feels it, the way Cal feels about her, the way I do. The fierce devotion, the concern, and way underneath, because I don't know where her head is at, the raging desire. It radiates off of us, thick waves of what if and if only. Silent questions that must go unanswered because I can't see a reality where we get to have her.

Where *I* get to have her *and* Cal.

Even as I surrender to my affection for Selene, I can't help but think about the hard lessons life has taught me. How it's shown me that I never get to keep anything good for long. How circumstance has mocked me when I got cocky enough to think I could have two good things at the same time. How every time I've had palms full of blessings, both things were ripped from me so quickly, so violently, that I wondered if I ever had them at all.

That's how it happened with my parents.

That's how it happened with Diana and Cameron.

And that's how it would happen with Cal and Selene.

It would be beautiful for a while, but then it'd break. We'd break.

I think that's why I fought these feelings so hard, denying the truth of my heart in hopes of maintaining the delicate balance of my dynamic with Cal. Stomping out the blooms of affection because I know I shouldn't have been able to keep him this long, and I'm scared that adding Selene to the mix might trigger whatever hex has been put over my life and cost me them both.

"I'm sorry I missed dinner," Selene breathes, lingering on the last step with her body angled like she's poised to run away. "I just didn't think I could hold down a full meal."

Cal pulls off his reading glasses, closing the book. "No apologies necessary. I made a grazing board for you just in case you wanted something lighter. Let me grab it for you."

He starts to stand, but she waves him off. "No. You've done enough. You both have." She splits a smile between us, and it's so thin, so brittle, it looks ready to disintegrate. I recognize it instantly as her First Lady smile and wonder how anyone could look at it and believe it to be genuine. "I really appreciate you taking this trip with me, for making sure I felt secure and protected every step of the way."

I want to touch her, to comfort her, but all I can do is say, "You don't have to thank us."

I intentionally stop myself from adding a qualifier about just doing our jobs because, whether she knows it or not, Selene is more than just a job to us. She's our family now. The quiet beat of our joined hearts. The person we'll do break oaths and bones for. Cal and I have only ever been that for each other, and I don't know if having that kind of intensity multiplied and focused solely on her will be too much for Selene.

I want to find out, though.

She clears her throat, stepping off the stairs. "Right, well, I still wanted to."

Part of me hopes that she'll cross the room and settle herself between us, allow us another moment like dinner the other night or breakfast this morning, but the other part of me knows she won't. She makes a beeline for the kitchen, and the quiet of the house makes her movements easy to track. There's the closing of the cabinet and the clinking of a glass against the countertop, followed by the opening of the refrigerator and the soft screech of the plastic pitcher filled with filtered water dragging across the glass shelves. Within seconds, the quiet is pierced by the soft glug of cascading water and then Selene's barely audible swallowing.

She finishes the glass and then pours another before returning the pitcher to its rightful place. Cal, who has been as tuned in with her movements as I am, shifts in his seat, glancing over his shoulder to see what she's doing now. I look too, conscious not to let my gaze linger on the long, powerful legs and the toned muscles on display as she bends at her waist to rummage through the still full shelves.

Cal stands, moving to the kitchen with a single-minded focus. It's the same way he approached me in the office, with the intent to comfort and reassure lining the span of his shoulders. He can't touch her like he touched me—that would be a step too far—so he'll do the next best thing: offer indirect care and aimless conversation meant to distract the person on the receiving end from the fact that he's doing anything at all.

"We still have so much food left, maybe we can arrange to have it donated to a food bank." He's at Selene's back, angling his body to the side as he reaches past her to assist with her search for what I assume is the grazing board he prepared for her. "Or a homeless shelter," he continues. "I'm sure one of the officers can help us arrange that before we leave in the morning."

"I'm sure they'd be happy to," I say, pushing to my feet to join them in the kitchen.

Selene straightens, obviously giving up on conducting her own search for the grazing board. She skirts around Cal, wary eyes on me as she reaches for the glass of water she left sitting on the counter. The second she goes to lift it to her mouth, it slips from her hand, careening toward the tiled floors and landing at Selene's feet in a shattered splash of glass and liquid that I notice immediately is tinged with red.

"You're bleeding."

"No," she protests as I approach, recklessly reaching for her hips and lifting her off the floor. "I'm fine."

Her voice is insistent, but there's a low note of pain hidden in the two words, and she winces when I sit her down on the island, making sure we're far away from the shards of glass Cal is already cleaning up.

"You're hurt," I shoot back, dropping down to my haunches in front of her. She gasps when I grip her right ankle and lift her foot to my face to examine it. There are no cuts or blood there, but I still lower it gingerly, in case there's something I can't see, before wrapping my fingers around her left ankle.

Selene whimpers, and I immediately loosen my grip, moving my fingers up to her calf to support the weight of her leg without agitating a clearly tender spot. My examination reveals a gash in the bottom of her foot and an angry line of broken skin on her ankle near where I was originally holding her.

Both of the wounds are bleeding, and it's only then that I notice crimson liquid on my skin, sinking into the lines of my fingertips. The sight makes my heart squeeze painfully while my mind floods with images of Diana's blood on my shaking and bruised hands, all over the floor and walls of our bedroom in the house I still can't bring myself to sell, while every cell in my body works to convince me I could have found Selene that same way tonight.

Cut open.

Gutted and bled like an animal.

Suddenly, I'm paralyzed, unable to move or think of anything that's not that day and how close I came to reliving the horror of finding someone I love....

Wait. Love? When did it become love?

My breath stalls in my lungs, as the word echoes in my mind, only coming when Selene calls my name.

"Beck." Her eyes run lazy lines over my features, confusion at my reaction riding high on her brows. "It's just a small cut. I'm fine."

Something about her calm affect settles the anxiety that's been swirling in my veins since I found her in the bathroom. Then, as if to provide further proof that this situation is nothing like the horror-filled thoughts that just seized my mind, Cal appears at my side with a first aid kit in hand. He pops it open, handing me an alcohol pad to clean the wounds and digging out two band aids to cover them. Their size serves as a reminder of how small and insignificant Selene's wounds are, and Cal's assistance as I clean and dress the wounds drives home the fact that we face every issue—big, small, or in between—together.

When I'm done, Cal puts everything away, and I scoop Selene off the counter, carrying her over to the couch. She holds herself rigid, refusing to let the lines of her body mesh with mine. It happens anyway. I hold her too close, my grip a little too tight as I pull in greedy lungfuls of her scent. Sugared wild berries and cherry blossoms accompanied by the nectar of ripe pears fill my nostrils, clinging to me even after I lower her to the couch.

"I could have walked," she says without meeting my eye.

"You don't have on shoes. I didn't want to risk you stepping on any microscopic shards."

Plus, I really wanted to hold you.

The errant thought begs to be set free, to move past the barrier of my lips and destroy every obstacle standing between what I want with Selene and what I get to have, which is nothing.

My sound logic seems to set her at ease, and she relaxes into the plush cushion in the middle of the couch. "Will you sit with me?"

I'm in the seat beside her before the question is fully formed, grabbing the remote from the coffee table and handing it to her. She flips through the channels with no real intention or purpose, which suits me just fine because the last thing I want to do is watch TV. I want to watch her, and I find myself sneaking glances, tracing the curve of her jaw and the details of her profile while Cal sweeps the floor for a second time and then runs a mop over it just to be safe.

He joins us a few minutes later, rounding the couch with the grazing board in one hand and a glass of wine in the other.

"Don't drop this one," he jokes, handing the wine to Selene.

"I didn't drop the other one. It *fell*."

"That's a weak defense," I quip, tossing a pillow on her lap so the grazing board has someplace to sit. "It definitely wouldn't hold up in court."

"Good thing no one is suing me for a broken glass," she remarks with a roll of her eyes. I can't tell if it's in response to our teasing or the obvious coddling, but I don't care. It could be either, both, or neither, and I'd still be biting back a smile at the mundane exchange.

This. I think as Cal sinks into the spot on Selene's other side and she stops the TV on a rerun of an old police procedural called *Bones*. *This is what life would be if I got to keep them both.*

One episode blends into another and another until we're sucked into an unexpected marathon filled with Temperance Brennan and Seeley Booth. We don't speak except to complain about the inaccuracies related to the Bureau, and each time we point out an error, Selene reprimands us for disparaging one of her comfort shows. She falls asleep with a fading scowl of annoyance on her lovely features, and I scoop her up in my arms for the second time tonight, carrying her to bed while Cal does the final perimeter check.

Selene doesn't so much as stir when I lay her on the bed and cover her with the blanket that's folded on the end of the bed. I back out of the room slowly, using the stealth getaway skills I perfected in preparation for Cameron and never got to use to make a clean escape. When I make it back downstairs, Cal is coming through the front door. We meet in the center of the open living space, both of us smiling like fools.

"I love her," I murmur.

He nods. "So do I."

We stare at each other, and it settles in the air between us. The impression of her presence. The things she's awakened in us that are both the same and different. The scent of her in the air and something more. A wispy billow of smoke. The result of a soldered bond crafted over the last two days, welded with words, forged in the fires of easy truths not lightly given, and care reluctantly accepted.

It explodes between us, demanding to be fed, and I've held back so much for so long. I cave instantly, lunging at Cal with a ferocity and fervor that catches him off guard. My hands go to his face, and I yank his lips down to mine as I urge him back, back, back, until he hits the wall with a groan I feel in my chest.

I pull back, biting his bottom lip as I go. "I love you."

"And I love you."

My lips are back on his in the span of a heartbeat, and this second kiss is more. More passionate. More sensual. More urgent. It goes on and on and on, only ending when it's broken by the sound of a shocked gasp.

26

———

SELENE

I'd never seen anything like it.

The two of them wrapped around each other, their lips pressed together. Cal's long fingers splayed across Beck's back. Beck's large hands gripping either of Cal's face. Their eyes clenched shut to block out the rest of the world.

And I did feel blocked out.

I fell asleep on the inside of their bubble and woke up to find myself cast out. An outsider. An intruder. No, worse, a desperate, incredibly turned intruder who had to hobble back into exile with a hurt foot, rapidly beating heart, and images of the two most attractive men she's ever known locked in a passionate kiss flashing in her mind.

Sleep evaded me after that, leaving me with no choice but to stare at the ceiling all night and surrender to a persistent loneliness that has permeated my bones, drilling deeper and deeper into my soul with every passing second. The past seven days have been nothing but a grind of agonizing obsession, playing the kiss over in my mind to the point of distraction.

It's a good thing I don't actually have much to do these days, because I wouldn't be able to dedicate any mental space to an actual task. Every inch of my brain is filled with them, every cell, every neuron, every pathway marked by their clear desire for each other and the ache of having none of that energy directed at me.

"Selene, are you even listening?" Monique asks, bringing my focus back to the screen of my computer where she's frowning at me. "Girl, where is your head right now?"

"Attached to my neck."

She's unbothered by my snarky remark and flat delivery, closing the tab on her shared screen that contains our QI projections for next year, so I have nothing to look at but her face.

"What has Aubrey done now?"

"Nothing."

I've barely seen the man since I returned from Houston, but I don't mention that to her. Just like I won't mention how much I'm dreading having to spend the evening acting like I love him when we're at this debate tonight.

She squints at me, like turning her eyes into slits will give her the ability to see through to the truth I'm holding deep inside. "Just spit it out, Sel. I've never seen you this distracted before."

I've never *been* this distracted during a conversation about work before. Most of the time, I'm *too* focused on it, unable to see anything past my daily tasks and weekly goals. Forgoing everything that will take me away from the things I need to finish, doing anything to avoid the grating discomfort of leaving something undone, running myself ragged so I don't have to live with the pinpricks of dissatisfaction firing underneath my skin when I can't check off all my boxes.

Work is usually what I hyper-focus on when I want to hide from things I don't want to face. I disappeared inside of it when AJ died and depended on it to keep me sane when I found out about the affair. The problem, I think, is that this time around I know I can't hide from this. I can't unsee what I saw. I can't unknow what I know, and most importantly, I can't bear the thought of going back to existing outside of their orbit even though that's where I've been forced to live for the last week.

The morning after the kiss, I came downstairs, hoping for a

conversation and got nothing but stilted sentences filled with things I didn't care to know like what time we were leaving and when we'd arrive in Las Vegas. Their bags were already by the door, and both of them were wearing suits instead of the leisure wear they'd flown in last time. As a result, I stuffed my Stanford hoodie and leggings into my suitcase and donned one of my pantsuits. Neither of them sat near me on the plane, opting for the back row where they spoke in hushed voices that were never aimed in my direction, and when they escorted me up to my suite they left me with nothing more than a curt nod and a clipped 'ma'am.'

Initially, the sudden shift back to the professional hurt my feelings, but now, after not seeing them for days and being robbed of a chance to discuss anything, I'm just mad.

At them for shutting me out.

At me for letting them in.

At Aubrey and his fucking campaign.

At everything.

That anger and the injustice of being punished for simply witnessing them in their truth swells inside me. I bite the inside of my jaw to stop the deluge of words climbing up my throat, sorting through them carefully before I lend my voice to them.

"Hypothetically speaking," I start, and Monique clasps her fingers together, leaning in close. "If you saw two of your friends kissing, and they knew that you saw them kissing and stopped speaking to you because of it, would you be upset?"

"Hell yeah. Why the hell are they mad at you for something they did all out in public for the world to see."

"I didn't say it was me, and it wasn't exactly in public."

She waves a dismissive hand at me. "Of course, it's you, Sel. Everyone knows you only ask hypothetical questions when you're trying to get someone's opinion on a situation without admitting you're at the center of it."

"If everyone knows that why do we even bother to phrase it as a hypothetical?"

"To keep the thrill alive," she tosses out impatiently, gesturing for me to keep going. "Who are these kissing friends?"

"I can't tell you that."

There's no part of me that would ever be okay with discussing Cal and Beck's private business with anyone without their express permission. Monique presses her lips together.

"Do I know them?"

"No, Mo."

"You don't have any friends that I don't know."

"Of course, I do."

Even as I say the words, I know it's a lie. My life has been intertwined with hers for decades. Everyone important to me has either been introduced to me by her or has been subjected to an interrogation she's conducted when I bring them around. She's even met Cal and Beck.

"Whatever. The who isn't nearly as important to me as what you did when you saw them. Did you, *hypothetically*, insert yourself into this *hypothetical* kiss?" She does air quotes and wiggles her brows dramatically every time she says hypothetical.

"Absolutely not."

She shrugs. "They sound a little uptight, so they might not have appreciated that anyway, but did you *want* to?"

I've pictured it a thousand times. Walking—okay, hobbling—down those stairs and going to them, plastering myself against Beck's back and Cal's hands leaving his waist to sink into the fabric of my shirt and pull me closer. All of us shifting until I was in between them, pressed against Cal's hard front with Beck's perfect stature and dense weight covering me.

A low whistle leaves my best friend's lips. "You dirty girl! You wanted to, didn't you?"

"What?!" The word is too loud and sharp to convey outrage convincingly, so I have to say more. "Of course not, I'm—"

Legally and contractually prohibited from being with any man except the only one in the world I don't want, I think.

"Don't say married," Monique wails. "Aubrey was married when he was fucking that speech writer. That didn't seem to slow him down any, so why should your broken vows stop you from having some fun?"

Before I can address the advice I agree with but can't take, the door to my bedroom is pushed open. I jump, rushing to end the call as Jordan and a group of women I don't know invade my space with a rolling rack of formal gowns in tow.

"Set it up over there," Jordan instructs the duo, maneuvering the rack with her eyes on her phone, fingers flying across the screen. They follow her direction without question while I look on, stunned by the audacity of it all.

"Jordan, what is all this?"

She has the decency to look up from her phone when I address her, and she keeps her eyes on me as I walk over to the rack. "Dresses for the fundraiser at the end of the month. You need to try them on and pick one so Zee can make alterations. We need it to fit perfectly."

Fundraising is a necessary evil of all political campaigns, and even though the election is less than a month away, fresh cash is still needed to cover things like last-minute marketing efforts and the numerous expenses that can be incurred once the ballots have been cast. Knowing this doesn't make me any less annoyed, though. I can the rack, seeing nothing but itchy fabrics and unflattering silhouettes then turn my back to it.

"I don't need a dress. We'll be back in Virginia by then, so I can pick something from the closet full of gowns we purchased when this whole charade began."

"Senator Barnes is bringing some key members of her party to show the public there's no support for the incumbent. There will be even more press than usual, so Aubrey wants you in something new."

I cross my arms over my chest, feeling less amenable than usual because my mind is still on that contract and the clause that would have stopped me from having my men even if they wanted me. "Jordan, let me be clear: I don't give a single fuck about what Aubrey wants."

Emerald eyes turn into saucers at my bluntness, and she pockets her phone, clearly needing her full faculties for this one. She clasps her hands together, approaching me with a caution she wouldn't normally use.

"*Selene.* I think we both know how important this last leg of the campaign is. I know you're tired from being pulled in a million different directions, but we're almost done." A disingenuous smile pulls up the corners of her thin lips, and her next words come through clenched teeth. "Just pick a dress, so we can get out of your hair."

"You're not in my hair, Jordan, you're in my bedroom without an invite and on my last nerve. I will not be picking a dress, so you can pack all of this up and leave."

WE END up locked in a standoff that she still resents me for winning hours after it's over. She shoots me dirty looks from the sidelines of the step and repeat Aubrey and I are posed in front of with Cordelia Barnes by her side, but as I smile for the cameras that have come to document Aubrey's debate against President Sanders, I find that I'm more concerned about the eyes that are *not* on me.

Cal and Beck are across the room, standing shoulder to shoulder. Two bodies in a wall of black formed by the agents in President Sander's detail and ours that lines the perimeter of the room. For everyone else they probably blend in with their colleagues, but to me they stand out, glowing like beacons of hope for all the things I shouldn't want.

They didn't spare me a single glance when Aubrey and I arrived, and they won't look at me now even though I can't stop my eyes from wandering in their direction.

"Right here, Mrs. Taylor," one of the photographers yells, snapping his fingers like I'm a dog and not a human. I make a show of turning in his direction and then focusing on the man to the left of him instead.

"Play nice," Aubrey grits out through his smile, shifting us to the right so the rude photographer can get his shot.

I don't respond because despite all the words I know, I don't have a single nice one for him. The photo op is done soon after, and Jordan and Cordelia immediately swoop in to whisk Aubrey off to some private corner to discuss things I don't care to know about. With them gone, I'm able to find a quiet place to breathe and, of course, covertly spy on the men who won't leave my mind.

I'm watching Cal speak into his comms and imagining the deep rumble of his voice washing over me when I'm suddenly surrounded by four large men in black that I don't recognize.

"Ma'am," the tallest one says, "President Sanders would like to speak with you."

"Why?" I blurt the word out, knowing it's the wrong thing to say but not really caring because I genuinely can't imagine what he'd want with me.

"Please follow us, ma'am. The President only has a few minutes before he's due on stage."

Saying no to Jordan earlier felt good, like something I should, and will, do more, but actively ignoring the request of this man who, for all intents and purposes, represents the interest of the leader of the free world feels like something I shouldn't do. With a dip of my chin, I signal my acquiescence, and the big guy turns on his heel while the others form a wall around me, herding me in the direction of their boss.

He's waiting in, what I assume is, the larger of the green rooms in the venue, holding court from a velvet armchair that faces the door with several agents at his back. They mark my entrance with little interest, but when the President sees me, his face lights up like we're old friends.

"Mrs. Taylor," he bellows, rising from his seat with surprising ease given his age and the low position of the chair. His fingers do shake a bit when he fastens the button on his suit jacket, and as he approaches me, I force the list of his suspected and confirmed medical issues that I heard on the news out of my mind. "You look lovely as ever," he says, gripping the tops of my arms lightly and laying a chaste kiss on each of my cheeks.

It's too familiar of a greeting for us to be strangers, but I allow it because, well, he's him. I wonder how many liberties he takes as a result of that kind of thinking, how many liberties Aubrey will take if he's ever fortunate enough to wield the type of power that affords you such a thing.

I step back to end the contact and force a smile to ease the blow. "Thank you, Mr. President. You look well."

He chuckles, running a wrinkled hand over silver hair. "Not too bad for a man who's, how did your husband put it? Knocking on death's door?"

The smile, which I'd been holding for too long anyway, drops, which only seems to humor him more. "Relax, darling, I didn't bring you here to visit the sins of the husband on the wife. We have much more important things to discuss. Come, let's have a seat."

With a grand sweep of his arm through the air, he directs me to the sitting area. The coffee table between the chairs is covered with an assortment of foods and drinks.

"Would you like something to eat? Maybe a drink? I always like to have a little whiskey before I take to the stage, helps soothe the nerves."

"No, thank you. I'd much rather you get to the point."

"A straight shooter," he muses, crossing one leg over the other and resting clasped hands on his knee. "I like that. I like that a lot."

"I prefer to think of myself as an efficient communicator."

"I'm sorry if I offended you with the use of that turn of phrase." The stretch of his eyes and the flare of his nostrils indicate genuine regret, but everything about this conversation feels intentional, including the word choice he's apologizing for. "I know how you feel about guns. I saw a clip of your speech about gun control on the day of your software launch. You spoke with so much conviction."

Keeping tabs on your opponent and everyone in their inner circle is basic strategy, but it still kind of creeps me out to know that he's this tuned in to what I'm doing and saying.

"Well, as you know, the issue is close to my heart."

"Yes, I was so sorry to hear about the loss of your son."

"Thank you."

I want to urge him to get to the point again, but I don't bother because he's working up to it slowly but surely. As soon as I accept that he'll drop the bomb when he's good and ready, it explodes right in my face.

"Selene, were you aware that your husband no longer shares your views on gun control?"

"I'm sorry?"

President Sanders drops his leg and sits up straight, the light overhead casting long shadows over his face. "Aubrey won't make a move against the NRA now that Cordelia is backing him. Any hopes you had for gun reform are dead in the water, darling, and your husband is the one holding the gun."

My head swings back and forth on its own volition. An involuntary rejection of the President's words, of a reality where the one thing I trusted Aubrey to give me is being ripped away.

"No. That's not true. That can't be true." I'm looking down on Sanders now, taking in his repressed smirk, but I don't know when I stood up. "He promised," I whisper, my voice weak but somehow still laced with anger.

"I'm sure he did," Sanders says although I'm sure he knows I'm not talking to him. "It's a shame really. How he keeps finding new ways to betray and embarrass you on the world's stage."

The final shot works like a charm, turning me into a heat-seeking missile tuned to the exact temperature of Aubrey's body. I find him just down the hall from Sanders, his name on the green room door that I burst through without knocking. I'm absently aware of the agents around the room with their hands on their holsters, ready to shoot down a threat. It occurs to me that they might view me as one, but that doesn't stop me. Doesn't make my steps falter or take the red out of my vision.

"Are you fucking serious?" I hiss, all rage now. My body vibrates with it as I slap the papers Aubrey's holding out of his hands. Out of the corner of my eye, I see Cordelia literally clutch her pearls, pleading blue eyes on Jordan who is just standing by waiting to see how this all plays out.

"What the fuck is your problem, Selene?"

He starts to bend down to pick up the papers, but I pin them underneath my heel. "You are my fucking problem, Aubrey Taylor. Were you seriously going to let me sit in that audience tonight and find out with the rest of the world that you're flipping on gun control? *Gun control*, Aubrey?"

"Selene." He pinches the bridge of his nose. "Our democracy doesn't work without bipartisanship, and bipartisanship only happens when you're willing to compromise."

"Where is the line?"

"What?"

"The line, Aubrey. The thing you won't do, the concession you won't make. Where is it? Do you even know? *Does it even exist*?" I shake my head, disgust twisting my stomach into knots. "You are a pathetic man. Weak-willed. Undisciplined. *Spineless*. I'm ashamed to have ever loved you, to have ever trusted you, and I know without a doubt that AJ would be ashamed to call you his father."

There aren't many things I can say to Aubrey these days that actually touch him, but that does. Too bad I'm far too disgusted with him to take in or appreciate the effects my words have. I stumble back, ripping the papers underneath my feet when I turn to head for the door.

No one tries to stop me from leaving or follows me out, and I'm grateful for that because it gives me time to compose myself. It only takes a few minutes to set myself back to rights, and I emerge from the darkest corner at the end of a long hallway feeling well enough to fake a few smiles for the cameras who will capture my early departure.

Only, it seems Jordan has other plans.

She intercepts me just as I'm about to enter the backstage area and request to be taken home, already aware of what I'm about to do. "You can't leave."

I take a step to my left to walk around her, and she mirrors the move, blocking me. I huff out a breath of frustration. "You need to get out of my way, Jordan."

"Aubrey needs you here."

"Aubrey has you and Cordelia Barnes; he doesn't need me."

"I'm not his wife and neither is Senator Barnes."

"But you're his partners. You know what he's going to get up there and say tonight, don't you? The points he's going to make, the stances he's going to take?"

"I mean, of course, I—"

"Then you can be the one to sit in the audience and cheer for his lies," I interject.

Exasperation writes itself into the lines of her face. "Selene, the media wants to see you here supporting your husband."

"Jordan, if I talk to a member of the press tonight, I will intentionally set fire to this entire charade and smile as the ashes rain down on your head."

For the second time today, we find ourselves locked in a standoff, and for the second time today, I win. The taste of victory only lasts for a second, though, ending with a bitter note when Jordan waves over the first agent she sees and orders him and his partner to take me back to the hotel.

"Stay with her," she says.

Cal nods. "Yes, ma'am."

"We won't let her leave our sight," Beck promises.

After so many days obsessing over and being mad at them, I want to feel nothing about being around them again. Instead, I feel everything. The press of safety that only exists for me when it's the three of us. The heavy weight of desire sitting low in my stomach. The searing burn of their rejection and subsequent abandonment.

All of it comes spilling out when we're back at the hotel, alone in my suite, and Cal sets twin pools of copper and brass on my face from across the room. Beck is looking at me too, puddles of onyx warming my skin as they ghost over my features. We're all standing. Me, lingering near the door of my bedroom. Them, just a few feet apart in the living area with their hands in their pockets.

"What's wrong?" Cal asks. "Why did you need to leave the debate?"

"Did someone else approach you?" Beck hedges. "Did they hurt you?"

"Would you care?"

Beck's head rears back. "Is that a serious question? Of course, we'd care."

"Yes, it's a serious question," I snap, my patience paper thin. "I'm not playing coy. I'm asking because I can't reconcile the apparent worry on display now with the behavior of the last few days."

"Apparent worry," he repeats, lifting up on his tip toes and then rocking back on his heels. "*Wow.*"

Cal takes a few steps forward, offering himself up as a mediator. "Our concern is genuine, Selene, and as for our behavior over the last few days, we were just giving you some space because we thought you were…"

He gazes heavenward, searching for the right term.

"Disgusted," Beck supplies.

"Disgusted?" I repeat. "Why would you think that?"

He rubs at the back of his neck. "Because you saw us kissing and ran away. What were we supposed to think?"

"I don't know." My shoulder rises and then falls, the muscles heavy from all the tension I've been carrying. "Not that, though. *Never that.*"

This conversation isn't going how any of us thought it would. I can tell by the way Cal and Beck keep looking at each other, having those non-verbal conversations they're so good at, by the way I keep pushing down the hope trying to bloom in my chest because it feels premature.

"Describe it for us then." Cal murmurs, still inching closer to me while Beck lingers in the distance. "What did you feel when you saw us together?"

"*Jealous.*"

The admission tumbles out of my mouth and lands on the floor between Cal and I. He turns his head slowly, looking at Beck. They have another silent exchange, and when Cal turns back to me, his eyes have dissolved into liquid heat.

"Tell me more, pet," he purrs, and the command combined with the nickname and the shrinking measure of his proximity creates the perfect conditions for uninhibited honesty.

I bite my bottom lip as his smoked spice scent invades my nostrils. "I was caught off guard at first, but then..." All of my thoughts fall away once Cal is finally in front of me. There are millimeters between the hardened peaks of my nipples and the defined lines of his pectorals, and even that disappears when my chest starts to heave as a result of his hands on my waist.

His touch is firm, but gentle, and I melt into him, whimpering as his palms skate over my hips, ribs, the sides of my breasts and the column of my neck before stopping at my jaw. There's a tenderness to his callused palms as he cradles my face, tipping it up so I have to meet his eye.

"But then, what?"

"Then I was turned on," I breathe, shuddering when Cal's dick pulses against my stomach. "I wanted to be between you, a part of your connection, not on the outside of it." A low, rumbling chuckle breaks free from his chest, and my brows pull together. "Why is that funny?"

"Because for months now, we've been building our world around you, Selene. Your smile. Your laugh. Your wants and needs. You aren't just a part of our connection, pet, you're the center of it."

My heart is so full it's close to bursting, and then Cal brings his lips to mine and it does exactly that. The world implodes, morphing into a bright symphony of color and sensation that I allow myself to get lost in. I'm overwhelmed in the best way, but not so much that I can't hear Beck behind us. The gasp he releases sounds like the one I let hit the air in Houston that night. I laugh at that as I break Cal's kiss and peer over his shoulder, extending a hand toward Beck.

He stares at the invitation but stays glued to his spot. His reluctance sends a spark of fear through me, making me wonder if we all want this, and I look to Cal for guidance. He drags his gaze away from my face, trading my wide, fearful eyes for Beck's low, hooded ones. Something passes between them. A kind of understanding that comes from years of knowing each other, of loving each other, in theory and praxis. I want that knowledge, but I don't have it yet.

Cal's eyes are back on my face, they're darker now, a blanket of need cast over the rich shades of brown. He brushes his thumb over my lip. "Don't ask. *Tell.*"

It's a simple directive that makes my thighs clench. The thought of ordering Beck around is thrilling, but it's also scary. I trust that Cal is right about what he needs, but I don't feel confident in my ability to give it to him successfully. I don't want to fail.

"I can't."

My need to be perfect before I think about trying something used to be a regular point of contention between Aubrey and I, especially in our sex life. He'd want me to dive head first into new kinks and role play scenarios with no information, instruction or confidence. When I'd refuse, he'd get pissed and accuse me of ruining the moment. I watch Cal's face as he processes my dissent, searching for signs of disappointment or annoyance and coming up empty.

A slow, menacingly carnal smile spreads across his face. "Don't worry, pet. I'll teach you," he says, dropping one hand from my cheek and extending it in Beck's direction.

Now, we're both reaching for our hesitant third, asking him to join us so we can finally indulge in this thing we've been running from for so long.

27

BECK

Cal is reaching for me. His long arm is a strong, steady line that runs parallel to Selene's. Her elegant fingers strain in my direction, wiggling just a little, relaying the need to connect, but I can't move.

I've been paralyzed since Selene let Cal touch her, since his hands on her body coaxed words I could only hope to one day hear from her lips, since weeks of longing and pining culminated in the breathtaking sight of them kissing. I knew then how Selene felt when she saw us in Houston because I wanted nothing more than their hands on me. Cal's lips on my neck. Selene's fingers cupping my hard dick through my pants. I can have all of those things right now. The two people in the world who own my heart are holding their hands out, offering themselves to me.

But I. Can't. Fucking. Move.

"Get over here, Beckham," Cal barks.

The bite to his tone is the key to the shackles on my feet. They fall to the floor, lying uselessly on the ground. My steps are slow, hesitant. My legs are leaden, and my mind is plagued with memories of walking into things I wanted, things I cherished and lost.

My new home with my adoptive parents.

The aisle that led to the altar where I married Diana.

The hallway of the doctor's office we visited to confirm Cameron's presence in the womb.

I have had so much, *lost* so much, and I'm scared to want anything again. Terrified, actually, which is why I stop short, just inches from them. Cal's eyes flash as he wages a war between impatience and concern. His lips part like he's going to issue another edict, and I wait for it, knowing it will be exactly what I need, but then Selene catches me by the hand and the need for further encouragement no longer exists.

She threads our fingers together, her eyes soft, her expression open, and I remember that she's lost too. That Cal has as well. And yet, by some miracle, they are both here, wanting. Wanting happiness. Wanting love. Wanting *me.*

If they can do that, then I have to believe that I can do the same.

Cal reaches for my other hand. He squeezes it for just a second before placing it on Selene's hip and stepping back, creating space for it to be just me and her for a moment. It's not something I knew I needed until I have it, until she's gazing up at me with eyes sharpened by lust and the blunt edges of her teeth digging into her lower lip.

She's still gripping one of my hands, her thumb running anxious circuits over the side of mine in what is, to me, a clear substitution for her finger flicking stim. I'm comforted by the way she's incorporated me into the self-soothing behavior, but I'm also worried that she feels the need to engage in it at all now that she's in my arms.

"Is this too much?" I whisper, searching her face. "Do you just want it to be...it's okay if this is just a you and Cal thing."

That's a lie, but I hope she can't tell. I don't want my potentially hurt feelings to influence her answer. There are so many parts of her life that aren't about choice, and I won't let this be one.

"Yes, it's too much," she says slowly, glancing at the ceiling for a beat. "But it's too much in the best way. I have wanted this for so long, Beck. I have wanted you for so long. *Both* of you."

Selene doesn't say things she doesn't mean, so her succinct answer is a salve that soaks into the last bit of my anxiety and relaxes it away. I let go of her hand, so I can plant both of mine on either side of her waist and hoist her up. Her legs wrap around my middle, the taut muscles of her inner thighs gripping me like a vice.

My heart beats wildly as she stares down at me, her arms draped around my neck. "Kiss me," she demands, her voice breaking on the last word as her confidence wavers. I don't want her doubting my commitment to doing whatever she asks of me, so I oblige happily, turning feral when our lips meet. Desperate for the lush wonderland of her mouth. Hungry for every swipe of her tongue while she moans and rocks against me.

Suddenly, Cal is at my back, liberating Selene's feet from the confines of her strappy heels. They hit the floor with light thuds I barely hear over Selene's panting and Cal's rasping moans as he grinds his dick into my ass.

"Couch. *Now*," he tells me, pushing me in the direction he wants to go.

I lower Selene onto the plush sofa, and we both drop to our knees in front of her. She's wearing another one of her fucking pantsuits, but I want her bare legs. I want her smooth skin. Cal shares that desire. Pushing up on the balls of his feet, he curves his body over hers and plants kisses along her jaw and neck.

"Will you let us undress you, pet?"

I don't know where the fuck the name came from, but Selene loves it. She whimpers when he says it, nodding while she stares at me. "Yes."

Her eyes fall shut as we work her out of the suit. Cal handles the top, while I take care of the bottom, and when it's done—her clothes in a heap somewhere behind the couch and the entirety of her gorgeous sable skin is on display—neither one of us knows who's luckier.

My fingers ghost over her feet, caressing her pretty toes and massaging their way up to the inside of her thighs, pushing them further and further apart until I'm looking at the slick, puffy lips of her pussy.

"She's already wet," I tell Cal. He's up on the couch now. His knees in the cushion next to the one Selene is splayed out on. His back bowed as he laves at her breasts, his only response a muffled moan around a mouthful of one of her berry brown nipples. The vibration of it puts an arch in Selene's back, and I watch her get even wetter, liquid arousal glistening against her skin, peeking at me from between the folds of the most sacred part of her.

"No one gets to see you like this," I whisper, voice full of awe at the truth of the statement, mouth hovering over her mound while her hips lift and churn, asking me to taste her.

One of her hands snakes down her body, fingers searching for her clit. I nudge them out of the way with my nose then nuzzle into her, memorizing the scent of desire on her skin. I'm thorough in my endeavor, moving slowly, breathing deeply, torturing her until her sex is dripping with need, and she's begging when I pull away.

"Beck, please," she cries, planting the heels of her feet on the edge of the couch to make the meal I'm seconds away from gorging myself on appear even more desirable. It's an unnecessary move, but I reward it, leaning in close before diving in.

I go straight for her clit, concentrating all of my efforts on the swollen bundle of nerves that throbs underneath my ministrations and grows more firm when I slip one finger inside her soaked channel. The strokes are shallow at first, light, almost teasing, because of how tight she is, but the more Cal and I worship her, the more her muscles relax. Eventually, I add in another finger, angling up until I find the spot I know will send her over the edge.

She curses loudly when I start to massage the ridged flesh, and if Cal wasn't up there, anchoring her to the couch with one hand pressing into her lower stomach and the other gripping her nape, I'm certain she would be levitating right now.

"Fuckkkkk." Her eyes roll back into her head, and I feel her walls pulsing around me. I suck harder on her clit, using long, deep pulls that cause her thighs to jerk repeatedly.

"Are you going to come for him?" Cal's voice is crushed velvet and sin layered over the obscene sounds of my fingers moving inside of Selene. Her eyes are low as she looks at him, her head lolling on her neck in a lazy nod. "Say it, pet. He needs to hear you."

My heart swells with love for him, and I don't even question how even in this moment, when he could simply be focused on his needs, he's managing to hold space for mine.

Selene stares down the long line of her body, trapping me in her gaze so intense it makes the declaration more intimate. "I'm going to come for you, Beck."

Seconds later, her head falls back on Cal's hand, and she comes apart at the seams. It's a quick, violent unraveling that sweeps in and takes over her entire body. She goes completely still, nothing but her throat moving, working to expel the quiet mewls of pleasure I will never not want the honor of hearing. When it passes, her muscles relax and she sinks into the couch, boneless and sated. I retreat from her slowly, my hand leaving her channel with a wet smack that garners Cal's attention.

He's sitting on his heels, stroking Selene's cheek, but his eyes are on me, stretching as I take the digits into my mouth and suck her essence off of them. "Does she taste good?" he asks, voice thick with need. We're both hard, but there's an unspoken agreement between us that we won't push her for more.

My fingers are still warm from my mouth when I reach for her center, coating my fingertips in her juices and then holding it out to Cal. "See for yourself."

He stands, towering over Selene and me. The move puts the bulge in his pants right in her line of sight. Her eyes flit from it to my outstretched hand like she can't decide which one she wants to pay more attention to. Cal's fingers close around my wrist, and the decision is made for her. She watches, completely entranced as he brings my offering to his lips, moaning just as loud as I do when they close around me.

I see the moment her unique flavor explodes on his tongue, feel his addiction to it snap into place, and then we're all moaning.

Him at the taste of her.

Her at the sight of us.

Me at the way the wet heat of his mouth makes my erection strain against my zipper.

A bead of pre-cum escapes from my tip as Cal pulls away. He lays kisses on my knuckles before dropping my hand. Selene sits up.

"I want more."

"More?" I ask.

"*More.*"

"Are you unsatisfied?"

Twin frowns appear on her face and Cal's at my question.

"No, but you are." She waves a hand between my dick and Cal's. "I want to fix that."

Before either of them can protest, she's on her knees in front of Cal, deft fingers undoing the buckle of his pants. There's an air of confidence around her that wasn't there just moments ago, and I watch as Cal yields to it, letting her tug him down to the ground and push him onto his back before setting his dick free. I've always told him how beautiful his dick is, but I've never gotten to see anyone else admire it before. Selene stares at his length with a reverence and hunger that makes me want to join her as she feasts on him.

I start to move, to take up space on the other side of Cal's body to do just that, but she glares at me over her shoulder. "Stay right there, Beck." For a second I think she's planning to handle us one at a time, but then she smiles. "I want you to fuck me from behind."

It doesn't surprise me that she's a quick study, that after seeing how I reacted to Cal's directions and experiencing my immediate obedience with the kiss, she feels comfortable saying exactly what she wants. Just like before, I obey, taking off my jacket and shirt, and bringing my pants and boxers down just far enough to free my dick before lining the swollen tip up with her core.

From my position, I have a view of everything. The muscles and veins in Selene's back as she holds the deepest arch I've ever fucking seen. The rise and fall of her head as she moves her mouth up and down the length of Cal's dick. I can even see his face, the deep wrinkle in his brow as he surrenders to pleasure.

What I can't see is Selene's face when I slide into her.

I can hear her moan clear as day, though. It pierces the cloud of lust that's blurring my vision, making it so I don't miss the moment when she pitches her voice low and says, "Yes, just like that, Beck. You're such a good fucking boy."

Sparks of electricity race down my spine, and I plunge into her harder on the next stroke. Cal sinks both sets of his fingers into her hair and pulls her mouth back down to his dick.

"You're right, pet. He's the best fucking boy."

"*Jesus,*" I moan at their shared praise, closing my eyes and trying to maintain some semblance of self-control. It's an impossible feat. Between the tight grip and slick heat of Selene's pussy, and her slurping on Cal's dick while he curses and shudders beneath her, I'm bound to lose it any second.

Fortunately for me, Cal goes over the edge first.

He comes with a string of long curses, while Selene holds steady, taking every drop of what I know from first hand experience is an endless rush of hot, creamy cum down her throat.

"Don't swallow," Cal rasps, barely recovered from the onslaught of pleasure. "Let him taste."

Selene looks back at me, her lips swollen and her cheeks bulging with Cal's load. The vacant look in her eye tells me she's too pleasure drunk to figure out how to accommodate the request, and I can't help but laugh.

"I've got you, gorgeous." Still stroking, I grip her hips, bringing her with me as I recline onto my back. I tap her leg, "Turn around." She spins slowly, clenching her walls to keep me inside. When she's facing me, I plant my feet flat on the ground so I can keep fucking up into her and grin at the way her breasts bounce from the force of my strokes. "Now, give me that cum."

The tips of her nails dig into my chest as she leans over me, trickling a slow stream of Cal's cum mixed with her saliva into my waiting mouth. Salt and sweat and satisfaction run down my throat, and I gulp it down greedily, swallowing every ounce Selene deigns to share. When her mouth is empty, and I've had my fill of them, her lips close over mine in a filthy kiss that breaks on a shared moan the second

Cal joins back in. He's fully recovered now, his eyes bright with determination as he straddles my legs, pressing his chest to Selene's back.

"She tastes like you, Drake," I pant.

"And she looks so good on top of you," he says, putting his hands on her hips and taking over the rhythm, pushing her up and pulling her down, essentially fucking me with her pussy. Selene throws her head back, exposing her neck, and I sit up, unable to resist the urge to sink my teeth into the delicate flesh.

"*Oh, God.*"

One of her hands goes to the back of my head, her grip weak and desperate as she holds me in place. The bite turns into a nibble and then a licking kiss. The most primal part of me wants to bite again, to suck on her skin until my mark blooms there.

I use the last thread of my self-control to make the decision not to, and then I'm lost to the sounds of her stuttered breaths, to the cracks of lightning rolling down my spine every time Cal guides her back down my shaft pausing just long enough to allow her to grind her clit into me, coating the lower part of my stomach in her arousal.

"Is his dick good?"

"It's amazing," she gasps into my ear. Both of her arms circle my neck, and she clings to me tightly, nipping at my lobe. "Your dick is amazing, Beck."

"Tell him again."

Selene's walls flutter when she processes Cal's demand, and my balls tighten with the threat of release as she repeats herself, every word punctuated by a bounce he facilitates. We're not in charge of our pleasure, Selene and I. Everything that's happening now is at his discretion, occurring only because he allows it to. That feels right somehow since he's the one who brought us together. The one who believed we could get here.

"You're getting close, aren't you, love?" My answer is a jerky nod. Cal drags his teeth along the top of Selene's shoulder. "Can he come in you, pet?"

The most delicious pressure is building up inside of me, but I don't give in, refusing to let go until I know where she wants me to do it. Her lips are still level with my ear, sweat from her temple soaking into my skin. *"Fuck, yes."*

Cal works Selene over me faster, *harder*, ushering us both to our releases with an urgency that doesn't feel impatient but is still hurried, desperate. Like he'll find pleasure at the peak as well. Selene breaks seconds before I do, walls pulsing while moisture pours out of her, finding a home in the minuscule spaces between her body and mine, mixing with the evidence of my desire when the last thread of my control is shredded and I flood her with thick ropes of cum.

We collapse into a spent heap on the floor. Sweaty chest to sweaty chest. Pounding heart to pounding heart. I run my hands down her back and kiss her temple, loving the feel of her lips curving into her grin at the show of affection. It's not long before Cal is touching her too, kneading at her ass and the backs of her thighs. Selene sighs, and the sound is laced with a contentment I've never heard from her before.

All three of us know our stolen moment is winding down, but none of us wants to be the first to acknowledge it. We're left with no choice when Cal's phone starts to ring. Unlike me, he's still mostly dressed, so he's able to access it easily, pulling it out of the interior pocket of his jacket.

"Back to life, back to reality," Selene mutters into my chest as Cal puts some distance between us to take the call. She tries to lift up, but I'm not ready to let her go just yet. I lock my fingers at the small of her back to keep her in place.

"One more minute, gorgeous."

"I like when you call me that."

"Then I'll say it more."

Another smile I can feel but don't see takes over her face. "Will you tell me something?"

There are any number of topics she could want to broach with me right now, but my answer is still immediate and without condition. "Anything."

When she tries to sit up this time, I loosen my grip to allow her to, wanting to see her face. She puts one palm over my heart and then the other over the top of that hand, creating a makeshift pillow to rest her chin on.

"How did it start with you and Cal?"

I brush errant strands of hair out of her face as I consider where to start with a story I never thought I'd share with anyone else. "After I lost my wife and son, I was hurt, broken, and alone. I didn't trust anyone, didn't want to know anyone, didn't want to love anyone. But he didn't give me a choice."

"So you two were always romantic?"

"Not immediately. We built a partnership first, and then a friendship. Things didn't change until we'd known each other for about a year. At that point, it felt like a natural evolution."

Selene nods. "He does that, doesn't he? Loves you to the point of inevitability."

"Yes, he does."

Once again, she's taken a complex, layered thing and made it simple, clean-cut. I'm jealous of her ability to see things so clearly, of the way she seems to have readily accepted that what Cal feels for her is love. It took me forever to see it, to appreciate it, and I hope her awareness will save him from the heartache I subjected him to.

Heavy footfalls announce Cal's return to the living room. He stands over our prone forms, his expression pure affection. "Talking about me?"

"Yep, nothing but bad things," I quip. "Are they on their way back?"

He gives a regretful dip of his chin. "Yes, roughly fifteen minutes out. They wanted an update on Selene's mood."

A derisive snort escapes her as she lifts up and stretches. "Did you tell them I'm fan-fucking-tastic?"

Cal helps her to her feet once she's disentangled herself from me, his eyes on the cum dripping down her leg. "I told them you were sleeping."

"That works too," she says, legs wobbling as she walks. "I was planning on going to bed once you two left. I don't want to be awake when Aubrey gets here."

Silence pools between us at the mention of her husband's name. Cal and I share a look as I rise to my feet and begin the work of making myself presentable again. I'm fastening the last button on my shirt when Selene gets fed up with all the things we aren't saying.

"What did I say wrong?"

She's standing behind the couch, clutching her clothes to her chest. The picture of anxious vulnerability, even though her facial features remain smooth.

"You didn't say anything wrong," Cal tells her. "I think we're both just wondering what exactly is going on with you and Aubrey."

"He's my husband," she says, simply, her matter of fact tone sending my heart plummeting toward my feet. It stops in the middle of its descent when she pulls in a deep breath and continues. "In name only."

I tuck my hands into my pockets. "Elaborate, please."

A lingering, worrying quiet greets my request, lasting for what feels like hours. Truthfully, a full minute doesn't even pass before she launches into her explanation, giving us all the details about an agreement that ended her marriage but linked her life to Aubrey in a new way. Cal and I both curse when we hear about the clause that forbids her from being with anyone else.

"I understand if you don't want to get involved with someone who can't offer you anything but complications," she says, concluding her speech just as she tucks her blouse back into her pants.

Now that we're dressed and the couch has been restored to its former glory, all the evidence of what we've done is gone. To the outside world, it appears that nothing has changed between us, but everything has. That truth ensures that my response to Selene's statement is all passion and no finesse.

"*Get* involved? Gorgeous, you've felt what we're like together. We *are* fucking involved. We can't walk this shit back even if we wanted to!"

"And we don't want to," Cal tacks on, his voice calm, his hand on my shoulder a demand to reel it the fuck in.

Selene crosses her arms over her chest, and I watch as she

squeezes herself tightly, pain lancing my chest at the thought of upsetting her. Even though she's hurt, she holds her head high.

"I appreciate the sentiment behind that statement. I'm simply trying to make sure you know that you both have a choice here. You have an out if you want it."

Cal starts to step forward to go to her, but I move first. I'm the one who hurt her, so I'll be the one to fix it. There's a wariness to her eyes as she watches me approach, but when I pull her into a tight hug, she melts for me, succumbing to the deep pressure of my embrace.

"We don't want an out," I whisper into her hair. "All we want is you."

28

CAL

Beck is asleep in my bed, and it took zero effort to get him here.

I should be relishing in that fact, should be marveling at the sound of his soft snores and the scent of Selene filling my nostrils because he refused to wash her off his skin. We worked the rest of our shift smelling like her and finished out the evening quietly indulging in each other. He let me fuck him against the wall, his cheek pressed to the portrait of a field of wildflowers hanging next to the TV while I held him open, listening as he described what it was like to be inside Selene in vivid detail.

We came together, collapsing into bed shortly after without even eating dinner.

He fell asleep in minutes, one arm thrown over my stomach. Normally, I'm the one who sleeps easily while Beck stays up pacing and worrying, but tonight we've traded places.

I blame Charlie.

She texted me right after Beck passed out, responding to a message I sent forty-eight hours ago asking for an update on Jacob Marsh.

Charlie: Nothing on JM. Going on
assignment. Will be in touch when I can.

The curtness of the message doesn't bother me so much as the content of it. I just find it hard to believe that she's having trouble learning anything about Jacob outside of what we shared with her. If the kid has the balls to be gunning for a high-profile figure like Selene and enough pull to get a Secret Service agent to violate their solemn oath, then he has to be on someone's radar.

Although I know she probably doesn't have her phone on her, I still write back and tell her to be safe. Then I put my phone face down on the nightstand and attempt to sleep. As soon as I close my eyes, it starts to ring, nearly falling to the floor from the force of the continuous vibrations. Thinking it might be Charlie, I rush to pick it up, partially deflating when I see my brother Hunter's name scrolling across the screen instead.

There was a time when I'd fully deflate at a call from Hunter, when I'd just let the phone ring or send him to voicemail because I didn't want to know about whatever problems were plaguing him that day. That time has passed, though, and I'm smiling as the call connects, hoping I'll get a chance to talk to Riley too.

"What's up, little Drake?"

I can practically see the scowl on his face. "Little? Nigga, I'm bigger than you."

Hunter is bigger than pretty much everyone, so there's not really a point to this line of conversation besides getting on his nerves. I didn't get to do enough of that when we were younger, at least not in the fun, playful way.

"True, but I'm the oldest."

"The fuck does that have to do with size?"

"Everything."

He scoffs. "You hit your head when you were taking down those bank robbers in Wisconsin?"

"You heard about that?"

"Yeah, Rae showed me an article about it. Imagine my surprise when I see the date and realized you almost died a few weeks ago."

I wince, understanding my mistake immediately. Part of working on our relationship means keeping each other abreast of significant events in our lives. I guess trading shots with some low-level criminals counts in his mind.

"Shit, I'm sorry for not keeping you in the loop."

"It's all good, bro. Just make sure you call your niece and let her know you're okay. Rae found the article on her iPad. Apparently, she googles you on the regular."

The article in question is a small-time publication in Madison, Wisconsin, that refused to comply with a request to remove my name from their write-up on the robbery. I registered the issue with Hicks, but of course, he brushed me off, saying a two line mention of my involvement wasn't a threat to national security. Learning that his nonchalance has once again cost someone I care about their peace of mind sets my teeth on edge.

"I will give her a call tomorrow after school," I promise Hunter. "We can FaceTime if she wants."

"She'll love that. Make sure Beck's there too."

I glance at the man I have to share every good thing in this life with and smile, knowing he won't pass up the chance to talk to Ri. "He'll be there."

Hunter hums his acknowledgment. Usually, this is the point where we end the call, but he's lingering, as if he has something more to say. Dread coils in the pit of my stomach, and I start to pray, pleading with every god, idol and deity that he's not about to tell me he's relapsed again.

After multiple stents of falling off and climbing back on the wagon, he's finally figured out how to make it stick. It's been over a decade since he last used. I can't think of a single reason why he'd throw all that progress away, but I also know that addiction doesn't abide by logic. It doesn't play by the rules, doesn't stop niggling at you just because you have everything you want. Hunter once told me that's when the thoughts get the loudest, when the fear of ruining everything becomes a breeding ground for self-sabotage.

God, I don't want that to be the case for him.

I clear my throat, interrupting the silence that's enveloped us. "Any updates on your end?"

My fingers are crossed for a simple, inconsequential change. Something small and not at all capable of disrupting the delicate balance of his life. That's not what I get though.

"Riley's officially a Drake."

"What?!" I whisper-shout, smiling so big my cheeks hurt. "Hunter, that's great news."

He and Rae—Riley's mom and Hunter's non-girlfriend, girlfriend—started the process of changing Riley's last name in August, right after her tenth birthday. I'm happy to hear that it's done.

"Yeah, I know. Rae is over the moon. Riley doesn't know just yet, but when she finds out she's going to be excited. We're going to have a party."

"And what about you? Are you excited?"

"I'm scared, man. Rae showed me the paper she got from the courts saying it's official, and all of a sudden I just panicked. What if I can't do this?"

There's a helpless quality to his voice that activates the paternal instincts I'm not sure I'll ever get to tap into for a child of my own. Suddenly, I'm certain that this is the reason sleep evaded me, so I could be awake for Hunter's call, so I could give him the kind of support only a brother can.

"You're already doing it," I remind him. "You've been doing it from the moment she walked into your life. Most people have months to prepare to be a parent, but you were thrown headfirst into the deep end. Anyone else would have drowned, but you started swimming and you never stopped."

"What am I? A shark?" he quips.

"Yeah, asshole, you're a fucking shark. Matter of fact, you're a great white. Big as hell and mean, ready to eat a motherfucker if they look at you or someone you love wrong."

"Hmm. I think this metaphor is growing on me."

"Good, because I'm not thinking of another one." We share a short laugh, and I soak in the moment of levity before turning serious again. "All I'm trying to say is that you are already knee deep in this dad thing, and you're killing it. That paper shouldn't scare you, it should affirm you."

"But what if I fuck up again? Do something stupid to make her ashamed to have my last name? To make Rae reconsider agreeing to take it one day?"

From my understanding, things with him and Rae are kind of up in the air. They're in some kind of holding period that won't end until June of next year when Rae will let Hunter know if she really wants to give them another chance. He's been doing extremely well with the whole being in limbo thing. I guess that's something we have in common.

"Hunter, you're going to fuck up in a million different ways, but none of them will ever make Rae and Riley stop loving you." I pause for a beat then continue. "Unless of course, you pull a Nicholas Drake and abandon them to start a whole new family."

"Fuck you, Cal. I would never do no dumb shit like that," he growls. His clear offense makes me laugh, which shakes the bed, and Beck stirs a bit, turning over on his other side. "Alright then, sounds like you don't have anything to worry about."

I've lowered my voice a bit, but now that Beck's been disturbed he's turned restless. He tosses the cover off of him and groans, rolling onto his stomach.

"Are you with someone?" Hunter asks.

"Just Beck."

"Is he alright?"

"Yeah, he's sleeping." I don't say anymore than that, leaving space for Hunter to draw his own conclusions. We haven't talked much about my love life, but he's known for a long time that I date men, so I'm sure it's crossed his mind once or twice that there might be something between Beck and me.

That something changed drastically tonight in Selene's suite, becoming something more. I don't know what it is yet, but I know what I want it to be: forever.

"Oh, is it late there?"

"Almost three."

We're three hours ahead, so it's only nearing midnight for him.

"Damn. I'm sorry. I wasn't thinking about the time difference when I called, I just wanted to talk to you."

Warmth bubbles up in my chest. "I'm glad you didn't think about it."

"Why because you wanted to talk shit to me in the wee hours of the morning?" he jokes, the way we tend to do when things are getting a little too emotional. Most of the time, I follow him into the comfort of humor, but I don't do it because just a few hours ago two people I love showed me the power of leaning into your feelings instead of hiding from them.

"No, Hunter, because I love you, and love means being willing to be inconvenienced. I'll gladly sacrifice sleep if it means having the chance to say something that might help ease your mind."

"Do me a favor, Cal?"

"What's up?"

"Don't bring all that sappy shit to New Haven the next time you come to visit."

Now, I'm sucking my teeth. "Go to hell, Hunter."

"Gladly, when I get there, I'll save you a seat right between me and Dad."

We both laugh at the idea of us spending an eternity suffering next to the man who kept us apart for so long. Hunter ends the call shortly after, citing the need for sleep. I let him go and curl up next to Beck, whispering a prayer for my brother and his family, hoping the same winds of fortune that brought him his daughter and a second chance with the love of his life will blow my way.

29

———

SELENE

An incessant buzzing wakes me from a dream about Cal and Beck that doesn't even come close to the reality of what we shared earlier tonight.

Well, yesterday, I correct myself when I pick up my phone and see that it's almost four in the morning. It feels wrong to already be so far removed from such a beautiful moment, but I've come to accept that joy is fleeting and the blows that come with being associated with Aubrey Taylor not only persist but linger.

I haven't even fully recovered from the shock of his shift on gun control, and now he's done something else. What that something is, I'm not exactly sure yet. I scroll through a long stream of unread texts from Monique, my mom, and, shockingly, my sisters to get to the news alerts I keep on even though they make me anxious.

There are several to choose from, but I click the first one I see, wincing at the brightness of the screen as the article loads. The headline—What _Does_ Aubrey Taylor Stand For?—doesn't bode well for him, but I'm incredibly amused by the fact that the reporter is asking the same question I did last night. The only difference is they're posing the question to the world, not the man himself, and using the words of President Sanders to do it.

After weeks of speculation about his health and ability to lead, President Sanders used the stage of last night's debate to remind the American people that he still has the same fire and zeal that got him elected four years ago.

Sanders delivered blow after fatal blow to his opponent, Democrat Aubrey Taylor. Attacking his voting record as a Senator, taking him to task on his 'fair weather politics' and mentioning his affair with campaign speechwriter, Sutton Ellsworth, as proof of Taylor's "lack of integrity and moral fortitude".....

The article goes into further detail about the points Sanders made, deeming him the clear victor of the night, but there's nothing in it that really warrants my phone being blown up. Closing the news app, I go to my messages, clicking on Monique's thread, which has the newest message.

> Monique: I'm sorry. You're probably sleeping. I hope you're sleeping. I shouldn't have bothered you, but I'm just so fucking pissed. I don't know how you're still with him.

Confused, I scroll back to the top of today's messages to figure out what she's apologizing for. The first one came in just ten minutes ago, and the rest flowed in, in rapid succession.

> Monique: Why won't they just let this Sutton shit die?

> Monique: They shouldn't even be allowed to publish photos like that.

> Monique: These are worse than the first ones.

> Monique: I'm going to kill him.

> Monique: Can I say that? Will the Secret Service come and arrest me or something?

> Monique: Ohh, do you think those two sexy ones will come put the cuffs on me? What are their names? Beckford and Dean? Blake and Drakeford? Shit, I don't remember, but if it has to be somebody, let it be them.

That message makes me laugh despite my continued confusion over what the hell she's talking about. I exit out of the texts and head to Google, finding what has her up in arms in a matter of seconds, and immediately becoming sick to my stomach. Apparently, President Sanders' mention of Sutton at the debate inspired the person who initially sent me proof of the affair to share what little leverage I had left with the rest of the world.

Scrambling to sit up, I let out a string of low curses as I scroll through the photos, seeing all of the ones I've been holding on to like a lifeline and a few that I've never laid eyes on before. If I were still in love with Aubrey, still invested in this marriage, Monique would be right in saying that these new ones are worse than the first release.

There are three in total. One of them is a selfie, probably taken on Sutton's phone. Her head is resting on Aubrey's bare chest while he sleeps, the arm not around her waist tucked underneath plush pillows with one word threaded into the fabric in a flowy, script font that's barely visible to the eye.

Taylor.

He fucked her in our bed.

I'm more disgusted than hurt by that. The next few photos are more of the same. Personal, intimate, adulterous moments they chose to capture, heedless of the fact that one day they could be found out. The last photo isn't a selfie. Like every other one I've seen of them together before right now, it's taken from afar. Aubrey and Sutton are both unaware that they're being watched, but they're exercising more discretion because they're in public, strolling through a park near my office, traversing the path we taught AJ to ride a bike on.

I used to walk that path after work, used to sit on the benches on spring afternoons and watch fretful parents promise their kids they wouldn't let go and smile right along with them when they broke that promise, confident their kid would succeed, and they did. That path used to be one of the places I could go and remember my son. It was sacred, and now it's been desecrated.

That hurts, but I'm used to losing things when it comes to AJ. With every year that passes, and despite my best efforts, he fades away a little more. My memory of his laugh is inaccurate. My recollection of the feel of the curls I used to ruffle all the time is dull. So, in the grand scheme of things, never being able to return to the park or that path again isn't that big of a deal, and the longer I sit with that, reminding myself of all the things I do still have left of him, the less it seems to matter.

I shoot off quick responses to Monique and both of my sisters, asking them to reassure Mama that I'm okay, and then turn off my phone, determined to go back to sleep. Only, I can't seem to find a comfortable spot, so I toss and turn, which only serves to highlight all the places on, and in, me that were touched by my men last night. Despite the shitty wake up call, I find myself smiling at the memories, at the ache between my thighs from being stretched open by Beck and the small, tender spots on my hips from Cal's grip. After they left me, I was far too exhausted to truly appreciate everything that transpired between us, but now I'm obsessing over every detail.

Knowing I won't be able to sleep now, I decide to grab a cup of coffee and use my good mood to start working on a new program I've been thinking about for a while now. I open my bedroom door, expecting to be greeted by darkness and finding light instead. It's a soft, ambient light, coming from the lamps on the dining area. I crane my neck to get a good look at the table without being spotted and see Aubrey, Jordan and Cordelia leaning in close, speaking in hushed tones. Wanting to know what's being said, I tiptoe a little closer, noting then that they're alone. No security. No staffers. Just the three of them.

The sight is so odd, so distracting, I step out a bit too far, bumping into a side table and calling all of their attention to me. Both Jordan and Cordelia are stunned by my sudden appearance, but Aubrey? Aubrey is pissed. He's on his feet and across the room before either of his companions can say a word. His rough, angry hands on my shoulders before I can blink.

"Who the fuck did you give those photos to?!" He's seething, face red, eyes bloodshot from a lack of sleep and misplaced anger. "You're working with him, aren't you?"

Everything about this moment—his rage, the pain shooting through my arms because of how tight his hold is, and the way my vision keeps blurring when he shakes me—calls for panic, for tears, for fear, but I don't have access to any of those things. All I have is this calm resonating inside of me, stemming from the knowledge that no matter how angry he is with me, he can't kill me because the women in this room won't let him. Not because they give a fuck about me. They don't. But because watching Aubrey murder me would land them in prison right beside him, and they can't run the world from a prison cell.

Well, Jordan probably could.

The random thought inspires an ill-timed smile to appear on my face, which only enrages Aubrey more.

"You think this shit is funny? Am I fucking joke to you?" He growls and spins me around, backing me into a wall. I hit it so hard that the framed artwork falls off, landing with a loud crash.

Jordan stands then, striding over to us with no sense of urgency. "Aubrey, that's enough. Let's all sit down and talk before the agents outside the door decide to come in here and see what all the commotion is about."

He does release me, but not without one final squeeze of my arms that conveys every ounce of hatred and dismay he holds for me. Jordan places herself between us, following closely behind Aubrey until he's back in his seat next to Cordelia, who, of course, doesn't look as upset by his show of violence as she did by the scene I made at the debate. I take a seat at the far end of the table, away from all of them. My ass has barely touched the seat when Jordan starts with her inquisition.

"I'm sure by now you're aware that new photos of Aubrey and Sutton have been made public."

"Of course she's aware," Aubrey gripes, glaring at me. "She's the one who fucking sent them out."

"Why would I do that, Aubrey? How would it serve me to provide the public with the only thing I had left to hold over you?"

"To get back at me for the shift in my stance on gun control."

Tilting my head to one side, I consider his logic. "I could see why you would think that. The timing of this definitely seems convenient, but surely you know I'm capable of exacting revenge without hurting myself in the process."

I haven't figured out how I'm going to get back at him yet, how I'm going to make sure that I still get everything I want out of this arrangement, especially with my leverage gone, but I will.

Jordan clasps her hands together and places them on the table, emerald eyes narrowed at me. "You're right, the timing is convenient. How did you learn about the shift anyway?"

"President Sanders—."

Aubrey slams his fist on the table, cutting me off. "See! I fucking told you. She's working with him."

"Working with him? I just met the man for the first time last night. Do you seriously think we developed a take-down strategy over the course of a five-minute conversation?"

"No," Jordan says. "Actually, I don't."

One of my brows lifts in surprise. "*You* believe me?"

"I believe that this strategy was developed way before last night, probably by President Sanders' team. I also believe you've played a key role in making it successful."

"How? I just told you I don't know the man. I didn't give him those pictures." My frustration pulls one last confession from me. "I don't even know who sent them to me."

Cordelia chimes in then. "But he knows you, or at least he thought he did. I'd bet my granddaddy's farm that Sanders had one of the people on his opposition research team take and send those pictures to you."

Jordan nods enthusiastically, eyes shining with understanding. "Of course, he did. He gets proof of the affair and sends it to you, hoping you'll go to the public and blow up Aubrey's campaign in its early stages, which keeps his hands clean."

"Except you didn't do that," Cordelia drawls. "Why?"

No part of me feels like explaining my thought process and decision making to this woman, so I volley an inquiry of my own back at her. "Why are you here?"

"Because I asked her to be," Aubrey says, glowering at me.

"No, I'm not talking about here, in this room, I mean here, in our lives. Why are you involved in this campaign? Why have you attached yourself to Aubrey?"

Instead of answering, the Senator just smiles and shakes her head like I wouldn't understand her motivations even if she wanted to explain them to me. Maybe she's right. Meanwhile, Jordan is still putting together the pieces of this puzzle. She shakes her head.

"I should have seen it before, really, I should have known when we couldn't find out where the photos came from."

"Why would your immediate assumption not be that they came from the opposition?"

"Because we thought they came from you. You've been against this campaign from the beginning. I thought it was a case of internal sabotage."

I huff out an outraged laugh. "Right, let's focus on the wife and not the man who's competing against him for the most powerful office in the world. *That* makes sense."

"Sanders isn't known for dirty politics," Cordelia says.

Aubrey pushes to his feet and begins pacing. "But he's playing dirty now, which is a good thing, right? It means he's desperate, means he knows I'm taking the fucking Oval."

I want to tell him that he couldn't even take the debate, but I decide not to risk his wrath again. "So, I don't go public with the photos, so he has to. Only, he doesn't send the press everything he sent to me. He didn't even send me everything he had. I never saw the selfies in our bed or the picture at the park. Why hold back?"

Jordan shrugs. "It's possible that he didn't have those photos until recently. Those selfies would have been hard to come by, and the one in park wasn't all that damning on its own. He probably didn't think it merited sharing."

"But he went scorched earth tonight," Cordelia mutters. "Driving home all the points he made on that stage with visual proof."

Jordan runs her hand through her hair. "Our only saving grace is that you two aren't actually romantically involved anymore."

My eyes fly to Cordelia's face, and I'm not surprised to see that she's not even a little caught off guard by that statement.

"How is that a good thing?" Aubrey asks.

"Because Sanders thinks telling Selene you're going back on your word will cause a rift between you two that will be evident to the public and continue to feed into the narrative he established at the debate. They're counting on Selene being so mad she disappears from the campaign, and all the Black female voters who have forgiven you because she has, will disappear right along with her."

"But you can't cause a rift in a thing that's already been broken," I say.

Jordan gives me a smile that's half respect and half condescension. "Exactly, so despite his best efforts, Sanders hasn't done any real damage. You two will continue to present a united, unaffected front, and it will carry us all the way to the White House."

Aubrey claps his hands like everything is settled, but I'm skeptical.

"Unless Sanders realizes his plan hasn't worked and decides to dig deeper."

"Let him dig," Jordan snaps. "Aubrey has told me everything, so I know there's nothing left for him to find."

I don't like Jordan, but I normally believe her when she speaks. Two things keep me from doing that this morning: her stunning lack of awareness regarding Sanders' plot to make me a pawn in his game and the look Aubrey and Cordelia share when she says there's nothing left to find.

30

SELENE

The only good thing that comes out of my pre-dawn meeting with the trio from hell is that I'm up early enough to insinuate myself into the jog I know Beck and Cal take every morning. They were surprised when I met them in the lobby with my workout gear on and an exhausted Agent Ortega at my back. Once he confirmed they had agreed to take me on a run, he took his leave, too tired to ask further questions.

We spent an hour out in the sunshine in fresh air, walking too close to each other, risking everything for the brush of a pinky or a graze of each other's skin. But mostly, we just talked. About everything. About nothing. About life and the things we wanted for ourselves while hinting at the things we wanted with each other. It was a beautiful morning, and when we return back to the hotel, I'm loathe to tuck the happiness I feel when I'm with them away, exchanging it for the quiet numbness that allows me to keep my features neutral when I face the swarm of cameras and reporters waiting for me outside the hotel.

"Selene! A moment, please!" Someone shouts from the crowd, shoving a microphone in my face. Cal slaps it out of their hand.

"Back the fuck up," he snarls, and the person stumbles back.

"Stay close," Beck tells me, using his body and the force of his will to part the crowd for me while Cal keeps people off my back, literally. I take measured steps, keeping my breaths even as the overlapping voices, flashing cameras, and crush of bodies create a sensory nightmare that makes me want to scream.

By the time we make it inside the elevator, my body and brain are buzzing, and I'm ready to come out of my skin.

"You need—" Beck asks, his question cut in half by the nod of my head. I don't just need the hug. I crave it. The compassion in the compression. The perfection of the pressure. No one has mastered it as quickly as Beck has. I thought Aubrey was good at it, but after this morning, I can't even fathom what it would be like to be calmed by his touch.

Cal steps in front of me, splitting an inquisitive gaze between Beck and I. "Can I try?"

There's no time to think—not that I need to spend a second considering his question—so I launch myself at him. He grunts at the force, and I can't even be bothered to apologize.

"It has to be tight," Beck tells him, the same patience in his voice that was present in Cal's last night when he would tell me what our partner needed. I like that he has enough of an understanding of me to recreate that kind of loving instruction, that Cal cares enough to learn. "Tighter than you would think," he adds when Cal wraps me up in his arms but hesitates to apply serious pressure.

Beck's reassurance bolsters him, and I whimper against his chest when the hug turns deep, almost bone-crushing. My eyes are squeezed shut, but I can feel him panicking, trying to let go. I hold on tight.

"No, please, don't let go yet."

We don't have enough time. We never have enough time, but we use this time wisely. Cal doesn't let me go until he absolutely has to. I step back from him, and he returns to his place at my side just before the doors open on the floor of my suite, revealing the last two people I expect to see sitting on the bench in front of the elevator bank.

"Mom? Mo?"

They both look up from their phones as Cal, Beck, and I step into their space. Both of them look a little haggard, like they've been up all night and traveling all day. Mo has bags under her eyes. Mama's blouse is wrinkled. Their purses are thrown on top of their suitcases, which have been shoved off to the side to keep the walkway clear.

"Selene!" Mama shouts, her voice loud and filled with worry, as she rushes up and pulls me into a hug that smells like Daddy and home. I haven't seen her in almost a year, probably since last Christmas, and although I don't understand why she's here, I'm glad she is.

"What are you doing here?" I pull back, holding her at arm's length. She looks good. Her mahogany skin wrinkled in some places but still mostly supple, making her appear younger than her almost seventy years.

"I came to see you!"

"*We* came to see you," Monique says, wiggling herself between us while Mama rolls her eyes. "Mama J was worried about you since you weren't answering your phone."

"Y'all got on a plane because I wasn't answering the phone?"

"No, we got on two *separate* planes because you weren't answering the phone after somebody plastered your husband laid up with his mistress in your bed all over the internet."

"Monique!" Mama swats her on the shoulder, cutting her eyes at Cal and Beck. "We don't need to get into this when we're standing in front of perfect strangers."

The thought of exercising discretion when everyone in the world knows my business is laughable, but the idea of keeping anything from the two men behind me feels ridiculous. And it would feel that way even if I didn't know what Beck feels like inside of me or what Cal's face looks like when he comes.

All Mama's admonishment does is draw Monique's attention to them. She bats her lashes and her mouth curves into her signature flirty grin. "Oh, MJ, these aren't perfect strangers. That's Agent—" she pauses, blanking on Cal's name while her hand hangs uselessly in the air in front of him.

"Drake," he supplies, the corners of his mouth pulling up into an indulgent smile.

Monique snaps her fingers and nods while Cal and Mama shake hands. "Right. Agent Drake and his partner, Agent—"

Beck lets her flounder for far longer than Cal did, laughing along with us when she starts tossing out random last names that start with a B. "Bradford. Bishop. Bennett. No, um, Beckford?"

"Beckham," he says, taking Mama's hand. "Nice to meet you, Mrs. Grant."

My mother, who has always had a thing for tall, dark, handsome, and bald men, is especially taken with him. She talks his ear off while they carry her and Monique's bags down to their respective rooms and looks genuinely displeased when he leaves to stand guard outside the door.

"Damn, those men are fine," Monique exclaims, plopping down on the couch. I'm still standing, my hands on my hips as I look between her and my mother.

"Did you come all the way to Las Vegas to fawn over my security?"

She throws an arm over her face, sighing dramatically. "We already told you that we came to check on you."

"And I already told both of you, via text, that I'm fine."

I'm more than fine. Actually, the more time that passes, the better I feel. Especially if that time is spent with my men.

"You didn't text me," Mama grumbles. "I got a phone call from Robin."

"But either way, you knew that I was okay."

"No, we know that you said you're okay, but you've been saying that since you first found out about the affair, Sel."

"I know that, Mo, and I've been telling the truth."

"How is that possible, baby?" Mama asks. "I mean, honestly, if you can tell me how you're just so okay with this level of betrayal, then I'll have that handsome young man take me to the airport right now and go home."

Monique sticks her tongue out the side of her mouth and does a body roll. "He can take me somewhere, but it won't be the airport."

Mama frowns. "Girl, have some respect for your elders, I'm sitting right here."

"MJ, don't act like you wouldn't take Beck for a ride if he offered you one."

I shudder at the thought. "Mo, please."

"You two are no fun," she pouts, leaving her spot on the couch to head for the mini bar. "We're in Vegas for God's sake, and if you—" she points at me with a miniature bottle of tequila "—aren't going to tell us what's going on with you and that monster in the Presidential suite, then we might as well have some fun. Have some drinks. Share a couple of laughs. Act like we care that it's been forever since we've seen each other."

I'll give Mo one thing: she's a hell of a saleswoman. Her little speech takes all the fight out of me, and I cross the room, pulling her into a tight hug, hoping she doesn't smell Cal on me.

"Thank you for making the trip."

"Of course, Sel. Anything for you."

Next, I go to Mama. She's already on her feet with open, waiting arms when I get to her. I settle into her embrace and let the fact that she was actually worried enough to get on a plane wash over me, heal a little piece of me that is still deeply wounded by all the times my buried emotions and unusual reactions cost me her affection and concern.

"I love you, Selene, and I'm here, baby, for whatever you need."

"I know, Ma, and I appreciate you. Right now, all I need is a shower."

She and Monique agree to allow me out of their sight long enough for me to go back up to my suite and shower. I rush through my routine, surprised at how eager I am to get back to them, which, of course, means that Aubrey appears out of nowhere to delay me.

When I emerge from the bathroom, wrapped in a towel and nothing more, he's in my room, leaning against the door. His presence throws me, but I don't let it show, even as images of the way he handled me this morning rush through my mind. Instead of addressing him, I move around the room like I normally would if I were alone, while the weight of his gaze haunts my every step.

I'm sitting at the foot of the bed, slathering on lotion, when he finally decides to speak.

"Did you enjoy your walk?"

"Yes."

"Did you call your mom and Monique here?"

Letting out a deep sigh, I stand and step into my panties, pulling them on underneath my towel. "I didn't, but I'm glad they're here."

"You need to get them to leave."

"Why would I do that?"

"Because them rushing in after the release of the pictures makes it look like you're seeking support from someone other than me."

I turn my back to him and drop my towel, lotioning my breasts and stomach before putting on my bra. "Well, you were seeking pussy from someone other than me, so I guess we're even."

"Maybe I wouldn't have had to get pussy from someone else if you weren't such a cold bitch," he spits.

The insult is an arrow launched straight at my heart, but it misses its mark by a mile. Months ago, hell, even yesterday, it probably would have wounded me, but after last night, it can't touch me. I'm insulated by the power that comes from holding two men's pleasure in my hands and leaving them both satisfied, protected by the memories of Cal's worshipful hands and Beck's reverent tongue.

They wanted me, desired me, *craved* me.

And I rest easy in the knowledge that whatever I am—cold, stoic, dispassionate—is safe with them. It was never safe with Aubrey, though, and I don't think I was either.

"We've already done this scene," I tell him, intentionally making my voice flatter. "I'm bored with it now."

His mouth drops, and maybe it's the lack of sleep or the stress from the campaign, but it takes him a full two minutes to come up with a response. I count the seconds in my head as I put on my clothes.

"That's quite the shift in attitude," he sneers. "What happened to the woman who used to beg me to explain why I fucked my speech writer and how many times I did it? What happened to the woman who wanted to analyze my state of mind and needed to understand the logistics of coordinating an affair and running a campaign?"

"She's gone." I wave my hands down my fully clothed body. "All you get now is me: the woman who doesn't give a fuck about where you stick your dick."

Wild blue eyes rush over my face, looking for a crack in my expression. "You're not even the least bit curious how I did it? How I fucked her in our bed without you even knowing?"

I press my lips into a flat line of disinterest and shake my head. "No."

His face is beet red. The muscle in his jaw pulses rapidly, and he swipes an agitated hand over his face as I move past him to get to the door. He doesn't try to stop me. He just turns, so he can watch me go.

"Does your new boyfriend have something to do with your change of heart?"

The question is so random, so out of left field, I'm actually convincing when I stop halfway out the door just to turn around and laugh in his face. "I don't have a new boyfriend, Aubrey. I just don't give a fuck about you."

He stands in stunned silence as I leave, and I spend the ride back down to Mama and Monique, hoping he didn't see right through me.

31

SELENE

I didn't know how much I needed time with my people until they forced themselves on me, giving me no option but to take their love, to laugh at Mo's jokes and lay my head in Mama's lap and let her give me the scalp massages I only tolerated as a kid but enjoy now.

Monique is curled up on the couch with us, her feet hanging off the arm of the chair while her head rests on my hip. The TV is on, playing one of the Lifetime movies Mama enjoys so much. She and Monique are discussing the wisdom of the choices the main character has made thus far. I have my eyes closed, just listening, wondering if this is what my life will be like if Aubrey loses the election. He's holding steady in the polls, thanks to an increase in the white, conservative vote, but it's still anyone's game. Over the last three days, I've been fighting an internal battle between the part of me that wants to honor AJ and the part of me that just wants to have peace.

To have more moments like this with my family.

To have more time with my men.

Of course, I know I can walk away, that Aubrey and Jordan could oust me in a second, but I can't reconcile the idea of leaving when there's still a chance he could win. When the contract we signed still guarantees support and funding for my First Lady initiative. When I could still do some good.

"Your hair is so healthy," Mama muses, holding up a section to her face to inspect my ends. "Who is this lady that does it for you?"

"Her name is Diane. You'd love her. She's one of those old school stylists like you."

Dropping one section, she picks up another, doing the same thing. "I can tell. Those new girls don't know nothing about growing hair."

She tsks her disapproval, and Monique hums her agreement. "Talk about it, MJ! They don't care nothing about your scalp, your ends, or your edges. All they want is a deposit and your understanding when they send that damn 'hey, boo' text."

I peek at her through one half-open eye. "What on Earth is a 'hey, boo' text? And why are they referring to clients in such a personal manner? Seems unprofessional."

"Girl, it's all unprofessional," she says, rolling her eyes. "And a 'hey, boo' text is exactly what it sounds like. They text you the morning of your appointment, or sometimes minutes before, and say 'hey, boo, I won't be able to do your hair today because I'm going to Miami'."

"Don't they have scheduling systems? Why wouldn't they block off that time?"

"Because they're not professionals, Sel."

Mama laughs at Monique's exasperation. "Jessica got a text from a braider once canceling her appointment but asking if she could go ahead and send payment for service because she wanted to go out for her friend's birthday."

Jessica is my baby sister. I love her to death but she's incredibly ditzy, so I have to ask: "Did she pay it?"

"Of course she did, even sent the girl a tip. She still ain't got the style she paid for. Every time she goes to book, the girl says her schedule is full."

"Poor, Jess," Monique laments, shaking her head. "That girl should be ashamed of herself, taking advantage of people like that."

"She should," I agree. "But Jess should also have more sense than to send someone money for services they hadn't rendered. It's illogical."

"Yeah, well, logic doesn't always apply to matters of the heart," Mama says through a yawn. She's been hanging tough with Monique and I, staying up late every night, braving the paparazzi and crowds to go on brief outings supervised by Cal and Beck. We kept it pretty low-key today, since they're leaving tomorrow, but I can tell it's all catching up with her. She pats my head, signaling the end of my scalp rub, and I sit up.

Since she's tired, I don't bother addressing the slight dig she took at me with the logic and heart thing. She and Monique are both frustrated that they're leaving me with no further understanding of what's happening in my marriage, so they've resorted to little comments like that to see if I will break.

I never do.

"Why don't you go to bed?" I ask softly.

She tries to wave me off, her lips parted to argue, but another yawn comes, stealing whatever it is she was going to say. "I guess I will," she says, pushing to her feet and grabbing her room key off the coffee table. Mo and I both stand to escort her the short distance to the door, accepting kisses on the cheeks.

"Goodnight, babies," she says.

"Goodnight," we call, waving as she crosses the hall and disappears behind the door.

Glancing at my watch and then at the agent posted at the end of the hall waiting to escort me back up to my room, I sigh. "I should probably head up too."

Monique frowns. "What? No!"

"Mo, it's getting late. You've got a flight in the morning, I have press all day, and a rally tomorrow night. We need to get some rest."

"Just stay with me. You're already in your pajamas, and it's not like we've never shared a bed," she points out, her eyes turning bright at the idea. Before I can protest, she's beckoning Agent Harris forward. "Hey, come here, please?"

"Yes, ma'am?" he asks, stopping in front of us.

"Could you please let the powers that be know Mrs. Taylor will be spending the night in my room tonight?"

Harris glances at me, and then back at her. "I don't think that's a good idea."

"Good thing I wasn't asking your opinion," Monique retorts, doubling down now just because Harris has hinted at denying her request. "She wants to sleep here. The room has been secured. We won't be ordering in room service or sneaking out, so you can let everyone know you tucked us in real tight before you got lost."

"Ma'am." He's looking at me now, but I'm of no help to him because I have no interest in going back to my suite. Cordelia has practically moved in with us now. I see her more than Jordan. If I cared, I'd wonder if she and Aubrey are fucking.

"You're dismissed, Agent Harris. Please let Hicks know we've requested to be left alone for the rest of the night."

"There will be another agent arriving—"

Monique waves her hand in his face, and he stops speaking. "Did you hear what she just said? Left *alone* for the rest of the night. Tell that other agent to stay where he's at, or I'm digging in his ass and yours before I get on my plane in the morning."

Over the last twenty-plus years, she's exhibited how good she is at putting the fear of God into even the most formidable men multiple times, and at this moment, Agent Harris is no exception. The tips of his ears are red as he nods and turns on his heel to march away without so much as a goodbye. We have the decency to wait until he's on the elevator and the doors have closed to burst out laughing.

"I can't believe that actually worked," she muses, closing and locking the door behind us.

"I can. You can be really scary sometimes."

"Probably doesn't hurt that he saw me curse Aubrey up one side and down the other yesterday."

She's butted heads with Aubrey a lot over the years, but the way she laid into him yesterday was something new entirely. We ended up on the elevator with him, and because it was her first time seeing him since she arrived, she took him to task for the old and new while everyone—me, Mama, Cal, Beck and Agents Hicks and Ortega—watched on silently.

"I'm sure that was a huge motivator," I say, sinking back into the couch while Monique rummages through her purse. "What are you looking for?"

"This!"

She holds the treasure up with a triumphant grin while I frown, trying to make it out. "Is that a brownie?"

"Even better." Her shoulders bounce as she dances over to me and plops down onto the couch, sitting close enough that she might as well be on my lap. "It's an edible," she whispers conspiratorially. "I've been saving it for when we get a moment alone."

"Because you didn't want your precious MJ to know you're trying to corrupt me with drugs?"

Unwrapping the packaging of the admittedly delicious-looking baked good, she snorts. "No, because I didn't think you'd want to get high with your mama."

"I don't want to get high with you."

Despite my expressed disinterest, she breaks the brownie into what's supposed to be halves and forces the biggest piece into my hand. "Just eat the damn brownie, Sel. You'll be all relaxed and mellow and sleep like a log."

"Or, I'll be paranoid and anxious like the last time."

"No," she says in the middle of a bite. "It's a different strain."

"I don't care." I try to hand it back to her, but she won't take it. "You can eat my piece."

"Girl, these things are strong as fuck. Eating the whole thing would have me on my ass."

"Well, just save it for later."

Her brows knitted together. "I can't take it on the plane, Sel, and there's no way I'm eating it in the morning before a flight."

"Moniqueeee," I groan, wanting to say no again but already feeling myself caving.

"Seleneeeeee."

Where my drawn-out version of her name was more of a whine of desperation, her exaggerated pronunciation is the beginning of a celebration. She nudges me with her shoulder repeatedly, smiling when I lift the edible to my mouth and then pumping her fist in the air once I've chewed and swallowed.

We rest our heads on the back of the couch and close our eyes, listening to the opening sounds of a movie about a rich white woman nearly losing her family to her crazed nanny. It's over a third of the way done when the edible kicks in, and I say the first thing that comes to mind.

"How many times are they going to make this same movie?"

Monique shifts, lying down with the soles of her feet pressed into my thigh. "They won't ever stop," she mumbles, and I don't even have to be looking at her to know that her eyes are low and heavy. Getting high always makes her sleepy. "What I don't understand is why the best friend always has to die. You know if your life was a Lifetime movie, I'd end up dead."

"I wouldn't let that happen. The best friend only ends up dead because the main character doesn't listen when she tries to warn them about the psycho, and she has no choice but to investigate on her own."

"You act like you always listen to me, Selene."

"Name a time when I haven't followed your advice, Monique," I say, realizing my mistake too late because my brain is moving slower than my mouth.

"I told you to leave, Aubrey."

"Monique, please."

"I did," she insists sleepily. "I hate him, and I love you. You deserve so much better."

"I love you too."

It's the only response I can give, the only thing I can address. I can't admit to her that I hate Aubrey too. That I spend a lot of my free time fantasizing about all of the people who want me dead turning their vitriol on him, that sometimes I hope someone will be brave enough to put the bullets they've etched my name into between his eyes so the choice between suffering through this life and keeping my promise to AJ is no longer mine to make.

"You can tell me, you know? What's really going on with you and Aubrey. How you really feel about him disrespecting your home? What's going on in your head and your life?"

I trust Monique implicitly, which is the only reason why I offer her the small bit of truth mixed with a lie. "The pictures aren't new to me, Mo. I saw them before the world did. All of them."

She shoots up, and I open my eyes to view her shocked expression. "*All* of them? You saw her in your bed?"

"Yes," I lie. "Things with Aubrey are tense right now, but that's mostly just the stress of the election. None of this stuff is new, and we're working through it privately. It's just his opponent trying to dredge up the past to hurt him in the polls."

My stomach turns. I hate this. The lying, the pretending, the constant pressure to perform. But I don't hate the peace my words bring Monique. She's not fully satisfied, but I've given her enough to hold on to.

"He needs to do a better job of protecting you, Sel, and if he ever hurts you again, I'm going to make you a widow."

The threat lingers in the air as she stretches back out on the couch. Soon, it's pushed out by the sound of Monique's snores. I'm glad she's resting, but I can't sleep because of the sudden craving for the bacon and cheddar potato skin chips I saw Agent Anderson polishing off before he escorted me up to my room last night. He still had some of the dust on his jacket when I said goodnight, and it reminded me of how messy AJ would get when he ate them. I never much cared for them, but right now, they're the only thing on my mind.

Without putting much thought into whether or not I should, I pull on Monique's hoodie, grab a few bucks out of her purse, and swipe a room key. The door clicks shut behind me, and I pull the hood over my head to avoid being spotted, hitting a brisk walk as I head for the vending area. What's supposed to be a quick trip turns into a descending, multi-floor hunt for the one machine in the building with the snack I want.

I find it on the fifth floor, and I'm in the midst of celebrating my victory when the machine decides to take my money and keep the bag of damn chips.

"What the hell?" I mutter under my breath, shoving the machine with my hand. It doesn't so much as budge, so I try again, and again, and again, until I'm panting and frustrated with myself for engaging in such futile behavior.

"Need some help?" A laughing, deeply familiar male voice asks.

I turn slowly, and my heart jumps into my throat when I see Cal standing in the doorway with an empty ice bucket in one hand. His arms and the defined lines of his chest are on full display thanks to the white tank top he's wearing, and there are gray sweats sitting low on his hips.

"Hi," I breathe, my eyes on the imprint in his pants. He's not hard, but the kind of length and girth he's working with is impossible to hide.

"My eyes are up here, pet," he whispers, chuckling lowly. The use of my nickname forces me to acknowledge that we're alone. That there is no one watching, and, thanks to Monique insisting that I spend the night, no one waiting for me to return.

I am, for all intents and purposes, free.

The thought, coupled with the heat in Cal's gaze when I finally manage to bring my eyes back to his face, makes my thighs clench with delicious anticipation.

"What are you doing down here alone?" he asks. "I thought Harris was on duty. I didn't see him in the hall."

My snack all but forgotten, I start to move toward him. There's no intention behind it, it's almost a helpless thing, like he's a magnet, and I'm a piece of metal. "We sent him away."

He watches my advance with cautious eyes. "We? Who's we?"

"Monique and I."

I'm close enough now to smell him. There's sweat on his skin and the faint scent of our lover. Cal is spice and smoke while Beck is a forest after a fresh rain, quiet and refreshing.

"You made love."

It's not an accusation, but an observation. Cal confirms with a dip of his chin, and I'm immediately struck with thoughts of what that might have looked like. They're both so beautiful, so powerful and strong. The idea of them devouring each other, surrendering to the most primal of needs, makes my pussy throb viciously.

"Are you angry?"

"No."

"Jealous again?"

I bite my lip, nodding as I inch even closer to him. I could touch him now, but I don't because I know what will happen next, and we can't risk it happening here. Cal pulls in a sharp breath as the reality of what we could do to each other passes between us.

"Where's Monique now, pet?"

Our hands dangle at our sides, knuckles grazing ever so lightly. It's a ghost of a touch, but there's raw potential hidden in it, echoing in the millimeters of space left between our skin when it ends.

"She's sleeping. The edible she forced me to take knocked her out."

His brows lift, reaching for his hairline. "You're high?"

I shake my head, not wanting to get sidetracked. "I was for about five minutes, but it wore off."

"Oh."

"I'm supposed to be staying in Monique's room tonight."

Cal blinks slowly, absorbing the meaning behind my words. "You're not going back to the suite?"

"No," I confirm, linking our fingers together, the decision made, my snack forgotten. "I'm coming with you."

32

SELENE

Beck is still in bed when Cal and I walk into the room hand in hand.

He's tangled in the sheets. His chest bare. His eyes closed with his hands behind his head and a soft, contented smile on his handsome face. I've never seen him this relaxed. He doesn't even tense when the door closes, like all thoughts of danger and vigilance cease to exist inside these walls.

I like that attitude so much, I adopt it for myself, pushing all of my worries and stresses out of my mind as I toe out of my shoes and slip out of my clothes quietly. Cal watches me strip, his eyes liquid heat as he sits the empty ice pail down with a clang.

"Did you get the ice?" Beck asks, still unaware that I'm here. I tiptoe over to the edge of the bed, and Cal fights back a laugh.

"No, love, I didn't get the ice, but I brought back something better."

Beck's eyes pop open, and he blinks rapidly at me like I'm a mirage he's trying to clear from his vision. I climb up the bed slowly, watching his face transform from disbelief to desire as he sits up to greet me.

"Gorgeous," he breathes, pulling me close as I straddle him. "How are you here right now?"

His hands are everywhere as I explain the circumstances that led me here, running down my sides and gripping my hips, snaking around to caress my breasts and tweak my nipples. But the whole time, his eyes are on my face, watching my reaction to his touch.

I dig my nails into his scalp, dragging them down until they're buried in the corded muscles of his neck. "I missed you."

We've seen each other every day, but we haven't had this closeness since the night of the debate. Beck growls his pleasure at my confession against my throat, kissing and licking his way up to my jaw and then my lips.

Then Cal is there, his bare chest against my back, his body a seat for me to relax into as Beck's tongue swirls into my mouth, plundering, tasting, ruining me.

"We missed you," Cal whispers into my ear, sucking gingerly on the lobe and then down my neck, layering kisses over the invisible imprint of Beck's lips on my skin. "You're all I think about."

"....in every single one of my dreams," Beck murmurs, biting my bottom lip, holding firm even when Cal turning my head in his direction causes it to stretch between us. He lets me go with an evil grin that sears itself into my mind. I see it when I close my eyes and surrender to Cal's kiss, whimpering gratefully when he swipes his tongue over the abused flesh to soothe it.

"He's being a bad boy today," he says, sliding his hand down my body to lift my breast to Beck's mouth. He accepts the offering instantly, peering up at us with grateful eyes as he pulls my nipple into his mouth, sucking with such force it makes me cry out loudly.

Cal silences me with another kiss, moving his hand from my chest to the apex of my thighs where he finds me wet. Callused fingertips part my folds, honing in on my clit with perfect accuracy. I moan into his mouth, and the sound is raw pleasure. Unchecked desire that turns into panic when Beck retreats. Out of the corner of my eye, I'm able to see that he's just laying down again, onyx eyes focused on Cal's hand between my legs as he works to get his dick out from underneath me.

I lift up just a bit, and Cal slides me back, anchoring me to him while Beck jerks off to and for us.

Everything happened so fast the other night, I didn't get to fully take in all of the details of either man's body. I felt Beck inside of me, lived with the slight ache in my core that he left me with, but I had no idea he was that fucking big. My jaw drops, disbelief rushing through me to mix with the pleasure pooling in the pit of my stomach.

"You fit all of that inside me?" I gasp.

"Yes, gorgeous, and you took it like a fucking champ." He pulls a bottle of lube from underneath a pillow and squeezes a generous amount into his palm, using it to cover his tip and every gloriously veined inch of his shaft. I watch, mesmerized, as he resumes stroking himself, imagining what he must have looked like disappearing inside of me.

"She wants you again," Cal says, clearly talking to Beck. "She's getting wetter watching you stroke that big fucking dick."

Both Beck and I moan. His strokes become faster, and Cal matches the tempo he sets with ease. Beck bites down on his lip hard, his hips bucking and legs twitching as long ropes of cum erupt from his tip. The sight of him milking his dick sends me over the edge, and I turn, smashing my lips against Cal's to keep from being too loud. The kiss and the orgasm go on forever, prolonged by his continuous touch and the sound of Beck's ragged pants.

My neck starts to burn from being stretched in such an awkward position for so long, but it doesn't matter because the rest of me is burning as well. I'm a flame, an inferno, and every touch, kiss, lick, from my lovers is a drop of gasoline and the strike of a match. I disappear inside the fire, resigning myself to a fate of being turned to ash as long as these men are destroyed too.

When the tremors have subsided, and my body is nothing but a pliant heap of skin and muscle, Cal flips me over onto my back. I stretch my arms above my head, reaching for something to hold on to as he disappears between my legs. What I find, or rather what finds me, is Beck's hand. He slides down the bed until he's next to me, threading our fingers together before propping himself up on one elbow to watch Cal.

I'm too tired to lift my head to see, but when his hands part my thighs and his breath is a warm wash over my skin, I have no choice but to muster up the energy to. Twin pools of copper and brass hold me hostage as he gives me one, long, heavy lick with the flat of his tongue. My back arches, and he pauses, looking to Beck.

"That's a good thing, Drake," he says, laughing ruefully. "Just remember what I told you: her body will tell you everything you need to know."

I'm swimming in sensation, nearing the point of the only kind of overstimulation I don't hate, so I'm not sure I'm reading into Beck's encouragement correctly.

"So, he's never..." I lose the thought when Cal slips a finger inside me and flicks his tongue over my clit.

Beck leans over and drops a kiss on my lips. "No, gorgeous, you're the first woman he's ever wanted," he whispers, a wicked smile on his face when he pulls away. "I taught him everything I know, so you won't be disappointed."

"Oh, God."

It's too much. They are too much. These two men who protect me, who learn me, who take the time to teach each other what they know. We haven't put a name to it yet, not officially, but I know what this is.

Love.

Pure and unadulterated.

Passionate and intentional.

I feel it everywhere, bubbling in my chest, trickling down my spine, wrapping itself like a vice around my heart, squeezing and squeezing until I combust, exploding into a thousand tiny pieces that fill the air and float down, returning me to my body just in time to see the pride shining in Cal's eyes when I coat his chin, neck, and chest in my juices.

Beck laughs and curses, stealing a kiss from Cal as he crawls up my body. My heart is racing when he presses his chest to mine, and

I'm so satisfied, more satisfied than I've ever been in my entire life, but I still want more. His eyes tell me he'll give it to me, that he'll give me whatever I want, so I don't bother asking, I just take.

I wrap my legs around his waist and lock my heels at his back, trapping him against me, urging him closer until the flared head of his dick is kissing my entrance. He's not as big as Beck, probably just a few inches shorter, but there's no part of me left untouched as he slides inside. There's no resistance either, just a slow glide made easy by two orgasms.

His jaw tenses as my walls squeeze around him involuntarily. He lays his forehead against mine. "Fuck, Selene. You'll have to tell me if I'm hurting you, okay?"

"You won't hurt her," Beck assures him. "You've never hurt me."

The inadvertent revelation reawakens the images of them fucking that only live in my mind. Before this moment, I've alternated between Beck curved over Cal's back and Cal curved over his. Now I know which it actually is, and my brain won't stop conjuring new scenarios that get filthier by the second.

Cal studies me, a slow smile appearing on his face as he reads me easily. "You like the idea of me fucking him, pet?" He pulls out and slides back in slowly, feeding me his length an inch at a time.

"She likes it," Beck says, moving to his knees and guiding the hand he was just holding to his erection, which is still slick from the lube and his cum. I fist his dick and he rocks into my grip, fucking my hand while Cal pumps into my pussy.

"One day you'll watch me fuck him, pet. Would you like that?"

"*Yes*," I moan, clawing helplessly at his back with my free hand and digging my heels into his ass. With a growl, he slides his arms between the mattress and my back and flips us over so I'm on top. The adjustment forces me to let go of Beck, but he doesn't breathe a word of complaint. He just stands and picks up where I left off, stroking his dick as he rounds the bed to watch me ride Cal.

"That's right, gorgeous," he whispers in my ear, his hand bumping into my ass every time he brings his fist to his tip. "Ride his dick just like that. Show him why this is the first pussy he's ever fucked."

Letting out a torturous moan, Cal throws his head back into the mattress. "If you keep talking to her like that, I'm going to come, love."

"Isn't that the point?" Beck quips, dropping to his knees. At first, I can't figure out what he's doing down there, and really, I'm too caught up in the way Cal is stretching and filling me to care, but then the slurping noises start, and Cal lets out a sound that can only be described as a howl, and I'm intrigued.

I lean forward, nearly lying flat on him to get to his ear. "Tell me what he's doing to you."

He's so far gone, so lost in the pleasure of us, he struggles to form a coherent thought. His throat works to expel the few words he has strung together. "Sucking balls," he gasps, swallowing hard. "Finger —" his eyes roll into the back of his head "—in ass."

I swirl my hips, feeling the beginnings of another release spawn when Cal's dick twitches inside me. "Does it feel good?"

"So good, pet. It's so good."

I believe him. The breaks in his voice and his fluttering eyelids leave me with no choice but to. He's holding so still for Beck, so it's up to me to take over our rhythm. Since I can't feel or see what Beck is doing, I have to count on Cal's reactions to let me know when we're in sync. As soon as his breath hitches, I know I've got him, and my movements become more about granting him his pleasure than finding mine.

Still, by some miracle, we come together, panting and laughing, when Beck climbs up on the bed, still hard but happy. He strokes his fingers along my back and Cal's legs. The touches are tender and caring at first, but then they turn incendiary when he follows a trail of Cal and I's mixed release back up to the place where we're still joined.

"Fuck, he made a mess of you."

He's right. I am a mess. The moisture from multiple orgasms and Cal's cum is all over us, leaking out of me, onto Cal and the bed and Beck's fucking fingers that are trying to work their way into me, rubbing against Cal's dick as they go.

Cal's strangled groan melts into a pleasure-filled sigh that I let soak into me, encouraging me to relax in the wake of this new sensation. It's not uncomfortable. There's the pinch of stretching skin and the weight of fullness that appears and disappears every time his finger retreats.

I sink my teeth into Cal's chest, rocking into the invasion helplessly. "Beck, please."

"I'm sorry," he says, sounding anything but. "You just look so good like this. Do you think—" He pauses for a second, and when he speaks again, his voice is all challenge and sin. "Could you handle us both like this, gorgeous?"

My answer is immediate, informed only by the fact that I want to give him this and not by any proof that I can. "Yes."

"Are you sure?" Beck asks.

I turn my head, meeting his eye. *"Yes."*

"Drake, is it okay with you?"

"I want whatever you two want," Cal says, his hands skating up and down my sides.

With everyone in agreement, Beck goes into full preparation mode. He gets the bottle of lube from the top of the bed and coats himself in it before squeezing an overly generous amount between my ass cheeks and working it into the place we most need it.

Then he climbs on top. His knees on either side of my thighs as I straddle Cal, the head of his dick pressing against the limited space of my opening. Beck strokes my back.

"You're doing so good, gorgeous."

I don't respond, mainly because I don't feel like I've done anything at all, but also because talking would stop me from breathing, from feeling the moment when it stops being uncomfortable and starts feeling so fucking good. That moment comes slowly, after multiple pauses and a thousand check-ins from Beck and Cal, too. It comes after several reapplications of lube and Cal slipping out of me, and us having to start again.

It takes forever, but it does come.

And as soon as Beck is in, his thick length pressed against Cal's thick length to form one massive, heavy weight inside of me, I know I'm going to come too. There's no way around it. No way to stop it when I'm fuller than I've ever been, when I've got the weight of Beck's body pressing me carefully into the firm foundation of Cal's form.

Four hands touch me, caress me.

Four lips kiss me, praise me.

Two dicks stretch me, fill me, but only one of them moves. Only one person drives us all towards the brink of ruinous pleasure, and this time it's not Cal, it's Beck. He goes so slowly, moves so gently that in any other circumstance it wouldn't be enough, but in this case, it's absolutely everything.

Tears prick my eyes as a wave of pleasure crests inside of me, threatening to drown us all. I try to hold it, to prolong this moment we worked so hard for, but neither of my men are having it.

"Let go," Cal murmurs softly.

"Let us feel you," Beck growls, his shallow strokes urgent.

I break again, shattering into the most beautiful pieces before falling asleep in the one spot I wish to be every time I wake up: in their arms.

33

CAL

There have been so many times in my life when peace has eluded me.

The months of my childhood leading up to my dad leaving, when the soundtrack of every day was a fight, harsh words that found me through the walls of our small apartment.

The summer weeks spent under the roof of my estranged father and his resentful new wife and son.

The years spent investigating heinous crimes, delving into the depraved depths of the human mind.

But right now, in the pale dawning of a brand new day, with Selene next to me and Beck on her other side. I am at peace. My heart is full. My mind is quiet. My body is still, and my soul, my soul is the bright, sweet hum of satisfaction that only comes with the joy of completion.

I am complete.

I don't think I've ever been that before. I've come as close as I thought I possibly could with Beck, but I think we both know Selene has changed us. The way we move. The way we work. The way we love each other. We haven't spent a night apart since the first time we had her because Beck hasn't wanted to. The wall he's been keeping between us has come down, and Selene is the force that sent it crumbling. I'm so grateful for the fall.

For her. For him. For this unlikely thing we've found in each other.

"Hey," Beck rasps softly from his side of the bed. He's been awake for a while now. I noticed the change in his breathing almost instantly, but thought he deserved a moment to contemplate our reality on his own before we dived into it together.

Rolling onto my side, I hold a hand out, gratitude bubbling up in my chest when he takes it without a moment's hesitation. "Morning, love."

Our fingers tangle together in the air above Selene's sleeping form, then come to rest on her back. Neither of us speaks. We just stare at each other and then at her, trading thoughts in the form of a conversation that needs no words. Serenity lines his features as he tucks an arm under his head.

"What time is it?"

"Not even five yet."

"We should wake her."

He's right. Selene has a day full of press appearances and then a rally with Aubrey this evening, which means it won't be long before the clock on the freedom Monique bought her runs out.

"I'm up," she mutters, stretching with a groan before rolling over onto her back, blessing us with the gift of witnessing her in the vulnerable state of fresh consciousness. She's so fucking beautiful. Her lips swollen from our kisses, midnight strands mussed and hugging one side of her head, the tiniest bit of dried drool at the corner of her mouth.

I want her all over again, and I can see the hunger building behind Beck's eyes. Before I can tell him we don't have time, that she's probably too sore, he's leaning in to kiss her. We should all be exhausted and past the point of sated, but the moment their lips connect, the air is thick with lust I'm not immune to. My lips find Selene's neck and travel over her collarbone down to her chest, closing over a nipple while Beck reaches for her parted legs.

She pulls in a sharp breath that holds an unmistakable note of pain, and everything stops. Beck and I both pull away, and his face twists with concern. "What's wrong? Are you sore?"

The tops of her cheeks take on a red undertone. "I think so, but it's fine. I can—"

"No, you can't, pet."

I don't even know what the rest of her statement was going to be, but I know I don't want to hear it. There's no reality where we touch her when there's even a chance it won't be completely pleasurable.

She looks between the two of us, and Beck's expression is even more severe than mine. It doesn't stop her from trying to argue, though. "But I want you," she says, running a hand down his chest with her eyes on me. "*Please.*"

He wraps his fingers around her wrist, pulling her hand up to his mouth, and laying a kiss in the center of her palm. "You have us, gorgeous."

"Mind, body, and soul," I murmur, which takes the fight out of her. Something about that surrender forces words I've been keeping at bay to the surface. "I love you, Selene."

I'll admit that I haven't spent much time thinking about how Selene would react to receiving those three little words from me, but even if I had, I don't think I would have come up with a single scenario that captures this. This, being her still expression and matter-of-fact tone when she says, "I know. I love you, too."

It's almost amusing, the level of nonchalance on display. The absolute confidence she has in my affection that keeps me from fully appreciating the fact that it's mutual.

"You know?" I ask, incredulously.

"Yes, of course, I know. Beck and I had this conversation the other night."

My eyes fly to Beck's face. "You did?"

"We might have touched on it briefly." He shrugs, the beginnings of a smug grin on his face. He's known for days that Selene was aware of how I felt about her, and yet, he said nothing.

The bastard.

"You didn't tell him?"

He shakes his head. "I wanted this to be a conversation that happened between the two of you. Face to face. Not through me."

"Oh. I guess that makes sense." She turns back to me, frowning. "Did I ruin the moment? Should I have just said I love you back and left it at that?"

I run a thumb over her lips, smoothing out the frown. "You haven't ruined anything. I am interested to hear how you're so sure, though."

The way her brain works is an endless source of fascination for me. I want to understand her, to speak her logic-based language with the ease that Beck does.

Selene pulls in a breath, setting her gaze on the ceiling as she explains. "I've spent my whole life learning how to decode people. Breaking them down into small pieces of information so I could understand them, so that I could turn myself into a mirror. Reflecting their language, mannerisms, and displays of emotion back at them to make myself seem more...human."

Her lips twist together, and my heart breaks for the little girl who spent her life performing normality while I marvel at the woman in front of me who no longer dedicates so much of her energy to masking even when the criticizes her for it.

"Every person is different, but most neurotypical people emote in the same way," she says. "Flared nostrils indicate anger or frustration. Furrowed brows mean confusion. I can name an emotion even if I don't understand why I'm seeing it, why they're feeling it." Her eyes find mine, and my chest swells, expands, damn near explodes with love for her. "I didn't understand why I kept seeing affection on your face, why your eyes would go soft even as your stare got more intense. Why you would go out of your way to touch me, to comfort me, to be gentle with me. I had an idea, of course, I mean I have been loved before, but never like this. Never by anyone who sees me the way the two of you do."

Beck has been quiet this entire time, letting the focus be on Selene and me, but she doesn't let him linger on the margins for long.

This thing is for the three of us. There's space for one-on-one moments, but it's never long before they expand to include the other person, ensuring they know they are an integral part of our connection.

Selene reaches for both of us, linking us together with her hands as she turns her attention to Beck. "You were harder to read. I thought you disliked me, but then everything changed in the dressing room. You showed me how much you understood me. You fashioned yourself into a vessel vast enough to hold my pain, strong enough to contain it. You let me know it was safe to put it down, if only for a second so that it could live beside yours, and I love you for that."

His eyes ripple with unchecked emotion as he leans in to give her a soft, chaste kiss. "I love you, too, gorgeous."

"He fought it for so long," I whisper, grinning when Beck glares at me. "It was such a relief when he finally admitted in Houston."

"In Houston?"

She tips her head to the side as if she's trying to figure out when we had time to have that conversation.

"It was on our last night there," Beck tells her. "After I carried you to bed, I came back downstairs, saw Cal, and the words just came tumbling out of my mouth."

"I told him I felt the same way."

"Then you kissed," Selene says, putting the last piece of the puzzle together. "And that kiss led us here."

We sit in silent observation of those facts, touching, kissing, and cuddling, until we have no choice but to leave the bed. Selene steals away to the bathroom for a quick shower while Beck and I get dressed for our morning run.

"I still can't believe they told Harris to fuck off for the night," he muses, pulling on a moisture wicking workout shirt he stole from me. "I wouldn't have gone for that shit."

"Me either. I'm glad he did, though."

"Me too, but at the same time, I'm kind of annoyed, you know?" He spins around, standing over me as I kneel on the ground to tie my shoe. I nod, already knowing where this conversation is going because I had the same thought when I saw Selene alone in the vending room. It was quickly erased by the prospect of having a whole night with her, but now it's back in full force.

"Yeah. I know." I push to my feet. "She shouldn't have been left alone for that amount of time. Anything could have happened."

"Exactly. I mean, we've got Marsh popping up everywhere she is, and we don't know what he wants or which of the bastards on our team is giving him information. We've got these trolls online who get off on typing out the sickest shit they can come up with in their twisted fucking minds."

The water in the shower turns off, and I narrow my eyes at Beck. "Bring your voice down. She'll hear you."

"Maybe she should!" He throws his hands up in the air, and all of the calm, peaceful energy that's been floating around in the room fades as his agitation grows. "It's her life that's in danger, Cal. Her back with a target on it. She has a right to know what's going on, and if we don't tell her, who will?"

I don't disagree with him. Truly, I don't. I just hate the thought of bringing Selene problems I don't have any solutions to. Beck doesn't wait for me to answer. He's on a roll now, and when he's like this— feral and angry, worried about someone he loves—there's very little that can be done to stop him.

"It won't be those fuckers upstairs. They didn't even tell her she's the reason we're here in the first place."

"They didn't need to," Selene says, stepping out of the bathroom wrapped in a towel with her skin still glistening. She's even washed her hair, so it's wet and curly, piled into a bun on top of her head. "Your appearance coincided with an uptick in worrying comments online that started after the press conference about Aubrey's affair, all of them aimed at me, of course. I assume things have gotten worse?"

The towel drops to the ground, and she steps over it, grabbing my bottle of lotion off the nightstand and pumping some into her hands. I'm obsessing over the thought of her smelling like me all day, when Beck answers.

"Yes."

She crosses the room, retrieving her clothes from the edge of the bed where I placed them after Beck made it. When she's dressed, she squares her shoulders. "Can I see?"

Beck and I look at each other, both of us hesitant to fulfill this request. Monique let it slip that Selene has been on a strict social media hiatus, so she doesn't know what she's asking us to subject her to.

It doesn't take her long to grow impatient with our silence. She crosses her arms. "You want me to be informed, but you don't want to give me any information?"

"You don't need that information, gorgeous."

"Yes, I do. I need all the information."

"Selene." My voice is a cautious plea that she gives no consideration.

"*Show me.*"

The command lands on my shoulders, heavy and impossible to fight. I'm turned on by her ferocity even as I regret the very moment I said the words 'Don't ask. *Tell*,' because now she's turned them into some sort of spell. My teeth grind against each other, and every cell in my body screams its dissent as I turn to my computer and call up the file that contains screenshots of every credible online threat I could find. It bothers me that it's so vast but still isn't comprehensive, that there are hundreds of thousands of posts we weren't able to find or capture in time.

"Sit down."

She does as I ask, sinking into the chair in front of the desk and breathing deeply. I step back, giving her space, watching her hands as she uses some keyboard magic to display multiple threats at a time. It helps her sort through them faster, which means she gets to the posts about her son before I have the chance to explain how popular they've become, with the anniversary of his death approaching.

All of the posts pertaining to her were viewed with a kind of numb disinterest. She scanned them quickly and objectively, like they were about someone else, but with these, she takes her time. She views them one by one, refusing to look away even though there's nothing good there, nothing kind.

My stomach is in knots, and I want nothing more than to close the computer and make her stop, but I rein that desire in. I let her keep her eyes on the screen even when a particular post—a school picture of Aubrey Jr. that's been edited to include blood dripping down his face and neck, Xs over his eyes, and a gunshot wound between them— makes them bulge out in horror.

"Oh my God."

Beck steps up, his expression grim and laced with regret as he starts to close the computer. "This was a bad idea. I'm sorry."

"Wait." Selene places a staying hand over his. "Look at the caption."

Most of the time I try to put the shit these people say out of my mind, but this seems to be important, so I steel myself and read the words aloud. "Hope his mama follows him to an early grave. She deserves a bullet between the eyes just like her mixed-breed son got."

I shudder at the bitter taste of hate on my tongue, revolted by the thought of a bullet even coming close to her. "Jesus."

Selene appears completely unmoved, but I know that isn't true. She feels everything deeply, sometimes too deeply, which means the pain is somewhere in there, trapped behind the wheels spinning in her mind.

"I've heard that before."

"We've been considering the possibility that a lot of these accounts are bots. That would account for the sheer number of posts and the uniform nature of the language," I offer.

She shakes her head. "No. Well, I mean, yes, there are absolutely bots at play here. Normally, their sole purpose is to amplify the reach of the person or people paying for them by tricking the algorithm into thinking they have all this engagement and pushing their content further. These are also programmed to create their posts, echoing the sentiments of the person who paid for them. In this case, that sentiment is that I deserve to die in the same manner as my son."

I gesture at the post. "So you're saying this is a bot?"

"No. A human wrote this post." She glances at the screen for a second. "It was, however, liked and shared by several of the bot accounts, which most likely means the person behind this account is the one paying for them. I think I know who it is."

Skepticism lines Beck's features. "You're incredible, Selene, but I don't think anyone, not even you, can identify someone after reading one caption on a photo. You just said the bots echo the language of the person who programmed them, so it stands to reason that you read a comment just like that as you were sorting through the other posts."

" I didn't say I read the words before, Beck, I said I *heard* them."

"Someone *said* that to you?"

"When?!" Beck asks, his face a mask of rage that matches the fury coursing through my veins. He drops to his haunches in front of her, turning the chair so she's facing him. "Who the fuck said that to you?"

Her answer is faint. "The woman who approached me in the bathroom at Feast."

Beck rears back as if he's been slapped, and there's a rough edge to his voice when he responds. "You never told me that. I asked you for all the details, and you left that out."

His righteous tone doesn't account for the details we've kept from her about the same woman, namely, the connection between her and Jacob.

"I know, but I kept it to myself because the last time we talked about AJ, it brought up memories of Cameron. I was trying to spare you."

"It's okay," I assure her, because we've been trying to spare her too, trying not to add more worry and stress onto her plate by telling her about Jacob and the threat he poses.

But now that we know he's had his sights set on Selene for far longer than we thought, keeping that information from her is no longer an option.

34

———

SELENE

Four days ago, I had no idea who Jacob Marsh was.

I'd heard of his father. Read all about his failed attempt to assassinate a sitting President and the hate that led him there. Hate, he has apparently passed down to his son, who now wants to kill me.

And for what?

Because my son died and his father took the resulting call for action as a personal attack on his way of life and wound up in prison? Because, almost five years after the fact, I dared to stand on a stage and express my belief that America's gun problem won't be solved with thoughts and prayers? Because I refuse to kill myself like so many of the posts he paid to have pushed to the masses say I should?

Beck would tell me not to try to make sense of this.

Cal would promise to fix it.

They would both stand in front of me, pledging vows of devotion and protection. That's what they did before they let me go back to Monique's room that morning. They swore on their lives they'd figure this out before Jacob Marsh ever gets close enough to hurt me, and I believed them.

It was easy to do when I was standing in the circle of their arms, but the moment I left them, my belief started to fade. Not because I doubted their commitment to keeping me safe, but because my mind wouldn't let me forget all the cards stacked against us. The team they can't trust. The investigation they're trying to run with nothing but the help of one FBI contact they can't get in touch with. The staggering number of unanswered questions about Jacob's plans for me and the size of his organization. We know so much, and yet, so little, and it's scary to be in the dark.

Scarier still to be fumbling through it without the only people I trust by my side.

I don't know how their day off happened to align with the anniversary of AJ's death, and the morning news segment Jordan committed me to, which she only thought to mention when we arrived in Detroit yesterday morning. The thought of venturing out into the world without Cal and Beck left me unable to sleep, so I'm tired and cranky when I arrive at the news station. Ayanna, the make-up artist, is a slight little thing with an effervescent glow about her and a work area filled with flowers. She is gracious enough not to say a thing about the bags under my eyes as I lower myself into her chair.

"Can I get you some coffee or tea before we get started?"

"No, thank you."

She turns to her station, selecting products while I dig my vibrating phone out of my purse. I'm caught between the urge to smile and groan when I see Monique's name on my screen. There's never a time when I'm not happy to talk to her, but she's been on my nerves lately, asking questions about where I disappeared to on the last night of her visit. I send the call to voicemail and make a mental note to return it later.

Of course, she refuses to be put off. She calls two more times, and I decline them both, then she sends me a text.

> Monique: I know you see me calling you.

> Selene: Obviously. I have my phone in my hand.

> Monique: Then why aren't you picking up?

> Selene: Because I'm getting my makeup
> done for this stupid interview Jordan
> scheduled for me.

Ayanna's touch is light as she rubs moisturizer into my skin. She's a consummate professional, focused on her work, never once acknowledging the incessant buzzing.

> Monique: You answer the phone when you're
> on the toilet.

> Monique: You don't care about talking when
> you're getting makeup done.

> Monique: You're avoiding me.

The texts come in so close together that I don't have time to respond to one before another arrives for me to address.

> Selene: You're harassing me.

> Monique: I'm your best friend. It's my job to
> harass you.

I start to type out a text containing her actual job title and description, but she knows me too well.

> Monique: Don't send me my fucking job
> description, Sel.

> Monique: Just tell me where you were the
> other night, and I'll leave you alone.

The huff of frustration I let out does cause Ayanna's brows to raise a bit, but she remains quiet. Regardless, I feel compelled to apologize for interrupting the peace of her workspace with all the noise.

"I'm sorry. It's my best friend."

"No worries," she says, smiling. "You should hear my phone when the group chat I have with my friends is popping. I'll put it down for five minutes and come back to a hundred messages."

I shudder at the thought. "I would find that so overwhelming." Holding up my phone, I say, "I find *this* overwhelming."

"You could always mute her."

"No." I sigh. "She's liable to get on a plane if I do that."

"She sounds like a good friend."

"She's a great friend."

Which is why I feel so bad about all the things I'm keeping from her. I want to tell Monique about Cal and Beck, truly I do, but I know that one answer will only come with more questions, and then the thread of lies holding my life together will unravel completely. That's the kind of stress I don't need right now, not when the danger feels more real now than it ever has.

Biting my lip and sending up a prayer that she'll forgive me for one more lie, I type out a response to Monique.

> Selene: I told you, I just took some time to clear my head. Time I wouldn't have gotten to myself if it wasn't for you. I'm sorry I don't have a more satisfactory answer. I love you, and I'll call you after the interview is done.

When the text goes through, I turn off my phone and put it back in my purse. I leave it there even after Ayanna is done with my makeup, and I'm back in my dressing room with Agents Anderson and Harris standing outside my door. Neither of them brings me the kind of comfort my men would, but I'm grateful to have them nonetheless. They stay close and quiet, one of them escorting me to the stage while the other stays behind.

The lights on the stage are bright, nearly blinding me when I walk on. One of the PAs instructs me to sit in the tall, rolling chair behind the counter next to a petite blonde with big hair and bigger teeth. I've never seen her before, but she clearly knows me. She holds out her hand, and I take it, holding it just long enough to appear polite before letting go.

"Mrs. Taylor, it's an honor to meet you. I'm Ursula Upshaw, and I'll be interviewing you for today's segment."

"Nice to meet you, Ursula."

"Did you have a chance to look over the questions we sent over?"

"No, I didn't receive them."

I honestly thought they didn't send any. Frustration blooms in my chest as I wonder if Jordan has set me up somehow. Then, I immediately dismiss the thought because I can't see her purposefully leaving this interview to chance. She doesn't trust me at all, but she trusts the media even less, so the fact that I'm sitting in front of Ursula when she doesn't have an approved question list, and I haven't been reminded a million times what my answers should be, means something isn't right.

Jordan is a lot of things, but she isn't disorganized. She has been incredibly distracted lately, though, dropping balls I know she needs in the air. Maybe this is just one of them.

Ursula presses her lips together, beaming as she puts her hand over mine. "We are going to have *so* much fun."

The interview is not fun.

Actually, it's anything but, and I leave the stage thinking that Ursula Upshaw makes the sea witch look like a teddy bear. She started out innocent enough, with questions about the campaign and my hopes as the Future First Lady, which was, predictably, used to segue into conversation about AJ's death and my gun control stance. After those were out of the way, though, she kept going, prolonging the segment in order to corner me into answering questions about the photos of Aubrey and Sutton that dropped when we were in Nevada. I hadn't commented on them publicly at all, and Ursula was practically bouncing out of her seat with pride at having gotten a coerced exclusive, where I assured her and the American people that Aubrey and I were stronger than ever.

The walk back to my dressing room is a blur of sound and movement that I'm not connected to. I don't know who's behind me or in front of me, who's speaking to me or trying to get my attention, all I know is I need to be alone. Except when I am actually alone, my chest heaving with suppressed anger and my back pressed against the door, I realize that's not exactly true.

I don't need to be alone.

I need to be with them.

I need the deep, decadent pressure of Beck's hug, and the tempered strength of Cal's embrace. I need their touch, their eyes, their hands because I haven't had it in days.

I wrap my arms around my middle, holding myself as tight as I can. It's a pale imitation of the real thing, but when I pair it with some square breathing, it works. I come back into my body reluctantly. Blinking slowly, I take in my surroundings. It's a detached appraisal, and I'm not looking for anything specific, but then my eyes snag on the white box sitting on the vanity I didn't have occasion to use.

Several slow seconds tick by before I approach it, noting the perfectly tied crimson bow wrapped around it. The fabric is thick and lush when I rub it between my fingertips, and it gives easily when I pull at one of the ends, falling away from the box with a quiet whoosh to reveal a small white card with my name written on it in a swirling font. Thinking it might be a gift from Ursula and the network for participating in this ambush of an interview, I move the card to the side and then lift the top.

The first thing that catches my attention is the red substance that looks so much like blood, it makes mine run cold. After I confirm the sticky, thick liquid isn't blood, all of my focus goes to the photos it's smeared all over.

Because I'm in every one.

Sometimes I'm alone, walking into Culture Code on a rainy day, or strolling down the path Aubrey and Sutton ruined for me in a summer dress. Other times, I'm at lunch with Monique, waving goodbye to Diane as I leave the salon with my hair freshly done, arriving at hotels or events, with Cal or Beck holding the doors open for me.

There are several of us in front of the hotel in Atlanta, and I hold them close to my face with shaky hands stained with red, recognizing the outfit I was wearing on the day the formation was broken on the highway. Knowing that we were being watched paints the already terrifying experience in a whole new light for me. Usually, I'm comforted when my assumptions are confirmed with proof, but this isn't one of those times. This time, the proof makes me sick to my stomach. This time, it sends threads of fear rippling through my gut, makes my brain scream for me to stop sorting through the box even as my fingers continue to move.

Carefully, I excavate every layer that serves as visual proof of an active threat, setting the pictures from my stalker aside until I'm staring at the bottom of the box. It's empty save for the remnants of the fake blood and the card that says: **SEE YOU SOON, HUMMINGBIRD.**

35

BECK

In every investigation, there's a moment, a single instance, when you're left with no choice but to throw caution, protocol, common fucking sense, to the wind and follow your gut. When you've exhausted whatever options you had and the only decision left to make is what you're willing to risk to close the case.

Four days ago was that point for our back-channel investigation into Jacob Marsh.

When Cal and I asked ourselves that question and the only answer was: whatever is necessary. Our careers, our connections, and the element of surprise that gives us somewhat of an upper hand over Jacob and whoever he has working for him on our team.

All of it.

Because the only thing we can't risk, the one thing neither of us can abide losing, is her.

Selene is over thirteen hundred miles away in Detroit, while I'm sitting next to Cal in a federal prison in Florence, Colorado, waiting for Leland Marsh to grace us with his presence. The decision to come and see him wasn't made lightly, and I'm still not sure how much information we'll be able to glean from our conversation, but we had to come. I wanted to look him in the eye and tell him to call his boy off before I put him down like the last man he sent after someone under my protection.

My leg bounces harder with every minute that passes. "I don't understand what's taking so long."

"He's fucking with us just like Valinsky did," Cal responds, flipping through the copies he made of Leland's visitor logs and the duplicates of the worrying amount of fan mail he's received over the years. So far, none of it has linked back to Jacob, but we know he likes to use proxies to do his dirty work, so that doesn't mean anything.

I grimace at the mention of the visit with the man who murdered my family. He wrote to me every day after his sentencing, asking me to come see him, taunting me with details of my wife's final moments that he would only share with me in person. For some reason, I got the wild idea to grant his request on the anniversary of Diana and Cameron's deaths. Cal and I were working together by then. Partners and friends, but not yet lovers. I didn't tell him I was going to see Valinsky, but somehow he still knew. He beat me to the prison, meeting me outside the gates.

We walked in together, and he sat beside me, stoic and silent for the entire hour it took for the guards to bring Valinsky down. And he pulled me off of the bastard when I snapped after hearing him say Diana used her final breaths to explain that she was far enough along for Cameron to survive outside of her, to beg him to save our son.

"You're probably right."

He closes the folder and sighs. "There's nothing useful here."

"So we'll have to depend on Leland to give us answers."

A vein in his temple throbs. "Unfortunately."

Another twenty minutes pass by before I hear the tell-tale clicking of secure doors sliding open and the slamming of them closing shut. Then the door to the windowless box we've been stuck inside swings open, and we're sharing air with Leland Marsh.

He's a short man, about five inches shy of six feet with beady blue eyes and a bald head that used to be covered in fine, blonde hairs.

What he lacks in height, he makes up for in width, slabs of hard muscles rippling under pale skin as he shuffles towards us with cuffs on his wrists and chains around his waist for the shackles on his ankles.

"Nice of you to join us, Leland," Cal says, watching with vague interest as the guard secures him to the table and pushes him down into the seat across from us.

Leland heaves a sigh, turning to look at the guard and exposing the confederate flag inked into his neck in the process. "Told you I didn't want to see these nig—" I slam my fist into the table, and he chuckles, cutting his eye at me. "You got a problem, boy?"

"Behave, Marsh," the guard warns, stepping out of the room with a shake of his head.

"Let's be clear," I bite out through clenched teeth. "There are no boys in this room, only two men and a hate monger who spends his days bartering for packs of noodles and single cigarettes. When you address me and my partner, you'll refer to us by our names and nothing else."

"That would be Agent Beckham." Cal points to me and then to himself. "And Agent Drake, respectively."

"I know who you are, bo—" The disrespectful moniker dies on his lips when I reach across and grab the back of his head, slamming his face into the metal table. Leland's groan of pain draws the guard's attention, and he opens the door, prepared to come to the rescue.

Cal stands, holding out his hand. "Don't."

"There's no need for your partner to handle him like that," the man says, shrinking back as Cal advances on him.

"Walk away," he growls. "Before your head is on the table next to his."

The officer retreats, but I can tell by the look on his face that he won't be gone long. It's highly likely he'll be back with the warden and a few of his buddies to escort us out of here. Apparently, Marsh is extremely litigious, and I just gave him grounds for a new excessive force claim. If the prison doesn't try to de-escalate the situation, then they'll be implicated too.

Leland struggles against my hold. "I've got rights. You can't treat me like this."

Since I'm already going to hell, and to court too, I apply more pressure, watching as his face turns red and the veins in his forehead start to pop. "Where's Jacob?"

"What?!" he sputters, spit flying out of his mouth. His eyes wild and pleading as Cal rounds the table. For a second there, he looks like he hopes Cal will help him, but then his face falls when Cal crosses his arms over his chest and looks down his nose at him.

"Your *boy,* Leland," he chides. "We know you've been in contact with him, know you're a part of whatever it is he's planning to do to Selene Taylor. Tell us where he is, so we can bring him in. If you cooperate now, I'll pull some strings, get him a cell next to you in this hellhole."

"Who is he working with?" I ask. "Are the Brothers back together?"

"I don't know anything about what Jake is up to," he groans, sweat blooming on his brow.

I grind the heel of my palm into his temple. "Don't fucking lie to me, Marsh."

"Not...lying," he pants.

"Yes, the fuck you are, and Jake's blood will be on your hands when we find him and put him down."

"Agent Beckham, that's enough!"

I glance up, unsurprised to find the warden, Ethan Bennett, standing in the door with the officer who, in my opinion, is far too empathetic with a prisoner, behind him with a smug smile turning up his thin lips.

Bennett marches into the room, hands on his hips. "I order you to release this prisoner at once."

"I don't take orders from you." The cords in my arms strain against the fabric of my shirt, and heat creeps up my neck, searing my anger and fear for Selene into my skin. "This man has information that we need, and we're not leaving until we have it."

Cal puts himself between me and Leland and the Calvary that's come to save him just to cover their own asses. "It's a matter of national security."

"So you said," Bennett barks at him. "But I'm afraid that even a matter of national security isn't enough to justify such excessive force. Agent Beckham, you need to let Mr. Marsh go. If you refuse again, I'll have no choice but to have you physically removed from the premises."

There's red in my vision. These days, it's all I seem to see. It paints the room, bathes Leland, Bennett, and the stupid fucking guard, turning darker when Leland's laughter reaches my ears and his face is level with mine. I don't remember letting him go, but I must have because no one is close enough to have made me. Not that the proximity would have mattered when none of them had the power.

I watch Leland run his hand over the lines of my palm that are etched into his skin. His eyes glow with contempt, and his bottom lip curls into a sneer. "I used to hunt your kind for sport, bunch of filthy fucking animals."

"And yet you're the one in a cage," I remind him, shrugging out of my jacket because it's far too warm in this room now. "Jacob will be caged up next. That is, if I don't put him in an early grave."

"That's enough," Bennett says, gesturing for the officer to come into the room when Leland tries to lunge at me. "Get him out of here."

He struggles against his restraints, trying to break free when the guard unhooks him, spitting empty threats at me and Cal. He is still shouting when they drag him out. "If you lay a hand on my son, you'll regret it, you hear me, you fuckers? You and that Black bitch will fucking regret it."

When he's gone, Bennett has us escorted out of the prison. The gates slam shut behind us, and Cal looks at me. "Well, that was pointless."

I tip my head to one side and then the other, cracking my neck. "No, it wasn't."

"We didn't learn anything, Beck."

"Yes, we did. Did you see the way Leland reacted when I threatened to kill Jacob?"

He nods, pulling the keys to our rental car out of his pocket as we approach the vehicle. "Yeah, and? Anyone would be upset if someone kept threatening to kill their kid."

"Right." I pause at the passenger door, my hand resting on the handle as I look over the top of the car at Cal. "But everything we've seen in his visitation records and contact logs suggests that he hasn't seen or spoken to Jacob in years. They were estranged before Leland went to prison. I re-read the transcripts of our interview with him and even found one with his mom after the arrest. She said Leland disowned Jacob for refusing to join the Brothers. He told anyone who would listen that he no longer had a son."

Understanding dawns on his features. "And now he's threatening two federal agents and the future First Lady for him, which you think he would only do if they've managed to somehow rekindle their relationship without anyone knowing."

"Exactly. Maybe Jacob is doing all of this in some misguided attempt to gain his daddy's love."

We pull our doors open at the same time, dropping into the car. Cal starts the engine and cranks up the AC. "So we know the why, now we just have to figure out... everything else."

"That would be so much easier if Charlie's ass would call us back."

I've never liked Charlie Monroe. She always had an unhealthy attachment to Cal, feeling entitled to his time and attention, growing resentful when he gave it to someone else. When we left the Bureau, I was glad to be done with her. I put her out of my mind, stuffed her entire existence into a box next to all the other things I can go months, if not my entire lifetime, without ever thinking about again. Lately, though, all I do is think about her. Hope Cal will mention her. Pray to hear her voice or, sometimes, when I'm really desperate, to see her face. I'll endure just about any interaction if it means getting answers that'll help us protect Selene. And yet, there have been none.

It's been over two weeks since Cal placed that first call, and while

I respect the fact that she has a job to do and its not investigating Jacob Marsh, I am tired of fucking waiting.

"Call Charlie again."

"Beck," he groans in exasperation. "I call or text her every day, and she doesn't pick up. She's probably still on assignment."

"Have you called her today?"

"We've been in that prison all day," he points out.

Reaching over, I slide my hands into his jacket, fingers traversing hard lines of muscle to find the interior pocket where he keeps his phone. He shakes his head as I pull it out and slap it into his palm.

"Sounds like it's time to do that. Make it quick, we have a flight to catch."

Instead of making a comment about how impatient I am, he connects his phone to the car's Bluetooth and pulls out of the lot after selecting Charlie's contact. The line rings several times before going straight to voicemail, and he hangs up.

"I told you she—"

The rest of his sentence is cut in half by the sound of an incoming call, and both of us wear stunned expressions when we see the name on the screen. Cal clicks the accept button with a quickness.

"Monroe?"

"Drake, I'm sorry I missed you."

I open my mouth to point out that she's been missing his calls for days now, but he holds a hand up to silence me. Since I've pushed enough boundaries for the day, I sit back in my seat and keep my mouth closed, listening as she spouts off some excuse about going dark for so long.

"You're good. I'm glad you're back safe," Cal says. His tight grip on the steering wheel the only indication of his impatience. "Do you have anything for us?"

"Jumping right in, huh, Drake?"

Charlie's voice is light and teasing, which only serves to further annoy me. Thankfully, that same feeling is growing in Cal. I watch as it writes itself into his features, hardening his jawline.

"I've been waiting to hear from you for weeks."

She lets the statement hang in the air for a second before addressing it with a sigh. "I know. I'm sorry about that, and I'm sorry that I don't have more for you right now."

My heart drops into my stomach. All this fucking time wasted on waiting for her just for her to come back with nothing?

"What *do* you have?"

"Beckkk," she drawls, her voice all sarcasm and loathing I'm not always sure is an act. "I was wondering where you were."

"What the fuck do you have, Monroe?"

I don't know if it's the repeated question or the venom in my tone, but suddenly she starts talking. For the duration of the drive to the airport, we listen to her drone on and on about Jacob's shitty childhood and his strained relationship with his dad. She tells us about him losing his job and room in her basement when his mom died. This resulted in him crashing on the couches of a few of his father's friends who managed to beat the charges from the Warner assassination attempt.

"So the Brothers are back?" Cal asks, merging into the car rental return lane.

"There has been an apparent revival, yes, and unfortunately, in today's political climate, there's no shortage of people looking for a reason to hurt or harm someone who is different from them."

Feeling the onset of a stress-induced headache, I massage my temple. "Do we know how extensive their network is?"

"Unfortunately, no. Jacob is nothing like his father, which means the organization looks much different under his rule. There are no meetings in the back of bars or abandoned warehouses. Everything is online. Everyone is hiding behind VPNs and bouncing their IPs. Jacob is very clever. He's brought a level of sophistication to the Brothers that was missing during his father's reign."

My eyes narrow at the wistful quality her tone takes on at the end. "You sound like you admire him."

"*What?*"

She heard me the first time, but I have no problem repeating myself, projecting my voice a bit to make sure she really absorbs my words. "You sound like you admire him."

"I have a healthy respect for his skills, and you should too," Charlie throws back, leaving it at that.

"That was a lot of information, Charlie," Cal says, ending the awkward silence. "Why did you make it seem like you didn't have anything?"

"I never said I didn't have anything, just that I was sorry I didn't have more. So far, no one can confirm Jacob has any plans to harm the Taylors. As you are aware, any credible threats identified by the Bureau are reported to the Service immediately. From what we can tell, his focus seems to be more on rebuilding the drug and sex-trafficking side of things."

Cal is parking now, his face grim. "You just said he's clever. Isn't it possible he's hiding those intentions behind a VPN or bouncing IP?"

"Or bot accounts and troll farms?" I add, thinking of the connection Selene helped us make. We still haven't been able to identify the woman, which means we don't have anything definitive linking her or Jacob to the online harassment.

"That's always a possibility," Charlie agrees, sounding distracted suddenly. "At this point, though, it is unconfirmed. I'm sorry, but I have to go."

The call ends abruptly, and we don't have time to dwell on it or discuss anything until we're on our flight to Detroit. Even then, we don't say much, both of us caught up in our own thoughts and the bone-deep exhaustion that haunts our steps to the hotel room we have to share, as our late arrival has ensured that all the single rooms are taken.

I used to be so concerned about the optics of sharing a room with Cal, but tonight I'm past the point of caring. I'm tired and stressed, and I just want the comfort of sharing space with one of the people I love.

"You can shower first," I tell Cal, dropping my bag on the bed closest to the door. He grunts his acknowledgment, slinging his things down and rummaging through his suitcase to dig out his toiletries bag while leaving everything else in disarray. Once he's disappeared behind the closed door, I set to work unpacking.

Hanging our suits in the closet, sorting our workout gear into the drawers of the dresser. I'm putting my phone on the charger when I hear a timid knock at the door. I cross the room and open it, surprised and delighted when I find the only other person I want to see right now on the other side of it.

36

SELENE

"**G**orgeous."

Beck's voice is a dark, relieved chorus of soft breaths against my neck. He's got me pinned to the door, my legs around his waist, the tote bag that was in my hands on the floor, completely forgotten.

I wrap my arms around his neck, fingers caressing his scalp, cupping the back of his skull lovingly before moving down to knead at the muscles in his shoulders. He's so tense, but his eyes are soft as he gazes up at me.

"I missed you," he says.

"I missed you, too."

And I did. I missed the peace that the circle of his arms brings. The way the fear and anxiety of the day leaves my body as he carries me deeper into the room and sits down on the edge of the bed closest to the door, with me on his lap. He's partially undressed, the neck of his button-down gaping open to expose his throat and the spattering of hair at the top of his chest. I can't stop myself from leaning in, from licking and sucking and nipping at every inch of skin I can reach while he pulls the hem of my blouse out of my pants and lays his hot palms over the bare skin of my lower back.

I didn't come here for this. I really don't have time for it, but I need it. I need him, and it's clear to me that he needs me. Not just because he's responding so vocally—deep, approving grunts vibrating from his chest—or because his dick is a hard press between my legs, but because he's clinging to me like I'm his lifeline, like he knows that he's mine.

That thought makes every touch a thousand times more potent, every kiss a million times more heated. Beck's hands move to my waist, holding me close even as I cling to him, rocking against him repeatedly until the friction sends arcs of electric pleasure racing through my veins.

I bury my moan against his racing pulse, panting as I come down from my release.

"What a beautiful display," Cal purrs. I peek over Beck's shoulder to see him leaning against the frame of the bathroom door in a towel. His arms are crossed, and there's a delicious smile curving his lips.

"Hi," I murmur, tipping my head back in offering when he approaches for a kiss. "I missed you."

He cups my face in his hands, holding me like I'm the most precious thing. "And I, you."

Beck nuzzles into my neck. "How long can you stay?"

Dread inspired by his question coils in my stomach, stealing what little joy I had found in this moment of respite. "Not long. I'm on my way to a dinner with Aubrey, Torrance, his wife, Anne, Jordan, and Cordelia." I roll my eyes, sliding off of Beck's lap. "I had to feign period cramps to get them to leave me alone long enough to stop by."

Aubrey's impatience and lack of empathy made the excuse work like a charm. He demanded everyone leave the suite with him and his entourage, not even leaving behind a single agent because he didn't want their time wasted on me and my antics. The rest of my plan went off without a hitch once they were gone. I took the stairs from the top floor to here, knowing I'd find them in this room because I overheard the number on the comms when the agent posted in the lobby confirmed their arrival.

It was a complicated plan, with lots of room for things to go wrong, but so far, nothing has. If I want to keep it that way, I have to make it to the lobby in the next ten minutes to avoid Agent Harris sounding the alarm. He's been a real stickler for the rules lately, trying to reassert some of the authority he lost when he caved to Monique so easily in Nevada.

"What do you need?" Cal asks, expression turning serious.

I feel bad about constantly bringing them stress, but I know there's no one else I trust with this. "This morning I did an interview with a local news station."

They both nod like this isn't new information to them, and I wonder why I thought it would be. With everything they have going on, they still keep tabs on me. They know my schedule even on their days off, and make it their business to know who is protecting me at any moment. Going so far as to report any missteps to Hicks even if it's a situation like Nevada when they're the ones who benefit from their team mates slacking off.

"Ursula Upshaw is on my shit list," Beck says.

"Oh, she's on mine too, but her little off-the-rails interview isn't even the problem."

He tilts his head to the side. "Then what is?"

Knowing we have limited time, I rush back over to the door and pick up the tote. Beck stands, following me over to the desk with Cal on his heels. They're both quiet as I slide the white box out, tossing the tote I stored it in aside before setting it down gingerly on the lacquered wood surface.

"*This* is the problem."

I step back to make room for their imposing frames, giving them the space they need to fully experience the horror I've been carrying around with me all day. After the initial shock wore off in the dressing room, I had the presence of mind to wash the fake blood off my hands and put everything back in the box the way it was. I carried it out of the news station as if it were a gift, not letting on for a single second that something was wrong, because I didn't trust anyone but the two men in front of me to handle it.

Cal turns around first, holding the note from the bottom of the box in his hand.

"Where?"

"Inside my dressing room. It was waiting on the vanity after the interview was done."

Beck is still sorting through the photos. "Where were Harris and Anderson?"

"I was upset when I left the stage. I wasn't paying attention to who was where." My teeth sink into my bottom lip. "I'm sorry. I should have—"

"*Don't apologize.*"

They issue the order together, voices layering over each other to form one, strong, undeniable force. Cal comes to me, taking my face in his hands once again. "You made the best decision you could in the moment, Selene. We weren't there, and we still don't know who we can trust."

"Not Anderson or fucking Harris," Beck growls, turning to lay a severe gaze on Cal. "We need to process that room."

He shakes his head. "No point. There's probably been fifteen different people in and out of there since she left."

Another apology slides up my throat. I knew I was being unwise, breaking some kind of protocol or evidence-gathering process by not alerting anyone to the breach. Now we've lost the chance to examine what is essentially a crime scene. I bite back the words, knowing they won't want to hear them, focusing on offering something that's not regret.

For some reason, I reach for positivity.

"This is a good thing, though, right?"

Both of them look at me. Confused and enraged onyx. Wild, murderous copper and brass.

"This is terrifying, Selene," Beck says, pointing at the box. "There's nothing good about it."

Everything about Cal's expression says that he agrees, and as much as I love these two men, as much as I value their expertise, I know they're not thinking clearly right now. All they see is the threat, and I see it too; I'm terrified by it as well, but I also see the potential. I have to make them see it now, too.

"You're right. It's terrifying, but it's also the first tangible, credible proof of a threat we've been able to find. If we take this to Hicks, if we show him, he won't be able to write it off. He won't be able to ignore you."

Cal's features twitch with agitation at the mention of going to Hicks, and I get it. They don't trust their team, and right now, I don't either, especially after the author of the note used the code name that only the men on my detail call me by. However, we're past the point of pretending this is something we can handle on our own.

We need help.

"They'll want to know why you waited, why you came to us with this and no one else." He searches my face. "What are you going to say? How will you explain?"

"I'll tell the truth."

Beck balks. "You're going to tell them you're in love with us?"

I let out the first real laugh that I've had in days. "No, I think I'll keep that between us for now. I'll tell them the other truth, which is that there's no one else in this world I trust more than the two of you."

37

CAL

Forty-eight hours.

That's how long it takes for everyone's schedules to align. The measure of time scrolls through my head on an endless loop as I stand at the head of the table with all the people who wouldn't recognize urgency if it were a loaded gun pointed right in their faces, settling into seats in front of me.

Most meetings like this start with the person running them thanking everyone for making the time to be here, but I already know those words won't come out of my mouth. I'm going to jump straight into the details and past any and all formalities, because if I don't, the first thing I'll do is ask if it would have taken this long if Aubrey had been the target and not Selene.

It would be a rhetorical question, of course, because we all know the answer is no.

The only things soothing my agitation are Beck at my side and Selene right in the center of my vision. She's sitting between Aubrey and Jordan, who both look like they have other things they'd rather be doing than learning about the very real threat to her safety.

Hicks is the last one to take his seat, and when he does he sighs heavily, letting us know he doesn't appreciate being on the receiving end of a security briefing instead of the one running it.

"Alright, Drake, Beckham, you've got us here. Now tell us what's going on." He glances at his watch. "And make it quick because we've got to get Mr. Taylor to a speaking engagement."

I grit my teeth, holding back the slew of expletives that want to come spilling out of me, and jumping straight into why we're here today. While I speak, detailing the security breach at the news network and the contents of the box Selene gave us, Beck circles the room, handing out folders with photos of everything we found in the box, copies of a written statement by Selene and a report stating that no prints besides Selene's and ours were found on any of the items.

My goal is to get a read on everyone in the room, but I focus most of my attention on the two men who were on duty during the breach. They're standing on opposite sides of the room, acting as bookends to the line of agents bracketing the space. Harris does a thorough examination of every item in the folder, his brows wrinkled in confusion, while the red flush of embarrassment creeps up his neck. It's the same way he looked when we took him to task for leaving Selene unattended that night in Vegas.

Anderson, on the other hand, looks bored. He hasn't bothered to open the folder, which strikes me as odd. I glance at Beck and see that he's clocked the disinterest too, and we make the silent agreement to focus on Anderson, to figure out if he simply doesn't care about the details laid out in the folder or if he hasn't bothered to open it because none of the information inside is new to him.

"Let me get this straight," Hicks says, resting one elbow on the table near the folder he just slammed shut and pinching the bridge of his nose. "Mrs. Taylor made you and Agent Beckham aware of an egregious breach of our security *hours* after the fact instead of notifying the agents on duty?" He swings his furious gaze in Selene's direction. "Why on Earth would you do that?"

Selene's eyes touch mine for the briefest of seconds, a small recognition of the fact that I was right about what everyone would focus on first. We're playing with fire here, risking exposing the depth of our connection for the sake of possibly saving her life. I hate that we'll have to be more careful now, that there will be more eyes and scrutiny than before, but I'll gladly bear it all as long as she's safe.

When she speaks, her voice is all power and not a hint of apology. "Agents Drake and Beckham have been a near constant in my life since the start of this detail. We have an established rapport and a strong sense of trust that simply doesn't exist between me and any of the other agents on your team."

Love for her surges through me, a hot rush of affection I can't let show on my face. Beck sees it, though, and he stretches his eyes ever so slightly, silently urging me to pull it together as he makes his way back to the front of the room. He crosses his arms over his chest, staring down at Hicks, who scoffs at Selene's answer.

"With all due respect, Mrs. Taylor, neither of these things justifies the course of action you took. Had you notified Agents Harris and Anderson of the problem, they could have conducted a thorough investigation that would have yielded far better results than this." He stabs the folder with the tip of his index finger.

Selene tilts her head to the side. "You expected me to trust the very men who allowed the breach to happen to investigate it and come up with anything other than excuses meant to cover their own asses?"

Hicks' nostrils flare. Everything about his posture suggests that he wants to refute the implication carved into Selene's question, but he knows he can't. If Selene had immediately alerted them to the issue, Harris and Anderson would have been removed from the scene and questioned separately while another team processed the room. Procedures like that exist specifically to prevent the kind of corruption and accountability avoidance she's hinting at. Hicks knows that.

If he weren't so busy trying to take her to task for coming to us, he would have been able to string together something other than a string of words that suggest he doesn't.

"You could have come to me directly," he offers lamely.

A derisive snort leaves Beck, which pulls Hicks' attention away from Selene and straight to him. "Right, because that's worked so well before."

Jordan, who's been quiet up until now, perks up then. "Before? There have been more of these?" She frowns, gesturing at a picture of the box.

"No, but there have been other incidents that have given us cause for concern," Beck says, the muscle in his jaw jumping. "We have documented and reported each one to Agent Hicks. Each time he's dismissed or ignored us."

"Aubrey, did you know about this?" Jordan asks in a pointed tone, meant to capture the man's attention and prompt him to play the role of the caring husband. The thought of her thinking he could pull that off almost makes me want to laugh. Aubrey's emotional detachment from Selene is clear. I knew something was off with them even before I was in love with his wife, but it's so apparent now, and he doesn't even try to hide it. He's been on his phone the entire time, and his folder sits in front of him, unopened.

He jolts at the sound of his name, smiling awkwardly as he pockets his phone and sits up straight like better posture will convince us he was listening. "Right, so, uh, how are we handling this issue?"

Everyone is confused by Aubrey's inability to follow the conversation, but Hicks' relief shows on his face. He grasps onto the lifeline the man has inadvertently thrown him, steering the conversation towards next steps so we don't spend any more time discussing his lack of action.

"That's an excellent question, Mr. Taylor. Drake, Beckham, I assume you have a list of suspects? Have you run any names?"

"We don't have suspects," Beck says. "We have *a* suspect."

Aubrey frowns. "One? Didn't this just happen? How could you narrow it down so fast?"

I scrub a hand down my face, not bothering to hide my frustration. "There have been a series of ongoing incidents involving your wife, Mr. Taylor. They date back to early September. Everything has been documented, including an obvious escalation as our suspect has grown more and more comfortable with terrorizing Mrs. Taylor. Given the note left in the box, we have reason to believe he is planning something even more bold than the stalking he's already engaged in."

Selene shifts in her seat, growing uncomfortable when I allude to what Jacob might do next. We ran through a few scenarios together before she left for dinner the other night, and none of them were good. After all, no one leaves a box filled with bloody photos and a note saying 'see you soon' if they don't want to do bodily harm.

Grabbing his folder, Hicks begins flipping through the pages, looking for a name. He's frustrated when he comes up empty, but I don't care. Beck and I both agreed it was important for us to be able to see the face of our suspected traitors when we said Jacob's name.

"Well, who is it?" Aubrey asks, more concerned about ending the suspense than hearing the name of the man trying to kill his wife.

I don't bother looking at him because I know he's not the one leaking information and putting Selene in danger. Instead, my gaze bounces from Hicks to Harris to Anderson and back again as the name passes through my lips.

"Jacob Marsh."

Anderson's expression is flat. Too flat. Like he's intentionally withholding a reaction.

Harris' brows pull together. Now that he's over the embarrassment inspired by the news of the breach, he's dialed in. "Marsh? Any relation to Leland Marsh?"

"His son," Beck says.

Hicks' leg bounces with agitation. "How'd you make this connection?"

I lay it all out for him, giving him every detail, including the things we couldn't confirm, such as the link between Jacob and the vitriol online. When I'm done, Aubrey appears to be genuinely concerned. Not for Selene, though, for himself.

"This kid's dad tried to assassinate a President, right? Do I need to be concerned?"

My mask of professionalism threatens to slip, but I hold it

together. Blowing out a breath, I shake my head. "No, Mr. Taylor. Jacob seems to be singularly focused on your wife. Not you."

Every time I call Selene his wife, the word burns its way up my throat, scorching my tongue and my lips on its way out. She shouldn't be his wife. She should be mine. She should be Beck's. She should be ours. Though I know it's not legally possible, the desire still lives in my heart, existing right beside the urge to murder Aubrey for breaking vows I would kill to take, vows I would rather die than break.

He's frowning now, his over-inflated sense of importance trumping what should be relief that he's not in the cross hairs of a potential killer. "That doesn't make sense," he says, looking at Selene. "I'm the one running for President. She's just—"

Beck's interruption of his sentence begins with a growl he has to work hard to temper into something else. "She is the person Jacob blames for his father being behind bars. In his mind, this all started the day Aubrey Jr. was killed. Selene's public grieving was the catalyst for President Warner's push for real change on the gun control front. That speech sent a tremor of fear and then outrage through Leland's organization, and the assassination plot was born."

"I grieved my son just as loudly and publicly as Selene did," Aubrey insists, his hand going to his chest to rest over his heart. "For the last five years, I've kept AJ at the center of my life, career, and this campaign. If his death has made Selene a target, then I don't understand why I wouldn't be one as well."

"Great, we'll be sure to let Jacob Marsh know you'd like him to divide his stalking efforts and murderous intentions evenly," I spit, my last shred of patience gone.

"Careful, Drake," Hicks warns while Aubrey flounders for a response. "Mr. Taylor makes a great point. You've made a solid case for why Marsh would want to go after Mrs. Taylor, but I haven't heard a single reason why you've ruled out Mr. Taylor as a target."

Beck jumps in, giving me a second to recover from engaging with this level of stupidity. "Because Jacob wouldn't see him as a threat,"

Jordan purses her lips. "A future President with the power to do the exact thing his father went to prison to stop from happening isn't a threat?"

"Yes, because this isn't about gun control laws," he replies. "No matter what Jacob tells himself. No matter what lies he's spouted to his followers to get them to help him with this plan. Deep down, he knows it's really about revenge."

"And logically, Selene is the easier target. She's a Black woman in America, so he can count on her to be deprioritized, dismissed and discounted at every turn," I add, raising a brow at Hicks to make it clear that everything he did, or didn't do, in regards to Selene serve to prove that point. "Mr. Taylor's whiteness, his growing popularity with conservative white males, and his alignment with Senator Barnes, who is well known for her relationship with the NRA, has insulated him and left Selene out in the cold."

My eyes touch her face, then, the softest of visual caresses to let her know she is not alone in this. Aubrey might have built in layers of protection, but she has us. Her expression gives nothing away, but I have to believe she feels the reassurance I'm offering.

Aubrey resents the answers Beck and I just gave him, I can tell by the way the vein in the middle of his forehead throbs. "So, it's my fault this Marsh kid wants to kill her?"

"Is that what he said, Aubrey?" Selene asks incredulously. "How do you manage to make everything, even someone trying to kill me, about you?"

He opens his mouth to respond. I have no desire to see the two of them arguing because I won't be able to stop myself, or Beck, from stepping in, so I interject. "There's one more thing."

Hicks sighs, sitting back in his chair. "What is it?"

"We have reason to believe that one or more of the agents on this team is providing information to Jacob Marsh."

Everyone in the room, except for Beck, Selene, and me, starts to look around the room. Disgruntled murmurs and pleas of innocence blend together, growing louder until Hicks stands and slams his fist on the table.

"Now wait a damn minute! You two circumventing an investigation and commandeering a security briefing is one thing, but with-holding information about a potentially corrupt agent is something else altogether. This is my fucking team, and I should be the first one to know if anyone even thinks someone under my command is dirty, so I can handle it."

"That's not your job, Hicks," Beck says from his spot near the door of the conference room. His hand rests on the knob, and he pulls it open just as Hicks growls, "Who's fucking job is it then? Yours?"

"No, it's mine."

The words are spoken by a petite Black woman in a perfectly tailored black suit and a blunt bob. We've never met in person, but I recognize her voice from the phone call we had yesterday when she arrived in Detroit. She strides into the room on sure feet, marching right up to Hicks and extending her hand.

"Althea Lennon, Office of Integrity of Professional Responsibility."

Anderson, Hicks and Harris all look sick to the stomach, which makes me want to laugh even as Agent Lennon's presence in this room, and our lives, turns my intestines into a ball of anxiety. She's a highly perceptive woman and a decorated investigator who always gets to the bottom of every situation, even those she's not tasked with resolving. All of which means, Beck and I will have to be more careful around Selene than ever.

Hicks takes her hand, introducing himself through clenched teeth. She makes her way through the rest of the room, learning everyone's names before she comes to stand beside me at the front of the room. I step aside, taking up the space at Beck's side while she takes command of the room.

"I'm not here to disrupt your lives or your work," she starts, spreading a piercing gaze over everyone in the room. "I am, however, here to find the answer to a straightforward question: which of you has decided to put hubris and selfish desire above oath and duty? And I will do whatever is necessary to find that answer. If you are the guilty party I seek, you can make all of our lives easier and confess now."

She pauses, brows raised expectantly. When no one steps forward, she sighs.

"Very well. We'll start with voluntary interviews. When no one signs up for those, my consultant and I will move on to mandatory interviews. You will be assigned a date and time, and, of course, you have the right to have a lawyer present."

Once again, the room erupts into murmurs and uneasy conversation. Although I knew Agent Lennon was coming, I feel a bit uneasy as well.

"Did she say consultant?" Beck asks. The question, which is an echo of the one that just formed in my head, is loud enough for her to hear.

"Oh, yes," she nods, looking to the conference room door and waving someone in. "The Bureau was kind enough to lend me one of their undercover agents. She's only here for a short while, though. Marsh is starting to trust her, so she can't be gone long."

The door opens as I run through all of my conversations with Charlie, trying to remember when, or if, she said anything to me about them having someone inside Jacob's organization. When the familiar figure steps into the room, tucking brown strands of a grown-out pixie cut behind her ear, the question changes.

Did Charlie ever say anything to me about being embedded in the Brothers?

38

SELENE

gents Lennon and Monroe make quite an effective team.
Within twenty-four hours of arriving in Detroit, they find a burner phone among Agent Anderson's things in the hotel room he was sharing with Agent Harris.

On it were texts that went back months, detailing everything from my daily routine to the frequency and duration of my hair appointments with Diane. The burner was more than enough for them to take him in, but what really sealed his fate was the video footage from the news station that showed him leaving the green room unattended. Moments after he left, the feed was cut, and it didn't come back on for twenty minutes when he was back at his post.

I wish his removal from my orbit brought me peace, but it doesn't. Mainly because Anderson refuses to talk, except to vehemently deny his involvement with Marsh, so we still don't know what he's planning or when it will happen. But also because I'm not as confident in the results of the investigation as everyone else seems to be. Of course, I can't express my lack of faith because it's rooted completely in the agents' inability to sniff out my most closely guarded secret.

Agent Lennon touched on it a bit when we sat down for my interview. All of her questions at the beginning were centered around the bond I have with Cal and Beck. She wanted to know how they became the people I trust most, if we had known each other before the detail was assigned, if there had ever been any instance of impropriety. It was the oddest sensation, watching her face as I lied through my teeth, hoping she would believe me and being disappointed when she did.

That disappointment has lingered, morphing into anxiety-fueled questions centered on what else could have been missed during the short-lived investigation. Those questions, but especially the lack of answers, are making it impossible for me to enjoy being back home without Aubrey, who flew to Georgia to attend some event with Cordelia when we all left Detroit yesterday.

They're on my television screen right now, all dressed up and smiling, his arm around her shoulder, one of hers around his waist. It's not exactly inappropriate—though I wouldn't care if it was—but it's not the distant professionalism you usually see in politicians from opposing parties. Then again, nothing about their relationship suggests that they're anything less than completely aligned on everything that matters.

Fed up with looking at and thinking about Aubrey and Cordelia, I turn the TV off. I get to relish in the quiet around me for all of a minute before my phone starts to vibrate. I pull it from between one of the lush cushions of the couch in the movie room I've been rotting on all day, smiling when I see that it's Mama calling. Our relationship has improved by leaps and bounds since she came to Las Vegas to see me. We talk almost every day, sometimes it's a quick text, others it's a phone call, more often than not, though, it's a FaceTime. She says she prefers those to everything else, and as I swipe to accept the video call, I find that I agree.

"Hey, Mama," I say, pulling my weighted blanket up around my chest. "How are you?"

"I'm good, baby. I'm glad to see you resting."

She's got me set up on a tripod that Robin or Jessica got her, so she can move around the kitchen while we talk. For all the time she spends telling me to sit down somewhere, she's always moving around doing something.

"You should be resting too," I tell her, eyeing her closely as she starts running dishwater. "Daddy can wash those dishes, or you can finally use the dishwasher for once."

She dismisses my suggestion just like I knew she would, and I laugh, thinking of Beck. "Your daddy is in there watching the news. I got tired of looking at Aubrey and that white woman, so I came in here to get some peace."

I have to hold this laugh back, knowing she'll pounce on anything I do or say that suggests I'm unhappy with Aubrey.

"What did you cook?" I ask, switching gears.

"Fried pork chop, macaroni and cheese, some cabbage, and cornbread."

"No candied yams?"

"Your daddy's trying to cut back on the sweets."

"You could have still made them. He just couldn't have any."

"Yeah, right," Daddy shouts from the living room, making us laugh.

"Hey, Daddy!"

"Oh, no, traitor," he hollers. "Don't try to hey—OH MY GOD!"

The shock in his voice sends Mama running to the living room. She's moving so fast she doesn't even grab the phone, so I'm stuck asking what's wrong until she comes back. Her face is a blur as she moves to the living room again.

"Mama, what's—"

She shushes me. "Albert, turn the volume up."

An increase in volume does nothing to aid in my understanding of what's going on, so I reach for my remote to turn the TV back on. My mind is racing as I search the cushions and under my blanket. All of my thoughts are on Aubrey. Mama said they were just watching him on the news, so whatever happened could have happened to him.

"Mama, is it—"

Once again, I'm silenced, but it doesn't matter now because I've found the remote. I click the power button, and the TV takes its sweet time loading while I wonder what exactly I'd feel if something happened to Aubrey. The truth is, I don't know. The reality is, it doesn't matter because the words scrolling across the screen don't have anything to do with Aubrey, even though they will directly impact his future and mine.

President Lucas Sanders, dead at 72.

TWO DAYS after the President of the United States dies in his sleep, I'm decked out in a formal gown with my hair piled artfully on top of my head, wearing a pair of heels that aren't meant for anything but walking from the house to the car and from the car to the dinner table because Aubrey refused to cancel the fundraiser.

A man is dead. The nation he was tasked with leading is aimless and confused. His Vice President is scrambling to reassure the country and his party that he can lead. His wife is now a widow. His children are fatherless. His body is in a morgue, and I'm standing in front of a mirror, mentally preparing to spend my night socializing with a bunch of people who, like my husband, don't care that a life and legacy have come to an abrupt end.

It's not even that I liked the man all that much, or at all. I'm just so unsettled by the way it doesn't seem to matter to Aubrey at all. His reaction to Sanders' death was like his reaction to his hospitalization all those months ago, except so much worse. There's no sympathy or compassion, no care or concern, no genuine emotion. No humanity. Just the stale breath of a dry mouth preparing for the thirst-quenching rush of power. I can see it in him, the glee, the dangerous confidence that comes from knowing your victory is inevitable.

I hate it.

I hate him.

I hate the part of me that understands his excitement, that is already plotting on how to stay in close proximity to the power he'll wield, hoping I can use it to my advantage. A shudder rolls through me at the thought, half thrill, half disgust, and I turn away from the mirror, tired of looking at myself.

Since returning home, I've started sleeping in the in-law suite on the main floor. It's one of my favorite rooms in the house because of the large French doors that open to the patio and lead to the backyard. What was once my favorite feature has now become a source of anxiety for me, though. I keep lying in bed and picturing Jacob Marsh standing there, watching me. The thought is a prevalent one, always at the front of my mind, which is why I nearly jump out of my skin when I see a large, looming figure on the other side of the glass.

My heart leaps into my throat, but I bury the scream between my lips when I realize it's Beck looking at me. I rush to the door, unlock it, and pull him in. He comes down for a kiss as soon as we're alone, his hands on my hips when I want them everywhere else.

"That one was from me," he murmurs against my lips before bringing our mouths together again. This kiss is just as slow, just as decadent, just as full of love. "That one was from Cal."

I smile so hard my cheeks hurt. The ridiculous grin stays in place even as he pulls away because the reward for allowing him to break contact is a square jewelry box that he takes from his pocket.

"This is from both of us," he whispers, opening the box to reveal a gold, diamond-encrusted tennis bracelet. I gasp, covering my mouth with one hand while he puts the bracelet on the opposite wrist. "Full transparency," he says, onyx eyes serious as he fixes the clasp. "This isn't just a gift, it's also a safety measure."

"A safety measure?" I repeat, squinting at the unassuming piece of jewelry.

"Yes, it has GPS capabilities that we've already turned on, so it's transmitting your location to Cal and me in real time." He runs a finger over the flat gold disc dangling off the excess links. "If you ever need us, and we're not there, all you have to do is press down on this, and we'll be alerted immediately."

It's such a sweet and moving thing; I find myself getting emotional. With all the anxiety I've been feeling lately, my emotions live a lot closer to the surface these days, so I'm not surprised when the tears start to blur my vision.

Beck's eyes stretch wide. "Don't cry, gorgeous. You'll make me want to pick you up and take you away from all of this if you do that." I almost want him to. He cups my cheek, a gentle thumb brushing away a freshly fallen tear as he reads my mind with ease. "We're not cut out for a life on the run, baby."

"We don't have to run," I say wistfully, running a hand down his chest. "We could just walk out of here. No one would chase us."

He wraps his fingers around my wrist, stopping my hand from going any further."If you knew how badly I wanted that, you wouldn't say it now when you don't really mean it."

My heart twists in on itself. "I'm sorry."

Lifting my hand to his mouth, he places a kiss on the center of my palm. "Don't be. You have work to do, a promise to keep. I understand, and so does Cal."

"I love you," I whisper, the words urgent and necessary.

Beck's answering smile soothes the ache in my chest. "I know. I love you, too."

With one last set of kisses, he leaves me to finish preparing for my night of misery. When I referred to it that way on a call with Monique, she laughed and said I was being dramatic, but I wasn't.

In fact, I was grossly underestimating just how awful the night would be. I spend hours standing in my beautiful, but uncomfortable heels, pretending to care about the people Aubrey introduces me to, smiling through the constant wave of disgust that comes from being touched by him, laughing like everything is fine when Jacob Marsh is somewhere out there plotting to kill me and the only people I trust to protect me are doing perimeter sweeps at my house instead of at my side.

My finger runs over the bracelet for probably the hundredth time tonight, and I force myself to stop fidgeting when it catches Aubrey's attention. His eyes linger on the bracelet for what feels like forever, but eventually he turns his focus back to Cordelia and the other group of Republican senators who have come here to kiss up to the future President.

"Excuse me," I say to no one in particular, slipping off to the bathroom with the two female agents Agent Lennon suggested be added to my detail in order to avoid incidents like the one at Feast hot on my heels.

One of them, Agent Shaw, a tall Black woman with a stunning face and a grumpy disposition, steps in front of me, taking the lead of the procession to the bathroom. She steps inside first, leaving me standing outside the door with Agent Morgan, another incredibly tall and beautiful Black woman, watching over me. When Agent Shaw emerges and nods that it's all clear, I go in and breathe a sigh of relief at the quiet that envelops me.

It doesn't last long.

I'm retouching my lipstick in the mirror when Cordelia comes breezing through the door. She's walking with purpose, not at all surprised to see me in here, almost like she was seeking me out. We've never been in a room alone before, so I'm interested to see how this will go.

"Selene," she drawls, sauntering up to the mirror beside me with a smile on her thin lips. "I was hoping to get a moment alone with you."

"Why?" I lean closer to the mirror, using my pinky finger to remove any smudging. I can feel her eyes on me, unsettling and expectant. When I can't take the silence anymore, I angle my body in her direction. "What do you want, Cordelia?"

She taps blood red nails on the stone counter. "To tell you a story."

Sufficiently creeped out, I close my lipstick and turn to leave. She grabs my arm, the tips of her nails digging ever so slightly into my skin. I look down, shocked at the sight of such an egregious violation of my personal space and bodily autonomy. When the shock wears off, though, I snatch away.

"Don't fucking touch me."

She holds her hands up, palms out in mock surrender. "Forgive me. I simply didn't want you to miss the opportunity to finally get an answer to your question."

"What question?"

"The one you posed in Las Vegas after the debate."

I don't need any more information than that. I cross my arms and take a step back from her. "Well, go on."

Cordelia grins, clearly enjoying dangling a carrot in front of my face. I wonder how often she does it to Aubrey, taunts him with the promise of something he wants. Maybe she'll include that tidbit in her little story.

"I was a lot like you when I was growing up."

I twist my lips to the side. "Doubtful."

"Okay, maybe I wasn't intellectually superior," she concedes. "But I was also the oldest of a working-class couple with three daughters and not enough money. My daddy was a long-haul truck driver, and my mama stayed at home with me and my sisters. The days at home when it was just us and Mama were the best. There was no fighting, no cursing, no broken glass or slaps across the face. My sisters fell into the traps of teenage pregnancy and marital hellscapes that I ducked and dodged, so I could pursue my own dreams."

"The longer you talk, the more differences I hear. My father never beat my mother. My mother ran a successful hair salon throughout my entire childhood, which remains a staple of the community today. My sisters married their high school sweethearts and, as fr as I know, are both happily married. As far as financial similarities, we weren't rich, by any means, but we were never—"

"*My point,*" Cordelia cuts in, eyes narrowing into slits in the face of my bluntness, but she continues. "We're both survivors, both incredibly strong women who overcame challenging upbringings and made it here."

I have so much more to say about her faulty comparisons but decide to swallow the words because I hope eventually things will turn to Aubrey and what she wants with him.

"When I lost the Republican nomination last election cycle, I took it extremely hard." Frustration flits across her features, and she shakes her head like she still can't believe it. "Men who want to go to war every time a world leader forgets to wish them a happy birthday said *I* was too emotional to lead," she scoffs. "They don't even understand how a uterus works, and yet they felt confident looking me in the eyes and expressing doubts about my ability to hold it together during 'that time of the month'. Un-fucking-believable."

"It's actually incredibly believable. Misogyny trumps everything, even your whiteness."

She doesn't appreciate my contributions to this conversation. That much is clear by the way her nostrils keep flaring every time I speak. Maybe I should feel bad about interrupting her little monologue, but I don't. There's nothing worse than being forced into a conversation and then expected not to participate in it.

"That experience taught me a lot. Namely, that you don't have to be the person in the seat to be the one in control. That sometimes the key to real power isn't holding it in your hands, it's sitting next to it, steering it in the direction you want it to go."

"And that's what you're doing with Aubrey? Manipulating him? Pacifying him with the illusion of power while you wield the real thing?"

Cordelia tilts her head to the side, examining me. "Isn't that what you plan to do?"

"No."

She pushes her lips out into a fake pout. "Oh, that's right. You can't, can you? You don't have his ear, his trust, or his secrets. It's a little hard to control a man, even one as weak-willed as Aubrey, without one of the three."

The shot she's just taken doesn't hurt as much as she wants it to. I'm too caught up wondering what secrets Cordelia knows that I don't, and whether or not I can find them out. If I can, then I might be able to persuade him to reconsider his stance on gun control. Hope rises in my chest, bright and bubbly despite the dark cloud around my present company.

"Thank you for the story, Cordelia," I mutter, flashing her a smile I'm sure is disconcerting when her plan was to come in here and make me cry. This time she doesn't delay my departure, and I'm glad to be free of her, returning to the party with just enough patience to make it through the rest of the night.

As soon as I step back into the room, Aubrey is at my side wearing a wide, false grin. He sweeps me into his arms, pulling me onto the dance floor, so we can put on a show for the donors.

"Smile," he growls through his exposed teeth, spinning us around the floor in wide circles while everyone watches with adoring expressions.

They watch, but they don't see. The straining muscles in my upturned lips. The truth of our embrace. They don't see the distance between our hearts, the cold expanse of hate that stretches between us and gets wider and wider every day.

They don't know that being this close to him is nauseating, that having to pretend I welcome his touch is an insult to everything I've built with Cal and Beck. As soon as my mind conjures their names, my eyes fall on the bracelet, and Aubrey's follow. He spins me out, holding the wrist with the bracelet tight, then pulls me back in so my back is to his front.

His lips are at my ear, his breath hot on my skin. "That's a beautiful bracelet. Is it new?"

"A gift from Monique," I lie, wanting nothing more than to remove myself from his grasp so he can stop touching the only reminder I have of my men tonight.

Aubrey goes quiet, and I assume the conversation is over. Then, the song ends, and he dips me low and follows me down, kissing my cheek as he whispers, "You're good at a lot of things, Selene, but lying has never been one of them."

39
─────

SELENE

There are few things scarier than a cemetery on Halloween day, or at least that's what I believed until I watched Aubrey offer his condolences to President Sanders' entire family and come across completely genuine.

His features collapsed in on themselves, his eyes rimmed with tears he doesn't let fall because that would be a step too far. He stands next to me, one hand on the small of my back and the other over his heart as he nods enthusiastically at whatever it is that Deborah Sanders is saying.

She's not hard to understand, I'm just not listening.

I've mostly been tuned out all day, refusing to take part in the mockery Aubrey is making of this family's very real grief. I've been stone-faced but polite, keeping mostly to myself. No one has seemed to mind. They're all too busy fawning over Aubrey or standing off to the side, whispering to each other about why we're here.

I'm wondering the same thing.

To me, the proper thing to do would have been to attend the State Funeral service and leave it at that, but Aubrey insisted on flying to Ohio for the Burial as well, and now we're standing in the Sanders' home like we're their family when we're not even their friends with Jordan and fucking Cordelia in tow.

As if he can sense me thinking their names, Aubrey turns to search the room for them. I turn too, watching Cordelia wave him over to a corner where she's holding court again. She seems completely at home here, among the very colleagues who probably helped Sanders edge her out of the Republican nomination.

Aubrey releases me, cupping Deborah's hands in both of his. "I'm so sorry, Mrs. Sanders, will you excuse me for a moment?"

"Of course, dear."

Since his permission slip to depart doesn't seem to include me, I linger awkwardly in front of the now former First Lady. We stare at each other, and I have no choice but to fill the silence around us.

"I'm sorry for your loss."

She dips her chin gracefully. "Thank you."

I could leave it at that. I could find a quiet corner to spend the rest of the afternoon or even go to the car where Cal and Beck are waiting, but instead of doing any of those things, I say more words.

"I didn't know your husband well, and I wasn't really a fan of his politics, but the one time I met him, he seemed kind enough."

Deborah's green eyes stretch wide the way people's always do when I forget to sugar coat things. I expect her to be offended, but she shocks me by letting out a short peal of laughter that draws the attention of everyone in the room. She covers her mouth with her hand.

"That was inappropriate, wasn't it?"

"It's your house and your husband's funeral. No one can tell you what is or isn't appropriate. If they're uncomfortable with you laughing on a day like today, then they can leave."

"You're very honest, aren't you, Mrs. Taylor?"

I shrug. "Not enough people say what they mean."

"And even less mean what they say," she returns. "You should be careful of that, though; the American people don't appreciate it, especially in women." She gives me a smile that I automatically read as sad. "I don't envy you one bit. Being the First Lady will be hard for a woman like you."

With a raised brow, I ask, "A Black woman?"

She nods, displaying her own penchant for honesty. "Yes, but also a woman who knows her own mind and has her own agenda. You must know it won't be valued in the White House, that when you're in the Oval, only he matters."

I follow her gaze across the room to Aubrey, my mind on the contract we signed and the secrets I need to uncover to get him to honor it, on the son we lost and the promise I'm now tasked with keeping on my own. None of that happens if Deborah's warning becomes a reality. I lift my chin, defiance swelling in my chest.

"Maybe that was true for you, but that won't be my reality."

Once again, Deborah reacts completely differently than I expected her to. She studies me with something close to admiration in her eyes. "Is that why you stayed after news of the affair broke? Because you thought you could be something other than ornamental?"

There's no condescension in her tone, just a curiosity that makes me comfortable enough to be honest. "Yes."

"I told Lucas," she says. "I told him the photos wouldn't sway you. I told him you were a determined woman with a plan for that platform, that you would use it to do something more meaningful than plant flowers and set fashion trends."

It takes me a minute to catch on to what she's saying, but when I do, my jaw drops. It's one thing to suspect that the late President was the one behind the distribution of the photos, but it's another thing entirely to have it confirmed by his wife.

She laughs once again, and this time it lasts longer, tapering off when she wants it to instead of when she thinks it should. "Oh, honey, please tell me this isn't news to you. Your camp should have figured out it was Luke behind the photos a long time ago, but it should have been glaringly obvious when new ones emerged after the debate."

"That's when they put it together," I admit, rolling my eyes. "Up until then, they suspected that I was the one behind it all."

"You? What on Earth would you get out of exposing the affair and then sticking around to be publicly ridiculed?"

"That's the same question I asked, Mrs. Sanders."

"Oh, please, dear, call me Deborah."

I smile. "Then, please, call me Selene."

"I must say, Selene, I was surprised to see how the news of the affair seemed to breathe new life into Aubrey's campaign. Lucas was especially frustrated by that. Every night, he went to bed fussing about inadvertently activating a new base of voters for his opponent."

"Yes, well, Aubrey does have a frustrating tendency to come out on top in every situation, even the ones that should destroy him."

"Listen." She grips my hand, squeezing tight as she steps in closer and lowers her voice. "Your husband is going to win this election. I know it, and you know it too. When that happens, there won't be a single thing in your world that's not about him."

"It already feels that way."

"I know, darling." She pats my hand, trying to offer some comfort. "I know, but trust me when I say, as soon as those results come in, it will be a million times worse. Suddenly, it's not just you, his team, and a gaggle of campaign staffers running yourselves ragged to please him; it's the entire world. That kind of power is intoxicating, and when, not if, but *when*, he gets drunk on it, he'll do anything to protect it. Lie. Cheat. Steal. *Kill*. And there will be no end to the number of people who will be in his corner, offering every resource and skill at their disposal." Her eyes are locked on mine, every ounce of humor from our earlier conversation forgotten as she issues a final warning. "You need to think about who will be in your corner if he ever decides you're someone he needs protection from."

40

BECK

My sigh of frustration pierces the quiet of Cal's living room, and he closes the file in his hand, peering at me over the rim of his glasses.

"Spit it out, Beckham."

I shift in my seat, angling my body so my legs are stretched out and tangled with his while my back rests against the arm of the couch. "I don't have anything new to say, Drake. It's just the same shit rolling through my mind over and over again."

"Do I look like I care?"

He doesn't. He'd happily sit here and let me talk about the same situation, listening intently the entire time, never interrupting or complaining.

"I care, though. I'm sick of hearing myself talk. I'm sick of asking the same questions and reading through the same files and finding nothing new."

To demonstrate my point, I shove the files in my lap to the floor, watching as they land in a useless heap. Cal doesn't say anything, just watches me like he knows it's inevitable that the words I'm sick of saying will end up coming out of my mouth.

I hate that he's right.

"I just don't understand—" I start, grimacing when he smirks and puts his file on the coffee table.

"Go on," he says, crossing his arms over his chest and nodding encouragingly.

My need to express my frustration outweighs the need to prove him wrong, so I do, in fact, continue, diving into a monologue he's heard a thousand times before. It always starts with questions about how Anderson got by us, how no one knew he was trading information with Jacob Marsh, how we still don't know where they met or what they were planning for Selene. Then, it shifts, focusing on Charlie and why she never told us the assignment that kept her from getting back to us actually involved the person we were asking her to provide information on.

I asked her after the briefing where we brought in Agent Lennon, but she was vague and defensive. Everything pretty much boiled down to her not having to tell us anything because there was no confirmed threat against Selene, and, according to the report she gave over the phone today, there still isn't. After leaving Detroit, Charlie returned to the Brothers, taking the risk of calling in at least once a day. So far, she's only been able to confirm that Jacob has gone to ground and that no one trusts her enough to tell her why or where he is.

"Honestly," I tell Cal, wrapping things up before I get too up in arms. "Having someone on the inside should mean more information flowing our way, not less. I feel like we had a better understanding of the situation when Charlie wasn't involved. Now we're more in the dark than ever."

"I don't disagree."

"Then what the fuck are we going to do about it?"

"Focus on what's in front of us."

I frown at him. "I hate when you get all reasonable and shit."

"I know, but someone has to be able to talk you down, love. I can't do that if I'm losing my shit right beside you."

"I like when you lose your shit right beside me. Everyone gets all scared and cooperative."

He laughs like I'm being ridiculous, but we both know it's true. When a calm, reserved person like Cal starts to raise hell, people tend to pay attention in a way that they don't when someone like me—who's known for wreaking havoc—does.

"Yeah, but that doesn't really work on Charlie. If she gets pushed too hard, she shuts down. That's why you two don't get along now."

"No, we don't get along because she's a liar."

"You didn't like her before you knew she was a liar."

"So you agree that she's a liar?"

He rolls his eyes. "She's kept some things from us for reasons I don't completely understand or agree with."

"Right. Because you're an honest person, and she's not."

A small chuckle escapes him just as a ping on both of our phones sounds off. We both scramble to grab them, Cal reaching over his shoulder to pluck his off the end table, me hopping up to rush to the kitchen and pull mine off the charger. The notification has a distinct chime, and it continues to play even after I unlock my screen and open the app connected to Selene's bracelet.

We set it to notify us anytime she is on the move, which isn't often these days because she's too anxious to leave the house. But she is on the move now, and I watch with avid interest as the small dot with her face on it moves closer and closer to where we are.

"Is she—" Cal says, his nose damn near touching the screen of his phone.

"She's coming here," I confirm, my heart doing a flip because I'm so desperate to see her.

"How?" he whispers in awe.

I smile. "I may have told her about the blind spots around the house, specifically the gaps in the camera coverage between the patio doors of the in-law suite and the garage."

We fall quiet then, tracking her drive the way we did her footsteps at the house in Houston: with devotion and without distraction. We don't breathe or speak or move until she's on Cal's street. Then we rush to the garage and open the door, so she can pull in.

The lights on her luxury SUV are bright, and I squint against the beams until she cuts them and the engine. With the car off, the only sounds in the air are our pants of anticipation and the clicking slide of the garage door closing. Cal makes it to her door before I can, so I stand back, watching as she steps out and immediately sinks into his embrace.

His hands bracket her waist, fingers digging into the soft fabric of her favorite hoodie before sliding down to grip her ass through the sweats she's wearing. All the while, they're kissing, trading happy laughs that warm my heart and draw me closer to them without even needing an invitation. Selene turns in Cal's arms when I approach, reaching for me with open arms. I take her face in my hands, holding her gingerly.

"Hello, gorgeous."

She beams. "Hi."

"I've missed you," I tell her, watching Cal lean in to kiss her neck.

"I've missed you," she says through a shaky breath that caresses my lips just before they touch her. She sighs into my mouth, injecting that familiar feeling of belonging to someone who belongs to you into my lungs. Cal lifts her up, and she wraps her arms around my waist, allowing me to carry her out of the garage and into the house.

"I can't believe I'm in your house, Cal," she gasps, breaking the kiss to look around. I stop in the kitchen, letting her slide down my body until she's back on her feet. "It's so beautiful."

He's standing with his hands in his pockets, watching as Selene runs her fingers over the tiled backsplash. "Thank you. How'd you know where to find us?"

"Aubrey had copies of all of your personnel files in his office. I came across them when I was in there snooping."

My brows rise. "Snooping?"

"Yes," she says, matter-of-factly. "The only thing I found of interest to me was those files. They included your addresses. I knew you'd be together at whichever one was closest to me, so that's where I came."

Like always, her thoughtful reasoning makes me smile, especially because it follows our line of thought so effortlessly. Cal's house isn't all that close to Selene's, but it is closer than my apartment by just a few minutes. Since we gave her the bracelet, I've been spending every night we're not working here, knowing that if she ever needed to press that button, those few minutes could be the difference between life and certain death.

"And what did you come here for, gorgeous?"

My voice is low, dripping with carnal decadence that Selene reacts to immediately. She is back in front of me in an instant with Cal closing in on her back, all thoughts of exploring his or complimenting his home forgotten as I pick her up again.

Cal's fingertips brush against my hand as he slaps her ass, making her yelp. "I think she came to get fucked, Beckham."

She moans loudly, eyes low and hazy with growing lust. "I did."

"Say it louder, pet," he commands, peeling her out of her hoodie, setting those perfect breasts free to bounce in my face.

"I came to get fucked."

Her declaration ends on a broken moan as my lips close around her nipple, but I'm satisfied and so is Cal. She's given us what we want, so the only thing left to do is return the favor. Which is what we do over the course of hours, using every stolen minute she's gifted us with to wrap her in love, to worship her body and feed her soul, to remind her that regardless of what finds her out there in the world the only thing she'll ever find here with us, is love, peace and protection.

We fall asleep in a tangle of boneless, sated limbs. I'm on my side with an arm around Selene's middle while her head rests on Cal's chest, and the most perfect, soul-soothing quiet surrounds us. I don't know how long we get to stay like that before Cal's phone starts ringing, vibrating loudly against the hardwood floors from somewhere inside his pants.

He rises with a groan, rolling onto the floor to find and silence the disruption. Knowing that he's taking care of it, I try to find rest again. Selene tries to do the same, turning over to snuggle into my chest now that Cal has left the bed.

Neither of us is successful because as soon as we hear Cal say Charlie's name, all thoughts of sleep are gone. I sit up first, swinging my legs over the side of the bed and then rounding it to sort through the clothes on the floor. I hand Selene her items first, then get dressed with my eyes on the grim set of Cal's jaw.

"What's going on?" Selene whispers, slipping into her sweats.

"I don't know."

Cal holds a finger to his lips, signaling us to be quiet before he puts the phone on speaker.

"Charlie, can you say that again?"

"Jacob is back. Anderson's arrest had him spooked, so he went to ground with the handful of people he still trusts."

"Do you know where they've been?" Cal asks, sliding into his clothes now that his hands are free.

"Negative. I don't think their hideout is important, Drake. Today, I saw them bringing in servers' uniforms. You know, like the kind caterers wear at galas?"

"So they're trying to blend in with catering staff at an event," I say, not even bothering to announce myself before I speak because at this point, Charlie's used to hearing my voice whenever she speaks with Cal.

"Not just any event, though, Beck, Aubrey's Election Day party. They're going to wait until the results are in, until she's standing on the stage beside him while he gives his acceptance speech, and then they're going to..." She trails off, like she doesn't have the stomach to finish the sentence.

Cal finishes for her. "And then they're going to kill her while the entire nation is watching."

Selene is so still beside me. The shallow rise and fall of her chest the only thing indicating that she hasn't died of shock. I slip my hand into hers, squeezing hard to get her attention. She looks at me, but I can tell she's not seeing me, not feeling the calm and reassurance I'm trying to press into her skin.

Maybe she can't feel it because of how badly I'm shaking.

"We won't let that happen."

I don't know who the words are for, but they don't seem to do anything for the two people in this room with me. We are caught up in this storm of fear, of anxiety that refuses to fade even though we finally have the answer to the questions that have been plaguing us for days. The knowing almost makes it worse because it forces you to acknowledge how much more time the other person has had to plan and how little time you have to cover all the ground you need to make up for.

Suddenly, I'm back chasing Valinsky. Following a series of clues that led me to my own home, to my wife's mutilated body, and my son's tiny, lifeless form. I'm running up the stairs and knowing by the silence that it's too late. I'm racing down the hall, rushing headfirst into tragedy. I'm...

Selene squeezes my hand, and I'm back, returning to reality where nothing bad has happened yet. Where nothing bad will happen, if I have anything to say about it.

"Where are you now, Monroe?"

It's only then that I hear the tell-tale clicking of a signal light. The quiet hum of a running engine. " I told them the Election Day plan was too much for me and bowed out as quickly as possible. I'm on my way to the Taylor residence now," she says. "They need to be briefed immediately."

"We're on the way," Cal barks, hanging up the phone.

The energy in the room turns frantic, and we rush Selene to the garage in hopes that she'll make it home before Charlie's arrival brings her absence to everyone's attention. Everything feels urgent and rushed, including our goodbye kisses, which happen in the driveway because Selene forgot to get them when we were still in the garage.

Once she's gone, I stand in the driveway next to Cal and close my eyes, whispering a prayer for her, for us. He indulges me for just a second, then turns to head back inside.

"Come on. We need to get ready to go."

I'm about to follow him when I feel it.

The eerie sensation of eyes on me.

I tense, scanning the quiet street for any sign of movement, but come up empty. I do one more visual sweep, straining my ears to see if I hear anything other than the gentle quiet of the early morning and the desperate, stuttering beats of my heart.

41

SELENE

I'm tired of people looking at me and talking to me, or worse, talking *around* me. Having whole conversations where I am the topic of discussion, while I sit there and say nothing. Do nothing. Just breathe and think and try to feel anything other than the paralyzing fear that's clawed its way into my chest and made itself at home.

Cal, Beck, and Charlie are doing it now, the whole talking around me thing. Discussing all the things that could go wrong today as we drive to the polling center, where I'll cast my ballot early because Jordan essentially forbade me from mailing it in the way Aubrey had. She even resorted to reminding me of my lack of leverage and, thus, precarious standing in this arrangement to silence my protests.

When she floated the idea in our now-daily security briefings earlier in the week, it was met with a lot more resistance than I'd been able to muster, mainly from Cal and Beck. Beck, specifically, had raised hell, asking Jordan if she'd lost her fucking mind while Cal followed up with a calmer, more strategic refute about needing to limit my exposure as we get closer to Election Day.

In the end, neither of their responses mattered. I knew they wouldn't. By the time the meeting started, I'd already accepted that danger was imminent, that Aubrey and Jordan would send me out like a lamb for slaughter just for the shot to burn the image of me walking into the polls to vote for my husband into the minds of every American. Hell, they're probably praying I'll catch a bullet between the eyes on my way in, that way they can shift the last days of their messaging to talk about how I died carrying out my civic and marital duties.

"Jordan's going to get her photo opp after all," I murmur, looking out the window at the news vans lining the street in front of the polling center. There are reporters and camera people everywhere. Some of them are interviewing people wearing 'I Voted' stickers, but most of them have their eyes and lenses trained on the line of SUVs we just arrived in.

Cal puts the car in park, turning a fierce gaze on me in the back seat. Beck does the same thing, and I return their stares, wishing we were alone so we could speak freely. I want to say that I love them and that if the worst should happen, four days from now or today, then I'll die the happiest I've been since losing AJ. I want them to know how much I appreciate them and how much I value the way they've fought and advocated for me. I want to tell Cal that he's a gentle fire, silent and lethal, and laugh with Beck about how loud he always is in his outrage.

I want so much, and in this moment, I can't have any of it because Charlie is sitting beside me, watching and listening, taking up space in the only moment of togetherness I've had with my men since sneaking out to Cal's house the other night. I'd visibly deflated when I heard she'd be riding with us today, so much so that I didn't bother to respond after she explained her supervisor thought it'd be necessary to have her on site, even if she couldn't get out of the car for fear of her cover being blown.

Not responding was rude, I recognize that, but I don't care. And I still don't care that we're technically being rude now, forcing her to sit on the outside of our bubble while we exchange gazes filled with longing and love, and hope it's enough.

"If you see anything that looks even remotely off," Cal says, forcing a calmness into his voice that is betrayed by the wild look in his eyes. "You press the button on that bracelet and get yourself somewhere safe."

"We'll get to you in seconds," Beck assures me, his jaw tight. "No matter where you are, we'll find you."

Charlie sits up, locking the screen of her phone. "Bracelet?"

I turn to look at her, registering the shock and dismay on her face, and my heart starts to beat wildly. Fear that the moment and mention of the bracelet have given something away rips through me. It grows stronger when her eyes travel down to my wrist, tracing over the line of gold and diamonds circling it, then dissipating swiftly when she nods her approval.

"Smart," she says, glancing at Cal and Beck. "Why wasn't it included in any of the reports of the precautions we're taking to keep Selene safe?"

Cal is stone-faced, offering up a lie quickly. "It's a new addition to her jewelry collection."

"A gift from Aubrey," I add, throwing in a tense smile.

Beck opens his door, ending the conversation before Charlie can see through our collective lie. "We should get her inside."

I fidget with the bracelet nervously, cognizant of Charlie's eyes on it. "It's a beautiful piece," she says as Cal pulls my door open. There's a disconcerting juxtaposition between her compliment and the heavy curve of her downturned lips. I try to make sense of it, but there's no time.

Beck holds the door handle, blocking the cameras and reporters with his body. Cal offers me his hand, and I take it, squeezing his fingers lightly before letting go. Suddenly, there's a wall around me made up of bodies in black suits with faces I can't see and names I don't remember because most of them have only just become part of my detail. Hicks, who has finally decided to take my safety seriously, thought it was necessary to increase security, even going so far as to have local police monitor my parents' and siblings' homes until the threat has passed.

Those numbers don't do me any good as I pass through the doors leading to the main voting area, though. I walk into that space alone, leaving Cal, Beck, and all of the other agents in the lobby because the woman at the door said their presence in the room could be considered voter interference. The doors slam shut behind me, and I'm essentially alone. I feel the vibration of it in my bones, and I am too aware of the vulnerability that comes with it, of being thrust into the world on your own after months of always having someone between you and it.

The line moves too slowly, and I can't shake the feeling that someone is watching me. Well, I mean, of course, people are watching me. I'm the wife of the man who cheated and is still going to be President. I'm the woman whose son died in a school shooting. I'm the future First Lady of the United States of America, and I'm standing here with them, voting in person like I'm a normal American.

It's such a ridiculous notion that I almost burst into laughter as I finally make my way into the booth. Standing in front of the ballot machine feels...weird. I've spent so long thinking about this day, this ballot. So much of my life has been determined by this election, and now it feels almost disappointing to be here, especially when the options on the ballot are what they are.

When the campaign started, I felt certain I would have no qualms about voting for Aubrey, but now my heart and my mind long for a better option. My muscles are tight with resentment and fury as I reach for the screen.

"Here goes nothing," I whisper as my finger hovers over the box beside Aubrey's name. Just before it connects with the screen to make my reluctant selection, a loud boom sounds out around me, and the building quakes, sending me flying into the machine.

I brace myself against the table, wincing as the blaring of car alarms outside causes my ears to ring. "Was that a bomb?" the man in the booth next to me asks. My already pounding heart starts to gallop, slapping against my ribs as I try to breathe, try to focus, try to make sense of the worried murmurs from the other voters and poll workers.

The word bomb is now rippling around the room, a fearful echo that sweeps through the crowd in a second.

"Everyone stay calm," someone says, but their demand is drowned out by the second explosion that sounds like it's on the other side of the doors I just walked through, in the exact spot I left Cal and Beck standing just a few minutes ago.

My hand goes to my mouth to stop the horrified groan crawling up my throat, but it's no match for the melody of fear. Fear for them. Fear for me because I might not know much right now—like how to put one foot in front of the other and get the fuck out of here—but I do know I'm the reason this is happening.

The awful truth of it resonates deep in my chest as a third bomb goes off. This time, in the room with us. Everyone screams as the ceiling comes crashing down, glass and drywall and smoke blanket the room, adding a haze to the layer of darkness that descended on us when the power went out. People are screaming, and they're not all fearful screams. Some of them are loud, guttural expressions of pain their body can't hold anymore, and my voice is among them.

I blink up at the broken beams and wiring hanging above me, wondering how I ended up on the floor, and when I hit my head hard enough for blood to be running into my eyes. I'm coughing through my disembodied screams, lifting the arm that's not pinned underneath several privacy screens and what looks like a ruined ballot machine to put pressure on the gash in my forehead. Unfortunately, that free hand isn't the one with the bracelet on it, and it wouldn't matter if it were because Cal and Beck know exactly where I am, but they haven't come for me yet, which means something is wrong.

Are they hurt? Are they dead?

The questions float around my head in a loop that never ends. Blood pools in the corner of my eye and rolls down, staining my skin with crimson tears as I lie waiting for whatever comes next. The screams have tapered off, and my body has gone numb with the acceptance that it won't be anything good.

Because I'm trapped, and I'm hurt, and I'm scared that whoever did this did it to get to me. It feels like the only logical explanation, even though Charlie's intel all but guaranteed that Jacob won't make his play for another four days. The FBI and the Department of Homeland Security opted to leave him free for a bit longer, wanting to catch him in the act like they did with his father in order to make sure the charges stick.

They're supposed to have eyes on him right now, but I have first-hand knowledge of how easy it is to slip a tail when you're determined, and Jacob is determined...to kill me.

"Selene."

My eyes flutter open at the feel of firm hands on my shoulders. I don't know when I closed them, don't know when the weight of all the things pinning me down was moved, don't know anything except that the person in front of me isn't one of the people I was hoping to see.

"Charlie?" I blink rapidly as she hoists me up and off the floor. My vision swims with red and blurs of the room around me.

"We have to get you out of here. Can you walk?"

I nod even though my neck aches with the effort, and she grabs me by my hurt wrist, yanking me away from the people clamoring to get out of the front door. Her hold is less than gentle, and she's moving far too fast for my staggering steps, but there's no time to complain about that. All I want to know is one thing.

"Are Cal and Beck okay?" I ask, not caring if my asking about them first makes me seem too attached, if my calling them anything other than Agent Drake and Agent Beckham lets on to the fact that I belong to them and they belong to me.

Charlie doesn't react to my use of the personal monikers. In fact, she doesn't react to any of my questions, continuing to drag me through a maze of hallways that takes us deeper into the building and further away from the last place I saw the loves of my life.

"Are they okay?!" I scream, snatching away from her to bring our march to a halt, realizing too late that she has her index finger looped through my bracelet. It snaps from the force of my pull and clatters to the floor.

"There's no time," she growls impatiently when I try to bend down to pick it up. I'm still reaching for it when she grabs my elbow and yanks me down the last stretch of hallway that leads to a door that's already propped open. I can only assume it's the entrance she used to breach the building, but I can't understand why no one else came with her, why the black SUV idling by the door doesn't have an agent waiting outside of it but there is a familiar face in the driver's seat, why as soon as we pass through the threshold the entire world goes black.

42

BECK

Selene is gone.

Selene is gone, and the only thing we have left of her is the bracelet we gave her to prevent this exact thing from happening. That was supposed to keep us from spending days on end chasing down fruitless leads and cycling through the same fucking questions every five seconds.

Where is she?

Is she hurt?

Is she scared?

Is she still alive?

My hand turns to a fist around the plastic evidence bag when that question pops into my head again. I can't get it out, can't get past the sight of the clasp of the bracelet lying in pieces at the bottom of the bag, broken like my heart.

Cal had been the one to find it. His hands shook around his shattered phone as we followed the dot with her face on it to a hallway near the only exit in the polling center without a camera. I kept asking him to let me hold it, to let me see, to let me lead us to her, knowing that life had already prepared me for what we might find. He refused. Whether to spare me from experiencing that same pain or to maintain some semblance of control, I don't know, but I appreciated it all the same.

Just like I appreciated the way he knocked me to the ground when the first explosion went off, using his body to shield me from harm. The bombs outside and in the lobby had been small but powerful. We were able to use footage from the camera people to determine that the initial blast originated from some black duffel bags that were strategically placed to blend in with the equipment bags belonging to the news crews. The two that went off inside the voting area were a little bigger, causing a few fatalities, collapsing part of the ceiling, and damaging a couple of machines.

We knew from the moment we entered the scene that Selene's body wouldn't be among the wreckage. The locator on her bracelet told us she'd gotten away from the blast site, and I held out hope that we'd find her in the hallway, hurt but alive. Instead, we ended up with nothing but a broken bracelet and, a few feet away in the alley, an unconscious Charlie Monroe with a nasty head wound.

Cal is reminding me about the severity of concussions right now, while we're standing outside of Charlie's apartment. I've placed the evidence bag in my pocket, and the hand that was just clenched around it is poised to knock on her door.

"The doctor said her concussion was pretty bad," he warns me when the knock is more of a bang.

"Don't care."

When I hear no movement on the other side of the door, I bang again. *Hard.*

"She already gave her statement to the FBI and Homeland."

"Don't care about that either."

"I know you don't." He shoves his hands in his pockets, his jaw rigid as I start pounding on the door. "Just figured I'd remind you anyway."

"You don't care either," I tell him, dropping my fist when I hear the sound of shuffling feet on the other side of the door. "You don't give a fuck about her concussion or her statement, you give a fuck about Selene."

"I do, but I also give a fuck about you, and we can't find her if you're in jail for harassing a federal agent."

My chance to address his concerns is stolen by the loud click of a dead bolt being undone. Charlie's face appears through the gap created by the chain on her door, and she squints against the sunlight.

"We need to talk," I say, by way of greeting.

She rubs at her temple. "You should have called first."

"No time. Unlock the door, Monroe."

Cal's urging gets the ball rolling. She closes the door and undoes the chain. This time, when she opens it, it's wide with a reluctant invitation. It stays that way as she tiptoes back down the hall gingerly, walking like her whole body hurts. I don't care if she's in pain, though, and I don't care if I'm being rude when I start questioning her before she even settles into the armchair across from the couch we make ourselves at home at.

"Do you know what day it is, Charlie?" I cross my legs, resting clasped hands on my knee. She frowns. "Tuesday, November 5th."

"Election Day, also known as the day Jacob Marsh plans to kill Selene Taylor."

We don't know that for sure because we haven't heard from him. There have been no ransom demands, no posts bragging about outsmarting the FBI and Secret Service, or mocking Aubrey for spending every minute he's not drumming up votes in front of a camera playing the role of the loving, panic-stricken husband.

The quiet is worrying. It makes every second longer, every day without her more unbearable, and yet, I understand it. Charlie said that Jacob was smart, that he wouldn't make the same mistakes his father did. Leland got found out because he overplayed his hand, so his son is being extra careful, playing things close to the vest, leaving us chasing our tails, ensuring we'll be scrambling to make a plan when he finally reaches out, which will be today.

I can feel it in my bones.

Charlie seems to be feeling something in her bones, too. She grips her ribs and winces as she adjusts in her chair.

"Listen, I'm sorry that things happened the way they did. I wish I could have—" she pauses, biting her lip. "I wish I could have stopped this. I tried. I swear, I did, but there were just too many of them."

Cal scoots to the edge of his seat, placing his elbows on his thighs. At first, I think he's going to try to empathize with her, but his tone is wrapped in impatience when he speaks.

"Walk us through it again, Monroe."

"Cal, I already have. I've given this statement *twice*."

"Then it won't be a problem to give it once more," he snaps. "Start with why you were out of the car when you had strict orders to wait inside the vehicle."

She blows a breath of frustration through flared nostrils. "I had to take a call from my mom's nurse. You probably don't know this since you only call when you need a favor, but she's sick."

Skipping right past her attempt to guilt-trip Cal, I ask, "Why did you have to take the call outside of the car?"

"Because I didn't have good reception." She looks between us, seeing what I'm guessing are matching frowns of disapproval. "I know it wasn't a good idea with all the cameras around, but that's why I walked down the block a bit, to keep them from seeing me and potentially blowing my cover."

"How long were you on the phone?"

"Three minutes and sixteen seconds."

Cal doesn't let her catch her breath, hitting her with another question immediately.

"When you heard the initial blast, why didn't you come to investigate?"

"I knew the threat was in front, so I went to the back to clear the entrance and find Selene because I knew she was the priority."

The use of 'was' grates against my nerves. "*Is*," I remind Charlie. "Selene is the priority. She's not dead, so don't talk about her in the past tense."

Her eyes flash with defiance, but she tempers her reaction with another heavy breath. "I didn't mean it like that, Beck. I was just trying to be as accurate in my language as possible."

Waving her off, I redirect the line of conversation. "Be accurate in your description of the events in the hallway. How did the bracelet get broken?"

As soon as I mention it, the evidence bag holding the bracelet seems to get heavier, weighing down the pocket in my jacket where it resides, pulling my shoulders down into a shameful slope.

We failed her.

We were right outside the room, on the other side of the door, and we couldn't get to her. Charlie said she had been hurt, that when she found her, she was pinned to the ground by debris. She wasn't able to confirm the extent of Selene's injuries, though. Everyone keeps floating the idea that we haven't heard from Jacob because she might have succumbed to her wounds, leaving Jacob with a body to dispose of and a country to flee.

No part of me wants to accept that possibility.

"I don't remember." She squeezes her eyes tight, trying to recall, shaking her head when the memory won't emerge. "Everything was moving so fast, and Selene was hurt. I just knew I needed to get her out of there. We approached the door, and that's when I saw the SUV. It was black like the ones from the detail, but a little older." Her nose wrinkles. "That's what made me stop short. It just looked off."

"But you still went out the door," Cal says. "Why?"

"Because Harris was behind the wheel."

That sentence resonates with me as intensely as it did the first time I heard it. Charlie wasn't able to identify all of her attackers, but she identified Harris because, unlike everyone else, he wasn't wearing a mask. She said it seemed to her that he wanted to be seen, that he wanted Selene to know he was the one betraying all of our confidences.

After Charlie pointed the finger at Harris, we paid Anderson a visit, digging deeper into the 'damning' evidence that had been gathered against him. He told us the same story he told Lennon and Charlie, which was that he'd never seen the phone before it was brought into the interrogation room in an evidence bag and that he'd only left the green room unattended at the news station because a breakfast burrito Harris got him wasn't sitting right on his stomach. Apparently, it had real cheese on it, and Anderson is lactose intolerant.

All of this information, coupled with the fact that Harris has been missing for as long as Selene has, should make it less shocking to hear the facts repeated, but it doesn't. It just gives me another thing to be mad about, another person to picture hurting the woman I love.

"And he wasn't alone?" I push the words past the lump in my throat that swells and throbs when Charlie shakes her head.

"No, there were several other men. All of them in masks, except Harris. Two of them carried Selene off while the rest of them attacked me. They didn't call me Rose Alton, my cover name. They called me Agent Monroe."

"You remember that, but not how many of them there were?"

"Yes, Beck, my blown cover happened to stick out to me," she grumbles. "They were on me so quick I didn't have time to count them, to pull my weapon or anything else. All I could do was lie there and take it, hoping they didn't kill me."

Tears pool in her eyes, but I blink at her, unmoved. "Why didn't they kill you?"

"What?!"

She tosses an outraged look at Cal, and he shrugs. "It's a fair question, Monroe. They had the time, and you were an incapacitated, and essentially unarmed, traitor who lied about who she is to get close to them. Finding out you're a fed would have constituted the ultimate act of betrayal, punishable by death."

"Or by torture and then death," I drop in. "They should have taken you to be dealt with by Jacob, who would have killed you after finding out everything he needed to know about what you shared with us."

Charlie bristles. "Why do you sound like you wanted that to happen?"

My answer is simple, perhaps the easiest words I'll speak today.

"Because I would much rather be chasing down your murderer than looking for Selene and her kidnapper."

She puts us out after that, and I'm not surprised, but I am annoyed that we have to go back to Selene and Aubrey's home with nothing new to report to her parents and siblings. They flew in as soon as the news of the kidnapping broke, joining the ranks of the countless groups of people now roaming the halls of the sprawling estate, which now feels too small because it's teeming with people and empty because the one person who belongs in the center of all of this is nowhere to be found.

After checking in with Hicks, the FBI and the rest of our team, Cal and I head to the kitchen, which Justine, Albert, Robin, Jessica and Monique have claimed as their domain. Well, Mama J claimed it, but the rest of the family is there to support. Every day, Albert sits in the breakfast nook with his eyes on the TV mounted in the corner. Monique takes over the space across from him, staring out the window instead of the laptop in front of her with emails from shareholders and investors asking for updates she doesn't have.

Mama J spends the entire day cooking on a stove I'm sure Selene has never used before. The meals range from extravagant to simple, and sometimes they make no sense for the time of day or the season, but no one complains. Selene's sisters, Robin and Jessica, jump in to help her when she allows it, but mostly they split their time between checking social media for updates and asking us for the details we leave out when talking to their parents.

When we walk into the kitchen, five pairs of hopeful eyes turn on us. Mama J is slicing vegetables at the island. The knife in her hand is sharp as hell, and yet it keeps rocking against the cutting board while her eyes are on us, pleading for answers about her child.

"Any news?"

Cal dips his head in shame. "No, ma'am."

Her chin wobbles as she tries to put on a brave smile. "That's okay. I know you two are working as hard as you can to get her home."

The idea of her comforting us when we should be out there getting answers for her makes my stomach turn. It rumbles loudly, struggling to digest guilt, and Mama J mistakes it for hunger.

"Here, sit. I'm sure you two need to eat."

She waves at the empty seats at the island next to Jessica and Robin, who are absently gnawing away at the assorted vegetables on their plates. There's a lack of cohesion to the pairings and the knife work that reflects the state of their mother's mind.

Robin, the middle child, notices me staring at her plate and purses her lips, waiting until the older woman has turned her back to us to address it. "She just needs something to do with her hands," she explains.

Jessica bites down on what looks like half of a red bell pepper with the core still intact and sighs. "She doesn't know how to sit still."

"Never did," Albert mutters gruffly from behind us while Monique hums her agreement.

Cal and I nod our understanding.

For four days now, we've been plagued with the need to do something, but have had no true idea of what exactly that something is. Outside of tracking down useless leads pouring in from tip lines, we haven't been doing anything besides this. Sharing somber meals and snacks with the most important people in Selene's life, wondering what it would be like to be an actual part of their family, if they would accept us as a unit. Every time I follow that line of thought, I end up with a heart twisted into knots when I realize we might never get the chance to find out.

"Cal, you have to have some of these," Mama J says, spinning around with a platter of something in her hands. It slips from her fingers before I have the chance to identify the contents, and everyone in the room jumps when the sound of glass shattering surrounds us. My eyes fly to her face only to find her gaze locked on a spot above my head. I turn then, finding Albert frozen in place as well, a mug of coffee halfway to his lips.

"OH, MY BABY," Mama J wails, stepping over glass and an assortment of Cal's favorite fruits to get to the table where her husband is, to set her eyes on the TV screen where a news segment about Aubrey's lead in the polls has shifted to a live stream that shows nothing but Selene's face.

43

CAL

Since I met her, there's never been a time when I didn't want to look at Selene.

When I didn't want to study the lines of her face and learn the intricacies of the few expressions she gives freely. When I didn't want to stare into her eyes and name every shade of brown and gold that resides there. When I didn't want to marvel at her beauty and thank God for allowing me the chance to witness her.

I don't want to witness her like this.

A gash in her forehead with dried blood around the edges. A bruise under her eye. A fresh cut on her lip that suggests someone recently hit her in the face. A gun pressed into her temple, the glint of silver menacing and loud even before the pale hand holding it pushes down, digging the metal into her skin.

Albert's breathing turns shallow, and Monique rushes around the table on wobbling knees to put her arms around his shoulders because his daughters are busy holding their mother up. She's wailing loudly. Her body nothing more than a crumpled heap that seems determined to sink to the floor. Jessica and Robin don't let that happen, though; they keep her upright even as their own tears fall, even as the weight of their own fear tries to collapse their muscles and steal their strength.

Finding the remote, I turn up the volume so I can hear what's being said. There's a paper in Selene's hands, but she's not the one speaking. She's staring into the camera with a resolute glare while the man beside her, whose face we can't see because the angle of the camera only captures his body from the waist up, and the hand holding the gun.

It doesn't matter that we can't see his face; I know the man is Jacob Marsh.

There's more confidence in his voice now than there was years ago when we interviewed him about his dad. No ripples of anxiety or stumbling over his words, just a cool, calm, and collected tone laced with hatred and entitlement while he recites his version of his father's rhetoric. He's updated it some, but at its core it's the same white supremacy, bullets, bloodshed and Second Amendment rights bullshit that has plagued this country for far too long.

"My father is a patriot," he's saying now. "He loves this country. He believes in the America that libtards like Mrs. Taylor here want to take from us...."

I tune him out, focusing on Selene, forcing myself to pay attention to her breathing and the size of her pupils. She hasn't been drugged, and she doesn't seem to be suffering from any worrying side effects of her injuries, which would be a relief if there wasn't a gun to her head. Beck is beside me, his body tense and his eyes on the TV. Unlike me, he's not staring at Selene but looking past her, taking in her surroundings. There's not much to see, but if there is anything to be found, he'll find it.

"That's enough from me, don't you think?" Jacob asks Selene, running a hand over her hair. She flinches away, and I feel my hands turn to fists, clenching with the need to find and hurt him as I make a silent promise to kiss her everywhere he's touched her, to use my love to erase her trauma. "You have something to say to the world, right, *Selene*?"

He says her name like a slur, desecrating every sacred syllable with his hateful tongue. She shakes her head in response, her eyes still hard, still locked on the screen. She's trying to be strong, but I know she's scared.

Jacob presses the muzzle of the gun into her temple so hard that I can see the skin and tissue underneath it caving. "Read it," he growls, leaning down to put his lips to her ear.

Everyone in the room takes a collective breath of shock as she brings the paper up and inadvertently exposes the ligature marks on her wrists. They had to have had her tied up for days. I'm sure the wounds are painful and probably close to being infected if they aren't already.

Mama J turns her head into Robin's neck. "I can't look."

Jessica rubs her back, cooing softly in her ear that everything will be okay. I wish someone would tell me that. I wish I could believe them if they did.

Selene inhales shakily, and the paper trembles under the weight of her breath when she exhales "My name is Selene Taylor. It is November 5th, and I'm going to die today. This is not hyperbole or exaggeration. This is a fact. My death—" her throat constricts, closing around the words that must feel so wrong in her mouth. Once again, there's the press of the gun, and Jacob's insistence, and she starts again, infusing steel into her vocal cords. "My death is imminent and will be televised. There will be no negotiations or ransom demands; there will be no saving me. By the time my husband, Aubrey Taylor, is elected President of the United States of America, he will be a widower, free from the constraints of the liberal idealism and political correctness I have imposed on him and planned to use my influence as First Lady to force on the rest of the world. Do not grieve me, this is what I deserve."

The feed cuts off instantly, revealing a terrified news anchor on the left side of the screen and Aubrey on the right.

"Is that motherfucker seriously on TV right now?" Monique shouts, letting go of Albert to storm out of the room, presumably to find Aubrey and curse him out for not even taking a moment to come and comfort his wife's family before he addressed the fucking world.

Jessica, Robin, and Mama J all go running behind her, leaving Beck and I alone in the kitchen with Albert. He's a man of few words, so it shocks me when his voice fills the quiet left by the departure of the women.

"Four days I've been here, watching my Justine flit from one corner of this house to the other. Four days I've sat at this table across from Monique, listening to her take calls and answer questions people don't have no damn business asking. Four days I've seen my girls whisper prayers for their big sister, hoping we'll get her back so they can have a chance to love each other better." He lifts a gnarled hand to his mouth and shakes his head as he fights back a wave of emotion. "Four days I've seen that husband of hers do everything but come in this room and face us. He don't even act like he misses her. All he cares about is this damn election while my baby is—"

The words won't come. We don't need them. Silence stretches between the three of us while Albert gathers himself. He's bouncing his leg and tapping his fist on the table at the same speed until his nervous system is regulated.

"Do you two care for my daughter as much as you look like you do?" he asks, shifting in his seat to turn wary brown eyes on us.

Beck and I both nod, unable to say more for a million different reasons. Chief among them is our awareness of the contract Aubrey and Selene signed. It feels stupid to think of it now, to be worried about legalities and potential public fallout when the very people Aubrey and Jordan plan to weaponize against Selene in the event of a breach of contract are the ones who might watch her die in a few hours.

Luckily, Albert doesn't want our verbal assurances. He rises from his seat, heading toward the opening that everyone else just disappeared through. He stops short, pausing just beside Beck and me so that we're all shoulder to shoulder. A line of men who have held Selene and kept her safe, who have comforted her with bone-crushing hugs when words wouldn't suffice, who love her more than anything and will be shattered if her ominous speech becomes a reality.

"Then please," he begs, voice breaking over the words. "Bring my baby girl home."

"We will," I promise, praying the vow isn't empty as the older man shuffles away.

As soon as we're alone, Beck starts to pace with his fingers linked behind his head.

"I'm going to kill that motherfucker."

"Not if I kill him first."

Onyx eyes flick to my face. "Your bullet in his head, mine in his heart?"

"Works for me."

With that settled, Beck shifts gears, running through everything he noticed.

"He's keeping her tied up. Did you see the ligature marks?"

I nod. "They're pretty deep. She's been restrained for days."

"Probably infected."

"That's what I was thinking, too. We'll need to have a medic with us when we find her."

Beck pauses in front of me, despair and worry rolling off of him in poignant waves that threaten to swallow us both whole. My heart aches for him, for the pieces of him that broke when he lost Diana and are threatening to shatter once more. I helped him put them back together once, and it wasn't easy, but it wasn't impossible because that grief wasn't mine, but this? If something happens to Selene, this grief will be mine, and I don't know if I'll be strong enough to put Beck back together because I'll be broken too.

"What if we don't?"

I want to tell him not to lend his voice to that possibility, not to even *think* it, but I can't because my mind is in the same place. I knew when I met Selene that I'd be forever changed by her. I thought it would be her life, then hoped it would be her love, and now I'm staring down a reality where her death destroys me. I don't know how I'll come back from that, how Beck will, but I'm sure that we'll do it like we worked the Marsh case, like we saved President Warner, like we fell in love with Selene Taylor: together.

"Come here."

I don't give him a chance to refuse because he needs the embrace as much as I do. I just wrap my fingers around the nape of his neck and pull him into me. He sinks into my shoulder and wraps his arms around my middle, not considering for even a moment, what might happen if someone walks in here and sees us. I wish I could appreciate the moment more, could fully bask in the freedom that comes with simply not giving a fuck, but I can't because I know the fear of being found out has only been suspended because the fear of losing Selene, of reliving the trauma he experienced when he lost Diana has taken precedence.

Not for the first time, I find myself wishing I had been a part of his life when he was hunting down Valinsky. We would have been able to stop him together, to reach him before he reached Diana. And it doesn't matter that her being alive would have changed what Beck and I are to each other, because I love him. I love him, and in every situation, in every instance, I will do whatever is necessary to spare him the pain of loss.

I wish I could guarantee that he will be spared today, that we both will.

As if on cue, my phone chooses that moment to start ringing. Beck pulls away so that I can take the call, a tempered hopefulness trying to take over his expression. I turn the phone to him so he can see the screen.

"Charlie's calling."

He frowns, still frustrated with her from earlier, then shrugs like he knows things can't get any worse, but they might get better. "Answer it."

I connect the call and put her on speaker.

"What's up, Monroe?"

She doesn't return my greeting, forging straight ahead to the reason for her call. "I know where they are."

44

———

SELENE

Eye contact has always been kind of uncomfortable for me, but holding eye contact with someone when they can't look away from you is something else entirely.

Technically, I could look away from Agent Harris. I could close my eyes or stare at the water-stained ceiling above me. I could count the lines of mortar between the bricks on the wall behind him, but then that would mean skipping the ones covered in his blood and brain matter *and* the ones I can't see because his rotting corpse is in the way.

He's been dead for days, how many I don't know. Jacob killed him right in front of me because he'd outlived his usefulness. I'd never seen anyone murdered in cold blood before, but I didn't even scream. It was just another horrible thing happening in a space full of horrible things. Plus, I wasn't exactly sad to see the man go, not after he helped Jacob kidnap me and took great pleasure in finally letting his disdain for me be known. He was almost worse than Jacob when it came to the whole racist monologue thing, but no one, and I mean no one, beats Leigh Anne.

Leigh Anne Davis, better known as the woman who accosted me in a restaurant bathroom back in Houston. Now, *that* girl loves a monologue. Every time she comes into the foul-smelling room where they're keeping me, she delivers one. Sometimes they're unprompted, sometimes I intentionally pull her into conversation just for the mental stimulation, but every time she delivers a speech. I'm not in the mood for one today, but I have to risk it to ask her a question.

"Is there anywhere else his body can be?" I ask between sips of the water she's dripping into my mouth from a dirty bottle. She glances at Harris and turns back to me, rough fingers holding my chin in place.

"No."

"There has to be more to this building than this room. Why can't you put him somewhere else?"

"Because I don't want to." She releases me, capping the bottle with a laugh. "God, you really are full of yourself, aren't you? You're going to die today, and you think you can make demands. No one here cares about your comfort, Selene."

I pull against the restraints digging into my wrists and arch a brow. "I'm well aware, Leigh Anne."

"Then act like it, bitch."

In the last however many days, she's called me everything but a child of God, so I don't even flinch at that. Honestly, I kind of appreciate the consistency because I know what to expect when I see her. With Jacob, it's always up in the air. He's never nice, he clearly hates me too much for that, but he does volley between a child-like glee that's the result of having pulled this whole thing off and a red-hot anger that ends with him hitting me.

My jaw aches at the thought of his last temper tantrum. I'd made the mistake of asking him if he thought my death would change anything for his coward of a father, and he slapped me across the face, busting my lip. That was right before we live-streamed my death announcement, and I haven't seen him since. Leigh Anne is cruel and impatient, but I'll take her over him any day.

Not that I have many of those left.

I try to breathe through the panic rising up in me, but it's so strong and insistent, I know I can't defeat it on my own. I need a distraction, so I ask Leigh Anne the only question I haven't yet.

"Why are you here?"

She pauses, her hand on the door, her feet lingering by Agent Harris' head. Then she turns slowly, grimacing at me like I've poured salt in an open wound. "What?"

"Well, I know why Jacob is here, and I know why I'm here, to a certain extent, I even knew why Agent Harris was here, but out of all the awful things you've said to me, your reason for risking your life and freedom hasn't been among them."

Leigh Anne crosses her arms, top lip curling in disgust. "And you think I need to explain myself to you?"

"I think you like to talk, and right now I need a distraction before I have a panic attack and die before you and your boyfriend can make a public spectacle of my murder."

Her answering smile is eerily happy. "I've dreamed of this day for years, you know."

"You've dreamed of the day I die for years?" Skepticism coats the question, even though it probably shouldn't. I don't doubt the depth of Leigh Anne's hatred for me, but I just find it hard to believe that she's been waiting for years to see me dead. Jacob? Yes, absolutely. But this girl, who can't be any older than twenty years old—not much older than AJ would be had he lived—hasn't lived enough life to be this angry at me.

She tucks a strand of hair behind her ears. "No. Jacob is the one obsessed with you. I mean, don't get me wrong, I hate you and everything you stand for, but your death means nothing to me."

"Then why exactly have you been waiting for this day?"

Green eyes dance with mischief and madness. "Because today is the day I finally get to watch Agent Callan Drake and Agent Lance Beckham die."

Oh, this conversation isn't helping curb my panic at all. I was prepared for more hate aimed at me. For more vitriol and teasing about my impending death, but I wasn't ready for this. For the guarantee that my men will come here, for the revelation that the people holding me hostage want to see them die alongside me.

"What?" I gasp finally. "What did they ever do to you?"

I don't see her having many opportunities to encounter either man. She doesn't seem like the type of person who runs in the same circles they do, so I'm genuinely interested in how their paths crossed and what they did to make her hate them so.

Her expression turns grim, and I swear I see flickers of sadness beneath everything else. "They killed my brother."

Considering how absolutely vile she was in reference to my son, I have a hard time mustering up condolences, but I do it. "I'm sorry for your loss."

She rolls her eyes. "No, you're not. You just hope acting like you are will make me move Harris' body, and it won't."

"I've already given up on that. What was your brother's name?"

Logically, I know Cal and Beck have taken lives. Their work with the Bureau all but guaranteed it, but putting a name and the face of a relative to an unconfirmed number on their body count lists sends chills up my spine.

"Chester Davis."

I suck in a sharp breath of recognition, remembering the name from Beck's file specifically. "He was the shooter, the one who tried to kill President Warner."

"The one who died trying to free this country from the tyranny of one of you liberal snowflakes."

"Scott Warner isn't liberal. Most of his policies are oppressive and heavily steeped in racism, take for example—"

Leigh Anne holds up a hand, taking away my chance to educate her. "I don't care! My brother is dead, and those agents are responsible. They killed him for having the balls to believe in something."

"Nooo, they killed him for trying to assassinate a President. You don't get a free pass for that, Leigh Anne, even if you really, really think he should be dead."

She lunges for me, fingers wrapping around the arms of the rolling desk chair I've been tied to for days. Her breath is hot on my face, and it stinks of garlic and tomato sauce. Those bastards have been eating pizza while I've been sitting here, starving and looking at a dead man.

"Listen, you can say whatever you want to say. It won't change the fact that you and your precious agents are going to die when they get here. Do you hear me? We're going to kill all of you and leave you in this room with Harris to fucking rot."

Bile rises in my throat at the image, and she bares her teeth in a threatening smile.

"Not so tough now, are you?" she asks, shoving the chair back so it hits the wall behind me with a thud that makes my head ache and my vision blur. Leigh Anne backs away, heading for the door again, stopping once again when I hit her with another question.

"How do you know they'll come?"

Every day that I've been here, I've wished for them. I've waited and watched and prayed that they would come bursting through the door and take me away from this place, but now the promise of their arrival makes me wish they would stay far away. I don't want them here. I don't want my fate to be theirs. I don't want to have to watch them lose each other or suffer through losing them, even if I only live that harsh reality for a few brief seconds before being released into the oblivion of eternal life.

Leigh Anne grins, hooking a thumb over her shoulder to point at Harris. "You didn't think *he* was our only man on the inside, did you?"

She slams the door, leaving me to ponder the question. I know that I'm close to losing my sanity when I start talking to Harris.

"Who else were you working with?" I ask, staring at him as if he could give me an answer, as if he could do anything other than lay there and....*wait*. As I look at Harris, my mind interposes the image of Charlie lying in the alley, hurt and alone.

I don't remember seeing her like that, not really, but Beck had explained to me before that our brains can hold images our memories don't. Now, I'm running through the events of the afternoon my life changed yet again. I went down first after being struck in the head. When I woke up, I was in the back of the black SUV I'd seen idling by the door. Harris was behind the wheel when we came outside, so it had to have been Leigh Anne who hit me. He was still behind the wheel when I came to. She was hopping in the passenger seat, cackling like a hyena as he drove away.

At some point, I must have looked out of the window at Charlie.

She was sprawled out in the alley, her arms at awkward angles around her, her hands empty. *She didn't draw her weapon?* I close my eyes, breathing deeply and immediately regretting it when I get a lungful of decaying flesh. Even with my stomach turning, I'm able to find an answer to my silent inquiry.

No, Charlie didn't draw her weapon.

She didn't pull it out in the alley, and now that I think of it, I never saw it in her hands as we moved through the hallway that led to certain doom. I don't know much about standard operating procedures across national law enforcement agencies, but I do know that anytime an officer or agent is moving through a space, they're supposed to assume there's a threat around every corner. That means they have to be prepared to engage at a moment's notice, and having your weapon in hand, or at least having your hand on your holster, is the best way to make sure you are.

Charlie did neither.

She moved through that hallway like she wasn't worried about encountering danger at all. Like she knew it was safe, and the only way she could have known that was if...

"Shit," I curse, kicking myself for only now putting it together when it was so obvious. Her sudden appearance at the polling center with no backup. Her weird reaction to the bracelet. Her lies of omission regarding her undercover status within Jacobs's organization. "Charlie is involved."

And Jacob is going to use her to get Cal and Beck here.

45

——————

BECK

"**S**omething's not right."

I whisper the words to Cal as we exit yet another empty building on the lot of the abandoned clothing factory, where Charlie told us to meet her.

There was no time to wait for backup, so it's just us and the eerie quiet of our dilapidated surroundings. We move slowly, our backs to each other, our steps in sync, our heads on a constant swivel, even though we've encountered no threats since we climbed over the gate we found Charlie's car outside of.

The doors were open, the engine still running, but she was nowhere to be found. We'd rushed our entry, fearing that someone had seen her coming and snatched her up. So far, we've found no evidence of that. Besides her car and the promise she'd meet us here, there's no evidence that she's here at all.

No one is.

Cal and I have cleared five buildings, all of them in various states of collapse and holding guns or drugs. My assumption is that this is one of the places the Brothers are using as a stash house. As far as chosen locations to conduct illegal activities go, this is a good one. It's a huge property in a rural area that makes it easy to see someone coming from a mile away, but that vantage point only works if you actually have bodies stationed around the perimeter to keep an eye out, and Jacob doesn't.

"It's too quiet," Cal agrees, pausing with his back to the exterior wall of the building we just cleared. He lowers his weapon, allowing it to hang at his hip from the strap around his shoulders so he can pull out his phone and call Charlie again. I step in front of him, sweeping cautious eyes and a loaded weapon over the empty stretch of road ahead to make sure we're both protected.

The line rings and rings before rolling over to voicemail. Frustration rolls off of him in palpable waves as he pockets the phone and picks up his weapon again. He taps my shoulder, signaling that he's ready to move, and we head for the last and largest building.

"Maybe she didn't hear it," I offer, shifting my focus to my left as we prepare to walk through a second set of gates that are wide open. "You know she keeps her phone on silent."

It's a habit she learned during years of undercover work. One, she continues to use even when she's not working a case.

Cal's gaze is pinned to our right side, and we've both slowed down significantly, taking half steps to make sure we're not missing anything. "Or they saw her coming and took her down."

"There's no one out here, Drake. Who would have done that?"

"I don't know. Maybe Harris?" He sighs, and our eyes meet briefly over our shoulders. He reads my skeptical gaze with ease. "You're right. If she'd encountered trouble, Charlie wouldn't have gone down without a fight."

I nod my agreement, and neither of us speaks to the fact that there are no shell casings on the ground and the air is free from the acrid smell of freshly discharged weapons. There's just us standing steps away from the set of doors that will take us inside the building where Selene has to be, and the question of whether or not Charlie is in there, too. There's just the weight of the tactical gear on our bodies and the weapons in our hands, we've yet to use. There's just the alarm bells ringing in my head and then the disembodied voice of Jacob Marsh coming through speakers I can't see.

"Don't be shy, boys. Come on in," he sneers while a woman laughs in the background.

It's not Selene. I know that much, but I don't think it's Charlie either. Not that I've ever had many occasions to hear her laugh. I start to ask Cal if he has, but the thought is interrupted by a loud buzzing and the sound of the doors parting to let us through.

My fingers tighten around my gun, and Cal and I both take a step back, prepared to be ambushed. Jacob laughs over the intercom. "There's no welcome committee, I promise. All of our partygoers are in one place, waiting for you. Isn't that right, Selene?"

He pitches his voice low when she says her name, and the whimper that follows makes it clear to me that he's hurting her. I picture the gun pressed to her temple, and red floods my vision. I shake it away, knowing I can't go to that place, that I can't surrender to my rage because I have to depend on my training. That's what Selene needs from me right now.

Cal is half a step ahead of me, and the resolute set of his shoulders tells me his mind is in the same place as mine. He's expelled all thoughts of loving her, all memories of holding her and kissing her, every desire to comfort her, trading it for the skill needed to save her.

"Turn to your right, Agent Drake."

The smugness in Jacob's voice sets fire to my blood. It burns hot and bright inside of me as we follow his directions to the letter, but it threatens to turn into a searing white flame every time he speaks to Selene.

"Agent Beckham doesn't look too excited about seeing you," he tells her as we climb a set of rusted metal steps that place us on a platform with another door he has to buzz us through. "Why do you think that is, Selene? Are you difficult to work with? Do you think he's dreading having to come here and die for you?"

For some reason, it gives me a sense of relief to know Jacob isn't aware of what we are to each other. It's not much in the way of upper hands, but maybe we'll be able to use it to our advantage. God knows we need every bit of leverage we can get.

"The only person dying here today is you, Marsh," I growl,

making him the same promise I made his father about ending his life. We've climbed another set of steps. According to the faded signage in the hallway, we're now on the production floor. There are no more locked doors or buzzers, just two sets of swinging doors at the left and right ends of the hall. Cal moves down to the right, and I take the left.

"Oh, this is adorable," Jacob muses. "You know I can see everything you're doing right?"

We ignore him. I look to Cal, signaling my preparedness to enter with my hand. He nods, squaring his shoulders and adjusting his hold on his weapon. I do the same, and we step through the doors at the same time. The first thing I notice when I enter the space is that I can no longer see Cal. The second thing I notice is that the machinery and work stations haven't been removed. Large cutting tables with fabric stacked high are to my right, blocking my view of the rest of the room and my partner.

Partner.

I'm intentional in my use of the word, knowing that just like Selene, Cal is depending on me to be everything but the man who loves him. In this moment, all I am is a weapon. I'm decades of training and lethal focus. I'm sharpened senses and unhurried movements, clearing my side of the room and then making my way to the enclosed platform that sits above the production floor and spans the length of it.

As I make my approach, climbing up yet another set of rusted metal steps, I look to my right to see if Cal is there. He's not. My heart sinks, and the familiar fear of losing him rises up in my chest. I have no choice but to push it back, though, to quiet it with reassurances about what I would have heard if he were gone.

A struggle of some sort, the pop of gunfire, a cry for help.

Focus, Beckham.

I push all those thoughts away, stopping on the last step before the small landing outside of the platform's wide-open door. I strain my ears but don't hear anything except for my own pounding heart and the sharp inhale of resignation I take before approaching the entrance. The barrel of my gun enters the room before I do, and I ensure there's no one waiting behind the door on my left before I press my back against it and swing my gaze to the right.

What I find waiting for me is enough to steal my breath and make my trigger finger twitch.

"Aht, aht," Jacob says, wagging the index finger of the hand not holding a gun to Selene's head in my direction. "I wouldn't do that if I were you."

The years haven't been kind to him. His features are scarred with hatred. His ruddy skin buckling under the weight of intolerance to form wrinkles that make no sense on a man his age. His hairline is receding as well, and several of his teeth seem to be decaying right in front of my face. For all intents and purposes, Jacob Marsh is an unattractive waste of space, and yet it doesn't change the fact that he has Selene tied to a rolling desk chair with duct tape over her mouth.

It also doesn't seem to have any bearing on the way the woman standing a couple of paces behind feels about him. She's beaming at him even though he hasn't once looked in her direction, green eyes swimming with emotion. I recognize her instantly from the red light camera photo we got from the police back in Houston. She's the blonde who accosted Selene, the one whose hateful remarks were recited verbatim on the social media post that created the link between Jacob and the online harassment. She's also the person standing over Cal's kneeling form, the one with the muzzle of a gun trained at the back of his head, her finger on the trigger even though his hands are up.

I can't breathe.

This moment, this scene, it's the stuff of my nightmares. It's every fear I've beaten back with Selene and Cal's love turned into the most horrific reality. It's the last thing I wanted when I let myself have them, and yet, it's exactly what I expected to come to pass.

"It's going to be alright, Beckham."

Cal's assurance makes Jacob and the woman laugh, and I hate them both so much in that second that I find myself, once again, caressing the trigger of my gun, wondering if shooting Jacob would give Cal enough time to get the jump on the woman. His weapon is only a few feet away from him, and she doesn't look particularly fast. He could probably put her down before Jacob's body hits the floor.

Knowing it might be our only option, I decide to give it a try. Cal's eyes go wide, and at first, I think it's because he doesn't understand what I'm about to do, but then I feel it. The cool press of metal against my bare scalp.

"Lower your weapon."

My heart sinks, and the dread coiling in my gut takes precedence over the satisfaction swelling in my chest at the sound of Charlie's voice.

"I knew your story was bullshit," I grit out through clenched teeth.

"Didn't stop you from coming here, though, did it? "she asks, applying more pressure. "Lower your weapon, Beck. I won't tell you again."

Selene whimpers when I let my gun fall to my side. Any semblance of hope is sucked out of the room as Charlie removes it from my shoulders, dropping it outside the door before rounding on me with a conniving smile on her face. With her gun still pointed at me, she backs further into the room, stopping at Jacob's side to kiss him, which makes the woman behind them grimace. Her scowl has no match for the one on Cal's face, though.

"Seriously, Monroe? You're going to betray your badge and sworn oath for this asshole?"

Righteous anger coats every syllable of his questions, and I know the emotion stems from somewhere deep inside of him. When Cal and Charlie met, she was a young agent with potential only he saw. He mentored her, helped her find a path where her skills would shine. This betrayal isn't professional, it's personal. Somehow, though, it isn't surprising. Not to me, anyway.

We've seen this happen before: undercover agents getting entangled in the organizations they're supposed to be investigating, forging friendships and, more often, romantic relationships that blur the lines between their cover identity and their duty. I know for a fact that Charlie isn't the first undercover to get caught up in the snare of one of the Brothers. Leland had a knack for converting agents, and it's clear he's passed that skill on to his son.

Charlie pulls away from Jacob, turning just enough to look down on Cal. "I've made a new oath. I've pledged my allegiance to the people who would never abandon me, who would never promise to always have my back and then forget all about me the moment the next big promotion came along."

"Oh, for fucks sake, Charlie," I groan. "Don't try to make this bullshit about us leaving the Bureau."

She glares at me. "I didn't give a fuck about you leaving, Beck, but Cal—" she turns back to him, shaking her head "—we were supposed to be family, and you tossed me to the side like I was nothing."

Jacob snakes an arm around her waist. "You know I would never do that to you, baby."

Her gaze is soft when it finds his, and she leans into his embrace. "I know, Jake. From the moment we met, you saw me, the real me, and you loved me for it."

"That's fucking right, baby." Jacob smacks her ass, and once again, the woman who's name I still don't know scowls. Charlie hasn't noticed, and Jacob doesn't seem to be paying attention to it either. They're both too busy telling the tale of their sordid love story, detailing how Charlie told Jacob who she was less than a month into the assignment, regaling us with the disgusting details of how they fucked in the pool of blood belonging to the person who brought her into the fold.

Apparently, they killed him together.

Selene looks like she's going to be sick, and while I hate the idea of her experiencing any kind of discomfort, I'm not concerned about that right now. The only thing I care about is the obvious disdain on the woman's face as she looks at the couple. It's clear to me that she's bothered by their affectionate behavior, which, in my mind, can only mean one thing: she's jealous.

I don't know how to use that to my advantage yet, but I'll figure it out.

"Where's Harris?" I ask, inching forward just to see how much attention the three of them are paying to me. Charlie is the fastest of them all, stepping forward to put herself between me, Jacob, and Selene.

"Harris is dead, and you'll be laid out beside him in just a second if you don't step the fuck back."

Lifting my hands in surrender, I do as I'm told, walking backwards until I collide with the wall. It's not good enough for Charlie.

"Get on the ground," she says, gesturing toward the floor with a wave of her hand. I lower myself down slowly, catching Cal's eye and then Selene's just for the comfort of their gazes. Both of their faces are masks of stoicism, but their eyes reveal so much. Their anger over the situation and the gun in my face. Their fear and love for me. I return everything they give me in silent spades, praying the last time I got to show them and tell them wasn't actually the last time.

It'd be a cruel twist of fate to have loved so significantly twice in my life, only to be robbed of the chance to actually say goodbye both times. I hadn't known with Diana. I can't even remember if I kissed her before I left for work that morning, don't recall if I took the time to palm her belly and feel Cameron kick before walking out the door. That's how preoccupied I was with catching Valinsky, how big of a rush I was in to put cuffs on him.

That same urgency has surrounded every stolen moment I've had with Selene and Cal. There's been no time to savor, to feel, to truly appreciate what we have. We've rushed through everything, including our reluctant departures from each other, and now we're here.

I bring my knees up, resting my arms on top of them while Charlie checks her watch. "It's almost time, Jake. Do you have the streaming link ready?"

"It's all set, baby," he says, crossing the room to the wall of monitors and screens that were more than likely used for oversight on the production floor. He's rigged the majority of the screens to display the feed of cameras throughout the factory, which is how he was able to see Cal and me as we approached. The screen in the lower right corner of the display is black, but it comes to life when Jacob sits down at the desk and wiggles the mouse. Now, it's showing a timer that's counting down to when he's going to kill Selene.

There's a little over ten minutes left on the clock, and my heart rate triples while Selene watches her time on this Earth dwindle down with wide eyes that show no relief when the screen glitches and then flickers off.

Jacob drops his gun, banging his fist on the desk. "The fuck?"

"Is the internet down again?" Charlie asks, glancing between Jacob, Cal, and me. She knows us well enough to know that we're watching their every move, waiting for an opening. With Jacob's gun out of play, it's a great time to try something. Assuming that's where my head is at, she puts her back to him and does a wide sweep of the room with her gun.

"Don't move a fucking muscle."

Cal holds my gaze for a second, pulling me into one of our infamous silent conversations while Selene stares at the screen Jacob is still trying to get back online. With nothing but my eyes, I tell him that brute force wasn't my plan, and he nods subtly, signaling that he'll wait for me to put what I'm thinking into motion.

"So you brought us here to watch you fail to live stream her murder?"

I aim the question at Jacob, or even Charlie, but to my surprise, it's the woman behind Cal who speaks. Her tone is icy and filled with contempt. "No, Agent Beckham, he brought you and Agent Drake here for me."

"And who exactly are you?" Cal asks, stealing the words from me.

His inquiry only seems to anger her more, and I flinch as she slams her gun into the back of his skull not once, not twice, but three times. Selene's screams of protest are muffled by the tape over her lips, but it's evident to everyone that she's not happy. I'm the only one who cares, though, the only one who sees the single tear escape her eye as Cal hits the ground with a thud.

The woman smiles, lifting her foot to step on his back. Then she looks at me. "My name is Leigh Anne Davis. My brother was Chester

Davis, and one of you—" she gestures between Cal and me "—killed him in cold blood."

"Cold blood suggests a lack of cause," I explain, lifting my chin so I'm looking her square in the eye. "I had plenty of cause when I killed your brother."

It's a risk, this confession, but I have to take it. I have to hope my instincts about Leigh Anne being emotional and, thus, irrational, are spot on. She presents as a textbook wildcard. The weaker personality that easily gets lost in a trio with people like Charlie and Jacob. The one who will do anything to stand out, to be noticed, to get her point across.

A wildness takes over her eyes the moment she processes my words, and in seconds, she's trying to cross the room to get to me. Charlie stops her with an arm to her chest, struggling to hold her and keep the gun focused on any one place.

"Leigh Anne, you stupid cunt. Don't let him get into your head."

She thrashes against Charlie's hold, clawing at her arms. "Don't tell me what the fuck to do, bitch. I want him dead! Jacob brought him here for me to kill him."

"Jake, tell her to calm the fuck down."

"Both of you shut the fuck up," he screams, slamming his fist into the desk once again because the screen has yet to come back online. He stands, pushing his chair back so hard it knocks into the back of Charlie's legs and sends her and Leigh Anne flying in Selene's direction.

I don't have time to see who lands where or if they actually collide with Selene because I have an opening I have to take. I rush Jacob, tackling him to the ground before he even registers what's going on. We land in a heap near the door closest to Cal, who is far too still for my liking, and Jacob locks his legs around my waist, trying to leverage my weight to flip me. I swing on him, landing blow after blow to alternating sides of his face in an unsuccessful attempt to stop that from happening.

The world spins, and then he's on top of me, his triumphant laughs barely audible over the sounds of Charlie and Leigh Anne screaming about who Jacob loves more. One glance in their direction tells me they're fighting each other inches away from Selene's toppled chair. Her eyes are closed, and there's a small puddle of blood forming under her temple, indicating she must have hit her head hard when they knocked her over.

I have to get her out of here.

I have to get Cal out of here.

I have to get *us* out of here.

"You think you can stop this, Beckham?" Jacob asks, rearing back and swinging so hard I feel one of my teeth dislodge. "You fucking can't! You're all going to die here. We're going to—"

The rest of his sentence is swallowed by the sound of a gunshot. It's muffled, but it's so close it's still loud. Jacob pauses, spinning around slowly in the direction of the women fighting over him. Charlie is on the ground. Leigh Anne is curled over her. Their arms and hands are all tangled up, making it hard to tell who's holding the gun and who's hurt.

I don't care either way.

With Jacob distracted, I reach blindly for my ankle, fingers searching frantically for the small blade I keep there. Relief floods me when I grip the handle, and I waste no time pulling it free, plunging it into the side of Jacob's neck. His blood is a hot spew of crimson that covers my face and chest, flowing constantly even as he tries to stop the bleeding with shaking hands, moving faster when he pulls the blade out before falling off of me.

He goes quickly after that, gasping and gurgling while I fight to catch my breath.

"Noooooo!"

The screams come from the corner where Charlie and Leigh Anne were, and I don't even have to sit up to know that it's Charlie who survived. But I do. In fact, I stand, watching as Charlie shoves Leigh Anne off of her. She rolls slowly, landing on her back to reveal a wound to her stomach that's not too different from the one her brother gave Cal all those years ago.

Except it is different because Cal survived, and Leigh Anne is very, very dead.

I look between her and Jacob and grin at Charlie. "And then there was one."

"Fuck you, Beck," she spits, wiping angrily at her bleeding nose. Looks like Leigh Anne was giving her a run for her money before she killed her, but she still seems to have no qualms about squaring up with me.

"You don't have to do this," I tell her, raising my fists because I know she won't listen. There's been too much animosity between us over the years. There's too much hate in her heart now, and I just killed the man that she loves. Of course, she wants to do this.

I don't know when we agreed to hand-to-hand combat, but neither of us reached for any of the weapons available to us. Charlie rolls her shoulders back, rocking from side to side on her tiptoes like a boxer. She's all tension and radiating anger, so I intentionally keep my stance loose and open, knowing it'll piss her off even more if she thinks I'm not taking the threat she poses to me seriously.

As predicted, she comes at me fast. Throwing a wild series of kicks and punches that are borderline sloppy but still incredibly vicious. I match every blow with the same amount of intensity, knowing it's either her or us, and it can't be us. It *won't* be us. She tries to work me into a corner, but I refuse to be boxed in, backing out of the door instead. Charlie trips over Jacob's body, and she wails loudly as she throws herself at me, catching me around the neck and using the momentum to swing herself onto my back as I stumble out onto the platform.

Her hands are wrapped around my neck, applying pressure to my carotid with lethal precision. Specks of black start to float in front of me, and I know I only have seconds to stop her from rendering me unconscious.

"Just go to sleep, Beck," she grunts, pressing harder when my knees start to buckle. "I promise I'll make Selene and Cal's deaths quick."

My next move isn't artful. It isn't well thought out or skillfully deployed; it's just desperate and determined. Reaching back, I grab what little hair Charlie has on her head and pull hard. She yelps in surprise, losing her grip on my neck while I search for a better hold. I find purchase in the fabric of her leather jacket and grasp it tight, using it to yank her over my shoulder and inadvertently sending her tumbling off the platform.

I watch her flailing limbs as she careens towards the ground, landing on her neck with a sickening crack that will haunt my dreams for the rest of my days. My breaths are rough and ragged as I rest my forehead on the railing and accept that it's finally done.

Jacob is dead.

Charlie is dead.

Leigh Anne is dead.

Their revenge plot has been foiled, the secrets and betrayals exposed, and we're still here. Relief swells in my chest, and I feel like I'm floating on air when I walk back into that room. Cal is up now. He has a huge gash in the back of his head from where Leigh Anne hit him, but he's tending to Selene's wounds instead. She's no longer tied to the chair, and she reaches for me when I collapse onto the floor between them.

I'm barely keeping myself upright, but I don't complain when they each rest their head on one of my shoulders because their added weight isn't destabilizing in the least. It's grounding. It's reassuring. It's proof that they're safe, that *I* saved them, that I haven't just held good things in my hands, I've used them to fight for them as well.

And yes, it's true that I've lost many of those battles, but the only thing that matters in this moment is that, this time, I won.

46

SELENE

It's official.

Aubrey Taylor has been elected as the next President of the United States of America.

While Cal and Beck were walking into a trap to save my life, he was in the comfort of our home, doing remote interviews about my kidnapping, pretending to be concerned about my well-being when all he really cared about were the votes being cast and counted.

And now he's being rewarded for it.

It's been a month, and I'm still shocked when someone in our orbit calls him Mr. President. Every time those two words are spoken, the rope around my neck seems to tighten. It's not lost on me that I've been free from my kidnappers for weeks, and I feel more trapped now than I did when I was tied to that desk chair.

Everyone is hovering.

My parents. My sisters. Monique. The press. Even Aubrey is constantly around, being suspiciously kind and patient with me. It started when I came home. He hugged me on the lawn, pulling me out of Cal's arms with a possessive glint in his eye. I thought that was just for show, a ploy for the cameras, but the attentiveness has persisted even behind closed doors. For the first two weeks, he'd bring me food and sit on the side of my bed to watch me eat. Lately, it's been less invasive, check-ins when he's on his way in or out of the house, but tonight, he's laying it on thick, which only makes me wonder what the hell he's up to.

"Your bruises have healed beautifully," he murmurs in my ear, spinning me around the dance floor while dreamy sighs ring out in the crowd gathered here for Cal and Beck's commendation ceremony.

Aubrey had insisted on honoring them for saving my life, and although no part of me wants to be in the spotlight any more than necessary, I couldn't pass up a chance to be in the same space with my men.

Even if it meant participating in this farce with Aubrey.

I smile politely, showing all of my teeth. "Thank you."

Out of the corner of my eye, I see Beck push away from the table we've all been assigned to, tossing his napkin down and excusing himself. Cal is only seconds behind him, and I wish like hell I could go to them. We haven't been in the same room in weeks. I've been sequestered away, surrounded by everyone but them, and they've been busy with psych evaluations and after-action reports. According to a conversation I overheard between Aubrey and Hicks, Beck's evaluation process has been especially gruesome since he killed an FBI agent.

I've lain awake almost every night wondering how he's doing with that. He and Charlie weren't close, but I know it has to be eating him up inside to have taken a life. I didn't get the chance to ask him that night, and part of me worries that I'll never have an opportunity to ask again. That fear sweeps through me, and I pull away from Aubrey seconds before the music ends. His happy mask slips momentarily, but he recovers quickly.

"I'm sorry. I need to go to the restroom."

He smiles. "Of course, darling. I'm sure Agent Shaw will be happy to escort you."

The agent is lingering near the edge of the dance floor, but she approaches when Aubrey nods in her direction. I listen to her relay our movements and destination to the rest of the team as we weave through the tables and enter the hallway. Cal and Beck are nowhere to be seen, and I turn to the right, even though the bathrooms are to the left, because I've read that people tend to go in the direction that matches their dominant hand when they leave a room with no clear destination in mind.

"Ma'am," Agent Shaw calls. "The bathrooms are this way."

I round on her. "I know. I just—I just need a moment."

Her features soften marginally, and she nods. "I understand, ma'am."

We haven't worked together long, and I'm not exactly chomping at the bit to trust anyone these days, but I don't have much of a choice here. I need to find my men, and I don't have a lot of time to do it.

"Can you raise Agents Beckham and Drake on the comms?" I ask.

"No, ma'am. Agents Beckham and Drake have not yet been cleared to return to duty. They do not have access to comms."

"Right. Of course." I sigh, all the urgency and hope for a moment alone with them leaking out of me.

"However," Agent Shaw says, glancing over her shoulder to make sure we're alone. "I am aware that they were both seen out on the terrace." She juts her chin in the direction we were heading. "I can give you five minutes."

I want to thank her, to hug her, to ask her how much she knows about me and my men, but I don't do any of those things. I turn and run to them, the hem of my dress billowing in the wind created by my swift movements. When I open the door to the terrace, a sharp, icy wind greets me, but I step out anyway, willing to bear the cold for a second in their heated gazes.

They turn like they were expecting me, and in the span of a heartbeat, I'm wrapped in their arms. My face buried in Beck's chest, my back pressed to Cal's front. They are heat and home and love all wrapped up in one, and I soak in as much of them as I can, only letting go so I can look at them both, so I can hold their faces in my hands.

Beck is first, and the stubble from his freshly shaven beard that's already growing in rubs against my palms. Moonlight streams over the smooth skin of his scalp, and onyx eyes run gentle lines over my features.

"Are you okay, gorgeous?"

"That's what I came here to ask you," I murmur, rising on my tiptoes to kiss him. "I'm so sorry you had to…"

I can't finish the sentence. In fact, I struggle to talk about the kidnapping and rescue in general. Cal and Beck won't discuss it with anyone they're not obligated to. It's just not their way, which leaves Aubrey to do interviews and dramatic re-tellings of a story he didn't even live through.

Beck shakes his head, cupping my face in return. "I'd do it all again. A million times over."

The truth of his statement is reflected in his eyes, and my heart aches. "I love you," I whisper fiercely. He leans down and plants the softest kiss on my lips. "And I love you."

Cal is next, and he's smiling when Beck spins me around to face him, keeping his hands on my hips. My hands come up to grip Cal's face, and he nuzzles into my palm. His eyes are so soft, so tender, so full of love as he looks at Beck and me, I nearly melt.

Brushing a thumb over his bottom lip, I ask, "How are you?"

"Perfect now that you're here."

"Does your head still hurt?"

He averts his gaze, and I look to Beck for an answer, which he doesn't hesitate to give me: "He's still having the occasional headache."

"The doctor says it's perfectly normal."

"He won't take anything for them," Beck adds.

"*Cal.*" I slide my hand around to the back of his head, fingers running over short black strands with the occasional gray one mixed in to cup the spot gingerly. "You need to take care of yourself."

The worry in my voice makes it more of a plea and less of an admonishment, but it seems to work for him better that way. He exhales and then nods. "I will, pet."

"Thank you."

One of the doors to the terrace opens, and Agent Shaw steps out, not even bothering to react to the scene in front of her. "Your time is up, ma'am."

Both men wear shocked expressions as I slip out of their hold, and I shrug to let them know I don't get Agent Shaw either. I am grateful for her, though, because she single-handedly orchestrated the first moment of alone time we've had in forever.

"Thanks, Shaw," Cal says, eyeing her suspiciously.

Beck is usually the skeptical one, but after the way Harris and, especially, Charlie betrayed them, it makes sense to me that Cal is turning into a bit of a cynic. Agent Shaw nods. "Drake. Beckham. You're needed inside as well."

"We'll give you a head start," Beck tells her.

"Sounds good. Let's go, ma'am."

She steps back to allow me into the warmth of the building. We're back at the doors of the banquet hall when I get the courage to say something to her.

"About what you saw back there," I start, but she holds up her hand.

"None of my business, ma'am. My job is to keep you safe, and that's a lot easier to do if you don't feel the need to hide things from me. I don't care what you do or who you do it with, but I do care if you die on my watch because you were trying to sneak out like a teenager."

"So what are you saying exactly?"

Looking around to make sure we're still alone, she pitches her voice low. "I'm saying that if seeing Agents Drake and Beckham is a priority for you, then I will do what I can to make that happen. You can trust me to be discreet and keep you safe."

When I found out I was going to be the First Lady of the United States, I found myself stressing about a lot of things, but mainly about the conversation I had with Deborah Sanders at her husband's funeral. She'd warned me that I'd need allies, people in my corner and on my side, and now it looks like the first one has presented themselves to me, taking one of my biggest concerns and making it sound like a simple matter of logistics. Could it really be that easy?

I dip my chin in acknowledgment of her promise. "Thank you, Agent Shaw."

"Of course, ma'am. Now, let's get you inside."

I return to my table to find a glass of champagne waiting for me. A glance around the table and then the rest of the room shows that everyone has received one, but no one is drinking them yet. When Cal and Beck come back to their seats, Aubrey grabs his glass and a butter knife and clinks the two together, drawing everyone's attention.

"I'd like to make a toast," he announces, projecting his voice across the room as he extends his glass to me. "To my beautiful wife, Selene. We have had a trying year, and I'm proud to say we've come out on the other side of it stronger and even more in love than before." My stomach turns as he continues, speaking about the depth of his feelings for me like he's not the same man who cheated on me and hasn't shared my bed in months. I can't help but slide uneasy looks to Cal and Beck to see how they're reacting, and it's not good. Cal's jaw is tense, and Beck's nostrils are flared, but they've both got their glasses raised and strained smiles pointed in my direction.

The smiles falter and crack when Aubrey finishes with me and turns to them.

"And to the two men who saved *my wife*, who put their own lives on the line to bring her home to me." He places his free hand over his heart, and his wedding band shines under the radiant light of the chandelier above us. "Agent Beckham. Agent Drake. There aren't enough words to express my gratitude, so I offer you this." From the table, he grabs two square, navy boxes and hands one to Cal and the other to Beck. Everyone watches, riveted, as they open them, but only the people closest to them can see the gold-plated American flag pins.

"Of course," Aubrey continues, "these are merely symbolic. You won't be able to wear them when you officially return to the Service as the heads of my Presidential detail because they don't meet official attire guidelines."

He lets out a hearty laugh that trickles through the room,

touching every person except for the three of us. Shock and displeasure roll across Cal and Beck's features, but I'm the only one who sees it. The only one who knows how unfair it is that their dream detail is being offered to them by my husband, of all people. The only one who hopes they will turn him down to prevent the creation of another obstacle between us. The only one who rejoices when they ask him for time to think about it.

Aubrey is surprisingly gracious in the face of what I pray is the beginning of their rejection, asking them to let him know by the morning. After that, the evening winds down, and we leave, riding home in silence that eats me alive the longer it goes on. When we enter the house, Aubrey heads for his office, and I dog his steps instead of going to my room. He doesn't even turn around when he hears my heels clicking on the tile, doesn't say a word when I stand behind him while he unlocks his office door.

He smiles.

He smiles as he lets me into the office first, and as he shuts the door behind us.

He smiles as he moves over to the bar in the far corner and pours us both two fingers of whiskey.

He smiles as he presses the tumbler into my hand and sits down on the edge of the desk in front of me, crossing his ankles before he takes a sip.

"It's a 1969 Macallan," he tells me, holding the glass up so light can filter through the amber liquid. I take a sip and gag, putting my glass on the desk beside him.

"It's gross."

"I like it." He polishes off his and then picks up my abandoned serving, sipping from it slowly. "Did you have something you wanted to discuss, darling? Perhaps the offer I made to your boyfriends?"

There's so much conviction in his tone, I know he's not speaking from a place of suspicion any longer, which means there's no point in pretending I don't know what he's talking about.

"They won't accept your offer."

"What makes you so sure? Because they love you? Because they've fucked you? Do you think some mediocre pussy is going to keep them from the detail of their dreams?"

Even in the face of his insults, I can't help but notice that Aubrey refers to Cal and Beck the way everyone does. As a unit. A singular entity. My mind goes to the day we met in the hallway, the kiss in Houston, the image of them on the terrace tonight, and the relationship they had before they ever knew who I was. All those times, all those instances, come together to remind me of a lifetime of standing on the margins of existing relationships, on the edges of bonds I should have been a part of, and suddenly I don't feel so sure.

I want to be.

I want to look at Aubrey and tell him they'll choose me and believe it, but all I know for certain is that Cal and Beck will always have each other. They'll always choose each other. And maybe this time they should. Maybe I should want them to choose their careers and the path Aubrey is offering them because how is it fair for me to want them to walk away from their dreams when I can't even leave this fucking marriage?

"I heard you," Aubrey says, pushing off the desk to pour himself another drink as he answers a question I haven't asked. "That night in the hotel, calling out their names."

His imitation of me moaning for Cal and Beck makes bile rise in my throat. I swallow it down, which is a mistake because it's tinged with the flavor of that awful whiskey that burns even worse the second time around.

"After that, I knew something was up. I just needed proof."

"That's why you sent them to Houston with me."

As grateful as I was for that time alone with Cal and Beck, I knew something was off about the whole situation. Aubrey and Jordan were too agreeable when it came to the tight turnaround time, and then, of course, there was the issue of us being sent out all on our own.

The crystal decanter clinks against the stone counter. Aubrey shoots me a slick grin over his shoulder. "That's the only reason I let you go to Houston."

"*Let* me?"

"Yes, Selene, let." He saunters from the bar to the chair behind his desk and sinks into the plush leather, regarding me with a smug smile. "You don't get it, do you? There's not a single thing you can do in this world without my permission, including have an affair."

Crossing my legs, I sit back in my seat, trying to understand where he's going with this. "So that's what this is about? You want to give me your blessing?"

He scoffs loudly. "Absolutely, not."

"Then what's the point, Aubrey? Are you going to force me out now that you have proof of me breaking the contract?" I pause, my brows wrinkling. "I assume you have proof, right?"

"Of course, I have proof."

In seconds, I'm holding a folder not too different from the one I presented to him and Jordan all those months ago. Inside it are photos of me leaving Cal's house in the wee hours of the morning. There are close-up shots of me kissing both men goodbye, and I'm struck with the strongest sense of yearning. Not just for them, but for every moment we shared that led up to that goodbye, for the softness of the kisses and the promise that we'd see each other soon, if only in passing.

"What happens now?" I ask, closing the folder. "Do you have Jordan sell these to the highest bidder and publicly humiliate me? Do you divorce me and move Sutton into the White House, let her be your perfect little, cookie-cutter First Lady?"

I'm so tired, so emotionally and mentally exhausted, I can't even bring myself to care. Part of me hopes he will do precisely that, so I can leave him. I'd be ruined, but I'd be free, and it would be his fault that I didn't change the world in the name of our son. My stomach twists at the thought, making it clear that I wouldn't be able to live with myself or that reality.

Aubrey drums his fingers on the desk near his empty glass. "No, Selene, I'm not going to do any of those things."

"Why not?"

Because Sutton's face isn't on the cover of every magazine right now. Her kidnapping, rescue, and subsequent recovery aren't the topic of millions of social media posts and countless news segments every day. Sutton is worthless to me, and you, my dear, have given me the most political capital I've had since AJ died, and I intend to use every bit of it. I can't do that if you're distracted with your boyfriends, so I'm dangling a carrot in front of their faces, giving them something better to do so you can focus on being my First Lady and making those changes you've been so desperate to see in the world."

I frown, hating everything he's just said, but especially hating how nonchalant he is about how he's benefited from our son's death. That hate sends me to my feet, and I slam my palms on his desk, leaning over to spit it in his face.

"You're a heartless bastard, do you know that? How do you take the most horrific things that have happened to me—AJ's death, being kidnapped and held hostage for days—and make them about you? Aren't you even a little bit ashamed of yourself, Aubrey? Don't you find it the least bit disturbing that you would go out of your way to take the one thing that's given me happiness since AJ died?"

He blinks slowly, completely unmoved. "I'm not taking anything away from you, Selene. You are free to leave whenever you want."

"You know I can't."

"*AND,*" he continues, talking over me. "All I've done is give your boyfriends a choice. It's up to them if they decide not to choose you."

47

______

CAL

I walk into Aubrey's home office with Beck one step behind me and the ball of our shared frustration bouncing between us. It's been there all morning, well, really, since last night, but it pulses and explodes when I see Selene sitting on the couch in the corner of his office.

She's wearing a soft purple sweater and some simple jeans. Her hair is curly like it's been freshly washed, and I can smell her pear and cherry blossom scent from over here. I want to go to her, to kiss her, to tell her I'm so fucking sorry for how this is about to go down.

"Gentleman!" Aubrey exclaims, standing to open us with a wide spread of his arms. He's all smiles despite the fact that he's completely broken the agreement we made late last night in my living room.

He'd shown up unannounced, didn't bat an eye when he saw Beck on my couch in nothing but a pair of low-slung pajama pants. While we were still reeling from his sudden appearance, he made himself at home, examining the pictures on the mantle over my fireplace while he explained that he knew all about our affair with Selene.

From there, the conversation quickly devolved. Beck asked him why he'd offer a job to the men he thought were sleeping with his wife. Aubrey proved it was more than an assumption with a folder full of photos of Selene leaving my house. Beck threatened to kill him. I had to put myself between them, saving Aubrey's life by keeping Beck at bay with one hand, and now I kind of wish I'd let the bastard die.

"Please, take a seat," he's saying now, gesturing to the armchairs in front of the desk.

"We'd prefer to stand," I respond, refusing to play into this little act of his more than I need to. The agreement was that we'd come in and formally accept the jobs he forced us to take by promising to make any one of the continuing threats aimed at Selene online come true. After what she'd just lived through, there wasn't a chance in hell that we'd gamble with her safety.

Aubrey knew that.

He had smiled so wide when we finally caved, and it occurred to me then that he wasn't even upset about the affair. In fact, he seemed happy about it, that we'd created circumstances he could use to get what he wanted. And what he wants is us at his beck and call. What he wants is Selene miserable and lonely. What he wants is to punish her, to break her spirit and her heart.

His eyes flare at the rejection of his command, but his smile doesn't fade even a little. "Very well." He shrugs, sinking into his own seat. "Tell me, where did you two put the medals of commendation you received last night?"

Beck has no patience for this; he brushes right over the question, getting to the point. "We're here to give you the answer you asked us for last night."

The subtle allusion to the coercion he subjected us to gives Aubrey pause. He glances at Selene, who shifts in her seat. She seems uncomfortable, but nothing about her expression suggests she's caught on to the meaning Beck's tried to hide in his words.

Aubrey chuckles. "Straight to the point, then? Go on, I've been *dying* to hear your answer."

My fingers dig into the leather of the armchair in front of me as anger swells in my gut. This is not how it was supposed to go. Selene wasn't supposed to be here. We'd specifically asked to have a private conversation with her, to give her some sense of closure, and Aubrey had agreed. He said we could speak with her after we gave him our answer in person. I should have known he had no intention of giving us the chance to make a clean break.

Clean breaks can be healed.

What Aubrey wants is a messy shattering of bone and fissures in flesh. He wants us to break her heart in front of him, so he can watch her bleed. The only kindness I can extend to her, to the only woman I've ever loved, is a swift gutting. A precisely placed blade that severs our bond and sets her free to start the part of her life where she incorrectly assumes we care more about a promotion than her.

I clear my throat, and Beck's spine straightens. His entire body is stiff with resentment. Mine is too. And yet, we have to act like we're at ease. We have to act like we want this when all we want is her.

Aubrey lifts his brows, silently imploring us to continue as if he doesn't already know what we're going to say, like he didn't tell us word for fucking word. Together, and through teeth we try not to clench, Beck and I seal our fates and break Selene's heart, our voices blending into one discordant sound as we say:

"It would be our honor to serve at the pleasure of the President."

THE END

A TASTE OF SIN

Our trio's story continues in A Taste of Sin: Passion and Politics #2. Coming soon!

ABOUT THE AUTHOR

J.L. Seegars is a dedicated smut peddler and lifelong nerd who's always had a love of words, storytelling and drama. When she isn't writing messy and emotionally complex characters like the ones she grew up around, she's watching reality TV, supporting her fellow authors by devouring their work or spending time with her husband and son.

ALSO BY J.L. SEEGARS

Restore Me: The New Haven Series (Book #1)

Again: A Marriage Redemption Novella

Revive Me Part One: The New Haven Series (Book #2)

Revive Me Part Two: The New Haven Series (Book #2)

Revive Me Part Three: The New Haven Series (Book #2)

Release Me: The New Haven Series (Book #3)

Reclaim Me: The New Haven Series (Book #4)

Speak: A Post Divorce Romance

www.ingramcontent.com/pod-product-compliance
Lightning Source LLC
Chambersburg PA
CBHW020326010826
48973CB00005B/1148